MESSERSCHMITT'S APPRENTICE

A Designer's Journey of Love and the First Fighter Jets during World War II

FOR RABBI SHAPIRO

Norman Emilio Barrientos
Bayside, WI, USA

Norman
9/27/18

Messerschmitt's Apprentice

Dedicated in loving memory to my father,
Julian A. Barrientos

PROLOGUE

The look in his eyes implore, they beg me to listen. He seems conflicted, troubled yet also intensely focused on what he is drawing. In my mind's eye I see a vision of a man looking up from a drafting table. The room is dark, candle-lit, yet outside the windows I can see that there are flashes of explosions.

The scene of this man at his drafting table has appeared to me many times over the last week. As I hone in on his setting I can see his drawing instruments and then I sense that he is working on a mechanical drawing of some complexity. Beyond him, outside the factory-like windows, there is the outline of a traditional European city with spires and tiled roofs. The man, this visitor in my mind, is in his mid-thirties and has dark hair. He is European but of what region, I can't tell. Maybe he is a mix of nationalities?

A perplexing memory comes to mind, finally. I was in Germany as a young man for an exchange program and I learned the language readily even though I had never taken any formal courses. More curious is the haunting memory of walking across the Rhine River Bridge in Mainz and being overwhelmed with a feeling of sadness and grief. Could this memory be connected to these recent visitations?

So, who is this person? Why does he keep reappearing to me, looking at me and insisting that I hear his story? 'I have a business to run, and I don't have time to listen to you. I can tell you want me to write this down but right now, I am too busy. Go away.' I say to myself as if to reason with this ephemeral visitor.

Finally, one night I give in to his persistence and I 'hear' him tell his story. Following this, I start my writing and go with the flow of thoughts and images he projects to me.

The author,

July 2015

FEBRUARY 25, 1944

The jet plane that has the potential to shield Germany from the Allied bombing campaign arises from the complex geometries I have drawn. Curved lines evolve into parts, parts group into a machine, the machine forms into a jet and the craft soars off into the skies. Taking Professor Messerschmitt's plane concepts, I crystalize them into detailed subcomponents that collectively give me an innate understanding of the whole jet. The spirit of his visions flows freely from my pens and I become part of the plane. The immersion is complete; my drawings breathe of me and I breathe of them.

Looking up from my table and at our design hall I see rows of drafting tables lined up like dominoes, the table tops extending up at full attention. Focused designers silently pincer their instruments looking intently at their drawings as if deciding on how to start an operation. Surrounding the walls of this vast hall are long rows of factory-type windows checkerboarded with black steel mullions.

Beyond the windows off in the distance, I can see the Cathedral tower of Augsburg piercing the late afternoon, winter sky while billows of smoke roll out of chimney stacks peering from darkened homes. I can practically see my apartment building from this fifth-floor level of the Messerschmitt design bureau in Haunstetten and wonder how my Vanessa is doing with our children.

Giving my pencil another twirl in the sharpener, I look back down at my drawing, lift my adjustable triangle and focus on the radar operator's cockpit plan. How can I modify the jet's frame to add a second seat without dampening its wonderful flight characteristics?

"Armand," says my friend Walter as I look up. "How is my radar panel attachment going?" Walter's wispy blonde hair and reddish cheeks contrasting with his prominent roman-nose are always a welcome sight for me. "Word is that the Air Ministry wants to accelerate the production of this two-seater radar jet. Shortly we will have the Messerschmitt directors breathing down our electrical department's back."

"We feel the same pressure in my production engineering group. Every variant of the Me 262 jet is a high priority," I say. "But if the Wehrmacht wouldn't keep calling up our engineering staff to the front lines, maybe we could get one of these done in time. "

"At least we haven't been called up like some of our other University friends," says Walter. "Hey, I didn't mean to pressure you. I just wanted to get a break from the men in the electrical department. Speaking of a break, how about later tonight we stop by the Froehlich Haus for a day-ending stein? Since I broke up with Karen last week, my nights will be free, and I am not going to waste anytime mulling over her."

"Walter, I do admire your voracity, but you sometimes seem to forget that I am married. I am sure my dear Vanessa would not like me to be spending an hour or two at Froehlich's helping you round up your next Fräulein. Especially since Angelika and Emil are both down with a bad cold right now and she could probably use my help."

"Fair enough, friend," says Walter. "Maybe this weekend and it would be great if both you and Vanessa could join along? I've known you two since our University days, so I would never do anything to lose her trust as a friend."

"Only thing, Walter, Vanessa knows you all too well. But you do keep me vicariously entertained with your adventures."

Looking down the rows of drafting tables, I see Professor Messerschmitt making conversation at another designer's table. His balding head is accentuated with a dome of a forehead and the taut lines on his face speak of tensioned thought. As he heads our way and I see a flash of his Nazi Party lapel reflecting the hall's light, signaling both his arrival and his Party pride. As usual, he is wearing one of his pin-striped grey suits with a vest, a white shirt and a black tie to match his role as a company director.

"How are the two boys from Mainz doing?" says Messerschmitt. "Collaborating on the night-fighter variant I see."

"Yes, Professor, I am trying to fit Walter's radar panel design into the dashboard of the radar operator's cockpit," I say. "But if he hadn't designed it so large I would've finished this last week." Walter gives me a smirk of a smile in silent response.

"Ha, I like your banter and relationship, Walter and Armand," says the Professor. "I know you guys are working fourteen-hour days on these jet variants and I appreciate it. But with the Air Ministry and the Luftwaffe's constantly changing the priority level of these planes, we all have a mess on our hands. I'd pull out my hair if I had any."

"So, what is the latest on production priority Professor?" I ask. "Should I be focusing on the Me 262 jet or the Me 163 rocket plane this week?"

"Which one is having more problems?" asks Messerschmitt with his palms facing upward. "That's the one that needs more work this week. No seriously gentlemen, this week the Air Ministry and Luftwaffe agreed that the Me 262 night-fighter jet is the one that has top priority. Hitler is certain this plane will hold off the Allied air bombing campaign."

"Sure, I can focus my production design department on that Professor," I say. "But you know we have not worked out all the wrinkles. We still need to gather more field testing data and incorporate them into our production drawings."

"I know that, Armand, but I already promised Göring that we would have these radar equipped planes by June this year. I had no choice but to commit to that date. It was that or have our production contract order pulled. Moreover, they have a point. The Allied planes are reaching deeper into southern Germany now, right into our Bavaria."

"Yes, it is a real and active threat." I respond to Messerschmitt. "My hometown of Mainz was bombed earlier this month and I still have not heard word of how my parents or their house has fared."

"In all seriousness, Professor," interjects Walter, "We are closing in on the two-seater radar jet and we will have production drawings ready by the end of March, just a month from now. From there we can get a few prototypes done by late May."

"Thanks for your effort, gentleman," responds Messerschmitt. "Your commitment will make the company's investments pay off in the long run."

"Professor, I have one question for you," I say motioning for him to come closer for some privacy. "I see that the plant has received a shipment of prisoners of war for factory duty." Walter, hangs back at a distance and continues standing in the aisle.

"Yes, that is right, Armand," responds Messerschmitt quietly. "The only way for us to meet our war production goals are to bring in peoples from other countries and put them to work here. Prisoners, concentration camp workers and hapless people rounded up from our conquered territories. Do you have a problem with that, Armand?"

"Well Professor, with all due respect to the Director's decisions," I say. "What I saw arrive today was a large group of Italian prisoners of war."

"Does that bother the Italian side in you, Armand?" asks the Professor as he puts a hand on my shoulder.

"Quite frankly it does sir." I respond. "And worse, I found out that my Genovesan cousin, a captain in the Italian army, is among the prisoners."

"This is a necessity of war," says Messerschmitt moving his hand onto my drafting table and forming a fist. Our company has tremendous contract obligations to meet and I have signed off on the use of slave and prisoners at out plants. I am sorry if you have relations caught in this net of the war."

"Well, if there is any way you can assure that the Italian prisoners are treated justly that would be greatly appreciated Professor."

"I will consider that. For your sake as you are a valued manager here. But, I will have to convince the SS guards to play along with that request and that may not be so easy."

"Whatever you can do, Professor, would be appreciated by my mother's family and me," I say.

Messerschmitt moves back into the aisle closer to Walter and says, "Time for me to move on. I have a Party function with Kreisleiter

Schiede this evening in Augsburg. Word is, Armand, that your old University comrade, Dieter Fleischen, has been elevated in the Party ranks and he is now Schiede's right-hand man."

"He may have been a school comrade but not since then," I say. "How the Party picked up on him even after he betrayed our company, confounds me, Professor."

"Welcome to Party politics," says the Professor. "If you can lie, cheat and steal then you have just the right traits needed by the National Socialist Party. Just leave this to one me though and I will handle him, so he doesn't damage our company any further. Very well, see you gentlemen, perhaps even later this evening."

As Messerschmitt strolls away Walter moves in closer to me, "Dieter, a Party official now? How disgusting. Your assessment of him in the University was correct except we didn't figure that one of his major strong suits would be, conniving. I'd better get back to my electrical group. Talk to you later, Armand."

As Walter pulls away toward the far end of the drafting hall, I am once again facing the problems brought about by making the cockpit longer. Where do I place the cockpit firewall, where do the hydraulic control lines go and how I can shove the fuel tank back any further into the tail? I bow my head down and look closely at my drawings. Perhaps if I prayed a bit a seminal idea will come forward and help me solve these mechanical problems.

Clicking off the distances between feet, inches and down to the fraction I draw away and connect two curved lines with a tangential line. I then grab the pencil sharpener, twirl my pencil around and then apply it to the vellum sheet. First, I draw a thin sharp line for the centerline guides and then I come back, applying more pressure for a thicker line that defines the outer profile of the housing.

As I continue peering over the details, I feel a slight rumble vibrating my feet, but I do not hear anything. Then I notice that the checkerboard of window panes are starting to rumble within their steel frames. My coffee cup starts rattling as if lifting up for a ghostly dance and then my pencils jump off their precarious ledge from my drawing ruler, racing down the table and tapping onto the floor.

Finally, a droning sound can be subtly heard in a low frequency, but it is now moving up into a higher tone where I can distinguish the humming of…propellers. The drone turns into an all-encompassing hum that palpitates within the whole space of the drafting hall. This must be a large fleet of planes and they are heading our way.

I yell out to my production team, "Air raid! Take cover in the shelters. Roll up your drawings and throw them into the vault." My team of designers lift their heads from their aborted operations, pens and triangles fly off their tables as they rip off their vellum drawings. Then a siren sound starts swirling through the factory complex riveting our attention on one thing, run fast and now. After a short jam at the drawing vault, I push along with everyone else in a rush toward the stairs. I can see search lights scowling the night sky then there is a retort bursting from the ground as anti-aircraft guns blast off to greet the bombers.

As I round the first set of stairs I realize that we still have five more floors before we make it to the shelters below. Looking out the stair windows I start seeing flashes of light off in the distance, flaring into the pitch-dark sky. As I round the next floor, the first set of explosion shock waves hit our building. As I and others from our design team scurry down the steps, the flashes of horizon-filling light become continuous and the shockwaves roll in one after another.

As the explosions converge into one large and fast-paced sequence of detonations the noise becomes deafening and the surge of vibrations throw us off our balance. I grip harder onto the stair railing and crouch lower to the ground to keep my movement steady.

Finally, we break into the darkened shelter below and it is already crammed with other Messerschmitt engineers and workers alike, all looking to the ceiling, praying that it will hold up. The wave of bombs are crashing onto the plant now and I curl down into a fetal position while covering my ears. As the bombs drop right around the plant, I feel reverberations of gripping explosions transmitting a horrific force into the bones of this bunker. The noise is deafening, the ground slab heaves, concrete walls crumble, steel beams splinter, dust falls from the ceiling. But the building over our heads does not collapse.

Another roar of planes is heard whining overhead coming along the same line. Sounding like angry giants pounding the earth with their footsteps, this sequence of bombs expresses an impending doom for our building. A call goes out to run into a section of the shelter that is not directly below this building. This next wave of bombs rips through the airfield first, then the hangars and finally onto our plant offices. A crack sounding like a lightning bolt is heard above followed by a thunderous roar of concrete and steel tumbling downward in a frenetic rush. The ceiling overhead holds in place.

As the last bombs fade off further downstream of the air attack line, I look around at the pallid faces. No one speaks, many are breathing heavily, most are still looking up at the ceiling, their ears alert to see if another wave is approaching. Not being able to recognize many people in this dim lighting and starting to feel claustrophobic, I crawl my way toward what I think is the exit.

Finally, finding the doorway I walk through the tunnel system and step over the chunks of concrete that have loosened from the walls. I grope in the dark with my hands running along the cold concrete, my fingers hitting cracks every arms length. 'How long is this tunnel?' I think as I push away more rubble with my feet. I noticer others are following me as well and I lead this shocked group of people into a headhouse and empty out onto what was the airfield twenty minutes earlier.

Surveying the landscape, I see the airfield is pockmarked with newly formed craters still giving forth smoke and small licks of flames. Further beyond, I can see that many of the plant buildings have been hit, their structural innards strewn out like a crashed airplane. In portions of the buildings, flames are tossing around, silhouetting collapsed walls and twisted trusses. The personnel streaming out of the headhouse are dumbfounded and not being able to comprehend how our plant world has been turned inside out, are stunned into silence.

As the sound of fire trucks and the shouts of emergency personnel comes into my consciousness I realize my duty is to start assisting with the rescue and retrieval of people who are likely trapped under this debris. Dashing over to a nearby fire truck, I look off into the horizon and glimpse toward the center of Augsburg. To my horror I see a devilish orange-red light leaping into the sky with swirls of flames engulfing the beloved and iconic Cathedral spire.

Why has the City been bombed as well? Our Messerschmitt plant is three miles to the south. A sinking feeling of dread overwhelms me as I have no way of knowing the fate of my Vanessa and our children.

PART 1
CONCEPTUAL DEVELOPMENTS

JULY 1924

The Mainz Bahnhof Train Station looms in the gray light of dawn while my father, my mother and I walk along Kaiserstrasse Boulevard. The Station's voluminous vaulted roof rises into the eeking purplish light as if to help lift the sun up. Through the arched windows, I can see pendant lights hanging high inside like quiet beacons guiding travelers. While the streets are empty of people, up ahead at the station's plaza, there is already a slow trickle of pedestrians gathering before it's large neo-classical facade. From this distance, the travelers appear like charcoal marks ticked off in front of a L'ecole de Beaux-Arts drawing.

"Keep up the pace Armand," says my father. "The train leaves for Genoa in the next forty-five minutes and we still have to load our months' worth of luggage." My father wears a light blue linen suit, a bow tie and a flat-topped straw hat while he gives my shoulder a little push. Being summer he is not wearing the dark grey suit that he usually wears to his waterworks engineering job.

"I am working on it father," I respond back. "It's just that waking up at 4:30 AM is not my usual Saturday morning. Plus, I didn't get to eat breakfast." I look up to my father as I am only up to his chin at my age of fourteen.

"Armando, I have brought a frittata for you to eat on the train," exclaims my mother in her sing-song Italian accent. In contrast to my father's light Hessian features, my Genovesan mother has dark hair and eyes along with an olive skin tone. As I walk between them, I am a mix of the two having chestnut brown hair, hazel eyes and bit of freckling on my face. "You can sleep on the train and when we arrive to Genoa, I am sure you will be all rested up for play with your cousins."

"Will my cousins Rodolfo and Aurelio be greeting us?"

"Most likely as we will be staying with them," mother says as we continue walking along at a quick pace. "Your uncle Vittorio was delighted to have us stay with them last time we visited three years ago, and he has extended his hospitality for us this time as well."

"I hope my Italian fares well," I say. "I only get to speak Italian with you Mama and I have a feeling I will need a few days to get up to speed."

"You still speak infinitely better than me," responds my father. "My Italian hasn't improved much since I was at the University of Genoa for that one semester. But I did garnish winning your mother's affections for a lifetime commitment over that summer."

"You know, Mama and Papa, did I ever tell you two about the fist-fight I got into with Rodolfo three summers ago?"

"No son, you didn't," says mother. "Tell us what had happened."

"Well, you know how Rodolfo can be a bit aggressive at times?

"He does have his gruff moments, son, but I am sure it is just in a competitive way," says mother. "It's ????age."

"He may be my age but he felt it necessary to show me who is the better fist fighter of the two, so he challenged me to one."

"And how did it turn out?" asks my father. "Where you able to fend for yourself son?"

"Sure did. After a few minutes of sparring around I socked him one right into his nose and made him bleed."

"Ha, good job and way to keep up the family honor," says my father.

"Well, that was the first part of the story. While Rodolfo was tending to his bleeding, Aurelio stepped in for his older brother and told me that the Lorenzini family hangs as one and that he would defend his brother's honor."

"Yes, us Lorenzini's are a proud family," says mother. "I see you experienced this first hand then."

"Sure did. After a minute of sparring with Aurelio, he socked me right in the eye and for the first time I saw blue stars floating around. It seemed to make them happy that at least one part of the duo could claim dominance."

"Feistiness and pride are a big part of being a Lorenzini my son," says father. "I only know too well after eighteen years of marriage with your mother. Ok, here is the luggage drop-off. Let's help the porter sort out our luggage and then head over to our train.

★★★

The train rumbles into Genoa's Brignole train station puffing its last bit of steam out as the wheels come to a halt. We disembark into the vaulted train shed while our luggage is loaded onto a pull-cart. Passing under the black steel trusses, we empty out onto the station's piazza. Searching the motorcars and horsecarts stationed along the piazza's edges, my mother lifts on her toes and yells out to me. "*Armando, vieni qui*. Would you go and look for your uncle's motorcar along the *strada*?"

"Sure mama. I will run over now. Just keep an eye out for me if I flag them down."

After a few minutes of searching the jostling crowds, I exclaim, "There they are, Mama, Papa. I have spotted Uncle Vittorio's motor coach."

Uncle Vittorio, aunt Elisabetta, Rodolfo, and Aurelio all start walking toward me across the piazza. Elisabetta's arms are already outstretched ready to receive me. My two cousins walk a little more composed alongside their father and extend to me a handshake followed by an embrace.

"*Armando. Che buono vederte di nuovo*," yells out my uncle Vittorio with his moustache revealing a large smile that balances well with his bald head. "You have grown much since we've seen you last. Are you still sketching automobiles and ships?" My uncle gives me a hug and his usual light chuckle. "You are like a little Da Vinci."

I give him a warm hug. "Yes uncle Vittorio, I still love sketching. I will show you my latest ship ideas later."

"Oh, really nephew? Will it be the biggest ship ever or the fastest one? "asks Vittorio.

"Probably the fastest, biggest one. I am getting there but I haven't figured out dimensions and the like. Maybe next year in secondary school I will draw it up for you to see."

Walking off the train station's piazza, the Italian architecture surrounds me. Compared to Mainz, Genoa's colors are more ochre; yellows, tans, and faded reds. The housing blocks are evenly faced with tall windows with green shutters and wrought iron balconies gracefully frame the bottoms. On the newer streets, there are large palazzo villas that are more symmetrical and even larger than those in Mainz. And in contrast to Mainz's flat terrain, Genoa is sloped toward the Mediterranean like a ship that is pitched into high seas. This change sets an air of excitement and anticipation for me of what this summer may portend.

As we walk our way to the Castelletto neighborhood we pass the medieval section, the Carrugi, where the arms-length wide alleys wind and twist. Children run by in groups making boisterous noises as they pass by and then they disappear into even more narrow stairways that lead to higher streets. A pungent air mixed with freshly cooked food and that of musty cobblestone and stucco merges into a sweet smell that is strangely comforting. As we emerge from the Carrugi, we come upon my uncle's neighborhood, the newer section of Castelletto with its streets that wind up the hills of Genoa.

★★★

I have settled into the little room which will be mine for the next month, and I start to unpack. The floors are a dark tile with the walls and ceilings being plastered smooth. While in Germany it is the custom to keep all the doors off the main corridor shut, in Italy all the doors are wide open. To my surprise, I look up at the doorway and see Rodolfo and Aurelio standing there. They enter the room and look over what I have brought from Mainz. Rodolfo picks up a few items as if to inspect them the way a customs official does and then he drops them down with no further interest.

"Armando," says Rodolfo. "We are going down to the Piazza Marsala to play some street games with our friends. Are you coming?"

"Sure, that sounds fun. I can always unpack later. Let's go."

As we stroll down the narrow and steep streets of Castelletto, Rodolfo leads the way with assuredness. He checks out each pack of boys we come upon and then dismisses them with a quick shake of his head. Finally, we come to a fountain on the intersection of Piazza Marsala and Via Palestro. There, around the water fountain, I see numerous boys and girls. On the perimeter of the basin the boys are playing ball games. At the center, there are various clusters of young girls. Some are standing alongside with their bikes while others are sitting on the fountain's base wall.

Rodolfo leads us to a boy who seems to be the ringleader of the ball games. He shouts out to him. "Hey, my German cousin is here to show you guys a few new ball tricks."

'Great, thanks Rodolfo for putting me on the spot' I think to myself. The next thing I know, there is a group of boys starting to approach me with their chests out.

"Hey, *Tedesco* boy," says one of the boys. "So, you think you can beat us at this game. Come on show us a few things." This is followed by a few laughs between themselves as if they have my demise already pegged down.

"That's right boys," I say. "I came here from Germany to coach you guys. German girls can play better ball than what I see here." I say with enough bluster to even surprise myself.

The Genovesan boys all look at each other, laugh with an accepting nod and then pull up to me and link their arms around my neck in friendly banter. As we stand there, I notice that the young girls in the middle start walking around the fountain and some are casting glances at the boys. It all seems like some ritual to me; *regazzi* on the outer circle, *regazze* on the inner circle twirling around till they meet in between.

While I chat with Aurelio about the teaming arrangements, I start to sense that a group of girls or someone is staring at me. Perhaps it is because I have different kinds of clothing on or maybe it is because they can hear my German accent. One girl is smiling toward me then smiling back to her friends with an even broader and more mischievous smile.

Aurelio taps my shoulder. "Looks like our neighborhood friends would rather wait to see your German tricks. So, let's wait here on the fountain until they finish this first round."

Good, I think to myself, I am off the hook to perform for now. Aurelio and I set ourselves down in the midst of the girls flocking around the fountain. As we wait there looking toward the other boys, two girls walk their bikes toward us, and then they place them along the wall. The two sit on the fountain wall with the one closest to me casting a quick glance. The girl is my age, has deep brown eyes, matching brown eyebrows and thick, curly hair. Taking a second glance at me first, she then scoots over closer to me.

"Are you from Genoa?" asks the girl.

"No, I am from Mainz, Germany. Why do you ask?"

"Well, you speak a little funny, ha."

"I don't think I speak funny. I know my Italian pretty well."

With her eyes getting wider with expression she responds,

"I can hear your accent twenty feet away. But don't worry. It sounds kind of cute. You know, different."

My face starts blushing at her 'cute' label. At my age, cute is not on my wish list of adjectives. "I am working at it. My Italian is a work in progress. German is my mother tongue so you should be impressed I can speak it as well as I do."

The curly-haired girl looks into my eyes. "I don't know any German boys so I wouldn't be able to tell the difference."

"Well, here I am. Direct from Mainz, Germany, Armando Kindermann. What's your name?"

"I am Sara Mattatia. My family lives in this neighborhood."

"Nice. And I see you have a whole group of friends here. Are you always biking around this piazza?"

"Most of the time. It's my favorite thing to do, be on a bicycle. You get to move fast, especially down all the hills here in Genoa. So, Armando, are you here for the summer?"

"For the whole month of July. My uncle Vittorio lives here, and that over there is my cousin Rodolfo and this is Aurelio. They are like brothers to me and they show me around Genoa."

Sara looks at me then she looks back at her friend for some girl-to-girl communication. Her friend seems to understand this, and she moves away to the other side of the fountain. Oh, oh, I think I am in for it now.

"So, Armando, do you have a bike here?"

"Well, my cousins have two, and I am sure I could use one of theirs. Why do you ask?"

You and your cousins should visit the harbor sometime. They have some delicious gelato stands down there."

"Sounds like an excellent idea. Thanks for mentioning it."

"There is also a festa going on at the harbor and there are a few carnival rides and shows."

"Really, I love carnivals. Mainz has a wonderful one and people from all over Germany come to see it."

"Interesting. My father makes carnival masks, and there is a stall where he sells them. He also makes costumes for *Purim*; you know the Jewish festival in March. If you guys go down there, let us know, and we will join you."

She smiles and then starts kicking her legs out from the fountain wall. With her smile broadening, she looks at me, waiting for me to pick up on the conversation. A lump forms in my throat and I am not quite sure where to take this. I also have never heard of 'Purim' but I am too embarrassed to admit that. She is pretty, and I have a strange urge to kiss her but how, where, when and what to do with all my cousins around? Such complexities of girls have not entered my mind nor am I ready to figure them out. Feeling a little over my head, I stand up.

"Hey, Rodolfo. Is it time for us to play now? Well, Sara, it was nice talking with you. I will catch you around the fountain later."

Looking a little surprised but still having some mischievousness in her eyes, Sara says, "Ok, Armando. I will see you later. Bring a bike next time you come here."

As I approach Rodolfo, he has a big smile on his face. "Ah, so you now have a girlfriend. When are you going to kiss her?"

Already I feel this has gone too far for my fourteen-year-old heart and mind to handle. Time to call this whole affair off I decide. With that, I exit the situation to my relief and start playing the ball game. While it was exciting to have a girl approach me, I am also a bit confused as to what to do next.

★★★

"Armando, *il mio nippote*. How did you enjoy the games with Rodolfo and Aurelio?", yells out my uncle Vittorio as I enter the main parlor of his apartment. The room is lined with wood paneling and bookshelves while a telescope and a globe stand rests on the glossy marbled-tiled floors.

"It was a lot of fun uncle. Rodolfo and Aurelio are quite the ball players. I also met a lot of their friends in the neighborhood."

"Great my nephew. We are having lunch soon so why don't you clean up a bit and come back to the dinner table *a presto*. Your mother is in the kitchen helping out."

I walk down the corridor and look into the kitchen seeing my mother with aunt Elisabetta stirring pots and cutting vegetables. A savory smell of olive oil merging with vegetables and sauces wafts through the air. Upon noticing me my mama says, "Armando, Rodolfo came by earlier and told me you boys played a few games with his friends."

"Yes, it was a bit challenging for me but I enjoyed myself."

Stopping her pot stirring, mama looks up at me, "Rodolfo also made a comment that you now have a girlfriend. Was he just joking son?"

My gosh, what a blabber-mouth he is. Everything in this Italian family moves very fast and nothing seems private.

"No mama, I don't have a girlfriend, ha. But there was a girl who did talk with me. That's about it though." I say hoping to close off this line of conversation.

"Armando, where about have you been when you saw this girl?"

"On Via Palestro at Piazza Marsala"

"Ah, that is right near the Jewish Synagogue of Genoa. Perhaps she is a Jewish girl son? That would be interesting."

"Why do you say that Mama? The other boys said the same thing about her."

"Well son, let's see you are fourteen now? Almost of age I'd say or at least getting there quickly. It may be just that family lore showing up in you," Mother says.

"I am not sure what you mean by that, mama."

"You see, and I can tell you now, with my family being from the Veneto province, it has been rumored that we are of Sephardic Jewish heritage. It's never been proven directly, and since we've been practicing Catholics for generations, we don't know for sure."

"So, are you saying we may have some Jewish blood in us?"

"Very possibly, son. The story is that during the 1848 Revolution against Austrian rule, our family converted to Catholicism so they could join the military. The only clue we have now is the candelabra with seven candle holders and one offset holder that has clung to our family treasures."

I ponder mother's point in that she alludes to the Jewish Hanukkah menorah, "Are you saying I may have an attraction to Jewish girls because of that possible heritage? Sounds a little funny mama."

"I know son, but I thought I'd better let you know just in case we find out more someday, and you aren't too surprised. Now go run along and clean up for our meal."

With that mama dismisses but I am shaken by what my mother's family heritage may be all about. I quickly exit the kitchen and walk down the hall toward my room to change. As I disrobe in my room, I look into the mirror and wonder if any of my features are of Jewish descent.

SEPTEMBER 1928

I look about the small room in this boarding apartment and decide I've done enough unpacking for the day. The room is packed with my luggage pieces, drawing equipment and clothing for my first semester at the Munich Technical University. I then move into the common parlor and address the landlady. "Frau Kessler, at what times will dinner be served?"

A woman in her fifties with a long work dress and loose blouse comes out of the kitchen with a broom in her hands. Strands of grey hair fall upon her forehead from her cleaning activity.

"I will have dinners served at seven most nights. But I know you students tend to wander on Friday and Saturdays, so I will not be serving any food those nights," says Frau Kessler.

"That sounds fine. Where can I store all these drawing tubes and portfolios? My room doesn't have any closets where I can stack them."

"All four of you boarders can use this closet here right off the main entrance. And you are welcome to study in the parlor or congregate there whenever you like. I won't be around much in your apartment as I live upstairs. You are attending the Munich *Technische Hochschule* right? What program are you enrolled in young man?"

"Yes. I am enrolled in mechanical and industrial design. It's a blend of mechanical engineering with an emphasis on designing machine parts and housings."

"Sounds like a very useful program, Armand. I hope your first year goes well and that I will be seeing you for all four years."

"Thanks, Frau Kessler, I hope so too. Your thoughts are appreciated."

Being that it is my first week of University here in Munich, I am still settling into my surroundings. A bit of angst surges into me as to what to do with my free-time in this new city.

"Have any other students moved in yet?" I ask the Frau.

"Why yes, one lad has. He was in here earlier unpacking his books. He said he was going to the art store to pick up some drawing supplies."knock on his door," says Frau Kessler as she bustles down the hall and knocks on a door. Sure enough, the fellow cracks open his door and says in a low tone,

"What is it what you want, Frau Kessler? I am getting my school supplies in order," he says from his darkened room.

"I thought it would be nice to introduce you to one of your fellow boarders. Looks like he is in some kind of design program as well."

As he pulls out of the darkened room into the brighter hallway, I see a young man about my age who is on the stocky side, of dark complexion and sporting a short mustache. "I am Dieter Fleischen. What's your name?" He says as he extends his hand to me.

"Hello. I am Armand Kindermann, I am from Mainz. You know, Germany's wine capital, the Rhineland-Palatinate. Where are you from?

"I am a *nazi*, country boy from a hamlet in southern Bavaria, near Oberammergau," says Dieter.

"I hear you have been buying art and drawing supplies. What program are you enrolled in?"

"I am in mechanical and industrial design."

"Well, so am I. Looks like we will have some of the same classes then."

"That will be nice having a roommate in the same program."

"Well, you boys settle in and get ready for your studies," says the Frau. "I am heading back up to my apartment and I will see you later at dinner."

As Frau Kessler closes the apartment door Dieter exclaims, "I hope she feeds us well. She seems like a nice enough lady but the word is that these widows can make for stingy cooking."

"Yes, I've heard the same thing. They take your boarding money and then serve you stale pretzels for dessert. Well if that does happen, I've noticed that there are some boisterous Biergartens nearby that serve some tasty brats and pretzels."

"Say no more. I will get hungry just thinking about those two. The only thing missing in that picture is a cold stein."

"Hey, Dieter. You are done unpacking, right?"

"Sure, you heard, I was just organizing my drawing supplies."

"Well, how about we walk over to the garten and have a beer before dinner is served? With classes starting tomorrow, I don't have any project assignments yet"

"Yes, let's do that. I'll grab my jacket and we can head downstairs."

Dieter and I walk down the winding streets of the University neighborhood. I share with him my reconnaissance of the Hochschule,

"I dropped off some of my drafting instruments at the Mechanical Engineering Hall and got to see our design studio. It's very modern and large with lots of drawing tables. And all of them are set up with drafting arms."

"This will be quite a step up from secondary school. I think we are in the big time now," responds Dieter. "There are people attending from all over Germany. We will have sixty students in our first year, but I've heard that usually twenty people will drop out by the second year. Not me, I am in here for the long haul."

Sensing Dieter's determination I respond, "I plan to stick this out till graduation as well. Nothing is going to get in my way from this degree. Not even a *nazi* from southern Bavaria," I say this making fun of Dieter's rural background and the country connotations that '*nazi*' has.

Dieter responds, "I suppose people from Mainz are known for their determination then? Or at least aging their wine casks."

"You bet, taking our time is one of our better traits. You will find out shortly."

Once we grab a beer and some pretzels, I share with Dieter my thoughts about our program, "I am not looking forward to taking structural analysis or fluid dynamics. I heard the amount of homework is tremendous."

"My thoughts are the same," responds Dieter. I am not bad at math it's just that I'd rather get on to the drawing classes. That's where the real action will be."

"Me too," I respond. We've come to this program to design machines and engines. That's what I enjoy most. I am only taking these engineering courses because you have to know the principals to come up with the designs."

After a few bites of our warm, soft pretzels, we look around the other students gathered in the Biergarten. I look at all the unfamiliar faces and I notice that most are in gregarious groups, laughing and having a good time together. But Dieter and I are new here and so far, we only know each other.

"This is a big university," I say, "but I like how we will have our own drafting studio with drawing tables assigned to us. It will be like having our own little office, a place that we can call our own within this sprawling campus."

"I agree. I feel most productive at my drafting table and having our place marked off in the University will be great. I heard that all-nighters are common in this program. Doesn't worry me though. I know I can pull a few off."

As Dieter and I prost to the beginning of the semester, I start realizing that I will be in a program of many highly ambitious students and that my sense of accomplishment will soon be challenged.

In the distance, I hear the rumbling of voices emanating from down the street and it grows progressively in power. Dieter and I look toward the noise and from around the curve of the street we see a column of men parading four abreast military style. In the front of the column standard-bearers carry red banners with the swastika symbol of the National Socialist Party. They are brown-shirted SA troopers and they are singing the 'Horst Wessel', their group's anthem. They march in step creating a loud punctuated clap on the cobblestone pavement. I see them lift their arms up in the 'Heil Hitler' salute. Immediately the people in the street respond back and salute to them with rousing cheers.

Dieter drops his beer and shoots up from his seat, his body posture turning rigid, his chin jutting out, chest puffed up and eyes squinting. What just happened to the easy-going, country Bavarian I was having a chat with? Dieter seems to have transformed into another persona, one that is totally disconnected from the one that existed a few seconds ago. As the SA troopers march by the Biergarten, Dieter exclaims,

"Arise, Armand and salute." He breaks into the SA anthem along with most people in the garten and I see there is an excited pulse running through Dieter. I get up and reluctantly join along.

As the parade moves along, Dieter says, "This is another good reason to be in Munich. We are in the center of the Hitler movement. Such wonderful potential for all of Germany."

"Well, I hadn't really thought of that myself, just the university life here. Were you part of the Hitler Youth Movement?"

"Why for sure. Weren't you?

"No, I wasn't. I was too busy with my after-school projects."

"This is Germany's future in front of you. You should be involved. I plan on presenting myself the local Party chapter and hopefully getting inducted into the Party."

"We were just talking about how much this design program is going to demand of us," I say. Are you sure you can make that level of time commitment to the National Socialist Party?"

"I've made sacrifices in my life already and making time for this movement will be worth it," says Dieter.

"Quite frankly, I am not sure they are the best Party out there for Germany. A lot of people in the Weimar Republic call these SA guys hoodlums and ruffians."

"Nonsense. They don't understand nor appreciate the National Socialist Party's vision and goals for Germany. We must re-build a strong Germany. Just like we were before the Great War. Just like before we were betrayed by the Communist and Jewish traitors in the end."

"Ok, I see where you are coming from. How about for the sake of our rooming together, we leave politics out of this relationship?"

Dieter sits back into his chair and seems to simmer down. He looks around and takes a sip of beer, "Alright, for now I will abide by that, but I can't guarantee that position for more than a semester. Maybe in due time you will see the way of the Party."

With that I lift my stein and offer a friendly token of truce on this matter. After a few minutes of silence Dieter asks, "So you up for this grueling program. You are not going to quit and be one of the thirty-percent that drop out?"

"I am determined," I say. "This is what I want to do and there is no looking back for me."

"Ha, that is just what I tell people," responds Dieter.

"The event that really kicked off my interest in industrial design," I say, "was when my father took me to the 1921 Rohn glider competition in Wasserkuppe. Watching all those wooden and canvas planes soar through the air and seeing how many of those could actually fly. It was then and there that I wanted to become an industrial designer of vehicles and planes."

"For me the moment came when I was working on the assembly floor of an engine company," says Dieter. "I started working there as a teen and I was looking at all the parts that went together in building an engine. I could see myself designing and improving these parts to make a faster machine."

"Must've been great to see how those engines were built," I say. I haven't worked yet but I am excited about the internships they have programmed for us in our second year."

Dieter asks, "So, tell me about your parents, Armand."

"My father is a waterworks engineer. Hydraulics and fluid dynamics are his specialty. He is tutored me on math and science classes." I respond.

"Interesting," says Dieter." My father is a wheat farmer and he is proud of it, as I am."

"I am sure it is an essential profession," I respond. "But having a father with an engineering background came in handy for math and science homework."

"Perhaps," says Dieter. "Having a father as a farmer didn't hinder me from applying myself at school. I can't say math came easily to me but I can say that I was determined to learn. What about your mother?"

"She is Italian, from Genoa and met my father in Genoa while he was taking a course there."

"That is quite an interesting mix," says Dieter. "So, you are not a pure German but a half-breed mixed with Mediterranean blood."

"I wouldn't use the word half-breed, more like a combination of cultures brought together by two loving parents."

"Do you speak Italian and eat lots of pasta for meals?" inquires Dieter.

"Yes, I do speak the language well and no, I do not eat pasta every night. That is quite a generalization. But I must admit that having a mother who speaks primarily Italian was very interesting while I was growing up."

"How so, Armand?"

"I didn't realize that my mother had an accent so I was confused when my neighborhood friends would make fun of her speech. And then all they had to do to poke fun at me was to yell out, 'A R M A N D O', with an affected accent."

"Very funny," says Dieter. "I can't say my mother's Polish accent caused any embarrassment. More so now that the Party is all about a pure Germany does this lineage make me feel a little uncomfortable.

"Ah, so you are a bit of a muddle yourself," I say. Dieter looks away and doesn't respond. I take a sip of beer and look around at the chatting beer patrons

"I've been working since I was sixteen," says Dieter finally. "I went to work at the engine plant to help my father out to keep the family fed and clothed after my mother died from influenza."

September 1930

The stations black vaulted trusses runs off repetitively into the distance covering lines of green train cars. Multitudes disgorge in a stream as porters and conductors shepherd them down the platforms.

"Hey Walter, over here." I flag my hands over my head to grab his attention from all the other people disembarking from the train. It is a busy time at the Munich Bahnhof and people are packed into every platform and lobby space.

Finally Walter notices me, "Armand! Let me grab my bags and I will be over in a minute," He then hands his tickets to the porter and collects his belongings. Following this, Walter walks down the platform and gives me a big embrace.

"Hey, friend. What a delight to have you come to Munich," I say in a boisterous tone belying our many years of secondary school experiences.

"Yes. I see you received my letter in time and I am glad you made it here to help me settle in," says Walter with a jaunty smile followed by a quick-paced walk out the Banhoff. "Well, Armand, looks like you and I are going to continue the saga of the adventures of the boys from Mainz."

We chuckle at this boyhood connection as I pull in step with Walter down the Luisenstrasse and start the half-mile walk toward the university. Walter and I continue conversing as we stroll past the Alter Botanical Garten. I ask him,

"How did you end up choosing the *Technische Hochschule* and electrical engineering?"

"I ran my course with European political history at the Sorbonne. Or should I say that I ran headlong into the professors there. Paris was lovely but my journey had come to an end. It was time to come back to Germany."

"There are only so many ways to 'run' into the faculty of an esteemed institution like the Sorbonne of Paris," I respond to Walter.

"Well, I did it. I wrote a lengthy paper analyzing Napoleon's invasion of the Lowlands and my professor accused me of plagiarism."

"No. Really? That's awful Walter. I am sure they didn't understand your in–depth insight and vocabulary."

"No they didn't appreciate it. And no matter how I argued the point, the professor and his department would not back down. So I threw my hands up and decided that I had enough of the faculty's arrogance."

"I would've been equally insulted. So I can't blame you for leaving. But I thought you loved Paris. You are such a francophile."

"Oh, yes I still love all things Paris. I will have to tell you over many steins of all the interesting people and incidents that happened. And oh, the ladies were exceptionally stylish and so cosmopolitan."

I am surprised at his commentary on women. This is not quite the same Walter I knew in secondary school back when we met in Wurzburg. Something significant must've transpired in Paris over the last two years. Back then Walter was only moderately interested in girls and he never noticed if she was 'worldly' or 'cosmopolitan'.

"I am sure my friends and I will find it entertaining to hear your stories Walter. So, you are making a switch over to electrical engineering too?"

"Yes, after a having a taste of French 'politics', I decided I had enough. Engineering seems like a straightforward science. You plug factors into an equation and out pops the forces required." I am surprised by Walter's turn of career choice but I can see how his experience in Paris transformed him. Changing subject, I add,

"It worked out well that you can move into our boarding flat," I say. "Over the summer an older fellow graduated and we thought it would be great to stock the place with mutual friends."

"I am looking forward to getting to know Dieter and your other roommates better," says Walter. "I've only met Dieter a few times when I've come to visit here. Things going well as roommates?"

"I think that the two years of rooming together has been stressful on our relationship. We see a lot of each other but sometimes we need our own space. We have engineering lectures together, design studio together and then we go back to the flat after long nights at our drafting tables. He is also very active with the SA movement in Munich. He even wears his brown shirt uniform on the weekends"

"Yes, I see how all of that could be that as being a bit too much," concurs Walter.

"Also, we are both highly-ranked students and this has created a keen sense of competition between us. I think that Dieter thinks he is the superior one."

"I guess I had no idea that design schools could get so cagey."

"Unfortunately, it has been that way with a few of my classmates. I have to warn you over one thing. Dieter views and treats his drafting tools and household goods as if they are family. Do not touch them."

"I gather you crossed that line?"

"You got it Walter. He lent me his adjustable triangle and then I accidentally chipped off the tip. You should've seen Dieter's face when I handed it back. I thought he was going to wail like a funeral mourner. I'm thinking, 'it's just a piece of wood, get over it'.

"But there is something else about Dieter. He stays in the apartment most Friday and Saturday nights when there aren't Party rallies. You know me, I love getting out and pressing the flesh in this university community. But I can rarely get him out and he seems to have little interest."

"I am sure you do like to get out," says Walter with a wink.

"Even more curious is that Dieter never mentions anything about girls. None of my business, but I guess after two years of university I've heard nothing. So I have been spending more time with a friend called Josef Manakin as we have more similar weekend interests. You will meet him soon enough. I think overall you will enjoy my studiomates Walter."

"Thanks, for offering to connect me with your friends here. I wonder what my electrical engineering classmates will be like. If they are too dry I will for sure be hanging out with your studio friends on the weekends."

"Here's the place. We are up on the fifth floor so it will take a few trips to bring up your luggage." With that Walter and I proceed up the apartment steps and in doing so we enter a new phase of our friendship.

MAY 1932

Within the high coffered ceilings of the design hall, my studio mates and I are relaxing after completing our last project for the semester. The rows of drafting tables are barely discernible with all the sheets and drafting equipment sprawled and piled on top. As I sit on my stool cleaning up my drawings and trace studies, Professor Wochen walks into our studio. At first all I see is the glint of light coming off his large black glasses framed by his pointy beard and short cropped hair.

"Armand Kindermann?"

"Yes, Professor Wochen. I am over here," I say as I wave my hand in the air. The professor approaches me with a letter in his hand, "Congratulations, Armand. You have done a great job."

"Really? Over what?"

Stopping in front of my drafting table, Professor Wochen says, "Your competition submittal for the motorcycle design won you second place in the nation."

Stunned by this news, my jaw drops. "You mean my drawings for the motorized bike won second place?"

"Yes, that is right. Your designs were exceptional, and the university is going to make some serious headway with the award. As your design professor, I also will be getting byline credit on all the publications that will be forthcoming. And I thought you would like to know that as the second place winner you have been awarded 500 Reichsmarks and our school will be awarded 2000 Reichsmarks."

"500 Reichsmarks awarded to me? What am I going to do with that kind of money? This is like three months of living expenses in one payment. I never even thought about the prize money when I made my submission."

Professor Wochen continues within earshot of most of my studiomates, "Apparently the panel of judges thought your design was ingenious and well documented. In fact, based on their comments they initially had you ranked as number one. But some other student's entry caught their attention for being more conceptual and suggestive. I saw it myself and I thought his drawings were rather incomplete and sketchy compared to yours. So, congratulations, Armand. Here is the letter from the BMW Foundation announcing your award."

"My God, I can't believe it. I am stunned but extremely happy, Professor. Thanks for delivering such good news to me. I will write to my parents and let them know right away."

"Armand, I didn't think your entry would go all the way to the national level but somehow you pulled it off on this one," says Wochen. "Or as we sometimes say, to me it looked like you pulled a rabbit out of the hat. Don't let this award get to your head and keep working hard for the remainder of the semester."

With that Professor Wochen leaves the studio with a wake of students who are all looking at me. I then look at my classmates and say,

"The first round of beers and pretzels are on me guys!"

Upon saying this my classmates move in closer to shake my hand and look over the award letter. As I am getting pats on my back I notice Dieter sitting quietly at his desk continuing to work on some drawing. He seems to be ignoring the announcement and keeps his head down.

Josef comes up and slaps yet another hand on my back. "Way to go big man, or should we say big Kindermann. Excellent work. That is amazing you came in second nationally with these drawings."

"I know. I can't believe it myself. But thanks for your comments."

"What did Wochen mean with that comment that you 'pulled a rabbit out of the hat'?" says Josef. "Was that a round-about way of critiquing your work?"

"I didn't see that comment coming, especially given that he was handing me the award letter. The university, Wochen and I will all get credit for the award, along with prize monies, so why he felt it necessary to give me a critique with the announcement is beyond me."

"These professors never let up on pushing us harder. There was always something more we could've explored or drawn up. It's never ending here in the studio. But time to celebrate my friend."

Josef looks out to the studio. "Hey. Who here wants to take up Armand on his first round of beers and pretzels!"

There is a crush of people heading out the door and I am swept into a maelstrom of twenty-something, male energy. Other friends shake my hand or pat my shoulders and offer their congratulations. I think this is a dream, this can't be real. How did I pull this one off is right?

We all head down to the Alter Botanical Garten beer halls where many other students will be celebrating the end of classes. It is a few blocks walk down the Katharina Bora Strasse from our Engineering Hall, and we gleefully stride down the streets as if we own the place. My chest and head are swelling with a buoyant confidence. My voice is loud, my comments are getting bolder and I see the humor in everyone's comments. This is reciprocated by my classmates who are giving way to my feelings of exuberance. As we walk toward the tents and serving tables, we decide to sit at a bench table near the band and dance floor. Time to collectively release our project stress with celebratory beers, and we waste no time.

An hour later, Walter joins in with the group, and we buy him a couple of rounds of beer for him to catch up with us. Groups of friends or other people's friends flow by as the night grows hazy. But, a young woman captures my attention. She is with a group of university women who know some fellows taking graphics courses. As the band starts in with a polka I decide with a flurry of energy to approach her.

As I walk closer to her, and I can see she has light brown hair, very soft pale skin, hazel eyes, and a slender, slight figure. She appears almost diminutive within her crowd as if she is afraid to stand out. Still, she has pretty, feminine curves to her and a slight, turning-away demeanor. Why this attracts me, I don't know. I am not like that myself, but I seem to desire someone who is different and not necessarily a striking beauty but an unusual beauty. My mind and heart sum her up in the ten paces I take to get to her.

"How are you Fräuleins doing tonight?" I say, keeping my eyes moving from one woman to the next. As they respond, I zero in on my target. She is a bit shy, but I hold her gaze. "What a beautiful night to be celebrating with friends at the end of the semester," I continue.

Turning to her specifically, I say, "My name is Armand, what is yours?"

"I am Vanessa."

"Nice to meet you, Vanessa

She casts her eyes down at first then looks up to respond, "We are also celebrating the end of classes. Are those your friends from the University?"

"Yes, these are my industrial design classmates. We just finished our year-end presentations." The air is brisk, the hall lights are shimmering, the beer is getting flat, but my eyes and heart are starting to race.

"Oh, how did the presentations go?" asks Vanessa.

"It was down to wire as usual along with a couple of late nights but hey, we all finished up."

"And I suppose yours went pretty well?"

"I would say I made a decent finish for the semester. So, I am happy." As I say this I notice that she is looking back toward her companions. Even so I decide to keep the conversation going. "But you should've seen this one poor fellow. He was not only dead, flat tired like the rest of us, he was also very nervous. He had a slight twitch going on with his eyes as he made his presentation. Then he accidentally knocked down two of his drawing easels. Boom! They come down right in front of the assembly of professors and they all jumped from their seats as if to clear out for their safety. Ha! We all started laughing breaking decorum on how these usually go."

She giggles and looks back at me. Having her attention again, I seize the moment to pursue another story and hope this one will be more comical and perhaps more telling of my character.

"You know when I grew up, I traveled to Italy many times to visit my mother's relatives. Not being a native speaker, it took me a while to catch on to the nuances of the Italian language," I start off looking her steadily in the eye while my stein swings over her shoulder. "So, one fine Sunday afternoon, my Nona asked me in Italian if I was hungry. Now in Italian, hungry is *fame* but it came across to my German ears as a banner, *fahne*. So, I told her no I wasn't a banner."

The young woman continues smiling and lets out a little laugh. This is good feedback I am getting so I continue, "But I was too intimidated to question our family matriarch. The result was that I didn't get lunch that day." Am I slurring and swaying right now? Maybe I am losing her?

No, it's working and her smile broadens. I can feel an energy of attraction from her, or is that the music pounding on my eardrums? The band switches to a more contemporary song and then I quickly reach for her hand and tell her. "This is my favorite song. We must dance to this one."

I grab her hand and without hesitation lead her to the dance floor. It is a whirl of lights, music, jostling people as her smile radiates outward toward me. I am holding her against me, my smile broad and feeling energetic, and I look into her eyes,

"Excuse my forwardness to ask you to dance but I am in a very festive mood." Is the floor tilting? I better keep my balance.

"Oh no, I like your enthusiasm, it's very infectious, says Vanessa. "I am from Munich, what about you?"

I respond between polka steps and heavy breathing. "I am from Mainz and I spent secondary school in Wurzburg. But I have traveled further east to find my profession and perhaps someone special to dance with me." The surrounding Biergarten is now swirling faster than our polka steps.

"Your words match your smile. I like that," says Vanessa while gripping my hand. "Oh, what is this next song, Armand?"

As we move straight into the next song I know from this moment on that tonight will be a memorable one. After our second dance finishes, I bring Vanessa over to the table where my friends are stationed. Seeing my opportunity, they do their part in talking up my accomplishments and character to impress Vanessa. Walter and Josef come up to us and Josef puts an arm around me.

"Well, who is this, Armand? Would you introduce me to your pretty friend?"

"This is Vanessa. She is from Munich and she is quite the polka dancer."

"Oh, thank you, Armand," exclaims Vanessa.

"Nice to meet you Vanessa, my name is Josef. Welcome to our after-studio celebration."

"Nice to meet you, Josef and to join in your gathering. I can see your group is quite excited tonight. I suppose it was a demanding semester?"

Josef leans in closer while keeping his arms tightly around my shoulder, "Sure was. But let me tell you. This man, Armand, is the toast of our studio tonight. He just bought a few rounds of beer for all of us."

"Really? That's awfully generous of you. Is there some special occasion or should I recognize your family name from a company sign?" she asks me.

Josef looks at me with a big smile. "This fellow, big man Kindermann, just won a national design competition and put our department on the map." Josef swings his stein and clinks a *prost* with Walter and me. Walter is also smiling broadly at me, his eyes half-closed as he extends out his beer.

"Ah, that must be why you are so excited. I am very impressed indeed," says Vanessa with widened eyes.

"Thanks Josef. And yes, I am going to celebrate tonight like there is no tomorrow. Well, at least there is no class tomorrow." I take a quick glance at our table and everyone seems happy. Everything is great. Even the background noise of people is buzzing with joy. From the corner of my eye I see that Dieter has finally arrived to join in our studio's celebration. While I am still chatting with Josef and Vanessa, I see Dieter making his way through the crowds and I exclaim to him,

"Dieter, you are finally here. I didn't think you were going to make it, especially since it is Friday night."

"I gave myself some time to consider the benefits of coming out to join everyone here," says Dieter casting a glance around. "I see you fellows have already made a good dent into the evening fracas."

"Sure," says Josef. And who wouldn't? Can I pour you a glass from our pitcher?"

"Yes, I will take half a stein's worth," says Dieter. "Who is this young lady, Armand?"

"Ah, this is Vanessa," I say extending my arm toward Vanessa. She is a graphic design student at our university. Her classes are just a few buildings over from us."

Dieter extends his hands out and greets Vanessa, "My pleasure. We definitely are not graced with any delightful woman like you in our program, Vanessa."

"Why thank you, Dieter," responds Vanessa with a smile and twist of her skirt. "Are you in Armand's studio and also finished with your design projects?"

"Yes, I am. But I did not have as glorious a finish as Armand did," say Dieter with a level tone. "Maybe next year. Just watch out, Armand."

"Why, I am sure your hard work will pay off Dieter," offers Vanessa sympathetically with a long glance at him.

Seeing that this newly found interest of mine is open to meet other men as well, I move in between the two and say to Vanessa, "How about another dance?"

Vanessa looks me over and says, "I am not sure you will make it through another dance. You are swaying a bit. How about we wait this one out and we can chat more with your studio mates?"

While I simmer on that comment, Walter comes up from behind and gives me a hug around my neck interrupting my lock on Vanessa. "Armand, you are the big man tonight. I love you like a brother. Cheers to you." Walter exclaims with glassy eyes and a sloppy smile, his rosy cheeks even more red than usual.

The dance music continues in the background and the Garten seems full to capacity. Is the music getting softer or is it more like a drone now? I peer into my stein then at Vanessa who's chatting with Josef and Dieter. My glass is empty, so I order another one. I take large gulps of beer as I consider how to keep this woman in my orbit. Then the Biergarten setting gets blurry, people's voices are undecipherable, the ground becomes unsteady and then I remember no more.

★★★

I wake up on the couch of the shared living room. My clothes are still on. Ouch, my head hurts as I try to lift it up. I give up and let gravity take my head back deep into the sofa pillow. Walter comes out of his room and looks at me with an overly cheerful smile.

"Hey. You put on quite the show last night."

"Oh no, what do you mean?" I ask.

Walter chuckles, "You were a raucous hit last evening. Dancing, drinking games, telling stories and I didn't know you could sing as well. My, my Armand. You are the man. I always thought you were just another engineer, but you had me wrong. *Prost* my friend."

"My body feels only weakness in every muscle and joint. I don't think I am ever going to get off this sofa."

"So how did you do with that cute, petite Vanessa gal? I thought you were making good progress with her until you finished your fourth stein and then knocked the waitress Fräuleins down in a stupor. I think that's about the time that Vanessa took an exit stage right with her friends and some other fellows from our studio. No worries for you, though, you just went right onto the next set of Fräuleins."

"Oh my God. Vanessa, that's right. I totally lost her for the evening."

"Maybe you did but I am not sure other guys in your studio lost track of her."

"Look, you need to help me. I made a big mistake by drinking so much last night, and I want to find Vanessa. Do you know any of her friends?" I plead with almost enough energy to almost lift up my head off the sofa.

41

"Ok, let me think dear, Armand. So, what's it to you to find out her address?"

"Oh, please, I am not in the mood to bargain, especially as prostrate as I am right now. Just be a good friend and give me some names of her friends." Walter scratches his chin and looks around aimlessly for dramatic effect.

"Ok, I believe one of her friends is in our graphics classes, and she seems to know Vanessa very well. But you never know if Josef and Dieter already have her number."

"Thanks, you are a friend for life but don't take advantage of me either you *scheisse*. I don't even want to consider the possibility that she left with either of them. Since when has Dieter ever shown any interest in women anyway?" With that, I set my head down and put my forearm across my forehead.

"I just have to think of a way," I mumble out, "to amend for my actions so she will find me respectable enough to want to see me again."

★★★

The following day, Sunday, I go into the school drafting hall to work on one last technical illustration and to enjoy the solitude. Thoughts of over how to reach Vanessa are still swirling in my mind and the angst ruptures the silence of the drafting hall. I tear off a sheet of vellum from a drawing roll, line up the sheet on my drafting table so it is squared off and then I tape the sheet down. I move my parallel ruler up and down as if to get my mind tuned in and then I reach for the engineering scale to start measuring the size of this piece of machinery. I strike a few parallel lines and then I take my 45' triangle and start drawing the vertical lines. As I draw with intent and focus, my brain in parallel starts analyzing my mess up with Vanessa,

Ok, she was beautiful, I felt so charmed with her being in my arms, she is just the kind of gal I've been looking for and then, then I had to blow it! How could you have lost your drinking control, Armand? Just when you had it all coming together, the conversation, the

42

dance, the introduction of friends and getting those welcoming looks from her.

I sharpen my pencil and then reach for the adjustable triangle to start laying out angled lines around the housing piece. Let's see, how will I get the radius of the curves figured out?

If only I hadn't drunk that fourth stein. Who said I was a big drinker anyway? I haven't had a date all year and that was my one chance and I fumbled it! Then to have Josef and Dieter pour the charm on her and she even seemed interested in them.

I lift the compass from its case, sharpen the lead on sandpaper, and then adjust the width of the pincers to match my desired radius. I spin the compass and drag the point at an angle so to keep it sharp and even.

Maybe I can reach this friend of hers in the graphics laboratory tomorrow afternoon as Walter had mentioned. I believe they hold their studios after our joint technical illustration courses.

Then I pull down the moveable drafting arm from the top of the table and rotate the hub, so the rulers are just in line with the ends of the curves I have just drawn. I line up the ruler with the tangent of the curve and away I draw a nice crisp line that shoots out of the radius.

'That's it, I will befriend the woman whom Walter knows, let her see that I am a great guy, and she will get word back to Vanessa. At the same time, I will ask her friend what Vanessa's class schedule is. I will then just 'happen' to meet her outside her class for a chat. Ok, time to execute this plan.

★★★

A few students are milling through the hallways taking final exams or finishing up their projects. I scan every woman that passes out of the technical illustration class hoping to spot the woman that Walter has described. I finally recognize one as having been at the Alter Botanical Gardens.

"Hello there. I hear you are a friend of Walter Ignaz. Yes?"

"Yes, I am," she says. How can I help you? Oh, wait, I think I recognize you from last Friday."

"Yes, you probably remember me, but unfortunately, I don't remember much of that night myself," I reply.

"I bet you don't. I am surprised guys like you get through the university, but somehow you do."

"I'm sorry. My name is Armand, Armand Kindermann. Thank you for your insight and honesty. I deserve it all. My friend Walter tells me that you may be a friend of Vanessa's."

"I may be. What is it to you if I am?"

Realizing that this may be like prying open clams, I respond, "Well, I am trying to locate her and give her a little message."

"Hmm... I don't think she is in the mood to receive a communication from your type."

"Ah, what is your name?"

"Me? I am Bonnie Colintroppo."

"Oh, really? You know my mother is Italian, are you Italian as well?" I ask.

"From my father's side. So, you are half Italian too?"

"*Si e vero, e per sempre no?* I don't think I've met another gal here at the University who is half Italian like me." Bonnie catches my sentiment and softens up her great wall of defense.

"Ah, well maybe that explains your inability to control your drinking. German men are usually pretty good at holding their beer, but you seem to have lost it very easily like a kid in a *dulceteria.*"

"Maybe you are right. Maybe I should stick to Chianti from my mother's homeland. Just the way my Nona would serve it at our Sunday dinners."

"Ah yes, the Nona. Sure, mine was quite the matriarch. She controlled all of our family gatherings and every adult relationship. My poor German mother was beside herself most of the time."

"Well, I couldn't even understand my Nona half the time. And if I didn't understand her I was always too afraid to ask her to repeat it. As a young boy, she seemed imposing and mean to me."

She laughs, "Yes, I know what you mean. They must make them all the same way in Italy; with a mean temperament and no humor. Just all raising and disciplining the children." As Bonnie says this, she lifts her hand up, cups her palm and acts as if she is swatting some hapless grandchild.

"Sounds like you traveled to Italy often then?" I inquire.

"Sure, many a summer. That's the best time to visit, isn't it? Late evenings with all your friends in the piazza or an afternoon on the *spiaggia* playing in the soft sand by the ocean."

"Same here. Couldn't have been better. Where in Italy did you go to visit your family?"

A slight smile appears on Bonnie's face as she tosses her hair one side to the other, "Pisa, where there is a beautiful beach just north of town."

Catching her universal body language of womanly interest, I move in a little closer and say, "Yes, I did envy those Pisano's for their beach. Genoa's beach was, ah, *cosi, cosi*, so, so." I underline the last part with articulated hand gestures.

We stop chatting for a second and look at each other with smiles. This isn't what I had expected from meeting Vanessa's friend.

"So how come I have never seen you in my technical illustration classes?" I ask her.

"Perhaps because I am only a second-year student. What year are you?"

"I am in my fourth year and I have another year to go. That would explain things."

Still staring at each other I note that her light olive complexion is very appealing. Her deep brown eyes are playful and swimming in attractiveness. Her brown hair is lush and long, framing her feminine upper body.

"Say, Bonnie I was heading over to the university dining hall and I would love to chat more about your Nonna and your Italian summers. Would you like to join me? *Per favore?*"

Bonnie twists her shoulders sidewise while slightly pressing her books into her chest. "Sure, that would be nice or should I say, *molto bello, un piacere.*"

★★★

It is the following week and the Engineering Ball at the university's performance center will wrap up our semester. The center's ballroom has been decorated with streamers and banners livening up the marble columns and wood coffered ceilings. I attend with my friends and we cluster together telling stories of our final exam week. Feeling a little restless, I turn away from my group and see Bonnie strolling by herself. Her thick dark hair and deep eyes arrest me and hold me in my place. She is wearing a long dress that gathers at her waist, high-heeled shoes and she is donning a silk hairpiece. I reach out to take her hand and greet her in a courteous manner. After a few pleasantries, I ask her to the dance floor.

It is a slow number, and I am holding her one hand up, and my other hand is resting on the small of her back. Bonnie seems content as we sway around the dance floor. I am starting to feel some warmth in my chest I as we pull in close to each other. I can just start seeing past her shoulders and onto her bare back.

As I dance with Bonnie, I look to the sides and see various grouping of engineering classmates. I then see Vanessa standing on the edge of the dance floor with Dieter at her side. I grip Bonnie's hand tightly while I also lock in eyes on Vanessa. As I do this, I see her and Dieter move out to the dance floor for the next slow number.

As the song ends, I escort Bonnie toward where Vanessa and Dieter are now standing. Our twosomes approach each other.

"Dieter and Vanessa. What a delight to see you both here," I say.

"The same, Armand," says Dieter. "So glad you introduced me to Vanessa earlier. We have so many design interests in common."

"Yes, it has been nice to get to know Dieter better over the last two weeks." smiles Vanessa. "I've learned so much about your design program." Turning to at look Bonnie, she continues, "Bonnie, I didn't know you were coming with Armand here tonight."

"We didn't come together," says Bonnie. "But we did meet briefly last week in the graphics lab. We just met up a few minutes ago ourselves, Vanessa."

"I see," says Vanessa continuing to stare at Bonnie. The music starts up again and I turn to Vanessa stating, "Bonnie and Dieter, do you mind if Vanessa and I have this next dance?" The two of them look at us and turn their heads toward the dance floor with polite approval.

As I clasp hands with Vanessa for the dance, I say, "Look, Vanessa, I know I gave you a bad impression at the Alter Botanical Gartens, but I am asking you to reconsider."

"Oh, really, Armand?" says Vanessa. "After you obviously drank too much, lost control and nearly got yourself thrown out of the Garten."

"I got a little too excited," I exclaim. "Finishing our projects, delivering our presentations and learning of my winning that national design competition, all made for a very exuberant Armand."

"Ha, exuberant you were. How do I know if you are not like that every Friday night?" say Vanessa as we continue dancing.

"I am a very studious and dedicated student here. What you saw was very unusual of me." I reason with Vanessa. "Look, I would appreciate your giving me another chance to show you more about myself and my character."

"I am already making plans with other men from the university. Why should I wait to verify your character when I can see there are others with good social behavior?"

"Because, I will make it worth your time. I am quite taken with you and I am expressing to you my sincere intent."

"Hmm, well-spoken," says Vanessa. "How do I know if that isn't just a line you tell all the woman you take an interest in?"

"Well, there aren't many other women of interest to be honest. In fact, there are no others."

The song ends, and I bring Vanessa off into the entry lobby for some privacy. "Vanessa, I made a total fool of myself that night, and I thought for sure you were unimpressed if not repulsed by my behavior."

"Oh, I was impressed." Vanessa takes a deep breath. "You were quite an energetic showman and I was very entertained by you. I just felt that after a point it was time for me to leave before you and your friends got out of hand."

"So, will give me another chance?"

"Perhaps, but I think we should take this step by step."

"Very well. How about we start off with this next song?"

"Don't get too far ahead of yourself, Armand, but sure, I can start there."

As I lead Vanessa back into the parquet dance floor, I now know that this will be the memorable night I have been waiting for.

APRIL 1933

Josef Manakin and I are lounging in the engineering student's hall chatting away when Josef notices a poster pinned on the announcement board,

"Hey, Armand. Looks like one of our famous alumn is going to speak in the main lecture hall this evening. Have you ever heard of Willy Messerschmitt, the plane designer?"

"Sure, I am quite familiar with his planes. I've even seen him at some glider competitions. What's his lecture about?"

"It says here that he will be going over the latest advancements in airplane design along with highlights of his company's achievements."

"I would love to go. You have an interest in planes too?"

"Sure. Who wouldn't want to design a plane. It would be a designer's dream job."

"I think so too," I respond. "I don't see myself getting stuck drawing up driveshaft parts all my life, so I think I should check out his lecture. We better head over soon then."

Josef and I gather up our books and head over a few buildings to the main engineering lecture hall.

"I've heard Messerschmitt has hired some recent graduates from our program along with mechanical and electrical engineers," Josef says. "Maybe we can get an in on what he is looking for in his hires."

"I like how you are thinking. All the more reason to attend this lecture. Maybe I will get a chance to shake his hand and get my name on his interview list."

As we walk down the rows of seats in the wood-paneled hall, I see Dieter seated up front by himself. Noticing this, Josef says, "Hey there is your roommate. I gather he has the same idea to get into aviation design."

"I wouldn't know as of lately," I say. "I haven't had a meaningful chat with him since the beginning of the semester."

We then take a seat mid-way back and listen as a mechanical engineering professor rises to the stage taking the podium while stating,

"We are pleased to present this lecture series on advances in German plane design over the last decade. Tonight's inaugural address will be by our esteemed alum Willy Emil Messerschmitt, *Technische Hochschule* class of 1923. Herr Messerschmitt will commence our guest lecturer series and we hope this will lay the groundwork for what will eventually become a new department. Due to his tremendous accomplishments in practical applications, Herr Messerschmitt has recently been designated a guest lecturer by our faculty. Please join me in welcoming our lecturer for this evening."

Messerschmitt enters the auditorium and we all stand and politely clap. He acknowledges the audience with a few waves over his head and proceeds to take the lectern up on the stage. I see before me a man in his mid-thirties with a slender physique, thinning hair, a prominent dome of a forehead, deep-set eyes, and thin lips with a jutting chin. As he gathers his papers for the lecture he lights a cigarette and takes a few puffs.

"Good evening faculty and students of the Munich *Technische Hochschule*. Just ten years ago I graduated from this esteemed institution, and I recognize many of my professors here in the audience. My sincerest and deepest gratitude to the entire faculty present. As you know, there is no school for aircraft design yet, but with this lecture series we are beginning to lay the groundwork for what I hope will become the first fully dedicated school of aeronautics in Germany."

There is a round of applause and Messerschmitt continues,

"It is my pleasure this evening to provide you with an overview of plane developments in the last five years and in particular, the direction of our company, BFW. First, a little history on how we arrived at this exciting point in aircraft design. And I say 'we' as a collective German aircraft industry. The truth of the matter is that Germany's aviation industry has been built on the sailplane experimentations over the past decade. Due to our restrictions outlined in the Versailles Treaty, we had to find a way to continue plane research and development without propeller engines. So fellows like myself tinkered around with sailplanes and then later lightly propelled gliders. The annual Rhön glider competitions at Wasserkuppe garnered our attention and brought us all together to show off our latest advances. Being focused on gliding principals for a good ten years has paid back to Germany ten-fold in the development of high-performance planes.

"Back in 1924, I completed my second Rhön Air Competition with my partner Frederic Harth, an architect, and from then on I developed various principals for advancing glider designs. Once Germany had the go-ahead to employ piston engines, we then transitioned to passenger planes, mail planes and sport planes. The best of these passenger plane developments has resulted in the M29 model which we have delivered to Luft Hansa for passenger plane service.

"From all this work, my company has developed these simple and few themes: clean aerodynamic lines, easy to construct, light of weight combined and streamlined profiles. Moreover, we have moved to all metal planes with lower, mono-wings and enclosed cockpits. I also firmly believe that the time of bi-planes and wood construction is long due for retirement."

Messerschmitt scans the room with a grin,

Through his lecture, I also learn that Professor Messerschmitt is from Frankfurt, a regional capital not far from my hometown of Mainz. Messerschmitt is a mere twelve years older than me, and he has now merged his Messerschmitt Flugzeugbau GmbH Bamberg company with Bayerische Flugzeugwerke AG in Augsburg, also located in the State of Bavaria. The resultant entity is now referred to as BFW. In return, he is the Chief Aircraft Designer, a shareholder, and a board member. He basically has full control of the design, development and direction of the airplanes and he seems intent on realizing exciting advances. He says that his engineers and industrial designers in their project bureaus are always working at top capacity and our need for design talent is tremendous.

And while Messerschmitt's background started with gliders, as of lately he has transitioned more into creating powered passenger, mail and sport planes. He says that he believes moving people and goods quickly between cities will be key to Germany's economic recovery.

What most catches me is that at such a young age, thirty-five, Messerschmitt is so confident to take on the well-established aircraft companies in Germany. Heinkel, Focke-Wulf, Dornier, and Arado, are all plane companies that have been around since the Great War. Their names are synonymous with aircraft, yet here is this upstart challenging the status quo with his new company and daring to take them on full bore.

The company has had a rocky financial history to date. BFW was near bankruptcy in 1931, but then they were able to secure orders for their M 20 and M 28 passenger aircraft from the nation's subsidized airlines, Luft Hansa. It seems, though that the company is pulling through, and I am captivated by his energy, drive and potential. My burgeoning sense of self starts seeing the possibility of grand proportions with this company making my current internship seem woefully inadequate for my ambitions. Fitting in more with my personal ideals, it appears more exciting to work with this underdog company rather than the established aircraft companies of Germany. Perhaps a risky idea for me but being only twenty-three, why not?

Messerschmitt ends his lecture with this strong statement on design: "The designer does not only see the aircraft that is flying today, or even the aircraft that is being built or that exists only as a project. No, he looks much further into the future. Long before an airplane is finished, he knows how it could have been improved. Our work will never cease."

I am taken by his design manifesto and find it ringing in harmony with my own design thoughts. It is a process in which you explore solutions, tackle multiple problems in many dimensions and then you are left wondering if your solution was the best or the final one. How many hours more could I have worked on a given solution only to be halted by the time on the clock? But finding excellence in design is always worth the extra effort.

A professor takes the stage next to Messerschmitt and asks the audience if they have questions for Herr Messerschmitt. One of the faculty asks him what he thinks of the newly formed Ministry of Aviation, (RLM), and if he has joined the National Socialist party.

"It is a beneficial thing that our government is putting such great emphasis on developing the aircraft industries. Up until now, there has been no significant government interest. So, I believe the best way to harness all the air design and manufacturing capacity in Germany is with a centralized control mechanism. I think this will end up accelerating research and development of planes. And we can see it already with the government taking the lead in setting performance criteria for new planes that far exceed current standards. So, the central government is challenging us aircraft companies to come forward with better ideas, better designs and in the end a stronger German aircraft industry."

There is slight murmur of positive response from the crowd.

"It is has been very hard for any aircraft company, much less mine, to develop and produce advanced planes in any quantity. There just isn't enough market demand or financing going around to seed our developments. I appreciate Führer Adolf Hitler and General Field Marshal Herman Göring's prioritization of the aircraft industry. They have committed millions of Reichsmarks toward new plane developments and our company is very excited to see where this will take us. Without Hitler and Göring's vision, our plane industry would still be building wooden bi-planes for another decade.

"As for joining the Nazi party, I have not yet to date, but I do have two good friends who are actively recruiting me, Ernest Udet and Rudolf Hess. Both have been long-time acquaintances and supporters of mine. In fact, recently, Herr Hess got me out of a jam with the City of Augsburg. Last year, the city burger meisters wanted to seize my plant due to back taxes owed. But Rudolf Hess stepped in and persuaded them to back off, giving me time to come through with eventual profits. So, I think I owe him a favor, yes? But, from a business perspective, I think joining the National Socialist Party will be a good move for our aircraft business. I am confident you will hear news on that front. Next question?"

A graduate student rises, "Herr Messerschmitt, do you think the underlying objective of the RLM is military planes more so than commercial ones?"

Messerschmitt smiles a bit and looks down at his rostrum, "Perhaps it is, but I believe what we can learn from military planes, and this will help the commercial and sport market in the end. Moreover, I believe that a commercial aviation company like ours will be able to switch over to military planes with ease. I have never designed a military plane before but given our high-performance sport plane background along with our design talent, I am confident we can figure this one out. Plus, I have plenty of talented students coming out of this University with a desire to achieve this."

A mild chuckle can be heard from the audience.

Another professor rises. "What recommendations do you have for our aspiring engineers who want to either work for you, start their own aircraft company or become managers in a company?"

"I will say from a business point of view that operating an aircraft company takes a lot of cash and investment into heavy equipment. For us to carry through the design and production of a passenger plane, we must spend thousands of design hours, prototyping, testing and then incur production expenses to bring a new plane to market. So, our company welcomes new contract orders to obtain cash and to seed our new planes under development. I am always working on the multiple plane designs and sometimes I just have to believe in myself and plunge forward with their advancement with or without investment backers.

"Currently, we have eighty employees with about half of them involved in research, design, experimental workshops and production design. I have set up project bureaus for each type of plane, and these bureaus are headed up by doctorate engineers who oversee their development. The time and cost it takes to bring one of these new planes to the production covers many years, and I must admit, I have not done a good job in projecting what these costs will be. For all of you up-and-coming engineers, I recommend you understand accounting or have a generous investor on your side."

Slight laughter runs through the audience. Messerschmitt then concludes the lecture by stepping down from the stage and stands in front of the seating. I then rise without further thought and cue up to a growing line of students seeking to speak with the lecturer. I see that Dieter's upfront seat has garnered him first position to speak with Messerschmitt and I mull over how I can sharpen my introduction. Luckily, Messerschmitt is keeping his student chats brief and within ten minutes I am standing before him.

"Herr Messerschmitt," I say with my hand out for a shake. "It is my pleasure to meet you. Your lecture was eye-opening and truly inspiring for a student like me."

Looking calm and with his chin out, Messerschmitt smiles politely and says, "Thank you young man. It has been quite a challenge developing all the gliders and sport planes I have presented."

"I was most impressed at how you keep coming up with new ideas for your planes," I say. "Our professors are always pushing us to try new ideas and approaches."

"That is how I approach design," responds Messerschmitt who then asks me, "What is your engineering major young man?"

"I am in mechanical engineering with a focus on industrial design."

"Interesting area and very practical application. We are just starting to land contracts with larger production volumes and developing fabrication drawings will be a critical effort for us."

"Turning mechanical concepts into working machines is my specialty and passion, sir."

"Well I see there are a few of your other fellow classmates are here. BFW will be needing to employ many new production designers over this summer. When are you graduating?"

"I finish up next month and I would be honored to have an opportunity to meet with your managing engineers."

"Very well," says Messerschmitt handing out a business calling card. "Why don't you write to my company, attention Herr Coulis and request an interview."

"Thank you, sir. I will follow up immediately." Messerschmitt looks over my shoulder to the next person so I shake his hand and step out of the line. With sudden clarity, I know this is the company I must pursue for employment.

May 1933

As I leave the Augsburg bus station, I double check my portfolio. Did I bring my most recent truck engine drawings from my internship? What about that rendered axonometric from our senior project? I flip through the pages and yes, there they are. Time to present myself not as a student anymore but as working man. I just bought this suit and tie last week, and they are barely creased. I feel like I snuck into my father's closet and absconded with his outfits. Ok, hold yourself together and think like you are meeting the faculty for a review of your thesis.

The bus drives three miles south of Augsburg till we are at the Messerschmitt plant. A sprawling complex that is under construction everywhere I look. Even the road is being ripped up and paved over.

"Haunstetten! Messerschmitt AG!" Yells out the bus driver as I quickly descend holding my portfolio against my chest for safety.

As the bus pulls away like a stage curtain, before me is revealed a complex of five buildings, with more under construction. I gather the company has been successful in landing more Air Ministry contracts. Out on the airfield, I see various vaulted hangars and outside are parked an array of M37s, a passenger plane being used by Luft Hansa for commercial flights. Other unfamiliar aircraft, large and small are strewn about the tarmacs further from the public entrance. Beyond the hangers, I catch a glimpse of an airfield and I hear the rumbling of propeller engines gearing up for flight.

Feeling like a foreign visitor who has no credentials to be here, I work toward to what must be the main administration building. If another construction truck breezes by my suit will change colors from gray to brown. I make my way to the administration offices and am told to wait in a long lobby outside a series of conference rooms.

Finally, I am asked to come forward and I am directed to Messerschmitt's personal office. Upon meeting the professor, I notice that he now dons a Nazi party lapel on his suit coat. Seeming to be rather busy, he has me sit down, and he reviews my portfolio to remind himself of our introduction at the lecture.

Flipping through my drawings from school and the trucking company internship, he looks up, pointing his chin toward me and asks, "What do you know about sheet metal fabrication and creating stressed skin plates?"

"I took a course in structural dynamics sir and I learned that it all depends on truss and rivet spacing. My truck company internship focused me on how to structure the engine hood of trucks in a similar fashion."

"Do you have some of those drawings to show me?"

"Yes," I say as I flip through my portfolio. "Here, for these aluminum hoods I structured the shape, supports and connections for the sheet metal. And then I worked up the fabrication drawings."

Messerschmitt looks over my drawings for a good minute, but it seems longer as I know he is looking at the practicality of my approach. "What about your ability to design industrial parts?"

"Sir, my best example is my competition submittal for the BMW motor bike design I completed last year." I open up my portfolio and place it in front of him. He looks them over turning his head sideways a few times. He then slides the portfolio back to me and I recall to connect with his past,

"I've been to the Rohn Air competition a few times; once in 1921 and again in 1924. Then our secondary school entered a glider for the competition in 1927. I saw your planes' performance there and that is impressive that you have won so many glider awards, sir."

Messerschmitt's eyes soften their look and a small smile comes across his face, "Why you should've told me that right away. Given your active interest in sailplanes and the BMW design award, we would love to have you here. Please take this note and ask to see our engineering superintendent, Gerhard Coulis and he will further review your work. I appreciate you stopping by and a have a good rest of your day." With that Messerschmitt dismisses me, leaving me to exit his offices unescorted and to make my way through the halls to Coulis' offices."

After waiting ten minutes in the executive lobby, I hear the assistant say, "Herr Kindermann, you may now pass onto our engineering superintendent, Gerhard Coulis. As I walk into his offices a see a slender man with long face, droopy cheeks, a receding chin line that matches is receding hairline. Without saying much and seeming to be in a hurry, he takes my portfolio and thumbs through it.

Looking up he says, "How long did you take on these motorcycle drawings and how well did you understand of the mechanics behind the design?" I notice that he tends to speak in short bursts and I struggle to make sure I did not miss something he stated.

I respond, "I worked closely with the design engineers and I made every effort to capture their engineering direction. Once I set my design scheme, it took me two weeks to develop the ink on vellum drawings and renderings. After a few quiet grunts, he looks up and says in a crisp and rapid pace,

"Young man, your work is fairly good, but I think you could do even better work here. When can you start working?"

Taking a breath to slow myself down, I respond, "Sir, I am finishing technical college this May along with my internship and I can be here by mid-June."

Herr Coulis seems pleased with the response and then passes me on to meet with an administrative assistant for some paperwork.

★★★

I return to Munich to tell Vanessa about the exciting day and interview I had with BFW and she asks me,

"Armand, it sounds great for you to be offered an entry-level position but are you sure this is the right company for you? Couldn't you also interview at Focke-Wulf or Dornier as well? They seem more established. Who knows if this Messerschmitt company will succeed? He just exited bankruptcy a few months ago."

"This company is going where I want to go. The future is wide open for BFW. They have a fresh outlook on plane design, and I think in the long run they will end up with more ingenious aircraft."

"But they are not a proven company yet. What if they fold up and go into bankruptcy again? Willy Messerschmitt seems too young to be running an aircraft company. Plus, I thought you wanted to design passenger and sport planes. From what you told me it sounds like they are gearing up to develop warplanes."

"I don't think Messerschmitt will move too far from his current base of commercial planes. That's what he is good at; gliders, sport planes, and passenger aircraft. And that's where I also want to go."

"Plus, they are not a military contractor," I continue. "I have no intention of getting involved in war machines. Haven't our parents had enough of war back in the teens? I do not want to get into a military-based company. I can tell that Herr Messerschmitt is focused on bringing the world of aviation and travel to us everyday people. A plane system that transports people around Bavaria, just like what Northern Bavarian Airlines is doing now with his airplanes."

Vanessa responds, "We would have to move to Augsburg some thirty-six miles away from Munich, and I will be that much further away from my family here."

I ponder Vanessa's point and realize that while I have been miles away from my family since I have been fourteen she, at age twenty-two, has never been away from her family.

"I am confident that Messerschmitt's BFW will be a successful growing company and that we will find suitable employment today and an even better future there tomorrow."

Vanessa seems to calm down. "Ok love. You appear to know what you are doing. I just want to make sure this is the right company for you. You are a talented man, and I totally believe in you. I just want to ensure you will be happy in the long run."

"That is sweet of you to think that way. We are not even married yet, but I already feel you have my best interests at heart."

With that, we embrace and give each other a kiss. For not having dated much, I feel grateful that I have met such a wise woman at such an early age. I know that I will ask her to marry me soon but for the next year we will be living in separate cities, she in Munich and I in Augsburg.

JUNE 1933

After settling into a one-room flat, I arrive at the Augsburg design offices and find myself stationed in a sea of drafting tables that stretch from one end to the other of a large hall. Smooth concrete walls and black mullioned windows box in the endless rows of tables. All the drafting surfaces are slanted up at a high angle and I hear the sound of paper being torn, triangles slapping the desk tops and the grinding of pencil sharpeners.

I am assigned to a supervisor, Wolfgang Degel a man of thirty-two who is slender of build while being focused on detail and precision. In the first hour of work he calls me over to his drafting table to assign my work. There he has sketches left by Professor Messerschmitt from the night before, and they are a sprawl of scribbles and notations on how to sweep back the wings and have disengaging ailerons. Wolfgang muses aloud while I stand at attention in front of his desk,

"I made calculations on the number of wing trusses needed to hold this wing in place, and I've selected there to be eighteen trusses, spaced twelve inches apart and they are to be open-webbed aluminum. So, my young man, do you know the section modulus of aluminum and can you determine if it can bear that much bending moment?"

"Herr Degel, I do recall from material properties class that aluminum is light, has a high melting temperature and is strong for its weight. I do not, though remember the coefficient offhand. I do know which reference book to obtain it from, the German Metals Standards book by Krupp Industries."

"Well guessed young man. Good points but we use the German Metals Industry coefficients here and from now on that will be your Bible."

"Yes, Herr Degel I will follow through on that," I say with much-stressed deference.

He smiles and relaxes his stance. "You will do fine here. Relax and call me Wolfgang. We have a lot of work to do, and I'm happy to put a graduate from the Munich *Technische Hochschule* to work."

I set myself down at my desk and pull out my portfolio of drafting instruments. As is the custom, designers are a bit like traveling tradesmen, perhaps a bit of heritage from the German Guild practices. To each job, we bring our own instruments; triangles of all sizes, rulers, compasses, mechanical pencils, adjustable triangles, French curves, various circle templates and my most valuable tool, the erasing shield.

★★★

I am closely focusing on the Bf 108's landing gear joint detail when I realize that someone is behind me. I turn my head while keeping my hands on the drawing instruments and there I see the Professor within a few feet of my table. I can see from his expression that he is scrutinizing my drawing.

"No, I don't think that is going to work," exclaims the Professor. "It will be too large to rotate within its housing. You seem to be proposing adding a third joint to the landing gear? Every part needs to be as light as possible and now you are proposing adding another joint? Have you run your shear calculations on those bolts? There appear to be too many, and they are so large. Don't you have any appreciation of how heavy this plane will get with those added design features you are proposing?"

"Ah, no sir, I was just taking your sketches and figuring these bolts needed to be of that size to hold the structure together."

"Well, you should be selecting the lightest and smallest size of every bolt and washer that will be needed to hold the landing gear together."

"Yes, sir. I will double check my calculations along with the holding capacity referenced in the manuals."

"Well, you better be doing that all the time young man. What is your name?"

"Armand Kindermann, sir. I started in June and if you recall, I met with you in May at your University lecture."

"Ah, yes, ok now I remember. Well, you young designers have a lot to learn and you should think more carefully when you draw. It's not just about the line work, you need to understand what is going on in three-dimensions. How does that bolt attach to the structure, how does it look from all three planes and what engineering principals are being carried through."

"Yes, sir. I will keep those in mind."

"It's alright. You are just out of the University. It takes an engineer ten years to really understand how a plane comes together. As a production engineer, you need to think about how a part can be most easily cast or cut, how it will all be assembled on the factory floor, and how the mechanics can access the parts for maintenance and replacements."

"Sir, I can only hope to achieve that level of competency within ten years. And at your company, Professor."

"Let's hope so, young man. Now explain to me your approach to this landing gear joint. You know we want to fold it up flat right into the wing profile."

"Well, I believe that if we added one more joint and leg to handle the folding action we could get this gear to lie flat down."

"Oh really. So, tell me what you are thinking of Kindermann? I am listening."

"The way I see the mechanical movements of this landing gear is a lot like a way a bird folds its leg when it roosts or sits in a nest. If you watch birds nestle into their nests you will see that their joints bend in three directions. So, I was thinking we could do the same thing with the Bf 109 landing gears."

Messerschmitt scratches his chin and looks over my initial drawings, "Ok, Kindermann. So, let me understand, you think this additional joint will accomplish the flat folding? Like a chicken in a nest I take it. Where did you come up with that idea? Not in industrial design courses I take it."

"No, sir, but in industrial design they did teach us to explore other analogies for a potential solution."

"Analogies? In industrial design? You must've had some interesting professors, Kindermann. But I buy it. It does seem to have some merit. Ok, go ahead and continue drawing up your concept."

"I am glad you like my concept. I will have it on Degel's desk by the end of day tomorrow."

"Alright, I look forward to reviewing this design at our production meeting in a few days. I hope I won't be disappointed."

Messerschmitt turns and moves onto the next drafting table and engages in a similar critique session with the designer next to me.

I have now been put under the gun to carry through my concept and draw it up for the senior design team to review it. The Professor seems to have some confidence in my proposal, but I don't know him well enough to be sure how it will be received.

★★★

The following week my group supervisor, Wolfgang, calls me into his area and has me sit across from him.

"Armand, good job on the Bf 108's landing gears. The Professor and other bureau chiefs loved it."

Feeling relieved, I let out a puff of air and relax my chest, "I am happy to hear they accepted my design proposal. I was starting to doubt the concept myself so it's good to get some buy-in from the doctorate engineers."

"I think you had a good approach and I wouldn't of have let you gone too far astray anyway," says Wolfgang putting a hand on my upper arm. "Professor Messerschmitt will be making a design presentation on a new plane with Walter Lusser's design bureau this afternoon. He would like you there to start off with this new project and be part of the wing team."

Shortly afterward, I am called into a wing section meeting with the Professor and Lusser present. Messerschmitt addresses us all and to his back, he has pinned up a series of hand drawings outlining a plane concept,

"Last year the Reichstag Luftszueg Ministerium, RLM, had asked us to enter a competition to design an advanced fighter plane. The design criteria are that it will exceed 400 miles per hour, have a range of 500 miles, carry two cannons, two machines guns each with 100 rounds, one pilot, achieve a steep rate of climb, and take tight turns."

He paces back and forth along the wall of drawings, his head looking down as if he's thinking over all the developments it has taken to get this far.

"We have been pitted against our competitors, Focke-Wulf Heinkel and Dornier and the flight trials were held earlier this year in February. It has now been announced that our fighter plane is one of two planes that meet the RLM's specifications, and we have a contract to develop the first production prototypes. The planes number will be the Bf 109.

"The initial prototype was developed by Robert Lusser and me and it has been kept secret from everyone except those in our research group. For one, this will be Germany's first military plane and doing such is not accepted by our European neighbors.

"Now we are happy to announce an all-out effort for the Lusser project bureau to take this plane into pre-production development where we will work out how to mass-produce this plane. This will be the final step before the RLM approves a full series production contract for the plane. Moreover, since the airframe is so promising, we will likely continue developing variations on this plane over many years."

Messerschmitt scans our group from one end to the other,

"Your wing team will be an essential component in its development. Finalizing the center of gravity, the lift forces, drag coefficients, wing aspect ratios, thrust capabilities and fuselage moment connections will all be critical to making our prototype the best of the submittals."

The Professor's then says in a low voice with his finger pointing at us. "As this RLM project is top secret, all of you assembled here are being asked to swear an oath of secrecy and silence of your work here. Not even your wives and parents can know what you are working on. Our company's success will depend on this secrecy."

Messerschmitt scans each one of us, drops his pointing hand, and then says,

"Now let's move onto what I enjoy most, aircraft design. Shall we? Turn your attention to these sketches and diagrams so I can relay to you my overall and approach.

"The key to this design is that we reduce the drag coefficients, lower the airframe weight, minimize the profile exposed to the airstream and simplify the airframe construction. We are placing the wings on the underside of the fuselage as I believe this will further eliminate drag along with streamlined fairing connections. The wings are shorter than our prior planes creating a lower wing-aspect ratio, and this will allow the aircraft to take tighter turns in a dogfight. Combining this with a high thrust piston engine and we will have a nimbler, more responsive and faster plane than any other fighter in Europe. But with this speed comes an enormous increase in structural stresses on the wing. So, I ask this group to help me finalize the wing truss geometry and determine how to structure its inner workings along with the placement of the ailerons."

Later that evening, I write a letter to Vanessa and tell her that everything is going well at the company and that I have been assigned to a big project. So, big that I cannot tell her anything about it. I also tell her that I will be coming to Munich at the beginning of July and that I would like to take her to a local Hessen restaurant for a romantic evening together. I then start thinking that I need to start saving money for a piece of special jewelry.

★★★

"Armando. *Che felicita vederti di novo*," Exclaims my mother as I disembark from the train at the Mainz Bahnhof. Her flowing black hair is cut shorter this time, making her curls seem tighter and giving them more bounce.

My father, in his typical grey work suit, follows with a warm embrace and says, "Good to see you, son. It's nice to have you come visit us after such long a time. How is your work going at Messerschmitt AG? I hear lots of news about their plane contracts."

"It's going well, father, very interesting work but also very demanding. Believe me, I am ready for a weekend break with the family and some of mother's Italian cuisine."

"*Mio figlio,*" says mother pulling up right in front of me, blocking father, "So you have found the woman of your dreams and you are engaged now. *Congratulazione.* I am excited to meet her later today."

As I carry my luggage off the train, I walk in step with my parents. "Yes, I feel Vanessa is the right woman for me and I am glad you will be able to finally meet her. No more mystery woman to my family."

"I think your mother is more excited than anyone," says my father. "She has completely cleaned up the house from top to bottom and put out the best of our houseware."

"She is a sweet woman but I don't think she is a very critical or a demanding type. Thanks, nonetheless."

"Well, *figlio,* this will be her first impression of us and of the home you grew up in. And hopefully, once you are two are married, she will be a frequent visitor to our house."

"I am sure Vanessa will like Mainz, our house and the parents that I love. Remember, she can be shy at first so take it easy on her with all the Italian *familgia* bonding. I don't want to overwhelm her either."

"Sure son," says my father, "we will keep ourselves somewhat reserved until she is all settled in. You know we are Germans as well." Mother then shoots him a look with a quick lifting of her head as if to say, 'oh we are?' As we walk along the Kaiserstrasse leading to our townhouse, my mother finally says, "You know your cousin Rodolfo has joined the Italian Army."

"Really? Somehow that doesn't surprise me."

"Yes, he has apparently enlisted into the officer training corp."

"I could see Rodolfo enjoying becoming an officer. He always did like bossing people around."

"True, Armando, he can be a bit pushy but I think this is a good move for him. Your uncle Vittorio has told me that he is very proud of his son. And you know, I am too."

Changing subject, my father says, "During lunch, I want to hear all about your plane designs. At least the ones you can tell us about."

"I will for sure. But I don't want to take too long at lunch. Vanessa's train arrives at 3:00 PM and I want to arrange some surprises I have in mind for her. Papa, do you remember where I stored away my glider plane models from secondary school?"

★★★

"Vanessa, my dear, welcome to my home." I say as I give her a quick hug. "These are my parents." Vanessa lowers her luggage onto the parlor floor and extends her hand out to my parents, "Herr und Frau Kindermann. My greatest pleasure to meet you both." Vanessa is wearing a light tan overcoat that reveals her cotton dress with floral patterns. Her is smile is broad but it also reveals some nervous energy on her part.

My mother steps forward first, embraces her and gives Vanessa a double kiss. "*Che bella regazza*. You are just as pretty as the photos that Armando showed us." As she is squeezed by my mother, Vanessa's eyes pop out with a surprised look on her face.

My father steps in closer and extends his hand and quickly bows his head to her, "Vanessa, it is our pleasure to meet our son's fiancé. Welcome to our house and please, make yourself at home."

Mother, with a smile beaming on her face, takes Vanessa by the hand and leads her into the house. "Dear, please leave your luggage right there. We will take care of bringing it up to your room. Here is our humble abode and on this first level is our parlor and dining room. Do you play any piano?"

Vanessa casts a quick glance at me as if asking me to join along but mother continues her tour unabated with a guiding arm around Vanessa's shoulders, "Upstairs is our guest bedroom and that is where you will be staying my dear. Armando's room is on the third floor along with his large collection of models and drawings. Do you enjoy the opera? Armando has been attending performances since he was little."

"Yes, he has told me of all the Italian composers that he admires and I believe Giuseppe Verdi is his favorite."

As mother walks away with Vanessa, I turn to my father and say, "I guess mama has been practicing this event for some time?"

"Oh yes son, I am not going to even tell you how long ago she started preparing for all of this. Why don't we head upstairs and start looking for the model plane you were talking about," says my father as we start walking up the wooden stairs.

★★★

"Armand, how far out are we biking?" asks Vanessa pedaling behind me while the floral prints of her dress flow around her legs. "It seems we are a good five miles away from Mainz. And what is in your bike satchel?" We wind our way on gravel roads with large trees bordering the sinuous route. Beyond the trees are endless fields of wheat and alfalfa just popping up in mid-season.

"A little surprise. We are almost there, love. We just need to bike to that church off in the distance."

Finally, we stroll up to a country church made of fieldstone and park our bikes in front of it. A meadow surrounds the church with the tall grasses swaying in lazy adoration. Further off to the west runs a creek that slowly meanders through willow trees that border its gently sloped banks. The warm July weather has made us both hot from the bike ride so Vanessa and I sit on a bench by the church to rest and cool down.

"So why did you want to come out here and what is in that bag?" asks Vanessa pulling her hair back into a bun.

"I want to climb up to the top of this church spire for a look at the countryside. There aren't as many hills here in Mainz as there are in Munich, so this tower will give us a grand view of my beloved Mainz. Come on, take my hand."

Vanessa and I then walk into the quiet structure and climb our way up the winding stone stairs till we reach the belfry landing. There I lay down the satchel and pull out my model wooden glider and hold it in front of her. A light breeze whistles past the spire and it swishes Vanessa's hair to and fro.

Holding the glider between my hands I say, "I brought you up here to share a special childhood memory. You know in the Wurzburg secondary school I took mechanical drafting and as part of that course we designed and built our own wooden gliders models."

"Yes, I do recall you telling me that. So, is this one of those class projects?

"Oh, it's more than that. This little guy flew the longest of any others in my school and garnered me the attention of the University of Munich. So, I owe much to this fine plane. It was my ticket east toward my industrial design school."

"Yes, I recall your industrial classes and your classmates as well," as Vanessa says this she looks out over the fields and stares off into the horizon, "Some of them were quite interesting characters."

Ignoring her disrupted attention, I continue, "But more importantly, this led me to where I would find you eventually."

Turning back to look at me, her eyes narrow with interest, and Vanessa says, "I see why this is special for you then and for us." Vanessa looks down, touches the wing, running a finger along its edge and then says, "This looks like quite a nice plane and it's solidly constructed. I can tell you are fond and proud of it."

"Yes, you are right. My drawings, my design work, my plane interest all led right to you." I place the glider to the side and I place my arm around her waist and pull her up to me.

"You didn't just come all way out and up here just to show me the glider, did you? I would love to see it fly off too," says Vanessa as she puts her hands on my arms, leans her head back with a slight shake and then smiles eagerly.

"That's exactly what I am going to do. And for both of our delight."

I take the plane in both hands and say, "To me this plane represents many things for me. My youthful ideals and ambitions to create machines that are exceptional and ones that push the boundaries of science. This also says a lot of how I see our lives coming together. We didn't know each other earlier in life but we each crafted our own vision and ideals with the expressed intent of finding beauty and truth in whatever we make and in whoever we love."

"I like how you put that," says Vanessa softening her look while looking into my eyes. 'Our relationship is an outcome of all we have strived for to this point in our lives."

"Yes, that is it, dear. I now am going to launch this plane and let it land wherever, a farmer's field, a road or even a creek. Where ever it travels, I don't care. It will have a life path all its own set by the intent that formed it. So too we will have a life path together formed by the bonds we are forming now."

I turn to look out over the fields, the trees look like dollhouse placards below, the wind rustles by shaking the leaves on the trees,

"Ready? Here it goes."

I cock my arm back and with a quick thrust forward, launch the plane into the air. The glider at first wavers and rolls side-to-side as if hesitant to stay aloft but then it picks up an upward air current lifting it higher. The plane starts to bank to the right forming a large circular path that is broad enough, so it does not come back crashing into the church. On its second circle, the plane starts heading straight but losing altitude rapidly.

Watching this flight demonstration, Vanessa squeezes my arm and jumps up on her toes as the glider makes another turn. The plane though is getting further away from us as it heads toward the trees bordering the creek. At first it hovers over the trees and then it turns into the open field. It looks like it will land there but as it comes over the grass it seems to pick up another uplift and it banks back toward the creek and the surrounding trees.

"Oh no, Armand, it's heading straight toward the stream. I hope it doesn't land in there," exclaims Vanessa with a gasp.

"Go little guy. You can do it!" As I say this, the plane heads straight for the stream and then losing its speed, it nose dives into the water.

"Quick, Vanessa, let's run down and try to pull it out of the water before it washes downstream."

We scramble round and round down the church spire and spill out onto the field, our legs dashing at full speed. We laugh along the way. "Just go ahead. You are a much faster runner than me," says Vanessa while still running.

As I pull up to the creek's edge, I see that the glider is still afloat and moving downstream as if on a barge. Good thing it is all made of pine or it would've sunk by now. Vanessa pulls up to me breathing heavily,

"It's floating away. Can you catch it somehow?"

I decide to take off my shoes, pants and shirt and I splash into the murky water of the creek. The water flow is gentle, and I can feel the oozy, muddy stream bed between my toes. Being already up to my navel in water, I dive in and break into a swim crawl.

Swimming downstream I pull up to the glider and yank it out of the water. "I got it! This little plane had a mind of its own. But it wasn't going to get away from us love. Not when you have a swimmer like me going after it," I say while swimming on my back and doing a frog kick.

From the bank Vanessa cheers me on and laughs, "Nice job, Armand."

I pull up to the bank and say, "I will need to dry out under the sun for a good thirty minutes. Good thing the road isn't full of travelers or I would have to find a bush to hide behind."

As Vanessa and I sit next to each other with the glider at our feet, we breathe with relief and start appreciating the sparkling water flowing by us while we contemplate our life ahead together.

MAY 22, 1934

I wake up to the sound of Munich streetcars clattering on their rails and immediately start with an exciting thought; today is Vanessa and mine's wedding eve party. Legally, Vanessa and I were already married at the City Rathaus and sworn in as man and wife by the clerk. But as is the custom and being Catholics, we will have a traditional Church wedding tomorrow for our invited family and friends.

I have taken a fourteen-day leave from the Messerschmitt company, my first long break since I started here last year. Earlier in the week in Augsburg, the men at the plant arranged a bachelor party for me. They tried to drink me into an oblivion but to no avail; I learned my lesson at the Hoffgarten Biergarten that night with Vanessa, and I was in no mood to repeat that escapade again. Then last night, Vanessa and I had a young people's informal gathering near the University student bar area. It was a social event of mainly for our University friends along with her siblings and cousins.

While I am in Munich, I am staying in Walter's apartment since he is still in the University finishing up his electrical engineering degree. As I rest in bed pondering my big day, I think about the pre-wedding banquet, the Polterabend. It will be quite surreal to see both sides, if not four sides of the family one for each parent, celebrating together. There will be many uncles and aunts from Vanessa's side that I have not met before, and the same will go for Vanessa with my family.

While I have gotten to know Vanessa's parents and sisters I have not spent much time getting to know her extended family members. Except for an occasional holiday or picnic they are just thinly developed characters that somehow know my beloved better than I do. For all that I love Vanessa, I am starting to realize that my marriage is much more than marrying Vanessa; I am marrying into her family.

As for Vanessa marrying into my family, I sense she will be quite taken with my Italian side mixed in with a bit of culture shock. A large contingency of my mother's siblings will be coming up for this significant family event, and this will be her first big exposure to that part of my heritage.

As I lay in bed pondering the coming together of our families, the cultural divide between my German half and the Italian one becomes apparent to me in one large social canvas; one that will be played out tonight and tomorrow. I then hear Walter stirring around and he pokes his head in my door,

"Armand, it's your big Polterabend today, and it's my job to get you to events on time and with the rings in my pocket. It's the hour for you to get up and start dressing. Where is your suit?"

Suddenly a memory of my father waking me up early to go the Wasserkuppe glider competitions comes to mind and I think, 'As soon as I get up, great things will happen today.'

"Thanks, Walter, you are doing your job very well. Even though I wondered if a party-man like you would stay low-key enough last night at the Alter Botanical Garden gathering. I now have no doubt as to your responsibility."

Walter responds back, "I was starting to wonder myself if I was cut out for this best man role. But so far, I am enjoying it. Vanessa has some cute University friends, and I enjoyed sharing my stories with them."

With some caution, I respond "Well, it's a good thing you didn't take things very far with those Fräuleins last night. I didn't need a back-story for my wedding of Walter running off into the twilight with one of the bridesmaids."

"No worry, it wasn't going to happen. Not that I didn't try," states Walter with a sly look and the beginning of a smile. I think that part of the fun Walter has is not only pursuing women but also playing this role to his male friends for our entertainment.

"Keep thinking like that until after our wedding toasts and the first waltzes then you will be free to be yourself. Ok my friend?"

Walter looks a little sheepish and responds,

"You have my word and I will get you through this day. Now, did you see where I put the ring case? I haven't seen it since we left the party last evening."

"Oh, Walter! Don't start playing with me now." I state as I pull out of the bed and start getting myself dressed.

★★★

Vanessa and I meet in the backroom of the Alter Botanical Garden's Banquet Hall, we embrace and then peek out to the gathering crowd waiting to receive us.

"Oh, Armand, it looks like such a large party. I am not good in front of crowds. You can do all the formalities and introductions for us."

I respond, "I will need you to introduce me to all your relatives as well. But sure, I will address the guests as etiquette requires.

Vanessa asks "How do I look? Do I look my best?"

"Dear, you look sparkling. I love the way you did your hair and that's a lovely dress you are wearing. It shows how slender you are."

"Thanks, love, you are a sweetie. I hear my father making an announcement. Hold my hand and let's get ready to walk in."

We face the double swinging doors, while waiters barge in out of them with drinks and appetizers on their platters. I hear Vanessa's father bellow out a "prost" which is followed by the attendees responding back in kind. It is our cue to saunter in now. I take Vanessa by the arm, lock our elbows and move slowly into the banquet with our smiles a glow. I hear a bit of clapping and "Congratulazione ai nuovi fidanzati!" being shouted out from my Italian relatives.

The attendees form a receiving line, and we start greeting our wedding party guests one by one now. My mother's family seems to have cued up quickest, and we start receiving them. In the line, I see my uncle Vittorio, my cousin Rodolfo and my aunt Elisabetta quickly coming up on us. They greet us with strong expressive embraces, kissing Vanessa on the cheek. Aunt Elisabetta looks at Vanessa adoringly and exclaims, "Lei e cosi bella" and then "La pele come la neve" and in turn lightly touching her light, brown hair. Uncle Vittorio then steps forward and opens his arms to me embrace me then bellows out, "Complimenti Armando!" and then "Buona fortuna mio nipote!" This all followed by another crushing hug and pat that momentarily stops my breath.

Uncle Vittorio adds an offer while cocking his head down,

"Armando my nephew, I hear you will be honeymooning in Italy.

His head then lifts with a big smile, "That is wonderful my nephew, and I am certain your lovely young wife will enjoy everything about Italy.

I happily reply, "Yes, I thought it would be good to share those wonderful memories of Italy with Vanessa and what better way than on our honeymoon trip."

Vittorio leans in toward me, close to my face, "Nephew, we would be honored if you could take a day or two to stop by and visit us in Genoa. It would be great for you to see the other family members who couldn't make it and let them share in a bit of the joy we are enjoying today."

I take a quick look at Vanessa, and I have a feeling this is one of those decisions that young couples work out together, but I am on the spot. Accept your beloved uncle's offer in good Italian form or tell him that you need to think about it. Making a quick calculation, I respond heartily,

"Si Zio! That is an excellent idea. Vanessa and I would love to stop by for a family visit along with a tour of Genoa."

I look to my side to see if Vanessa is going to throw daggers at me with her looks but if any are forthcoming I don't seem them in her countenance, just the beginning of smile fatigue. Vittorio then happily states,

"Eccelente! I am so happy you have accepted our little offering of family hospitality that we can provide you two. We will talk later about your trip dates."

And with that, Uncle Vittorio moves along and now I have just altered our honeymoon on the spot.

When the German family members come to greet us, they are a bit more restrained upon meeting Vanessa and me. They are equally happy in their Germanic way but until the beer and waltz music starts, they will likely stay a bit reserved.

Uncle Peter, from Wurzburg, comes up looking proud as if he were my own father. He practically was for the four years I was in the Wurzburg secondary school. He already appears a little red faced with a big smile coming through his closed lips.

"Armand and Vanessa, I am so happy for you both, congratulations! You know Vanessa, I got to know Armand as a young man in Wurzburg, and you have picked a studious and ambitious companion. I am sure he will go far and bring you a happy home. And you, Vanessa, you are so lovely and finishing your University studies as well. Armando is very lucky to have you as his wife, and I am sure the two of you will make each other fulfilled for many years."

I respond back starting to realize that I may get choked up more than I thought I would over the next two days,

"Uncle Peter, that is so sweet of you to state that. I was just a kid when I came to live in your house. I think your proper guardianship will pay off someday."

Peter responds,

"I am sure it will soon Armand. And you Vanessa, I am so looking forward to you being part of our family."

Vanessa states quietly but with a smile,

"I am not surprised to hear you say that about Armand. I have full trust in his skills and his determination to get to where he wants to go."

Uncle Peter gives us each a hug, a light kiss on Vanessa's cheek and a healthy double pat on my shoulder.

Following the receiving line, our guests mingle drinking beer or wine. One side of the banquet hall is Vanessa's Bavarian family members; they are of a taller height, of fair complexion, blue or green eyes and have light brown hair coloring. On my side is my father's Hessian family members from Frankfurt and they are of similar appearance to the

Bavarians. Being they both speak German, they more readily mingle and get to know each other.

But my mother's family, being primarily Italian speakers, take some stilted moments in broken German to introduce themselves . They stand out from the rest of the party with their light olive complexions, dark-brown to black hair, broad smiles and lots of hand gesturing as they talk. And the festive fashionwear between the two countries is different as the Germans tend to wear materials of distinct patterns and colors while the Italians tend to favor black and straightforward formal attire for major family events.

As is the tradition in German wedding eve parties, there is the breaking of porcelain ware, followed by the mock clean-up by the bride and groom. To this, the Italian relatives are a bit amused and somewhat befuddled by everyone enjoying breaking perfectly good dishes with such zest. But it is supposed to be good luck for the couple and Vanessa, and I play along with tradition and clean up in good fun.

May 30, 1934

The train rumbles through the Tuscan landscape as vineyards and villas peer out on hillsides framing the endless olive fields. Vanessa sits next to me in our train compartment, and we are content to just watch the scenery roll by. Our honeymoon through Italy has been fantastic, and we are in a relaxed state enjoying being together. To date, we have traveled through Lake Como, Bolzano, Venice and then to Florence. And now for the final leg of our journey, we are going to stop in Genoa and visit my relatives. As I promised my uncle Vittorio, we are going to spend two nights in Genoa and stay at his house. Being a good family member, I couldn't say no plus I thought this would be a good way to share with Vanessa some of my childhood memories.

As the train pulls into the Genoa terminal, we are greeted not only by my Zio Vittorio but also what looks like a whole neighborhood of people. Vanessa and I are overwhelmed upon seeing this large reception and Vanessa braces up as if for a downpour of rain. Once we descend onto the platform, we are surrounded by relatives and their cheers of "Tanta felicta" and "Evviva gli sposi!" followed by a long series of hugs and kisses. We feel a bit like radio stars meeting their adoring audience fans. Vanessa looks around at everyone beholding her, and her smile is broad but also showing some signs of being embarrassed to be under such attention. I break the reception and state out in Italian,

"My loving relatives! Vanessa and I are so happy to see all of you all and to feel the warmth of our family love. We had a beautiful wedding with many of you present and to the ones who were not Vanessa and I are delighted to share some time with you here in my beloved second home of Genoa."

With that last comment, I can see my relatives' smiles broaden, and some of the men let out a little 'salute.' I then wrap it up by the stating,

"Vanessa and I are a bit tired but after a good rest we look forward to having lunch with all of you". As my family moves en masse off the platform, Vanessa looks at me and asks, "What did you tell them? And I didn't know you had this many relatives here."

I respond back while continuing to smile to the relatives around us, "I didn't know this many would come out to greet us either. So, I told them that we are looking forward to spending the next two days with them and I am happy to be here in my second home of Genoa."

Vanessa quizzically asks, "I never heard you state before that Genoa was like a second home?"

I shrug my shoulders a bit and respond, "To be honest, I have never thought of it that way either but standing there in front of all my Genovese family greeting us, it just dawned on me that maybe it is so. And it felt like the right thing to say."

As we move from the station, we descend out onto the piazza in front of the train terminal, and I feel an excitement to be here. Memories of arriving here with my parents and getting my first glimpses of Genoa's grand architecture all seem vivid in my mind. Genoa is like a second home.

As we drive over to uncle Vittorio's house, he starts chatting about my aircraft design career,

"Armando, I understand you have a good job with an airplane company in Augsburg. How is it going?"

I reply,

"It is going great Uncle. We are designing many kinds of planes, way more than I realized from when I first joined. The environment is very intense, focused and I am learning a lot. The owner of the company is pretty hands-on and I get to meet with him weekly in group meetings."

Vittorio nods his head and then puts his finger to his mouth as if thinking of a word,

"Is that the company 'Messer-kmit'?"

Yes, Uncle, it's pronounced 'mess-ser-shmit'.

My Uncle continues, "Well you know, up in Milano we have Fiat, and they are producing planes for the Regia Aeronautica, our Royal Airforce."

"I have heard of them and I am familiar with some of their aircraft products."

Vittorio pursues this further, "Have you ever thought of working for Fiat? I am sure they could use a talented young man like you."

Luckily Vanessa cannot understand this conversation or that fact that Italians believe that the husband can decide on significant career decisions without much consideration from the spouse. I then respond politely,

"That is an excellent idea, but I am very content in Augsburg with the Messerschmitt company. Plus, I don't know how Vanessa would take to moving to Italy. It's all very new to her." Perhaps if I could tell my uncle, it's all a little foreign to her is more accurate of an assessment.

Vittorio replies, "I am sure she will love it here. I recently read that Fiat is expanding their Milano plant and word is out that they are hiring engineers. But more importantly, Italy needs intelligent, highly skilled men like you, Armand. You would be giving back to your heritage my nephew. And besides, I believe Fiat will be producing some advanced planes over the next few years, and it would be very challenging for a young man like you."

I must take a second on how best to respond back. I don't want to sound resistant or ungrateful to an uncle's suggestion, but I really have no interest in working in Italy. Let's see, how should I say this?

"Zio, that is very thoughtful of you to be thinking of my future. Especially one that ties in with my Italian heritage. It's an interesting idea, but I would have to think long and hard about it before I left the Messerschmitt company."

Vittorio finally picks up on my drift and wraps it up,

"Ok Nipote, you know best. It was just a thought. I am certain you know your industry well enough and that this Messer-skmit company is a good one."

With that, we pull into their drive leading into their first-floor courtyard. Time to unpack, refresh and enjoy some tasty cucine Italiana!

OCTOBER 1934

"Your friend Walter Ignaz is done with his interview and is waiting for you in the lobby," says Frau Schnelling standing over my drafting table.

"Thanks, Frau. Tell him I will be over in five minutes."

With that I wrap up one last set of lines that I am drawing for the folding wing mechanism on the Bf 109 and head toward the visitor entry. The reception lobby's black marbled tiled floors are set off by the white concrete walls that surround it. Black leather seating with aluminum frames are clustered throughout for visitor seating where I see Walter looking surprisingly mature; he is wearing a dark suit and tie and his hair is parted and slicked back.

I approach him and say, "Walter. Great to see you here."

Walter, looking a little dazed from the interview, gives me a big smile and hug. "Armand, great to see you too. So, this is your work home? Very nice looking and I didn't realize there were so many people working here."

"Every month we add around fifty new people. The company must be pulling in every engineering graduate out there. So how did the interview go?

"I think it went pretty well. I first met with Gerhard Coulis and then he passed me onto the chief electrical engineer of the company. Coulis seemed eager to fill the ranks with electrical engineers and the lead electrical engineer seemed interested in my radio communications background. He mentioned that they will be developing far more sophisticated avionic controls systems to track flights and communicate with the pilots than what I've seen to date."

"Is that something you are interested in doing?"

"Sure, I would love it. Working on communications for just stationery radios has lost some of its excitement lately. You know a fellow like me needs a new challenge to tackle every so often," says Walter with a smirk.

"Fine, whatever gets you going, Walter. And if that attracts you to work here that would be wonderful."

"You know I see they have factory housing for the workers here," observes Walter. "With all the company apartments going up It looks like a Messerschmitt village here in Haunstetten. Best of all, I was told they are building an exclusive bachelor's apartment and that would be highly attractive to me."

"Imagine that," I say, "poor Walter all alone in his bachelor complex. Somehow I think this would be a good base for you."

"First, I must get a job offer and second, accept the offer. But let's see, it could be great fun for us to be working together."

"I welcome that idea. That's why I suggested you apply here in the first place. The boys from Mainz would continue their saga in Augsburg. Did mentioning my name help you in any way?"

"Oh, sure. They said, 'you are friends with him'?" chides Walter.

"Just wait till they ask me for a personal reference about your character. How truthful will I have to be? 'Oh yes, Walter Ignaz, he is quite a character. His joining the Messerschmitt family will provide us a lot of color. Just keep the young secretaries far away from him, such as on the other side of the plant'."

Walter smiles. "Oh, come on. It's just because you are a married man that they don't have to worry about things like that from you. But with Walter here, he will bring a new level of sophistication activity to Haunstetten," says Walter as he runs his hand over his slicked back hair.

"That's just what I am afraid of, Walter," I concur and I ask him, "How is it going on the lady front?"

Walter puts on a grin and leans back, "Where do you want me to begin? Since I last saw you or since the beginning of this year?"

"Why don't we finish this conversation next time I am in Munich," I say adroitly. "And let's hope you get a job offer. Truthfully, I will put in an excellent word for you."

"I like the sound of that and I appreciate your opening the door for me. I am going to head back to Munich now so let's hope this actually happens." And with that Walter gives me a quick hug, a shoulder pat and a thumb up as he exits the Messerschmitt AG lobby.

August 1935

A limousine approaches the plant; a flag is waving on the hood, and dust flies up in vortexes. It careens onto the compound's main entrance and zips past a slow-moving truck. The limo is in a hurry and continues its direct attack on the factory offices like a rocket with a tail of spewing smoke.

"Who could that be?" I ask Wolfgang as we lift our heads from our morning coffee inside the commissary. "They are definitely in a hurry, and they must have some urgent business with Messerschmitt."

The limo comes to an abrupt stop, and a chauffeur steps out and opens the rear door with his hand out to help the passenger. Out comes a fashionably dressed lady with an air of natural elegance. She is wearing long white gloves, a gathered tight cap; a draping dress that comes past her knees, and a mink stole drapes here delicate shoulders. Finishing off her outfit is a pair of sleek black shoes with silver buckles.

Recognizing her from past visits Wolfgang exclaims, "It's the Baroness. She is here to visit Professor Messerschmitt but she only comes when there is critical business. I've rarely seen her here, but I've heard she is of money and has invested heavily into the plant. She and Willy are tied financially to the company and to each other emotionally."

"You mean as in a relationship?" I ask Wolfgang. "I didn't know the Professor had any relations outside of the plant."

"They have been living together for eight years and they haven't married yet," says Wolfgang who has now leaned in closer to me over the table with his voice lowered to a whisper. While looking out the window at the Baroness approaching our building he adds in, "You know she is six years older than the Professor and she left her husband, Baron Strohmeyer, to pursue their affair."

Following our coffee break, Wolfgang and I get back to our work table but then we hear a bustle of people descending the stairs from the executive offices. I try not to stare but the Baroness is amongst the entourage as her beauty and fashion wear stand out like a freshly milled propeller. They are in a hurry to see something based on the looks of their faces and their agitated voices. Time to keep my head down and not to stare.

As they determinedly walk by I realize they are heading over to Robert Lusser's project bureau offices. Being only around twenty feet away I can catch snippets of their excited talk. Something about that the Bf 109 needs a more powerful engine, perhaps a radical redesign and that it has been selected to be put on show for the Olympics. But more than that I cannot tell. I then see them filing out with Professor Messerschmitt and the Baroness at the tail end.

The Baroness calls out to Messerschmitt and I overhear her say in a pleading voice, "Willy, you must be careful about this decision. The Party members are all watching you and that Eduard Milch character at the Air Ministry is ready to sink you at any time. You cannot afford one bad design move at this point."

Messerschmitt stops and turns to face her. "Love, this will be our biggest opportunity yet, and I must spend every effort to advance the plane to another level. Even if we must pay for it ourselves. If the 109 passes through RLM testing with flying colors, we will be all set as the mainstay provider of warplanes. There is nothing to stop us, my dear. We are simply the best out there."

"Willy, please be prudent. I know you are a good, if not a great designer. But this Eduard Milch fellow has it out for you, and he could conspire to undermine any of your planes' field trials in whatever way he can. Maybe it would be best for you to stick with what you know best, glider and passenger planes. That is your background love, right?"

"Lily, I have grown beyond that," says Messerschmitt. The time to reconsider commercial planes has passed. And how else can I pay for my pet projects except with the money we could gain from the military contracts. The company and I are ready to take on these high-performance military planes. And I do have a supporter at the Air Ministry, Ernst Udet. I have asked him personally to be there at the test trials, so nothing is looked over. Or as I believe, that our exceptional performance will be duly noted."

"I believe in you, Willy, so I trust you will do the right thing," exclaims the Baroness. It's just happening so fast, going from producing twenty or so passenger planes to producing thousands of fighter planes. The Strohmeyer's are making a huge investment in you. And while Raulino and I are no longer married, I do not wish to be the fool that dithers away their family estate," she says this with conviction but also with a hint of a threat as well.

Messerschmitt looks at the Baroness with his eyes widened; he tightens his grip on her arms, "My love, we will always come out on top, there is no other alternative. We are this close to handing the Heinkel and Arado companies the shirts off their backs. Don't you see, we have come out of nowhere onto those stiff, arrogant aircraft companies. And now our company is about to beat them at their own game. They have snickered at me for the last ten years, and I am going to show them what I am really all about."

"Yes, you have what it takes, and I will support you all the way through," says the Baroness with softness and understanding. 'But please don't make this about besting out your competition. This should not be about Willy proving himself over the established companies. In the end, your planes have to be exceedingly good and make a profit for the corporation."

With that, they walk away and back up to the executive offices. A few minutes later, Lusser comes out of his office looking a bit flustered as if he promised the moon and now he must figure out how to deliver it. He then casts a glance upon the drafting floor, and I put my head back down as I know this means we will have a lot of work to do.

Shortly afterward, the Professor comes back down to Lusser's office and gathers a quick meeting of the production team. Messerschmitt starts off,

"We don't have full government go-ahead to continue developing the Bf 109, but our Board has just voted to move ahead with a prototype using our own funds. They have full confidence that our fighter plane design will outperform the Heinkel He 112 entry and be approved by the Technical Bureau. We have also just learned that the Arado aircraft has been dropped out of the competition so it is now just us two finalists.

"In September, we plan on having the first test flights of the Bf 109 right here at our Augsburg airfield and from there ten of our prototypes will be shipped off to the Rechlin test center. Luftwaffe test pilots will then put the planes through weeks of flying tests. What we, and what your design team will address, is that there is reported ground looping as the plane descends for landing and tipping on its wings. It also appears that the tail wheel is castoring, spinning around, upon landing and making for an unsteady run. The other problem being reported by our own test pilots is that the plane has tipped over its landing gears indicating they are too close to the middle of the plane and need to be spread out. I think our attachment of the landing undercarriage to the fuselage is an innovative and a safe one, so I am going to stick with that as we move forward."

"But aside from these maneuvering issues, the plane is doing exceedingly well in other areas. The rate of climb is fast, the turning radius is tight, and it's been achieving faster speeds than we even predicted. I also have heard that our plane is lighter, uses less quantity of materials to build and is quicker to assemble than the Heinkel entry."

Messerschmitt paces in front of the row of drafting tables looking at the floor and then addresses us again, "So, your Project Bureau for the next few months will be focusing on how to re-position the undercarriage, stiffen the tail wheel and figure out why the plane loops at landing. From there you will continue designing modifications to the Bf 109 following the Rechlin test trials.

"If all goes well, I've been given a heads up that the winning plane will be showcased at the 1936 Berlin Olympics and from there the model would go into series production." He stops, turns to face our assembly and spreads his arms out, "Is this not what we all have dreamed of gentlemen?"

Messerschmitt's scans the room, his eyes focused and alert as he glances into each of our eyes. I feel like I am ready to stand up and commit every hour of my life until we ship this plane off. The design team stands up and starts talking amongst themselves in excited tones as we ponder how to address all these issues in a short two months.

Robert Lusser then comes to the head of the table. "Thank you, Professor, for that spirited challenge. Staff, now that the Board and the Professor have set the bar for us, we are now going to set up a work plan of how we are going to accomplish this. I am excited as everyone here at this table. The opportunity to have our plane design be exhibited at the Olympics and then be the standard fighter for Germany is a once in a lifetime opportunity."

As Lusser goes through a schedule of events and team assignments, my mind races off with excitement, and I barely comprehend what Lusser is saying. Only that our team will make or break the company's success within the next few months.

JUNE 1938

I've been working at Messerschmitt AG now for five years now, and I've been rewarded for my loyalty with a promotion to section chief of wing design within Lusser's construction and design group. I am in charge of a crew of three designers, a structural engineer and six draftsmen. An aerodynamist reports directly to Lusser and he will be forming the wing and fuselage shapes. My role now is to make the aeronautical engineer's sizing and shapes into a buildable plane while integrating all the other structures and systems. These include the fuselage group, the fuel groups, the landing gear team and the avionics group where Walter Ignaz is now working.

With my recent promotion comes another knock on the door, this time, it is the local National Socialist Party leader, Kreisleiter Schiede. He has been a regular visitor to Messerschmitt's executive office, more so to pester him with requests for attendance at rallies and contributions to the Party. Messerschmitt is polite with him, but he has extended his stay often, and the welcome mat is worn thin. Even Frau Schnelling, Messerschmitt's personal secretary, knows how to distract Schiede and cover for the Professor's whereabouts. Shortly after my promotion to section manager of wing production, I receive a summons from Frau Schnelling informing me that the local Party leader wants to have a short chat with me.

Upon coming up to the wood paneled executive offices, I see that Schiede is waiting for me at the head of the conference table, the position where usually Messerschmitt sits or the other Board members. Schiede is a roundish, stout man who obviously hasn't done a hard day's worth of labor in years based on his soft, pudgy fingers. He has thinning hair, round wire-rim glasses, eyes that protrude from his sagging eyelids, thickish lips that pout out and a double chin that sags over his collar. As he speaks, he has a thin, raspy voice that is windy and in an unusually high vocal range. Schiede wears a brown Party tunic with insignias of his party rank sewn onto his collar along with a red armband with a swastika emblazoned on it.

As I sit down, Schiede pulls out a portfolio, slaps it on the table and opens, "Herr Kindermann, congratulations on being promoted to section chief here at Messerschmitt AG. I've been reviewing your personal dossier that we have accumulated at the Party offices."

"Thank you, sir, for taking notice. I am very excited to execute more of the design work that we have under development here."

"Great my young man. I am sure you will do wonders for the company and by extension our Party efforts. You see with every man who reaches your level in this industrialist operation, I pay a visit and explain how things work here.

"You see, Armand, if that is alright with you, this company's contracting and dollar flow all comes because our Party has set the course and priorities for Germany's war effort. And while you and your fellow engineers put all your good energies into designing our next fighter plane, we at the Party believe it is all because we have directed you to do so and you are only following through on our vision.

"It is, therefore, essential that you keep in good communication with the Party and that you help us back in return. And in following, I am asking, and that may be too polite of a term, to start attending our events. I am confident you will enjoy the comradery of like-minded individuals all of whom want Germany to be superior over all."

"Why of course, yes Herr Schiede, I am honored that you have come to me personally and requested my services to the Party," I state with stressed enthusiasm but inside I am horrified this request is being put upon me. I just want to design planes. I have never participated with any of the Party's events nor even agree with their purist ideology and hooligan methods. Why else did I evade them during secondary school and skip out on the Hitler Youth Movement?

Taking my simple response, Herr Schiede assumes that I am on board, "Good, I just wanted to make sure that we are on the same page and that there was no doubt as to your complete loyalty to the cause. Let me tell you something, Armand, as you seem like a well-educated and intelligent man. We at the Party believe that smarts are important but loyalty, unquestioning loyalty, is even more important. And when we at the Party want an action taken, our members do everything they can to help us. *Verstehen sie?*"

"Yes, of course, sir. I would not think of doing otherwise." This is Messerschmitt's doing I think with revulsion. He is a Party member and he has probably committed management's participation as a demonstration of his own loyalty.

"Just one other thing, Armand. We've noted that you have not participated in Party events to date on your own, and I am disappointed that it took us this long to meet."

I hesitate for a second, "Well, us designer folks are quite bookish and all physics, you know. It takes us a while to appreciate the higher level philosophies of Party manifestos. And besides with us working twelve-hour days, we just have time to head home after work for a night of sleep."

"Well, how about you consider spending some of that after twelve-hour time at a few of our rallies or readings? I am sure you will find them inspiring and refreshing to your mind."

"Of course, Kreisleiter Schiede. You can count on my attendance and support from this day forward," I state this with forced enthusiasm. How could I commit to these Party activities? I despise their unruliness and lack of civil order. I imagine I am getting myself involved with a bunch of thugs, but I have no choice. Messerschmitt's allegiance to the Party and the plane contracts he has been awarded are all integrally tied together. And now us mid-level managers must buy into it as well.

Kreisleiter flips through my dossier and pulls out a page, "Herr Kindermann, your father is German, yes?"

"Yes, from Frankfurt and I grew up in Mainz."

"But your mother is Italian; at least that is what our files have found out so far. Is this correct?"

"Yes, my Kreisleiter, she is from Genoa, and I am fairly fluent in the language."

Schiede scratches his chin and looks over the file in his hands, "Well it's a good thing that Germany and Italy have formed a treaty some two years back, but it remains to be seen whether Italy will be our military partner as well. I suspect things are going that way and if so, both of your lineages will be tied into our goals.

"I think your background will be very useful to the Party. I am glad we had this talk, Herr Kindermann. I may call upon you for your specific tasks in the future given your unique dual allegiance."

"However I can help the Party, Herr Schiede."

"There is a rally this Friday evening and we could use some young men to hand out pamphlets. You know," pauses Schiede with his forefinger pointing up. "An Italian delegation of the Fascist party will be visiting us this weekend. I think you would make the perfect host and guide for them, Armand. We will present them at our reading at the Brucke Beer Hall this Friday.

"What better way for me to start out my Party activities Kreisleiter," the irony of this brewing inside me.

"Yes, we need to provide them some hospitality and good old German *gemutlichkeit*. But more importantly, we need the Fascist Italians to buy into our German mission of purity, dominance and European manifest. Those Italian Fascist speak our socialist language but at the core they don't quite appreciate our ideals of racial purity and the exclusion of Semites. They are tepid about the German *Lebensraum* and even fear our ambitions to dominate the continent. But with your dual German-Italian background, people like you can help us win them over to our cause.

This is what Schiede has been hoping from me all along and now my moment to help the Party has finally arrived.

"Good, young man. I knew this would be a pleasant and productive talk. I look forward to seeing you at the rally, Herr Kindermann."

Schiede pulls back from the table, grabs my dossier and then raps it on the table. I stand up and give him a salutation. He smiles but with no emotion in his eyes and then leaves the rooms with a tight smile breaching his thin lips and round face.

I stand alone and still in the conference room for a minute. Not seeing this coming with my promotion, I am shocked. I want to share this with Vanessa in complete confidence and let her know how chilling the meeting with the Party leader was.

★★★

It is evening in our apartment with Vanessa and I share the details of my conversation with the local party official. I have an insidious and unsettling feeling that I am now part of a large military contractor that is hand-in-glove with the Party's ambitions. I tell Vanessa,

"I had no idea that after five years here that I would be designing warplanes that can blast a plane or twenty people in one short three-second burst of machine-gun fire. But here I am and there is no way out for me now."

"I am glad the Professor entrusted more responsibilities in you," states Vanessa, "but I am still leery of where all of this is going. I mean our whole country. From what you are telling me, Messerschmitt and all the other plane companies are gearing up to produce more and more warplanes. What happened to your vision of working on passenger and sport planes?"

"They have gone out the window, dear. Messerschmitt is no longer designing passenger planes or sport or glider planes for that matter. It's like they have morphed into a different kind of company over the last five years."

"I appreciate your having a stable job, but you know for me it's more than just having steady pay. A man with your talents could do so much to help our economy and the common folk. And designing attack planes with four or six machine guns seems a bit removed from where you started."

"I am in this company deep now, and I see no other alternative for me career-wise. It is exciting and challenging, it's just that I am now designing planes of destruction. Another development that is bothering me is the way our country is treating non-Aryans, especially the Jews. Why do we need to do this? What's the point?"

"How can we prosper on the back of hatred toward another people?" concurs Vanessa. "I don't understand why this is such an important part of the National Socialist movement. Not that I know many Jewish people, but I don't have anything against them either."

"I think about all the Jewish engineers and technicians we have lost at the company over the last three years," I state, "and it seems crazy to purge out people because of their being Jewish. Plus, I am torn by these new laws as I see myself as half German and the other half Italian, and I do not feel the Aryan ideals always include people of Mediterranean background."

"I don't think the Purity Laws will extend to Italians, dear. Just folks south and east of there."

"They still makes me feel uncomfortable. I think my German friends have long forgotten that I am half Italian and just think me as part of their nationality. But inside I do not forget."

I ponder my identity, am I Italian or am I German? Blood-wise I am both, but culturally, it is a little more ambiguous. Where is all this Fatherland pride going? It makes me feel like I am denying if not turning my back on my Italian heritage as I watch these Party rallies. "Deutschland uber alles" rings ominously in my ears.

Finally, I say to Vanessa, "I have ambitions to be an advanced industrial designer of planes within Messerschmitt AG. For the time being, I will have to play along with the Party's ideals and their escalating anti-Semitic edicts. I am only 28 years old, and I am dead-set on rising up the ranks to lead design of some section. I will have to deal with the Party step by step."

★★★

It is Friday evening and I find myself attending my first National Socialist Party meeting. The dark beer hall has a series of arched openings between various smoke-stained rooms with one room in the center having a higher, coffered ceiling. The stuccoed walls are decorated with murals and there is old-German lettering spelling out portions of song lyrics. As Herr Schiede had 'offered' my participation, I have obediently followed through with my attendance. I am not a Party member and I hope to dodge the bullet on that one. So what are these meetings all about and what will they expect of me?

As I settle down in the main hall, a parade of SA brown shirts files in from what appears to have been a parade through the streets of Augsburg. As the men file in, I notice Dieter Fleischen is amongst the ranks of brown shirts. Not having seen him in five years I gather he has continued his Party affiliations and desire to climb within its ranks.

As I sit toward the back of the beer hall on a wooden bench amongst the eighty men, Kreisleiter Schiede enters the Hall triumphantly as if he is some Roman consul ready to address the Senate. He opens the meeting with a 'Heil Hitler' salute and initiates an opening song, '*Deutschland Uber Alles*'. Schiede then addresses the crowd,

"The National Socialist Party has come so far and there is palbable groundswell of the German people's support for ss our goal to make us the dominant people of Europe.

"Much has been accomplished since our Party has taken control of the government back in 1932. The most important being, the subjugation of Jewish peoples and their elimination from our public and industry ranks. Let me give you a quick overview of how far we have come.

"In April of 1933 our Government retaliated against an international Jewish boycott of Germany with our own boycott on Jewish stores and professional businesses. Then later in April came a law called the Restoration of the Professional Civil Service, which has banned Jews from being employed in the Government. This included Jews in academia and the science professors. Good riddance to Jewish science."

"Then in May of 1935, the Government proclaimed that Jews were no longer allowed to enlist in the Wehrmacht for military service. In September, following the Nuremberg rallies, a law was passed forbidding marriage and sexual relations between Aryan Germans and Jews. Later in November, we adopted a law denying Jewish people full citizenship, and now they are subjects of the State.

"In 1936, the Jews were banned from all professional jobs. And now, in this year of 1938, Jewish businesses have been prohibited from obtaining government contracts. Currently, the Reich government is drafting up laws that will require Jews to add Israel and Sarah to their names so as to publicly identify themselves. Moreover, another law is in the works that will ban Jewish children from attending normal schools. This gentleman, is progress for a pure Germany."

With that, the audience stands, starts cheering and shouting with their hands up and their faces full of reddened zeal. I am in the back rows standing up as well clapping but staying quiet.

Schiede then ask the Italian delegation to come forward for a short presentation. I see about twelve men with some dressed with Mussolini black shirts and some in military garb. As they face us, it dawns upon me that I recognize one of the military members; it is Rodolfo, my cousin.

The delegation's leader calls out, "Comrades in Socialism and Fascism. We are proud to be here representing your political brethren from northern Italy. Our *Il Duce* has promoted a Fascist platform that will transform Italy's political landscape into one of Socialism and central control of all resources. Like your government's control of all the heavy industries, we are executing the same and aligning all sectors toward an authoritarian government. One that is for a pure Italy and a militarily strong one. From our tour to date throughout your Fatherland, we have been deeply impressed at your stupendous progress in advancing your military industrial output to levels beyond what any other European countries can muster."

"Similarly, Mussolini is advancing our output of military weaponry so that eventually Italy and Germany can fight together in what will be the greatest victory in National Socialism. Together Hitler and Mussolini will subjugate the weak of Europe and make us the cleansed and fittest survivors of Europe"

This whips up the German crowd into hoots of cheers and they stand to pump their fists into the air while stomping their feet. The Italian delegation leader wraps up his speech by expressing their desire to keep this bond of political brotherhood together throughout our next advances. With the completion of his speech, the Kreisleiter takes the podium and asks that we take a break to welcome their Socialist brethren and enjoy a beer together.

At that point, I walk up to the delegation and approach Rodolfo, "*Cugino. Che fa fratello primo?*" Doing so we embrace and pat each other on the back. Rodolfo is wearing a Captain's outfit with three golden stars and he looks sharply dressed, down to the neatly pressed tunic and his polished black boots.

"*Cugino* Armando," says Rodolfo. *Che cosa bella vederti qui.* I thought you might show up at this rally and I am sorry I did not write to you earlier cousin. Our tour of cities was not fully revealed to us until we left Italy last week."

"Well Rodolfo, or should I say *Capitano* Lorenzini? I didn't know you were promoted to Captain. Wonderful cousin! Here let's grab one of these beers. It's not like Peroni beer but you will get used to it."

We head over toward the bar, grab a small stein and then Rodolfo and I pull aside into a corner.

"Yes, the promotion was recent. Once I took on more Party duties, this promotion came next. But that is the way things work in Italy. You have to play your politics carefully and hope that you end up on the winning side."

"Looks like you played a good hand cousin. Is the military treating you well?

"Yes, it suits my character perfectly. I appreciate a clear chain of command, ranks to work your way up, total respect from your subordinates and I must admit the ladies love these officer uniforms," he says this with a wink and a crack of a smile.

"I can see this fitting your character very well, cousin," I say.

"But aside from that," says Rodolfo. "I am very excited by Mussolini's vision for Italy. Central control of the government is what we need. There are too many incompetents in Italy, be it in the government or industry. It is time for our Government to take charge and to get things done. It's the only way Italy will get out of this depression, clear out the Communists and jump-start our military economy."

"Well, that is exactly what we are doing here in Germany, Rodolfo. My company is booming with warplane contracts. We can't hire enough engineers."

"Actually, Fiat's airplane division is in a similar situation. After we produced all those planes for the Spanish Nationalist's war, our Milano Fiat plant has established quite the advanced aviation design group."

"I hope you aren't going to tell that I should move down to Milano and work for Fiat. Your father tried that one on me, and right at the end of my honeymoon."

"No, no, Armando," he pauses. "But you know, Italy would love to have some plane engineers like you in its plants. Anyway *Cugino*, how is Vanessa and I hear you have one bambino and another one on the way. *Congratulazione. Cin, cin cugino.*"

"Thanks, Rodolfo." With that we clink our beer glasses and I have a flashback of us as kids biking around Genoa. Rodolfo owned that neighborhood, he was a natural-born leader and now I sense he has found the right place to be in: A Fascist-controlled army that has set its sights on dominating its colonial land and resources.

As we speak, Schiede walks toward us with a big smile, "Herr Kindermann, how do you know Captain Lorenzini? You seem to be rather friendly together."

"Yes Kreisleiter, the Captain is my cousin from Genoa. Can you believe it that he shows up at this Party rally?"

Schiede pats both our backs. "Ah, the brotherhood is only getting deeper. You two are a great harbinger of what is to become between Italy and Germany. Armand, I am so glad you came tonight. Your Party involvement and role is far clearer in my mind than ever before."

"However, I can help Kreisleiter," I respond nodding my head toward him.

"Good Herr Kindermann," says Schiede. "By the way, if I can pull you away from Captain Lorenzini for a minute."

"Sure, Herr Schiede," I say as I excuse myself from Rodolfo.

"I would like to introduce you to one of our rising stars within the Party ranks. Perhaps he can be a bit of a mentor for you." As Schiede says this, he turns around and taps the shoulder of a man's indicating for him to turn around. As he does so, I see that it is Dieter Fleischen.

"Why hello, Armand," says Dieter as he extends his hand out for a shake. "I was wondering when we would see the likes of your kind finally joining Party events." Underneath his short moustache, I see a forced yet unfriendly smile coming through.

Looking at Schiede I say, "I know this gentleman from the University, Herr Schiede. How are you doing Dieter?"

"Excellent. I am still working in the aviation industry but as in the University days, I have committed my life to the Nationalist Party."

"Armand," says Schiede. "You are full of surprising connections. Dieter here has been demonstrating his Party involvement by taking leadership at our weekend rally events and readings. I think he would be a good role model for your development with our Party district."

Dieter and I continue staring at each other as I say, "It is a pleasure to see you after some time. Perhaps since our days at the University, Dieter?"

"Why I think so, Armand," responds Dieter. "You were always a little slow to catch on to the Party's manifestos, but I see you have finally come appreciate them now."

"Most certainly and I hope to make myself useful to the Party with my after-work time." I say with forced conviction as I am only here to keep in good standing with my company.

"After work time?" questions Dieter. How about after work and your work time as well? That would be a better response."

"I am happy to see how you have stayed on course for your values. Looks like they are paying off," I say with cloaked irony.

"Oh, they are paying off," says Dieter. "And for all of Germany. This is just the beginning of something big for our country and the next few years will see total fulfillment of the Party's goals."

"How wonderful that I have started participating just in time with the Party, at this moment," I lift my stein and think that my career has been overtaken by the National Socialists agenda.

Schiede continues to smile and puts his arm around Dieter's shoulders, "Men like Dieter will carry through our Party ambitions and you, Armand, will learn from the most dedicated."

November 1938

It is dark along Mainz's Kaiserstrasse as I walk up to my parent's townhouse. A burnt stench seeps through the air from every street corner while wisps of smoke rise out of piles of shattered architecture. My shoes crunch over broken glass and brick shards as I pick my way over street debris. I see that there are many storefronts that have had their windows knocked out along with the store innards having been ransacked of goods. Down one narrow street, I see that what was once the Mainz synagogue, is now a smoldering heap of timbers and stone. This was the same situation in Augsburg where there was an equal vehemence of violence against the Jewish community last week.

I knock on the door and wait. I notice how much more quiet and inactive the streets of Mainz are these days. Even my parent's house seems dark, reclusive and introspective. People just don't wander about freely or aimlessly for fun these days. All German people have a rigid purpose and every aspect of our lives are becoming militarized or Party controlled.

The house's door finally creaks open and a small feeble light emanates out to meekly welcome me. My mother peers out and slowly opens the door. Upon seeing me, she says, "*A che buono,* Armando, it is you. Hello, my son and welcome home." Moving into the parlor, she continues, "We never know which party official may come knocking upon our door or what neighbor may turn on us for being unpatriotic. But please come in *mio figlio*."

"Sit down in the dining room, Armando. How is Vanessa and our little Emil? I will call down your father. Here, let me get a pot of tea going for us."

"Thanks mama. I am happy to see you. Vanessa and my Emil are doing fine. He is already walking and starting to babble a few words." As I scan the parlor room, I comment, "Mama, the house seems dark."

"Well you know, Armando, electricity has just started to be rationed in Mainz, so they can use it for the factories instead. And we don't want nosy neighbors spying on us anyway. So, best to keep the curtains drawn and the lights low. Please sit my son."

My father comes down the stairs checking out who is here besides me. He seems apprehensive as he approaches but upon seeing me he opens with an embrace. "Oh, Armand. Good it is just you. So nice to see you my son."

We sit around the kitchen table and my mother pours tea from a pot and places some cookies on the table. No one speaks and all I hear is the clinking of spoons hitting the porcelain cups.

"You both look worried mama and papa. How bad is it here in Mainz?"

"Life in Mainz has changed a lot in the last year, son. Your father and I are not happy with it and we are uncomfortable with the direction of the National Socialists," says my mother.

Father then looks up from his tea. "Armand, you know I fought in the Great War and I never thought I would see Germany prepare itself for another full-scale European war. You were a young boy when I went off to fight in the trenches. Given the casualty count amongst my regiment, it's lucky that I even came back to continue raising you."

"I know, father. I remember nights of feeling sad because you could not come home and that I didn't have a father in our house."

Mother then says, "And that I had to hold the house together for those two years, were some of the toughest years of my life, son."

"I understand you are both worried about where Germany is going after five years of Hitler's Chancellorship. And I totally agree with you. Even though I am working at Messerschmitt AG, a prime, military industrialist, I can see the writing on the wall. Germany is scaling up for huge war, maybe on two to three fronts."

"We just didn't know where you stood on this, Armand, at least privately," says my father. "With your employer being a key contractor of warplanes, we can understand you may have interests in this weaponry build-up.'

"Oh no, I have grave misgivings about where my company is going and what we are producing," I say. These are exciting planes, it's just that the programs are all about warplanes or transporting soldiers or bombing cities. There is no civilian plane production going on. It is all heading toward one direction. I can see it when I look out my design bureau windows and look upon all the prototypes being tested. They are all military oriented."

"We have to keep this conversation and our thoughts very private," says my father. "There are people turning in their neighbors for anti-Party sentiments all the time. It's like a cruel game of revenge for whatever pet peeve you may have with your neighbor. And once people are turned into the police or Gestapo stations, we never see them again."

Mother frowns and says, "Worse yet, Armando, is the prosecution of the Jewish people. Last week the SA went on a wild rampage of breaking into Jewish stores and synagogues. There was so much debris and smoke in the air the next day, you would've thought that a battle had been fought here."

"Yes, it was frightening in Augsburg as well, mama" I respond. "Vanessa and I couldn't believe what was going on. But I could see that people that I have met at Party events were actively out in the streets leading the violence." My thoughts turn to how I saw Dieter leading a group of SA marauders demonically breaking storefronts and throwing torches into Jewish-owned buildings.

"The brown shirts are showing their true, ugly nature and spite for the Jews," says mama. "How much further can they go in their subjugation of the Jews? They have had all their civil rights stripped and now they are stripping them from our land. We just watched a parade go by in which they tarred and feathered a German woman for having a Jewish lover. And then everyone just railed at the poor woman and enjoyed seeing the punishment being dealt upon her."

"Those public punishments in the form of a spectacle are awful. I've seen them in Augsburg as well. Making matters more uncomfortable for me, my promotion at Messerschmitt requires me to participate in National Socialist Party events."

"Yes," my mother says, "I read your letter that you saw cousin Rodolfo at a rally. Seems like both sides of my family are now getting involved with Nationalist Parties. I had heard from Vittorio shortly afterward about Rodolfo's promotion to Captain as well."

"So, mama did you find out more about your family's religious heritage?" I ask.

"I did son," says my mother as she twirls her teaspoon around her tea cup. "Uncle Vittorio and I did some more research into our northern Italian heritage. Turns out the city we are from, Verona, is where there once was a large Jewish population. There is still a synagogue there and a small Sephardic community. Vittorio was able to find our families' surname on the list of Jews buried in their cemetery. It's not a direct link but a likely one given the family lore that we converted after the 1848 revolutions."

I ponder this point and feel a slight swirl of confusion run around inside me, "Well this brings home our country's anti-Semitism, right into our family. Oh my God." I stare blankly at the table.

"Yes, Armando, it is terrible for us to be living through these times. Now, the likelihood of the government persecuting us is slim but ethically son, how can we tolerate what is being done now to our brethren?"

Father extends his hand over to mother and strokes her shoulder in a show of support for this dilemma. He then says,

"We understand you have a good job with Messerschmitt AG and that you are playing a more critical role there as well. So realistically, we don't expect you to take any action about this family heritage, but we thought we should let you know. May this guide your moral compass for the upcoming years as Germany plunges itself into a another major conflict."

"While this news is hard to take, I appreciate knowing it," I state. "But I almost have no choice but to continue working at Messerschmitt. There are so many Air Ministry contracts being issued to my company that the war build-up is an integral part of Messerschmitt AG's essence."

Father says, "Also, I must express my fear that we do not want to lose our only child to a military conflict. Already the rate of conscription is increasing beyond just younger twenty-four-year-old men. Soon it may reach your age of twenty-eight."

"I know father. There is a possibility that I may have to serve in our country's military. Although, likely my status as an essential armament personnel will protect me for some time."

"Armando," says my mother, "I have a little something special for you. I feel with Germany on the brink of war that you could use this token of protection from me." She hands me a small jewelry box wrapped in brown paper and I start to unwrap it.

"Why mama," I say, "What is this?"

"It's a religious relic I picked up in Verona when I was with your Uncle Vittorio. Open it up son."

As I look at the piece I see that it is a small glazed clay tube that has Hebraic script carved into it.

"When Vittorio and I went into to the Verona synagogue," says my mother, "The Rabbi who helped locate our family name, presented one to each of us. It's called a 'mezuzah'."

"But, there is only one for our family and it was meant for you," I respond.

"At this point, son, I can think of no other person who will need this more in the upcoming years, than you. Bind this to your doorpost for a remembrance of your connection to our God and our family lineage. But given these times, only do this figuratively, son."

DECEMBER 1938

I see a handwritten message left on my desk that I am to report to Professor Messerschmitt's office. This is unusual I think; I hope I am not in trouble. I immediately jump off my drawing stool and walk past rows of drafting tables toward the administration offices. Usually, I am only here for conferences but never to the Professor's suite alone.

I am met by Frau Schnelling, and she has me shown into his private conference room, the room where he usually meets high officials from the Luftwaffe and the Air Ministry. I sit on one side of the wooden conference table noticing all the photos and awards on the wall. There are pictures of Messerschmitt with the Führer visiting our plant earlier this year, along with pictures of Göring, Udet and Major Galland. There are recognitions from the Ministry for exceptional design services contributing to Germany' success in the Spanish Civil War. Just this year the Munich *Technische Hochschule* conferred upon Messerschmitt the official title of full professor and the newly framed degree tops all of them.

Off to the side, is Professor Messerschmitt's plaque commemorating his official membership into the National Socialist Party. I had heard that Messerschmitt at first resisted joining the Party until 1932 and he would've rather stayed out politics. But when the government started issuing requests for designs with the potential to win large plane contracts, he joined the Party and since has not looked back. Nor have I have ever seen him without his Party pin on his lapel. I can't quite tell where he stands on this; is he a Party member to conveniently acquire contracts or does he fully adhere to their goals of European dominance and subjugation of non-Aryans?

The door opens, and I hear the Professor speaking to someone out of my sight as if they are still finishing up a conversation. He is wearing a gray wool, pinstripe suit with a vest, white shirt and a black tie; his usual uniform for being at the plant. Messerschmitt is thirty-nine years old, but his thinning hair and facial lines indicate a man who is older. Certainly, compared to my twenty-eight years of age, I feel like he is more accomplished a man than myself.

He closes the door and says, "Good morning Herr Kindermann. It's been over five years that you have been with us, and I am content to see your continued loyalty toward Messerschmitt AG. Now that we are working more closely together, I've been able to get a measure of the designer that you are, and I think your supervisors have done a good job in training you and advancing you to where you are. Your ability to put together cohesive, buildable drawings of our planes indicates to me that you have a good understanding of what is driving the design and more importantly how they can they be built quickly and efficiently."

"Thank you Professor for those positive observations."

He reaches into his suit coat pocket, pulls out a lighter and a cigarette, takes a puff and then taps it on the ashtray. For a moment, he stares off at the ceiling while he exhales out smoke. I sense his mind is visualizing some plane design issue. From what I can tell we have at least twelve under development and I wonder how he keeps track of them.

"Moving forward, Armand, I have some plans for your future here at Messerschmitt AG. I believe you would be an asset for our project bureau teams that are working on the early development of plane prototypes. The aero-dynamists and structural engineers do not always have a good sense of what it takes to build these planes and to make them sturdy for field use, particularly combat use.

"I've noticed your work on the Bf 109 Frederich, and I think you did a stupendous job on pulling together the designs for a fuselage to hold a stronger engine. And your wing design work on integrating the machine guns was uncanny. Much the same way I would've gone about it. In fact, I wish I could've said I came up with the solution myself, but as you know, I am much too busy these days with RLM and Party politics. They play such games with each other and our company that it's a full-time job for me to figure what they mean and anticipate when they will change their minds next. I don't know how we are going to take on a major war if the RLM and Luftwaffe continue with their petty politics and favoritism."

"I leave the politics of our contracts to you Directors," I say. "Yet I also appreciate your efforts to win new contracts for the company."

"Thank you. You know, I firmly believe that Messerschmitt AG is the *best* plane design company in Germany. Damn those fellows at Heinkel and Focke-Wulf. War or no war, the real war is with our plane competitors. Our company's battlefront will be in competing with those entities while the RLM and Luftwaffe shift the ground rules beneath our feet. It is imperative that our firm comes out on top because we are destined to. We have hired the best talent with young people like you, and soon we will test the mettle of every man in the design bureaus. We shall and you shall come on top with the best designs and production schemes so we can achieve our visions of the fastest, strongest fighter planes ever supplied to the Luftwaffe.

"Not to ignore the fact that I am thoroughly behind our Third Reich's goal to dominate Europe, its airspace and to make living room for the German people. I also believe our National Socialist Party ideals are the best for the German people so by extension, my vision to create a supportive factory community.

"Now with that preamble, the RLM will be issuing more requests for proposals for fighter planes that succeed the Bf 109. So sometimes we will be working on multiple planes in development. I expect your full effort in contributing your skills to these various endeavors. As such, I have two projects in mind for you, both of which are top secret."

"Yes sir," I respond. "You have my word as a good German that all this information will stay in the plant."

"Good, the first project is a delta-wing rocket aircraft that Doctor Lippisch will be bringing into the company. At the German Sail Plane Institute, the DFS, Lippisch tested it out solely as a glider plane. We are now going to combine it with a Walters Company rocket engine, so it can climb fast into the atmosphere and then glide down upon our enemy aircraft. We are referring to this plane as the Komet.

"Lippisch is an exceptionally intelligent aerodynamist and mathematician, perhaps as good as me," he says. "But he has been researching this plane at the Darmstadt DFS center for the last ten years with no operational fighter to date. That is where we come in. We and the likes of you are much better suited to bringing this plane into a production reality while the DFS folks keep their heads in the clouds, so to speak.

"Now the unusual thing, is that this delta-wing has no tail to it, and Lippisch that this may be just what is best suited for breaking the sound barrier. Could you imagine that, Messerschmitt AG breaking the sound barrier?

To be honest, this is the main reason I bought into the marriage with Lippisch. I want our 'Me' designation on the fastest plane out there, and Lippisch may be our ticket there. Plus, our own research team has already concluded that piston propeller planes can never fly faster than 500 miles per hour. And it's even worse at altitudes over 30,000 feet. The propeller efficiency hits a limit and the only way we can break it is through either rocket propulsion or a jet turbine."

My eyebrows pop up. "Yes, breaking Mach 1, that would be an impressive feat for our company. I would love to be part of that effort."

With a pen in his hand pointing at me, Messerschmitt moves onto the next assignment.

"And on the note of approaching the sound barrier but with jet turbines, the second project I have for you is working on just that. While we don't have a working jet turbine in Germany, the RLM has asked Messerschmitt AG to develop an airframe that will be eventually matched up with a future turbine. I must hand it to the fellows in the Technical Bureau at the RLM for their forward vision. Designing a plane for which the engines don't even exist yet. But with the turbine prototypes that Hans von Ohain has developed to date, BMW and Junkers are furiously working away on a factory producible turbine.

Internally, Voldemar Voigt will be heading up this project bureau, and you will report to him as chief of wing production.

"Now, the Komet project is a bit more problematic for me as Doctor Lippisch's rocket plane is not something I conjured up or even sponsored here. Instead, Doctor Lippisch is being matched up with us, and he is bringing in a whole project team with him. And while I have met Dr. Lippisch at many events and even know him from back in my gliding days, I sense we have very different approaches to plane design. We both want to create fast and swift aircraft; we just have very different ideas on how to achieve this.

"Lippisch is convinced that the future of supersonic flight is delta-wings without tails, and I see no advantage in this. If anything, I firmly believe a jet or rocket plane needs tail fins. So, we are coming at this goal from two very different mindsets.

"Lippisch's has a team of seventy people, and they will be stationed up on the 6th floor. There will be guards posted at all entries as the RLM has sanctioned this as a top-secret effort. Being that I do not know Lippisch or his team members working methods, I want you to work on the project with them and help them to conform to our company standards. But, confidentially, I am not sure I fully trust where Doctor Lippisch is taking this. So I want you to be my eyes and ears. Report to me any actions that you think are not in the company's overall best interests. Can I have your word on that, Armand?"

"Most certainly, Professor," I say. "I will do so as I only want to see good project results come out of our design bureaus."

Professor Messerschmitt puts down his pen and extends me a hand, and we shake on it.

"So, you will expect me to work on both projects," I ask, "making myself available to both project design chiefs?"

"Yes, I know you can handle the pressure of juggling these two. Plus, there will be periods of time where we will be building mock-ups and prototypes and then the endless round of RLM technical testing. So, I think you will have some downtime between the two."

I must leave now, the Baroness is coming to meet me here and then later, some Party officials are coming to our estate for a reception. A grand life that I have. All these Party and Ministry events keeping from me from doing what I do best. But with good designers such as you, we will get there. Tell me, are you married?"

"Yes, my wife's name is Vanessa, and we have two children and the youngest, a girl, was born just this year. My daughter's name is Angelika while my boy's name is Emil, in honor of you, Herr Professor."

"I am very honored to hear that," he says. Perhaps he will be a plane designer someday like both of us."

"I would be a happy parent if he did but for now he is mostly under the care of my Vanessa."

Messerschmitt responds, "With the Baroness, we have our hands full with her grown children. In fact, one of her boys has graduated from engineering school, and shortly he will be working here. But aside from the Baroness' children, Messerschmitt AG is my baby and many times I stay up all night to nurse it to health. Well, I enjoyed our chat, and I must head out now. Thank you, Armand."

With that he dismisses me, and I can see his attention is already drawn into another matter. A secretary enters the room and hands him a file bulging with memos. I imagine the Professor will be sorting through those next. I head back to my drafting table excited to have had this conversation with the Professor. It is also a little scary that he put upon me the effort of working on two significant projects. Both are full of technology that I don't quite comprehend yet; planes powered by jet and rocket propulsion.

★★★

"Armand, is that you?' says Vanessa emerging from the kitchen. You came home earlier than usual. Here, Angelika has been fussy all day for her bottle . Can you hold her while I finish up the potato salad?"

As I enter our second story flat, I say to Vanessa, "Sure but I wanted to chat with you about a new assignment that the Professor gave me." I say with the hope of having a quiet and adult conversation."

"Dada," exclaims my son Emil as he waddles over toward me towing a wooden duck family tied together by a rope. Emil also motions to be picked up so I shift Angelika to one arm and then lift up Emil.

"Oh my," I exclaim to Vanessa, "It seems that our little boy is growing in weight so fast. "You must love mama's food." Emil looks straight at me and bangs a little wooden duck onto my arm in a show of playful interest.

Vanessa then finishes in the kitchen, grabs the children from my arms and places them down into their playpen. "So, Armand. What was this chat about today?" she says as she brushes her light brown hair off her forehead

"For the first time the Professor called me in for a private conversation about taking on new key assignments. I can't tell you the specifics of the planes, but I can tell you that for these projects I am going to be the lead fabrication engineer and work more closely with the design bureau chiefs."

"Well, that sounds wonderful. Messerschmitt must trust you a lot to hand these tasks to you."

"I think so and I now feel me more 'in' with the company leadership. This was the first time he had me come to his offices and review key development issues like this."

"Does this mean you may be working longer hours?"

"I think everyone will be working longer hours. The way we are stacking up new Air Ministry contracts there will be no way to produce all these designs without more hours on everyone's part. But I don't mind the hours that will come this new assignment."

"Well maybe Emil and Angelicka will miss seeing their father day-to-day," says Vanessa with a hint of frustration.

"I know dear. They won't get to see their father that much if I have longer hours. But hopefully we can catch up on the weekends." Vanessa looks at me with her chin down but doesn't say anything, so I continue, "Still Vanessa, this will be all worth it in the end. I can feel that my potential to rise up the ranks is increasing." As we finish up the conversation Vanessa heads back over to the children not looking as excited as I had hope. I think how these new assignments will force me to cross a threshold that pits my family time up against my career ambitions and company commitments.

JANUARY 1939

It is January 2nd and Doctor Lippisch along with an initial retinue of twenty engineers will soon be showing up at the plant. I am curious to see who I will be working with and surreptitiously, watching out for the Professor.

As I gather up my drafting tools and manuals for moving up to the sixth floor, I say to Wolfgang, "Keep a look out for me in case I disappear into a no-man's land of secrecy and defunct science."

Wolfgang responds, "Do, you think this Doctor Lippisch fellow knows what he is doing?" A rocket strapped to a plane sounds terribly wild even by Messerschmitt standards."

"I hope he does. Otherwise, I am going to be wasting a good year of my life chasing the moon with this Lippisch Bureau. I've heard that he's been at this rocket plane with delta wings for the last ten years. So far, no luck and I think the DFS didn't want him burning up their development hours anymore. How he got assigned to Messerschmitt I don't know, probably some highly 'intelligent' RLM official who knows better."

"Probably, it seems to be the way things are working these days," chimes in Wolfgang, "But really, come on, Lippisch's ideas of a solid fuel plane with huge triangular wings and no tailfins is just so, so Buck Rogers-like. You know that American movie character?"

"You know," I start recalling, "I once saw Lippisch at a glider competition back in 1924. I went there with my dad and Walter Ignaz. We saw Messerschmitt fly a powered glider that was later picked up by Theo Croneiss for production. Lippisch was the director of the Glider Club and he announced the flying teams as they took off. Surprising that I ever ended up in aviation given the number of crashes we saw. Ok, Wolfgang, I will see you around the halls. Don't be a stranger and come over and visit me once and a while." I salute off to Wolfgang.

Shortly after I am finished setting up my drafting table on the sixth floor, Doctor Lippisch's team files in one by one. Immediately I recognize someone, it is Dieter Fleischen.

Dieter and the other Lippisch engineers walk past my drafting table and place their drawing instruments on their assigned tables. It takes Dieter a minute or so to pull out all his triangles and rulers. I notice that he is carefully wiping each one and inspecting their edges as if they are his own children. My eyes also catch a flash of metal Dieter's lapel. It is a National Socialist Party pin. He has followed through on his University years' aspirations.

Dieter notices me at my table, and he comes over beaming a strong smile under his mustache, "Well, well, what do we have here? Armand, the 'star' designer. You better be ready yourself for a little competition." Dieter chuckles to himself. "I didn't know you were going to be assigned to our Lippisch bureau. Such a pleasant surprise. What, are you going to do, keep an eye on us advanced delta wing engineers?"

"You got it Dieter," I respond looking straight at him, "And I will be watching your every move while I advance my way through and out of this bureau."

"I will be well on my way to the next high-speed plane before you can blink an eye." responds Dieter curtly. " I know your work habits from school and I don't think they will get you far here or help you keep up with us."

"Your sense of self-worth hasn't diminished one Mark since our university days. But if your assessment of me is correct, then why did Messerschmitt plant me here?"

"That's just it. You probably are here as a plant and your main role will likely be to bungle up our works."

"Really Dieter? Do you think I would stoop to take such a role given my experience with Messerschmitt AG? I have plenty of other planes I could be working on but the Professor entrusted with this to me for a reason."

"Well, I will be keeping an eye on you just as much as you will be on us."

Alexander Lippisch finally enters the studio along with a few other Messerschmitt directors including Gerhard Coulis, Ratathan Kokathi and Herr Schmedemann. However, I am the only engineer-level person attending for the company. Lippisch is a slender fellow with an equally drawn out and thin face, a receding hairline and an unusually dark skin-tone for being German. He is of moderate height and he keeps looking down at his pad as if he is ready to go back to making calculations.

Lippisch introduces everyone to his rocket engineer, Doctor Helmuth Walters and the two of them explain to the Messerschmitt/Lippisch assembly what the plane's design parameters will be, "Gentlemen from the Messerschmitt company," starts Lippisch. "I am pleased to give you an overview of the Komet. It is a delta wing, rocket-powered plane of modest proportions but huge flight capability. Overall the entire plane is 22 feet long and the wingspan is 31 feet. The swept-back wings run along the fuselage much longer than your typical piston-engine fighter as there is no tail wing. It's main role will be as a fighter interceptor that is propelled by rocket combustion.

As Lippisch says this, I think the plane looks stubby and the cockpit canopy looks like a boil on a nose. Not a very pretty looking plane much less flight-worthy in my opinion. The physics behind this plane confound me but obviously Lippisch has been mulling this one over for years. The drawings he shows still have the DFS Institute title block on them but soon we will make this a Messerschmitt AG plane.

Then Lippisch goes over the flight characteristics of this rocket plane, "It will use a rocket engine to not only lift off but to travel through the atmosphere at very high speeds, over 550 miles per hour. Its rate of climb will be stupendous and unmatched by any piston engine plane as it will climb to 30,000 feet in three minutes. From there it will glide in for attacks using its short, swept-back wings for tight turns even at high speeds.

"The airframe for the Komet started off as a glider plane so the rocket-propelled version will have excellent gliding characteristics once it reaches the top of its apogee. In fact, the plane is being designed to glide back from high altitudes and land that way as well. The glide ratio is 15 to 1 meaning it can fly for fifteen miles with only a mile drop in altitude.

"This plane has been named the Komet, and our prior plane number at the German Sailplane Institute was DFS 194. But now here at Messerschmitt AG, I've been instructed that it will be numbered the Me 163. You are of course welcome to still refer to it as the 'Komet' as I think it is an appropriate moniker for what will be the fastest plane ever to hit the skies. Our timeline goal is to get a prototype flying by 1941 and then secure RLM contracts for a production series by 1942.

"Now I understand we have some Messerschmitt AG staff here in our Bureau, and I believe there is an Armand Kindermann here in the room?"

I raise my hand much the way a student does when called upon the first day of school. "Greetings Doctor Lippisch, I am Armand and Professor Messerschmitt assigned me to work on the production drawings of the wings and the fuselage. I look forward to working with all of you."

I notice a slight amount of staring between the Lippisch team members, perhaps they are questioning why I have been placed amongst them. Lippisch then says. "I am glad that Mtt, been so generous to contribute some extra manpower to our team."

I realize that Lippisch has referred to Messerschmitt as 'Mtt' and pronounces out the letters, 'em te te' as if he is a chemical abbreviation or a plane designation. I think this group is going to need some coaching on how everyone here addresses Messerschmitt as 'Professor' and I then respond back,

"Yes, Professor Messerschmitt has directed me to provide at least half my time to this rocket plane team. Additionally, I will be happy to instruct you on our drawing and production standards in Augsburg, so this plane can be readily factory produced."

The group as a whole looks to each other and then to Doctor Lippisch. After some mutterings with some of his crew, Lippisch responds,

"Thank you, Armand for that offering of production assistance. And along those lines, do you know where our workshop tools are? We need to continue building mock-ups of the Komet, and I told Mtt that we would need the shop equipment in place the day we arrived."

Lippisch is right, the workshop is empty of machinery. Even the Professor said to me that the experimental shop would be ready, but it's not. I look at the Lippisch team with slight embarrassment, and I am scrambling on what to say. I then turn toward the company directors, and they start rambling off some excuse about the equipment being held up in transit. I am starting to realize that I am going to be right in the middle of two aeronautic Titans and both are going to play me against the other.

APRIL 1939

While in the Lippisch bureau, I lift my head up from my drafting table and think to myself that I need more structural information on the wing forces. I approach Dieter's table and lay out my drawing,

"Dieter, I need to go over the wing strengthening detail of the 163. The latest directive is to augment the bolt connections with glue between the wood wings and the wood strip on the fuselage. The only thing is, I don't know of any design institute that specifies the flexural strength of glue."

"Ok, Armand. Let me see how I can explain this to you. I mean it's obvious that these delta wings have a high wing-aspect ratio, so I would think you could figure the stresses out by applying some good old Newtonian physics on it. Right? So, once you figure out the bonding area and assume the glue will be like a bolted plate of steel, I think you will be able to calculate it."

"Maybe I can but there is no institute that has documented glue's strength levels."

"Figures," says Dieter changing his tone to sarcasm, "That Lippisch has asked for a design that has no standards we can rely on."

"What do you mean by that?" I inquire of Dieter.

"I mean that Lippisch is pushing us into design areas that have no basis of testing. There are no industry standards available for much of what we are doing. We have to just guess and figure things out all the time."

"Well, that is what being in research is all about, Dieter."

"I know. I don't need you to tell me that. I am starting to wonder if Lippisch really knows what he is doing with these glider rockets. Will this Komet really hang together after it exceeds 500 miles per hour or will it fall apart?"

"I have come around to trust what Doctor Lippisch is projecting these rocket planes will do. Don't you Dieter? You are one of his main design engineers."

"Yes, but it doesn't mean I have totally bought into his plane design direction. The actual test flights better show equal or stronger results than Lippisch's calculation, otherwise, I will have been wasting my time here."

As Dieter says this, I see that he slides another drawing under his layers of sheets. I don't think much of it right away; maybe it's something between him and Lippisch. After all these years, project bureau Lippisch still feels like a separate company that happens to be housed in Messerschmitt AG.

We continue our chat on the wing mountings and then I notice the sheet he hid has slipped down just enough to reveal the title sheet information. I see an unfamiliar title block and an Arado Plane company logo with an aircraft project number that I don't recognize. I think Dieter has realized I have seen it, and he pushes the drawing back under the other sheets. I go back to my drafting table wondering what I have just seen.

My suspicion being aroused, I decide to check back at Dieter's table later when no one is around. It is Ten PM and being one of the few night owls I find myself back at his table with the Lippisch bureau empty. I approach Dieter's table and look through his sheets until I find the Arado logo. Once I pull the drawing out, I look it over, but I don't recognize the plane I am looking at. It is a jet plane based on the turbine shown in the drawings, but it is not one of our plane designs.

What is Dieter doing with our competitor's designs at the Messerschmitt company? The drawing is under progress as I can see there are still the guidelines softly drawn in of what is to be drawn in eventually. Then my mind rapidly turns to, what is Dieter doing here with Messerschmitt and Arado drawings together?

Instinctively I head to the executive offices hoping to speak with someone. I find the Gerhard Coulis, the superintendent engineer still there under a lamplight at his desk,

"Is the Professor still in the plant?" I ask.

"No, he went to a dinner meeting at six, but you never know, he may come back to haunt the halls and mull over your tables."

I decide to wait back at my table for another hour and finally I see the Professor. Sure enough, his bewitching hour has begun, and he is ambling through the sea of tables looking with his chin bobbing up and down as he looks over the drawings. I see him stop at a desk and then he starts scribbling notes over the drawing. I approach him and exclaim,

"Professor, I am glad to see you here, now. I have something urgent I want to share with you."

"Armand, what a surprise to see you here. You must be like me, a night owl. What is bothering you?"

"I was at Dieter Fleischen's desk today and noticed he was hiding some Arado plane drawings on his desk. I can't think of a good reason for him to be holding onto these blueprints as they are our competitor in putting out a jet plane proposal. We are in a race to beat out Arado's jet with our Swallow so why would he be working on an Arado drawing?

The Professor's face looks surprised, next gray and then anger spreads across his face.

"*Mein Gott!* How could he be working on our competitor's design while working for me? Or is he sharing our jet designs with Arado? Haven't I given those fellows in the Lippisch team full opportunity to prove their designs and I get this, a stab in the back. Where is the ethics of these young engineers?"

Messerschmitt slaps his forehead with his palm and places his elbow on the nearest drafting table. Staring at the ground his eyes go blank as he starts realizing the depth of the betrayal by his own staff. He continues with his teeth gritting.

"We are in a pitted battle to win this fighter jet contract and Arado's design is rumored to have better payload capacity than ours. Some of the test pilot reports also say that their jet turns more tightly than our Swallow and is easier to fly. It is neck and neck and if Arado gets any more legs up on us, our whole jet project will be abandoned.

And that would be a calamity for you, for me and for the story of the German jet.

"Ok, we are not to say anything to Dieter or Lippisch for that matter," he continues. Let's monitor him first and see who he is communicating with. Perhaps if we trace him, we can find out if there are other collaborators or an Arado gateway in this plant. Still, the gall of these people to turn on me like this. It's been the plague of my career, Armand. Either my own employees betray me, or my ministry supporters pull out and jump sides like rabbits in a hunt. Their white tails bouncing away through the snow."

"Well, Professor, if it helps, I have known Dieter for some time. We went to university together and were friends for some period."

Messerschmitt looks up. "Oh yes? Tell me more."

"Well, Dieter was always an ambitious student and had big dreams for himself. He was very talented and put many hours into his school projects, so I can vouch for his discipline. But his drive comes from a sense of destiny to be the best designer, ever.

"So, Professor, what I am thinking is that Dieter was not seeing his due advancement coming fast enough with our company nor with the Lippisch team. I believe he started to see that Doctor Lippisch's theories on delta wings were just too far out there for them to be practical for contemporary aviation. And because of that, he felt that his work here would be a waste of his career.

Messerschmitt follows my chain of logic and then chimes in,

"So, you think he shared our Swallow's secrets with Arado to get a big step into their company? Something he didn't see himself getting here at Messerschmitt AG?"

"Knowing Dieter, I think that would be a consistent set of motivations. Your company wasn't giving him enough stepping stone upwards. Sorry if I am being disrespectful Professor."

Messerschmitt lifts his body off the drafting table and straightens out his stance with some authority, as if he has recovered from a punch thrown by a weaker opponent.

"No, Armand, I appreciate your observation and it sounds like a probable reason. But why give away our secrets to our competitor? Why slap me in the face after I took the whole Lippisch crew on without really wanting them here in the first place."

"Perhaps because they know you really don't welcome them here. Maybe they feel a bit of spite like step-children do toward their step-parents. They need your protection, but they resent your lack of full acceptance."

"I think you have made me realize that I need to change my tune with the Department 'L' team. I need to make them feel more welcome here, or we will be getting more of these friendly gestures.

"Ok, here's my plan," says Messerschmitt. Let's keep this quite for a week, I will have my closest confidants in the company, all three of them, watch Dieter carefully and see who he is interacting with. Especially off the plant grounds. When we figure out his collaborators, we will then swoop in and catch them red-handed."

"However, I can help. I surely do not want Arado walking off with our jet's technology."

"Now you are talking. I like that you take ownership of it. The jet is a beautiful machine, and it is ours to beget and to behold. Never lose sight of that. We will round these fellows up eventually, root them out and leave Arado in the dust. Now, I think you should go home, rest and I will contact you in the next few days with our plan to scrub out this illness from our company."

"Yes, and I am glad to help."

With that, I leave the drafting hall with Messerschmitt still standing deep in his thoughts. I am certain he is already thinking out a chain of actions on how to catch Dieter and others in this scandal. As I bike home, I think to myself that I will now have to 'fake' cooperation with Dieter for the next week or so and then we will turn on him as he did to us. Perhaps a sad ending to our University based relationship but at this point in my career I am only too happy to have him moved out of my way. And to think, he did it on his volition.

★★★

Messerschmitt's secretary, Frau Schnelling calls me up to the conference room. When I arrive in the room, Doctor Lippisch and Messerschmitt are already seated around the meeting table. The Professor has me sit down,

"Armand, I just finished having a revealing conversation with Doctor Lippisch here, and I believe we have an idea of where this Arado spying is coming from. Doctor Lippisch has been very forthright about Dieter's behavior in the last month, and he too had his suspicions about his loyalties to the company. Thus, we are going to move Dieter to our Regensburg plant."

Being caught off guard by this I say, "What, he is not being fired but being transferred?"

"You see, Armand, it's not such a clear-cut matter," responds Messerschmitt.

"What, that he was spying on us for Arado? He should be let go immediately," I state sharply with my fingers gripping the chair's armrests.

Messerschmitt looks down at his pen and twirls it around. "We've determined that Dieter was not only spying for Arado but that he is also a Gestapo informant. A plant to spy on our industrial operations and to inform Party officials at the highest level as to what we are really up to."

"So, he is going to be rewarded for this with a job transfer? Professor, he was willfully sharing our company plans to the potential detriment of us winning new contracts."

"Yes, Armand, but you see I cannot upset Party officials too greatly. Obviously, they knew that Dieter was spying on us, if not informing on us. It's part and parcel of this whole government contracting business. It's the government's way of keeping tabs on us. Unfortunately, we must tolerate it so we can keep our contracts in place."

I am stunned that my revealing the spying by my old competitor has turned into a 'turn the cheek the other way' event to appease others.

Dieter should've been penalized but he had his back covered by Party officials.

Doctor Lippisch then interjects, "I know, Armand, I feel somewhat like you, a little confused but this will be the best course for our department as well. I do appreciate your being diligent about this and I value the technical skills you bring to our Komet team. However, I agree with Willy here that it is best for our overall relationship with contracting officials."

"Nevertheless," says Messerschmitt, "you showed true loyalty and commitment to Messerschmitt AG. So, I am rewarding you with a promotion to chief production engineer for both the jet and rocket planes. All production designers and draftsmen on these projects will be reporting to you directly from now on. And, you can take the station along the window near the executive offices as well."

"Thank you, sirs. I am glad to accept this assignment, and I understand your decision on Dieter. I look forward to serving Messerschmitt AG in this higher capacity."

I rise and extend out my hand to shake their hands and seal the compact they have offered me. Inside, I feel a little sore, though, that Dieter got off this scandal so unscathed. At least I have the backing of the two lead directors. In turn, I am getting more of what I want; design input, authority and control over my career while having gotten rid of that irritant in my life.

PART 2
FIELD TRIALS

AUGUST 1943

"Alright, Herr Messerschmitt. Hold still while I adjust the lights. Ok, now look the other way while I frame the camera's view. Would you reposition that third light and instead put it behind him above his head? We need some highlight to contrast out his head against all the white drafting tables in the back."

From the film camera's viewer, up pops the director and he looks at the Professor with one eyebrow furled up as if he is some still-life to be painted.

"No," the director says. "I think we need a better backdrop to accentuate his importance in the design studios. How about we move the Professor over toward those drafting tables, the ones where the super-long drawings are pinned up? They nicely portray the complexity and beauty of these planes. Professor, would you sit across from one of your designers, hold a pencil and point at their drawings. You know, like you are directing them to undertake a significant design change."

With that directional cue, the whole film crew shifts over toward the grouping of drafting tables next to mine. While I am not the designer that Messerschmitt will be pointing at, I am just behind them, and thus I must 'act' along with the filming.

The Professor walks over to a stool opposite my co-worker. I can see on his face a slight irritation at having to take up a whole morning for the Ministry of Public Enlightenment and Propaganda. But Messerschmitt has become a poster-child for the National Socialist Party as a highly-accomplished, technical virtuoso. To the German public and to the outside world, the Party wants to craft Messerschmitt as the plane designer *par excellence*. Especially for our enemies when they hear our Bf 109's screaming overhead strafing their troops or pursuing their Spitfires.

Messerschmitt understands his selected role and obliges to help the Party, but he also knows that it is good public relations for the company. He appears to relish being glamorized in these riveting, authentic portrayals of accomplished Germans.

"Ok, Herr Messerschmitt, I would like you to start talking with the designer and carry on some form of conversation with him, but of course, you oversee the conversation and you, Mr. designer, just smile, nod your head and continue to draft away."

As the filming gets underway I continue to conduct my real work. I hear the director yell 'cut' and he seems satisfied with the take. The camera and light crews then move around toward the corner to the drafting hall with Messerschmitt's back to us designers while he recites from a rehearsed script the essence of his company's superior design approach. Messerschmitt begins in a forced acting tone,

"My dear Germans. The National Socialist Party extolls everyone to work one-hundred and ten percent for the armament of our war effort. The more weapons we produce, the more, we can obtain our Germanic living space. And we at Messerschmitt AG in Augsburg are a shining example of Socialism and technology at work, producing aircraft that excel all others. This is because our centralized government has made every planning measure needed to design, test and build military aircraft that exceeds our enemies' planes. It is the German way, and it is a superior one.

"Our Augsburg plant demonstrates how National Socialism can obtain high levels of creativity, output, and motivation. We have not only a talented workforce but a highly productive one that operates in harmony. Our workers are well taken care of with clean housing, adequate health support, and plenty of exercise and community activities for all. These Party ideals have resulted in our producing Europe's most exceptional planes, the Bf 108, the BF 109, the Me 110, the Me 410, the and the Gigant transport glider.

"With these exceptional warplanes being under massive production programs, Germany is sure to maintain the upper hand in this war. We will bring the war to our enemy's front line, wherever they shift. And we know at Messerschmitt AG that a strong aviation industry makes for a strong Germany. What is good for the aircraft industry is good for Germany. Heil Hitler!"

"Cut," the film director barks out. "Let's take that one more time Herr Messerschmitt. I think you need to cut that last line about what is good for the aircraft industry. So, let's run that again minus that statement, shall we please?"

"Of course, Herr Director," says Messerschmitt through tightened lips.

For the next scene, the film director looks over the script with another assistant and they ponder if this scene is still appropriate. After some looking around they decide to keep the framing as is and say,

"Alright, Herr Messerschmitt now I am moving to the lines that will be used for updates on our cinema newsreels. Remember these next scenes will be utilized in the future to tell people how we have already progressed. This way we won't have to come back and restage this set. Are you ready for this now?"

After a short breath in, Messerschmitt refocuses his attention on the director and the film crew before him. I only see his back and beyond that the large filming camera, three lights, a microphone boom and the crew facing intently toward Messerschmitt. I notice how glaring these lights are and they are distracting my drafting activities; too many shadows and I am catching glare off the triangles.

"Action, begin," the director says, pointing toward Messerschmitt.

"Good to see you again my Germans and your National Socialist Party plans are well at work at Messerschmitt. We have just produced our 20,000th Bf 109 among all our factories, and we are confident to hound the Allies back to their lands with these planes. Moreover, we have come out with even more advanced planes that you will see shortly over our skies defending us from this terrorist bombing campaign. We the German people are fighting the principled war; the Allies are fighting a dirty war with their bombing of the populace. But in response, we are at Messerschmitt AG have developed the next generation fighter planes that will knock down the heavy bombers by the dozens in one sortie. The Fatherland must be preserved from these invading hordes and at Messerschmitt AG we have the tools to achieve this goal. My blessings to all us Germans and Heil Hitler!"

"Excellent!" snaps the director. "Your energy and conviction is palpable Herr Messerschmitt. You believe in what you say and that makes our filming job all the easier."

★★★

I am resting at home listening to the radio as the announcers' talk of Germany's military successes in Africa, France, and Russia. Sounds like the country is holding on to all the captured territories well. I then hear a knock on the door and Vanessa gets up to greet our visitor. Vanessa walks back into the living rooms looking like she just saw a ghost.

"Armand, it's Josef Manakin, your old classmate and he is on leave from the Wehrmacht." I bolt up from my chair thinking, 'Josef? I hadn't heard from him in two years, ever since he shipped out for the Russian front'. I walk to the apartment door and there I see I haggard, sun-beaten version of my old university friend, now a lieutenant. His eyes are lined with a pink rim, and they seem deeply sunken. What has the war done to him? I greet him with affected normalness,

"Josef, my old friend, good to see you."

Josef holds onto his cap, slowly looks up at me and hesitates a second. "Armand and Vanessa, it is a relief to see you both. I know you didn't expect me, but I was passing through Augsburg, and I had a few hours to wait for my next train. I am being transferred to the Western front."

"Oh Josef," Vanessa says, "please come in and rest while you can. We are so happy you stopped by. Please sit over here. Armand, would you clean off the sofa."

Josef slowly walks over with a slow gait and then slumps into the couch his long body falling deeply into the cushions. He paws his cap in his hand and stares outward toward our window. I take a quick look at Vanessa and off she wheels into the kitchen to set the teapot on.

I sit across from Josef and take my time before I press anything out of him,

"Josef, you can rest here as long as you would like. Vanessa and I will provide you whatever traveling comforts you need."

Josef turns his glare from the floor and looks toward me but his focus is way past me. He begins tepidly with long pauses in between his sentences, "Our regiment, or what is left of it, was at the Battle of Kursk. If you haven't heard correctly yet, it was a total massacre of our men. It was a complete rout, every man for himself. The Russians broke our attack, and I believe they have broken our backs. Worse yet, they destroyed our ability to go on the offensive again."

As Josef says this, he again turns his gaze back into his hands and fumbles his cap. I reach out and place my hand on his shoulder hoping to offer him some comfort,

"I did hear something of a setback on the Russian front but here in the homeland, details are far and few. All we have is the Government radio broadcasts and the weekly newsreels." I pause and then change my line of conversation, "My old friend I can see you are very shaken. Take your time. Sip some of this tea."

Josef takes a sip of tea and for the first time, he looks at what is in front of him, "Armand and Vanessa, I need to know what the propaganda ministry is telling folks back in the homeland. Since I've been transiting through Germany, I sense there is a disconnect between what is being told here and how the war is actually going."

I respond to Josef, "We hear that our brave soldiers and their impenetrable tanks are overrunning the Russian horde day and night. Although, lately some of the reports indicate that we have reached a standstill in further offenses. What we heard about the Battle of Kursk is that it was a great German offensive of thousands of Panzer tanks, and that we pushed the Bolsheviks back to the Caucuses."

Josef nods his head. "Well, that was partially correct, up until the second day of fighting. But then the Russians counter-attacked with more vehemence than we put into our offense, and they ground our attack to a halt. Then on the third day, they continued their assault and busted up most of our tanks and troops over miles of flat plains.

"My platoon was decimated, out of forty men, only sixteen of us walked out of the battlefront. Further, our regiment lost sixty-percent of its tanks and trucks, so we have little attacking force left. The retreat of the next two days set us back to where we started. A net gain of nothing. Only that we lost almost a thousand tanks in the seesaw action. As the Russian pressed their pursuit, many broke ranks and fled further west away from the front. It was chaos, fear, massacre, and the loss of hope. The loss of hope that we could ever pull off another attack on Russia." Josef puts the teacup down and then buries his face into his hands.

Vanessa seems shocked. "Oh my, Josef. This is not the picture we have been given. This is very worrisome."

Josef looks up at Vanessa, gathers some composure and says with kindness. "I am sorry Vanessa. I did not mean to worry you and your family but at the same time, you should probably know the real state of the war. Just don't let anyone know that I told you."

I think to myself about our warplane effort and if only we could've had more planes out in action to cover these poor men. But now, RLM indecisions have left us with not enough planes or fast enough ones to provide an adequate air offense. I turn to Josef,

"Josef, my old friend, I am very proud of you for battling on the front. In fact, I must admit at times I feel guilty that I am sitting at my desk safe and sound out of harm's way."

"It's alright. I understand and appreciate the role you have with the aviation industry. You are a designer of advanced fighter planes and I am a combat officer. We each have our part in this war. And for sure, we need the best planes to cover our men and go after the Cossack mongrels. I will continue doing my part to preserve our Fatherland and leading my platoon of men to safety if not victory."

I am touched by Josef's understanding our situations. I think back to our University days when I admired Josef's technical drawing hand and his natural leadership skills within the studio. He then stands up and we give each other an embrace. Vanessa comes forward and does likewise. Josef heads toward the door,

"Armand and Vanessa, it meant so much to see some old school friends amidst my journey. You don't know how much comfort this brought to me to see you two together, in your apartment with children running around and a household full of love. I see so little of this while commanding my platoon through battles. I will think of this on the train to France and keep the thought of this with me as I lay in my tent or a trench or whatever I find for the night. I don't mean to sound bitter or ironic. This really was heartening, and I am glad I came to visit you two. *Auf wieder sehen mienen freunden.*" Josef places his officer cap back on and walks out the door.

Vanessa and I look at each other, contemplating the drastic change in Josef's demeanor, knowing that the war has already sucked out a portion of his life. He will never be the same Josef, in war or in peace.

SEPTEMBER, 1943

Voldemar Voigt keeps shifting from one side to the other as we drive up to the Leipheim airfield near Ulm. I finally ask him, "A little nervous, Doctor Voigt?

"Sure," he responds, "if this jet crashes on this test flight, I will sure to be rooted out by the SS for some treacherous reason."

"Oh, you are beyond that Voldemar. You are one of Messerschmitt's prize designers. I can tell everyone wants to be in your project bureau and I feel particularly grateful to be in it"

"Thanks, Armand, but us plane designers are fallible. Isn't your ten-year anniversary coming up?"

"Actually, my ninth anniversary is approaching but thanks for asking."

"It's a good thing you have stuck it out with us, Armand. Once we get the Swallow up and off the runway, your real work will begin. I am just an airframe aero dynamist and my work will be completed soon. From here, it will be up to you and other in production engineering to make the bird an operational fighter."

"That's why I am sticking it out, Voldemar. I want to see this beauty fly."

As we approach the airbase, we see there are already a long line of Ministry and Luftwaffe staff cars parked along the security checkpoint. Voldemar looks out the window and says,

"Either, I will be a hero today or I will be thrown to the wind and forgotten about. Let's hope for the best. The only things that are worrying me are the landing gears and the BMW turbines. Both are not flight tested to date."

As we step out onto the Leipheim tarmac we see clusters of people representing different aspects of the industry; RLM planners, Luftwaffe officers, BMW managers and our

Messerschmitt engineers. Finally, Fritz Wendel comes out his barracks with his flight suit and parachute on. The crowd turns quiet, breaks open a path and allows a quiet and stoic Fritz to walk toward his altar, the Me 262 jet. The test pilot par excellence, Fritz, remains calm as the airfield mechanics prestart the jet turbines. They bring a ladder over for him to climb into the cockpit and Fritz slips in and buckles up. After the mechanics close his canopy, they pull away allowing the jet to rev up its engines.

Fritz has been with Messerschmitt since 1940 testing planes and I have been getting to know him better these days. Perhaps because his life and safety depend on our good engineering senses, he occasionally makes his way back to the project bureau and chats with my design team.

Fritz is relatively young, as he is twenty-seven years old and *Flugkapitän* of our Augsburg test pilots. As I am also one of the younger designers, at age thirty-two, Fritz and I occasionally spend after work hours sharing steins of beer and adventurous stories.

The jet that Fritz will fly is labeled as the Me 262V1, PC+UA. It's already our second prototype of the Me 262, but this one has both jet turbines as wing pods and a piston engine mounted in the nose. After taxing around, he finally pulls the jet straight down the runway and slowly but surely pulls up it into the air. The jet has a high-pitched whir that is much sharper than any piston engine. Once the wheels are off the ground, Fritz pulls the plane into a steep ascent accelerating all along. He pulls level at around 5,000 feet and then starts banking into a large circle.

Fritz is up in the air for fifteen minutes and then suddenly we hear the jet engines cut out and only the sound of the small propeller engine kicks in. Fritz is losing altitude and speed rapidly, but he is able to bring the plane down on the runway. Since the jet was moving so slowly, it comes to a halt rather quickly after touchdown. As it stops, the engines continue to flame and then spew out smoke, but Fritz is able to kill them after a few seconds. We are all ecstatic he has made it back and that our Swallow flew so well. First, the mechanic crew runs out to the jet, followed by Luftwaffe officers and RLM personnel. Then seeing a celebration erupt on the field, we designers also decide to go and join the joyous melee. Fritz is the hero today, and it is well deserved. His athletic build and face beam with confidence and energy and his usual restrained manner is left behind for this precious moment.

October, 1943

The Leipheim Airfield stretches flat out before me as I stroll between the hangars and the concrete runway. A constant hissing sound pierced by an occasional blast-off of a rocket permeates and activates the scenery. Emerging out of the officer's barracks, a rather tall pilot walks toward me donning what looks like a white, full-body skiing outfit. I notice that he is entirely covered in this baggy, fabric as he shuffles over to me. "Armand Kindermann? I am First Lieutenant Wolfgang Spate, commander of Operational Test Unit 16 for the Me 163 Komet.

"My pleasure to meet you Lieutentant. I didn't realize Komet pilots wore such baggy flight suits."

"I know, it looks like I am wearing an old lady's blouse and pantaloon set. Not the most militaristic looking but hopefully it will do the job."

"And that job being what?"

"These flight suits are made from a unique fabric that will protect us from the concoction of rocket fuels used in the Komet. If ever one of us pilots crashes a Komet, the rocket fuel will be sure to leak out. And one splash of that fluid on our skin will rapidly melt our body and bones like water to sand."

"I see, not an attractive prospect. Well, I came up from the Augsburg design bureau to work with your Operational Test Unit to redesign the landing skids, wing mounts and other items from your field reports."

"Yes, we have been waiting for you or someone from Messerschmitt AG to come up and start addressing these problems. Not to put you on the spot Kindermann but we in the Test Unit are feeling a bit like step-children compared to say, the Bf 109 or the Me 262. Am I just imagining that?"

"I can see how you may feel that way but has not been our intent Lieutenant. We are stretched thin as a drum designing modifications to all existing airframe lines. And recently a few of our key technicians have been called up for duty. So, trust me, we are doing whatever we can to keep the improvements going for the Komet."

"Well, let executive management at Messerschmitt AG know that I not only have this test command, but I have also been authorized to train up our first fighter units by year's end. Pilots are being assigned to me now but there are no combat-ready planes in sight. What am I supposed to have them train on? A reindeer sled?"

"I tell you what. After you take your test flight, I will be officing here at Leipheim airfield for a week. Why you don't come over and we can have a longer chat about this. I do want your Operational Command Unit to complete the testing of the Komet, so we can see this plane off into the air."

Lieutenant Spate seems a little more settled. "Ok Herr Kindermann, I like that offer. Why don't you and I spend a good amount of time at our hangar and speak frankly about the plane's issues, production schedules and how your staff and mine can be on the same page. Sounds good?"

"Excellent approach, Lieutenant. I will come over at your convenience. In the meantime, I will enjoy watching my first take-off of a Me 163. I see you are cued up and waiting for the fueling process to be completed."

"Yes, I am next once Heini Ditmar lands. He is a regular test pilot but me, I am a combat pilot. I am only learning how to fly this so when I take command of my fighter unit, I will be able to competently lead them into battle. Provided I don't crash land this little bird first. "

I am always impressed at these officers of the Luftwaffe. Even the commanders are always actively leading missions and engaging in aerial combat, Spate being no different. Then from the field there is a flagging motion and Wolfgang starts walking off saying,

"It's my birthday today so wish me luck on my first powered flight of the Komet." For being a bit grumpy, Spate does seem to have a good sense of humor, perhaps a dark one given his fighter pilot's role to date. He is no one to sneeze at either. He has had 79 plane kills to date and he has been awarded the Iron Cross with oak leaves, meaning Hitler handed it to him personally. And prior to that, he was a champion glider pilot in the Wasserkuppe competitions.

As Spate walks up to the Komet, I see a group of technicians surrounding the craft parked on the grass. They are tending with two different fueling trucks in sequence. One has the T-Agent, hydrogen peroxide, and the other is the C-Agent, a mix of liquid carbons. As they pour out their fuels into the Komet I see steam evaporating out like a wicked sorcerer's brew. Cloaked in white suits, the men have fire extinguishers packed on their backs. They appear to be closely following the fueling operation as they continuously splash water around the craft. Surrounding Spate's Komet I notice that the grassy runway has ruts in it where the soil has been blown off by prior rocket lift-offs. Unexpectedly for a runway, there are also green and purple splotches stained into the grass. I am assuming that is from the spillage of the rocket fuel.

Ditmar's plane comes in for a landing and finally it is time for Spate to climb into the cockpit. I see the technicians open the bubble of a canopy and the lanky Spate fits into this midget of a plane. It is then that I notice that a few other officers and pilots have gathered up next to me. They are from Spate's unit and they seem eager to have their leader test out the newly fangled craft.

As the second fuel truck and electric starter cart pull away, the rocket engine is engaged by Spate. With a low hiss, I see at first an alternating white smoke pulsing out the rocket's nozzles. Then it picks up in consistency, thickness and sound; a deafening, high-pitch hiss that makes me cover my ears. I was already warned that it can reach 120 decibels. Spate's plane starts moving forward with steady acceleration and heads down the grass runway. A tail of rocket combustion spews out some 200 feet in length.

At about 600 feet down the runway, but nowhere near take-off speed, the Komet jumps up into the air 30 feet up but then descends quickly slamming into the ground. It appears that Spate has hit a dip in the runway before reaching take-off speed. With the rocket increasing its thrust, the Komet continues moving on the runway and finally starts to lift off the ground. Spate must be a little shook up at this point, but he seems to have the plane placed into a low climb now. The undercarriage wheels' release allowing the plane to take on a more streamlined profile. The wheels go bouncing down past the runway while a kubelwagen drives out to chase the set down.

The rocket engines increase in thrust and a robust climb begins. Spate is heading up at 45 degrees and in a matter of three minutes he should reach the stratosphere. As the Komet screams upward and further away from sight, all I can see is an ever-expanding column of billowing smoke that points toward the heaven. It as if the Komet is being boomed up into space by a large and mushrooming column.

I look over at the other flight officers and they are waving their caps and cheering Spate on. They know that soon they will be next to ride this screamer of a craft and they can't wait.

About twenty minutes later we see his Komet gliding toward the runway and with Spate having been a champion Rhön glider this should be a piece of cake for him. The extending skids are out from the fuselage and he run the Komet along the grass strip for a good 400 feet. Time for me to pull my notepad out and start observing what needs to be improved on the craft.

★★★

"Armand, please come in." waves Lieutenant Spate. "Glad you got to see some take-offs of the Komet today."

"It was very impressive how that little bird can handle so much thrust and speed."

"Oh, yes. It is quite an amazing flying machine. The minute you sit in the cockpit, it demands to be flown. Not only under its rocket propulsion but also as a swift glider. Nothing like what we had at Wasserkuppe though. Do you know that Heini Ditmar hit Mach one with the Komet last year? We can't tell anyone because we don't want our enemies to find out. But this bird can fly super-fast and not break into any vibrations."

"So, I take it Lieutenant that the rest of your flight was stupendous?"

"Very much so. Once the rocket's thrust cut out, rather abruptly I might add, I was in a wonderful state of gliding. The flight characteristics were excellent. I took some fast dives and swung back up without losing much altitude. Lippisch can really design a fast glider. And I will acknowledge your production engineers at Messerschmitt for helping this become a reality. But we must now talk about improvements to the plane."

"Sure, Lieutenant, let's run through the checklist of items needing improvement. We received your memo last month and we have been making progress on many items."

Spate raises his eyebrow and says, "Oh, really? Now, the airframe model flies very well and I understand you fellows are already working on a variant that will have a larger fuselage, so more fuel can be stored. Good to hear. The items needing work though, are more on the operating side. I will run through the list and see how far you have come." Spate then reads through a list of items uninterrupted,

"The landing skids need a suspension and release system. The current landing skid of wood should be made of steel. The tail skid should be replaced with a steerable tail wheel. The wood wings need strengthening at their attachment to the fuselage. Tactical speed brakes are needed to adjust the glide path. That or we need to develop a drag chute for landings. The 30mm cannons need alignment testing. The current Plexiglas canopy needs side viewing bubbles and better clarity overall. Antennae near the engine get corroded from the hydrogen peroxide so they need to get relocated. Let's see is there anything else?", asks Spate to himself. "Oh yes, some wise ass in Berlin insisted that the jettisonable undercarriage be equipped with wheel brakes. Can you believe the Air Ministries' meddling? That they have all these people assigned to review one little element of a plane and then they each set up a requirement."

"Oh, we are totally frustrated with the Ministry's Technical Office, Lieutenant Spate. But your list is pretty long. That is a lot for us to work on in say three months' time."

"And you see, Armand, that is the point. We have been demanding action on these items for six months now and no one from Messerschmitt has responded to us or shown us any progress to date. I have a fighter unit to assemble and I need planes that will take off and land with reliability. Not to mention, be able to fire weapons straight and with confidence."

"I understand your situation, Lieutenant but to our defense, we have been working away on some of these issues and we are making progress on them." I know as I say this, I may be making our company look worse. But Spate has a point, maybe we are side shunting his plane for other priorities. But this is not what I have been told by superintendent Coulis. I had no idea the list of issues was so long. Even I have not been updated with all these issues needing improvement. Conceding his point, I finally say,

"On the other hand, I do see your point. These are critical items needed for full deployment and I honestly can't say that I was aware of them until now. It almost seems as if someone has been holding back on getting this information to us engineers."

"Exactly, that's what I think. I know that you've been working with the Lippisch's Department 'L' team for three years now, but can you honestly tell me if the directors of Messerschmitt have placed this craft on a priority list. Or more likely a 'de-prioritized' list."

"Lieutenant Spate, when I arrive back to Augsburg, I will speak with the superintendent about the allocation of our resources to properly address the Komet's development."

"These are the most encouraging words I have heard to date. I sense your sincerity and I much prefer hearing this than some bullshit about 'yes, we will get to your plane in no time' and 'oh sure, we will assign the proper number of engineers to the problem.' Because if it isn't happening, I need to know now. I am a combat officer and I will be going into battle with these planes hopefully in the next year and for my men's sake, I will do everything I can to pull together a combat-worthy fighter unit. Understood Herr Kindermann?"

Spate's military decorum with me is understood. This is not the way civilian engineers communicate usually but I get the gist of his message and the urgency of the matter. Rising from the table, I then extend my hand to Spate.

"Lieutenant, I want to see this Komet take to the air in great numbers and as the production engineering manager I will do what I can to make that happen."

Spate rises and gives me a strong handshake, "Your efforts for our fighting cause will be deeply appreciated. Herr Kindermann, the pleasure has been mine. Time for me to address my incoming recruits and orient them on flying the Komet to be. Oh, and Kindermann, next time you come to the airfield, we should take some time to enjoy a stash of wine booty that we have locked up in a nearby hotel. It's wonderfully decadent wine and I am sure you will enjoy a bottle or two."

"I like that offer Lieutenant Spate very much. Perhaps that will provide me the extra motivation to get your list addressed in three months."

"I thought it would Kindermann. Whatever I need to do get my job done, you see."

With that I exit the Leipheim Airfield barracks and start working my way back to Augsburg.

★★★

"Professor Messerschmitt, may I have some of your time to go over my field investigations of the 163 Komet from last week?"

I catch the Professor as he is walking between meetings on the drafting floor. I seem to have broken his concentration, but he looks up, thinks about my question and then says, "Alright Armand. How about right now? Let's pull into this open meeting room over here."

I follow Messerschmitt into the conference room, close the door behind me and sit down across from him.

"Professor, as you had asked I have been conducting operational investigations into the field improvements needed for the 163 and I wanted to give a few key summary points."

Messerschmitt looks a little agitated and says, "Alright, Armand. Let me hear it. I have five minutes I can spare on this topic."

"Ok, I met with Test Unit Commander, Lieutenant Spate," I start off, "And I also observed many flights of the Komet. The pilots were all in agreement about one thing; this craft can fly fast, and the flight controls are superbly connected."

"Yes, I've gathered that Lippisch designed a slippery and responsive airframe. I am glad that all his time calculating and musing over this delta wing approach is paying off. Ok, continue." Messerschmitt clasps his hands in front of himself.

"The testing unit though has a long list of items that need to be improved or changed so the Komet can become a fully-functional fighter interceptor. Here is a list of the items on this paper." I place a memo in front of Messerschmitt and he looks it over with a bit of a scowl. "Professor, I personally looked over the plane after flight tests and I concur with Spate's summary of items needing improvement. If we don't get to them in time, he will have forty pilots all trained up but with no planes to take them into combat."

"Yes, we all know that Test Unit 16 is to be transitioned into a fighter unit by the beginning of 1944. But they must wait for their improvements."

"But, sir, I understood from company directives that we were supposed to be diligently working away on finalizing the Komet. For us to implement these enhancements will take months of work. As such, I confirmed with Lieutenant Spate that we would do our utmost to meet these timelines."

"Armand, look. This is not how things are working out. There is a war going on and the whole aviation industry is short of materials, short of technicians and short of transport services."

"Sir, just two months ago, we told the Air Ministry and the Test Unit that we would have the planes to them by September. With what you're saying, we are going to let this deadline slide. If that is so, then I need to appropriate my staff accordingly."

"There are forces far above you that are re-prioritizing our planes' efforts. Unfortunately, we internally at Messerschmitt have placed the 163 as a low priority plane. And that's the way it is. Understood?" says Messerschmitt as he places both his palms flat on the table.

"Professor, I just made a gentleman's commitment to that unit commander and now I must lie to him about our efforts on it."

"Unfortunately, yes, that is what you must do. I am sorry. Besides, it's Lippisch's design and he receives all the royalties for the 163. And now that he is gone, out of Messerschmitt AG, I'd rather put my effort into planes that are under my license."

Feeling a bit indignant that I have found myself caught in this battle of resources, politics and royalties, I let my resentment show through,

"Professor, if I could argue that we should do differently, let me do so now."

"Alright, go ahead," says Messerschmitt leaning back into his chair as if he will give me just one moment to make my case, his fingers forming a tent.

"Look, I had very little to do with the development of this plane. I took over production engineering at your request back in 1939. And while Lippisch is gone now, I do find merit in the technology of this plane. It performs its job superbly and being rocket-propelled not even a jet could catch it. If the English came up with a jet tomorrow, we could throw this rocket plane at them the very next day and we would keep the balance of power in our favor. I know we have the 262 jet too but the turbines are not fully developed for combat demands. Here we have a tested rocket engine with advanced delta airframe that is swifter than any jet. My God, it already has surpassed Mach One."

"Enough, Armand." say Messerschmitt while raising hand up. He sits up and I see the veins on his forehead start to come through. With sparse punctuality, Messerschmitt says, "Given our limited resources, some of the plane projects must take a backseat, regardless of what we told the Air Ministry. These are decisions that are being made at the director level and you are to follow through.

Taking a breath of air and leaning back into his chair, he continues, "I probably should've informed you earlier, but we don't want too many people knowing our real capabilities and our internal priorities. It's a corporate decision of what is best for the company."

My shoulders drop and I sink into my chair feeling deflated in that my challenge to the company has just been slapped right back at me. I have worked so hard on both projects and to see them off into the air. And especially with the Komet team, I did everything to make them feel like they were part of the Messerschmitt team. But the director level support is not fully behind the Komet. Or is it because Lippisch receives royalties for every Komet delivered into combat use and Messerschmitt would receive none? I dare not broach him on that financial matter. Messerschmitt continues,

"I foresee that it's only going to get worse. With the Allied bombing campaign ripping up our rail lines and fuel depots, I don't know how we are going to get enough manufacturing material in place to produce all the planes that we are already committed to. When I look at the production schedules the Ministry demands of us, I just think about where are we going to get all the labor and supplies to make these planes?

"Ok, Professor. I appreciate your dose of reality on our production situation. But don't you see the value of the rocket plane for Germany's defense?"

"Quite frankly, I think both the rocket plane and the jet are too far out there to immediately help us with this war. They are wonderful pieces of technology but with the Allies looming for an attack on Europe, we must choose planes with more immediate results. In fact, I am thinking we should just try strapping on a jet turbine to the Bf 109 airframe. We have all the jigs and assembly lines in place for it. We would just need to change the wing mounts."

"Professor, are you saying you think the rocket and jet planes are not going to help win the war?"

"Yes, I am sorry to say that. I know you have put your heart and soul into these planes and we will keep developing them. But for the sake of dividing up what resources Germany has left, we must make expedient choices on what planes should be allocated resources. And while I love the technology of the rocket and the jet, I am concluding that they are too late for this war."

I can't believe it. The father of the first fighter jet is about to disown his own offspring, or at least let them go to pasture for now. Is it because Lusser and Voigt really masterminded the Me 262 and Lippisch spawned the Me 163? And perhaps because the Bf 109 was the last plane that Messerschmitt fully conceived of on his own? But this can't be, he has fought with all his spirit and time for all these planes. Maybe the Professor has become a realist and understands the stark supply position that German is in. Now difficult priorities must be made, and the rocket and jet may not make it.

NOVEMBER 1943

Messerschmitt's personal secretary hails me down as I am heading toward the commissary.

"Herr Kindermann. Please wait a minute. I have something to hand to you personally from the Professor." Heaves the busty lady as she quickly approaches me.

I halt in my tracks. "Yes, Frau, how can I help you or the Professor?"

As she gathers her breath, she hands me an envelope of personal stationery and then says, "The Professor and the Baroness are hosting a dinner party for RLM and Party officials, so they can lobby support for obtaining the government contract for the Me 262. Herren Messerschmitt and Gerhard Coulis have asked for the senior members of the jet team to be present for a personal showing of the plane's design drawings. The Professor has asked for four of you from the team to attend, and he wrote your name down on the list. And of course, your wife can attend the dinner party as well."

"Thank you, Frau, I am delighted to be invited. This is such a surprise to me. I have never been to their estate. Vanessa, my wife, will be so delighted. Thank you so much, Frau."

Thinking over my prior conversation with Messerschmitt, I ask, "So, the Board is continuing to push for development and contracting of the 262 jet?"

"It looks that way. Plus, there are Luftwaffe supporters of this jet, General Galland being on the key ones. He and some other pilots have send in glowing letters of support for the jet and the tide is turning in our favor."

★★★

That night I rush home on my bike back to our flat on Stretten Strasse and break in with my arms wide open and exclaim at the top of my lungs,

"Honey, we are in! We have been invited to the Professor and the Baroness' estate for next Saturday. Get your finest clothes lined up."

"Darling, you are so excited. Oh, love, please settle down, the kids will think something is wrong." Turning to our children, she then says, "Come along Emil and Angelika, it is time for your beds. Into your rooms." Vanessa grabs the children from the kitchen and pushes them along into their bedroom and shuts their door.

"Wrong?" I say. "My god, things could only be so right, Vanessa. Do you know what this means? For the Professor to invite me to his exclusive estate for the sake of his schmoozing military and Party elite. Imagine who we will see there, Göring, Milch, General Galland and perhaps that Munitions Minister, the up and coming Albert Speer. And imagine being in such luxury and God knows what they will serve for food."

"Ok, dear, settle down. It's just a dinner," soothes Vanessa. "I am sure you will be given plenty of business to do there so it's not as if you are there to be sold to. You are the ones doing the selling, and you must be on your sales' toes all evening, no slip-ups."

Coming down from my excited pitch I concur, slightly,

"I know hon, but for once just let me dream this one out. I've been with the company now for nine years and only recently has upper management been taking my ideas seriously enough to put me in charge of critical tasks. This jet will be the next great thing to both the military and civilian world. And it will be our team working on it. Now we just have to persuade the RLM and Luftwaffe that they should invest in our jet over the Arado one and then we will be all set. My, we could even regain dominance of the skies if we can get this Swallow out there in full force."

★★★

I pull out my airbrush machine and start going to town on the illustrations. My design team and I start assembling plans, sections, renderings and cutaways, some in perspective as well as simulated action scenes of the jet already taking on Allied bombers. It is my intent for these drawings and illustration to technically and emotionally persuade the audience with a compelling argument that the Me 262 is the future of the Luftwaffe and to our defending our homeland from the bombing campaign.

On the Saturday before the dinner, the four of us and our wives are picked up by a limousine at the plant and taken to the Baroness' estate. Having been at the plant earlier, we made last minute assemblies of our drawings and ran through our presentations. Following an introduction by the Professor, we will have twenty minutes to make our point.

As we approach the driveway, we see that there is already a long, line of chauffeured cars leading up to a grand staircase flowing down from an entrance portico.

The main house is an Italian Renaissance villa complete with colonnades, pergolas and extensive molding framing the windows. As we enter, we are shown to a drawing room and told to wait for the Professor.

Our team disassembles the drawings and easels, and we put them in order of presenting. After a few minutes, the door opens, and Messerschmitt enters in wearing a dark suit, a cigarette cocked in his mouth and a large broad smile. "Gentleman, good you are here and welcome to my humble abode." His expression turns a little more business-like as he transitions from the hot lights of entertaining the high-level guests outside. "Now, Voldemar, did you remember to bring a summary sheet on the key flight characteristics of the jet? And Gerhard, what about the latest information on the power plants being provided by Junkers? Remember not to knock the BMW turbines, even though we would like to, but they have too much political clout with this group. Wolfgang, do you have your key points on the armaments, landing gear, radio controls and fuel systems? And finally, Armand, it is essential for you to stress how simple it will be to produce this machine and mount the turbines. Especially since you spent so much time on how we could section up the plane and assemble it in a wheat field if we had to."

Norman Emilio Barrientos

We each take our turn in responding affirmatively to him and point to our drawing boards where our core points will be made.

"Ok then, after you hear me toast the Führer, the Party, and the war effort, that will be your cue to come out. At that point they should all be three champagne glasses into the evening. They will not have lost their rational abilities, but they will be softened up enough to accept our arguments. Following your presentations, I welcome you to join in for drinks, fraternize with the mid-level or whoever approaches and keep a positive outlook on our jet's capabilities. If someone approaches and asks you if the turbines are too unstable or that the wings will likely vibrate at such high speeds, tell them we have been testing prototypes at the largest and most technically advanced wind tunnel in all of Germany. And I know that I have some of the smartest aviation designers in Germany assembled right here, including you fellows from the Munich Technical University."

Messerschmitt swings back outside and shortly afterwards, we hear our cue of toasts and salutes. Walking out into the entry foyer I see wood-paneled walls bathed in soft lights from candelabras, wall sconces and torches. The marble flooring glistens as highlights bounce off the black and white checkered pattern. Dominating the end of the foyer is a large red Party flag unfurled from the stair landing. There are waiters rushing by us with their eyes and chins pointed straight ahead carrying silver plates of sumptuous hors d'oeuvres; pate, cheeses, sliced hams, truffles, deviled eggs and smoked fish. The plates are placed in front of small groups of four to five people dressed in evening wear. They are many military staffers from the Luftwaffe, along with men from the RLM, the Technical Bureau, Luft Hansa, the Armament Ministry, and both local and national Party officials. And in following with the military personnel, there are SS guards posted at the entry of each room, their shiny black steel helmets glistening with military might.

In one corner is a rotund man holding court with at least six men around him. It is Göring, our *dicke* head (fat head) and oh does he look just like what everyone says about him now. Large, avaricious and pig-like in his behavior but a royal pig at that, greedily gobbling up the hors-d'oeuvres as he is with the attention he commands. He is larger than I recall seeing in photos, almost appearing elephantine in his lower half. He is wearing purple felt boots, with gold embroidery and a cumbersome number of medals giving the impression that he just walked off the Nutcracker dance stage.

There are many finely dressed ladies here too; I assume the wives of the gentlemen although upon closer inspection some of these women seem much younger than their companions, and they seem a bit compliant as well. Eagerly affirming their man's statements by grabbing his arm with unnecessary firmness and flashing quick, toothy smiles. Perhaps too, do I notice a bit of too much make-up on some of these women?

But all these thoughts are changed as I see the Professor and the Baroness in the center of the large salon. This was probably the dance hall in days of old and intended to impress a Baron's guests. Only having seen Lily Strohmeyer dressed for plant business, tonight she radiates beauty, class, dignity and most of all, complete adoration for her Willy. This much is evident as she stands by him always not as a bauble but as his equal in this business. I can see her dive into conversation with the top officials and then break into a charming smile. Occasionally I hear affected French, *"enchante"* and then see a uniformed man bowing his head while taking the hand of the Baroness in both reverence and acknowledgment of her class.

The Baroness wears an evening dress of black with an outer layer of lace hiding the inner layer of silk dressing. The dress is gathered up high at the waist with pleats splashing down to just below her knees. Above, her sleeves gather at the shoulders and on top she dons a lacy hair bonnet to gracefully finish off her hairstyle.

The four of us design team members gather around our easels. As the lead designer, Voldemar Voigt, starts off discussing the design of the airframe. Wolfgang Degel then addresses the design of the cockpit, pilot controls, weaponry and communications systems. It is my turn and I come up to the center of the easels and face the audience,

"The design of the Me 262 is a radical departure from any other plane in the lexicon of German aviation. Not only are we employing jet turbines, but we have developed a profile of a plane that has a low drag coefficient, swept wings for faster speeds, a flat underbelly to control airlift and a wing assembly that is strong yet light in weight.

"As the lead production engineer, I have put every effort into making this plane one that is easy to assemble not only in the factory but also in the open field. We envision that our jet will be produced in various locations, each have varying degrees of assembly facilities. To that end, my design team has produced extensive amounts of drawings so that any one of our factories can readily assemble the jigs and start cutting metal for a finished jet. We have also segmented the fuselage body into five parts, such that each of the five parts can be assembled separately and then brought together at one final assembly plant. Labor-wise, the jet can be assembled by semi-skilled workers working on an assembly line where each of them installs only one distinct component.

"Mechanically, we have structured the wings to hold the jet turbines in place with only four large bolts. This will allow for changing out of the turbines in a matter of thirty minutes and right in a field. With one large spar supporting the main wing structure, we have been able to devise a framing structure that can support all the weaponry and control systems along with the retractable landing gear. And the wings are designed so that they can be assembled in one plant and then shipped to another where their final attachment will take place.

"In summary, *meinen Herren und Damen*, this advanced jet not only incorporates the latest in power plant technology, an aerodynamic profile that can reach speeds over 560 miles per hour, and cannons that will shred a Liberator in three seconds, we have also designed a jet that can be readily produced by many factories dispersed throughout Germany. A formidable fighter jet that is easily mass-produced to meet our war demands. This is the jet of Germany's future."

I take a slight bow and I hear a ripple of applause coming from the audience.

Messerschmitt approaches me with a broad smile on his face, shakes my hand and then says loud enough for everyone to hear, "Thank you, Herr Kindermann. That was an excellent summary of both the design and production features of the Swallow. I would now like the General of the Fighters, Adolf Galland, to come forward to speak about his experience in flying the Swallow."

With an assured step, his chin up and of course, his cigar wagging from his mouth, General Galland, now age thirty-one, approaches our drawings and easels. He positions himself in the center of the hall and starts off sharply,

"I flew the Bf 109 Emil in the Spanish Civil and I owe many of my ninety-four kills to their responsiveness to my critiques. I told them what was needed to improve the plane, and they listened keenly. Now I have flown the Bf 109 Gustav and not only did the Messerschmitt team understand our needs, but they also the led the design process far beyond our expectations. We now have the most exceptional, agile, flying workhorse in the whole European Theater and it has empowered us to dominate the skies. All of this is due to the exemplary Bf 109 plane design engineered by these gentlemen.

"Now, in May this year, I took the Me 262 out for seven test trials and here is what I conclude. As a seasoned Ace and the General of the Fighters, I am positive that the Me 262 opens new tactical advantages for Germany over the Allied forces. Being in this jet accelerating up to high speeds is like having an angel push you along. It is a pure delight to fly."

Galland pulls in a drag of his cigar and exhales out with a smile on his face as if he is enjoying a fine cognac.

"It gathers speed so strongly creating a rate of climb far faster than any other plane I have flown, and it sustains this power at high altitudes. The control stick and the ailerons are so smoothly connected that you feel you are one with the plane. The armament of four cannons and two machine guns is amazingly large enough to blast a bomber out of the air in three short seconds.

"This jet provides pilots with a whole new array of tactics that will turn the tables against the Allies. It is not only 120 miles an hour faster than a Spitfire, but it can climb up to a higher altitude, allowing it to drop down on them like a falcon catching its prey in mid-flight. I find that its short wings enable it to achieve high speeds, take tight turns and allow our pilots to come around on the enemy and end up on their tail. This powerful tactic of turning so tightly on your pursuer that you end up on their tail is one I have used successfully with the Bf 109. I am confident that in dogfights the Me 262 will provide us the same tactical advantage."

"Now I am not a consultant to Messerschmitt, and I have no financial gains from endorsing this plane. I am only here as the General of Fighters and I want Germany to pick the best fighter so we can defend our skies and dominate the European air war. I urge my fellow officers and ministry friends to recommend this jet as our plane of choice and move into full production. And not only as the aircraft of choice but specifically as a fighter plane that will intercept other fighters and bombers over our skies."

I see Göring's face go from a happy, rolly face to a lumpy, quizzical face with his dangling jowls adding a downward tug for more effect. There was something he didn't agree with Galland on that last sentence, and I believe it was that the jet should be a fighter plane. I can see it now, they all seem to like the jet but tactically, what kind of plane should it be? A bomber, an interceptor, a night fighter, a reconnaissance plane or a bit of all?

Messerschmitt comes to the center again and addresses the guests with a big smile and warm tone,

"Thanks, General Galland for your unequaled endorsement. And no, I did not promise the General any caviar from our estate, but I did promise him a ride in our next top-secret jet."

Chuckles ripple through the audience as the waiters walk out with another round of green champagne bottles.

Standing in the middle of the parquet wood flooring, Messerschmitt says, "My esteemed friends from the Air Ministry, the

Party and the Luftwaffe, we sincerely appreciate your attendance at our estate to hear this summary of the Me 262. I would now like to conclude our technical presentation by saying that all lead members of our design team are personally committed to developing for Germany the most advanced military plane that Europe has ever seen. One that will match our own Teutonic race's natural superiority in technology, industry and military prowess. As we have done since 1939, we will continue dominating the skies of not only Europe but also those of the Atlantic Ocean, the North Sea, Russia, the Middle East and Africa. Is it not Germany's place is to rule Europe? Warplanes are critical to this dominance and our company, Messerschmitt AG, is completely committed, heart and soul, to achieving this mission."

I see the Luftwaffe and Party officials bolster and heave up their chests in unison as if getting ready for the national anthem.

"Is it not also Germany's place to lead the world in technical advances, in designing the fastest and swiftest plane, to lead the world in setting bold new visions for what can become of aircraft? We have it right here in the palm of our hands with the design of the Swallow. This is our future, painted out for us in these outstanding blueprints and illustrations. For these embody science of the highest degree, one that only German scientists could have reached and we at Messerschmitt have developed it first. Aeronautical engineering is a new field, and we have the shown the ability to dominate aircraft in much the same way that we are dominating Europe."

There is another round of applause and Messerschmitt realizes he has started to work the crowd with his magic. He becomes bolder with each audience affirmation and my only fear now that he doesn't oversell what our design team can do.

But Göring interrupts Messerschmitt with a low, bass grunt. Sounding like something of a bullfrog in a swamp at night, Göring bellows out, "It is true that our race can excel in all things technical Herr Messerschmitt. But tell me why the focus on being an interceptor jet? You know the Führer has requested offensive planes that can go on the attack. We are not to just defend our homeland but also attack. At no time has the Führer given us orders to retreat and defend Germany, at least not while we also continue our plans of aggression. Can your Me 262 also carry out bombing missions? Because, this is what we strategically want to do? We want to bring the war to England, Russia, even America. Can this jet also act as a fighter-bomber?"

With these words, our whole design team tenses up because we know the Swallow's swiftness is most useful as an interceptor fighter. But we see in Messerschmitt a desire to close the transaction so he may say whatever the Luftwaffe wants, and seal the deal. This is what this whole evening is about, right?

The Professor maintains his confidence and a broad smile appears along with a forced, upbeat affirmative tone, "Certainly Air Marshall. This plane can hold up to 2,000 pounds of bombs, and it can carry them out to any target within 250 miles."

With that, our design team drops our shoulders instinctively as we realize Messerschmitt has just undersold the jet. It's not intended to be a bomber, it wants to soar through the air like a hawk and swoop down on its prey. But we realize that the only way for us to finalize the contract with the RLM will be to also provide a bomber version of the jet. And with that comment the Professor has cast our design direction into a big loop away from our primary goal of a fighter plane.

"Very well, Herr Messerschmitt. I like the sound of that." Emphasizes Göring looking pleased with himself as he looks around to his retinue for confirmation of his comments, of which they do so.

"Well enough," says Messerschmitt. "Then a toast to our first jet, the Swallow." The audience throngs in a hearty, reverberating 'Prost' as they all lift their champagne flutes and then bottom them down. Time for our design team to break ranks and mingle with the crowd. The guests also disassemble and form smaller circles within the main salon.

I see Vanessa looking at me from across the hall beaming a smile of congratulations. Walking over to her, I take her by the arm and lead her over toward the dining hall where we are greeted by Baroness Lily Strohmeyer-Raulino. I take the Baroness' hand and bow to her, "Baroness, Armand and Vanessa Kindermann. My greatest pleasure to be your guest here at this distinctive affair. My wife, Vanessa and I are honored that Herr Messerschmitt invited us to your evening soiree."

The Baroness is very much at ease, and her pleasure at Willy's performance is evident. "It is our family's pleasure equally. Kindermann? Yes, I do believe I have heard Willy mention your name from time to time. He is very delighted to have you has as his employee and as one of the key production designers. Willy has such a soft spot for men who stick by him through thick and thin. And you are one of the outstanding men he so values."

"I am happy to serve the company and help meet its goals. I have been with the company ten years now, and I will gladly stay for at least another ten years my Baroness. May I introduce my wife, Vanessa."

Vanessa takes Lily's hand and bows.

"You are a lovely couple, and I am always happy to meet the design staff's spouses. Such sacrifices all of you must make while we demand so much of your men's time. I am so glad you can enjoy this bit of recognition and involvement in tonight's important effort. Armand, I thought you and the rest of your team's presentation was very thoughtful and convincing. In fact, I think the rest of Board needs to hear this same presentation about the Swallow. My dear Willy has so many management items to attend to that he must rely heavily on the design team's smarts to pull together all these planes."

"I feel that over the last ten years the Professor has entrusted a lot to me. I feel the burden of this responsibility every morning I start work, your Baroness."

"We on the board realize this, and we know my dear Willy has so much going on so I am happy to hear this affirmation. By the way Armand and Vanessa, do enjoy a good wine? Willy and I maintain a cellar stocked with wines from all over Europe. You might've known that Willy's father was a wine merchant. Here, come follow me down this corridor and I would love for you to pick out a bottle. We will then have it ready for you in your car when you leave."

As the Baroness walks down the corridor of marble flooring, Vanessa and I cast surprised and happy glances at each other expressing our excitement to be among such wealthy settings. At the end of the corridor we see Messerschmitt engaged in a conversation with some Luftwaffe staff members. As we approach, he breaks away from them and comes over to the three of us.

"Dear Willy," the Baroness explains, "I just had the pleasure of finally meeting Armand Kindermann and his lovely wife Vanessa. I am taking them down to our wine cellar so they can select two of our aged wines."

Messerschmitt seems pleased by this. "Wonderful my dear Lilly, thank you for attending to Armand and his wife. If it weren't for having an older brother to take over my father wine store, I would be a wine merchant instead. I was only a teenager when my father passed away and my older brother to took over the business, so I could go back to meddling with glider models." Vanessa and I chuckle. "Good thing or this whole aircraft company and all our designs would've never happened. Funny how I dodged the bullet on that one.

Never having seen the Professor in such a chatty mood, I relish the situation and wait pleasantly for what he may say next. Messerschmitt continues,

"Actually, I didn't dodge the bullet on being drafted into the Army for the Great War. I was only seventeen when they got me, and they placed me in some artillery unit. Can you believe that? With all my plane skills developed to that point they ignored the young man in front of them and cast me away to some no-name unit. But luckily, I got word out that I was very adept at glider planes. So, finally I was transferred to an airplane unit where I handled field communications. Which back in those days meant waving around big flags on an airstrip."

Vanessa and I look at each other and we both seem delighted to be hearing this youthful story from the company icon. Messerschmitt suddenly changes gear with his tone of voice. "Ladies, do you mind if I have a few minutes with Armand?" Putting his arm around my shoulder, Messerschmitt then walks me down toward a drawing room and in a confidential tone says, "Armand, the presentation was excellent. Your delivery was just what the RLM and Luftwaffe needed to hear. You nailed it on the head. Thank you so much."

"I felt well prepared for the presentation and must acknowledge many of my own staff for pulling together all these drawings."

"Oh no, Armand. I know that you were the key man in defining the presentation and delivering it. Now, I just spoke with Erhard Milch and for the first time I sense that he is in full support of producing the Me 262 at a mass production level."

"That's great to hear, Professor. I know he has been one of our main detractors, so this is key."

"Yes, it is. But beyond that though, I can see that I will need you for other critical upcoming meetings."

"As in presentations at our Augsburg plant?"

"Yes, but even more importantly, meetings in Berlin with the top RLM command. I have a meeting next week coming up and I'd like you to join along."

"Yes, Professor. I am starting to get a hang for this public speaking role." With that Messerschmitt pats my back, nods his head and then walks off to greet another Ministry official. I turn around to see Vanessa chatting away with the Baroness, both smiling, and I think to myself, "my wife is beautiful."

DECEMBER 1943

As we break from our Monday morning production meeting, Professor Messerschmitt walks up to me and in a hurried tone says, "Armand, I am worried that your design for the fuel tanks is not going to provide the jet with enough flight time. Fifty minutes of flight time is barely enough to make two passes at a bomber fleet. And don't you think it will be unsafe to crowd the pilot with fuel tanks on the aft and under seat areas."

"Professor, we've explored other locations, but the wing assembly is already jammed tight with control equipment."

"What if we put it in the tail section?" asks the Professor. "You see I've come up with a sketch on how we could fit another set of fuel tanks in the tail section and in the wings too."

"Have you shown this to Voldemar Voigt?"

"No, he doesn't seem open to my ideas on it but I think this will do the trick in extending our airtime."

The Professor pulls into my office and we look over a cross-section view of the latest Swallow variant, the Stormbird bomber. "Professor, Voigt has instructed me to submit any design concepts through him. I just can't take ideas not generated by him and have him review my production designs as an afterthought."

The Professor looks a little desperate. "Look, Voldemar thinks this jet is his. Granted, he did concept the airframe back in '39 but it's my company name on the Me 262 and I still have good ideas to contribute to the team."

Not wanting to get in the middle of Messerschmitt's changing role in the company, I offer, "Yes, but ever since the Directors have reassigned you to your technical role, Voldemar has become more independent in his design leadership."

"I know what you are referring to, Armand. With the Board having demoted me from President to Technical Director, I've lost some respect with the design staff."

Messerschmitt alludes to the fateful decision by our Board of Directors to punish Messerschmitt for his poor handling of the next generation Bf 109 propeller fighter planes. To save face with the RLM they had the Professor fall on his sword and demote himself down in the executive ranks. But still, Messerschmitt's fire for design and his sense of ownership over all the planes remains unabated. For me as a production manager, it can be confusing to have him jump all over our methods when organizationally this is not his role anymore.

Knowing the Professor can't let go of his 'babies' I get back to our discussion, "Alright so you think we can fit a fuel tank in the wing root and tail assemblies?"

"Yes, look here at these sketches. I am actually thinking there would be two wing tanks, one on each side of the spar and around the landing wheels."

"Ok, but where would I move all the hydraulic controls to? We would then need two more sets of fuel pumps and more controls for the pilot's console."

Messerschmitt considers my comments and looks over a wing assembly plan. "Well, if we could slide the landing gear in closer to the fuselage, then we could move the control lines over to the trailing edge of the wing." Messerschmitt pulls up straight, grabs his concept sketch. "Alright, Armand. I'll back off this proposal. I just can't seem to get a good design idea into this one. It's like Voldemar has locked it up and I feel a bit irrelevant design-wise to the jet."

"Professor, I've been working with you for ten years now and you have come up with many exceptional designs. This jet is a different animal though."

"It is. I just don't know how I was there when we conceived it in '39 but now four years later, I have lost touch with its detailed design. Instead, I am left with dealing with RLM politics, winning contracts, making sure we have enough cash and keeping our labor supply at high levels."

"At my position in the company, sir, I most appreciate what you are doing for all us. I am sure I would not want to take all that on myself.

It's sometimes easier to keep your nose to the grindstone and let others deal with the big strategic issues."

"Thanks, Armand. I appreciate your understanding. Let's keep this conversation confidential and I will keep on being Technical Director for all of our planes."

The Professor leaves and as he does, I realize that his physical features reflect a man who is racing against the clock. He looks more haggard, forlorn and hunched over now. He is a man who cannot escape the huge commitments his company has made to help Germany win this war.

January 1944

I am in my design office looking over drawings for the Me 262 two-seater variant. The cockpit is longer than the previous version and this will allow it to hold either a training pilot or a radar operator. As I page through the drawings, I hear a knock on my door and I see an executive assistant standing before me,

"Herr Kindermann, you are requested to come up to the executive offices immediately."

I put down my pencil and follow her up the stairs. As I enter the executive conference room there are three other production managers present. Then Baroness Lily Strohmeyer enters the room looking somber as she takes the head chair. After looking at one of us silently and with some hesitation she says,

"We've called up the production engineering managers from the Me 262, Me 163, the Gigant Glider, and the Amerika Bomber to ask for your participation on a sensitive matter. You see, and this is highly confidential, my Willy has collapsed from exhaustion." As Lilly Strohmeyer says this she puts her clenched hand up to her mouth as if to stifle a cry. She then looks up with determination and gathers her composure, "After years of working fourteen-hour days my poor Willy's health had enough and needs a break. It's not that he wanted to take a break, his body demanded it."

Strohmeyer looks up as if appealing us to understand the situation. "The doctors at the sanitarium have ordered two weeks' rest at the Rennerhaus Lodge. To assure a solid recovery no one is to contact him and he is not to attend any meetings onsite or offsite. Nonetheless, we are to carry on with our duties and schedules as planned without any hesitation or delay.

I am not too shocked to hear this news. The Professor has looked exhausted and worried sick for the last six months. Although the fire in his eyes and the passion in his voice has always been at full pitch. Lilly continues,

"Now, the company is under demanding production schedules along with testing and prototype development timelines. And for every project, the schedules are compressed, if not hectic in pace. While my Willy is out I will be looking to you to keep the development of the advanced planes at full pace."

Seeing that the Baroness needs assurance that development will continue on schedule, I interject,

"Your Baroness, you have our total support to meet the commitments of the company. We understand the urgency of the war and we are familiar with the terms of production we are under with the Air Ministry."

Lily seems pleased with this. "Herr Kindermann, thank you for that note of encouragement and reinforcement of your commitment. I do have one other task for all of you to handle though. You see, Field Marshall Göring indicated to Willy that he would drop by unannounced someday next week to confirm our development and production timelines. Based on what we agreed to last year on many of our planes, we are to have full production drawings ready by the end of this month. Plus, all fabrication and assembly plans are to be laid out and detailed output schedules committed to. Göring, though, has been carefully watching our company's progress and if we don't convince him as to our progress, he could pull the plug on any one of the planes."

The thought of that possibility reverberates inside me harshly like a broken bell. Wolfgang Degel then interjects,

"Your Baroness, we are all working at full capacity and with due diligence, but to be frank, we are behind in many areas. I am not sure how much the Professor informed you, but both the Swallow and the Komet have much untested technology and we have much more development and prototyping to do. I am not sure how we can hide that fact from Göring."

Lily stiffens, "Messerschmitt AG is relying heavily on the initial payments for the jet and the rocket plane. They are critical to our cash flow to cover other projects that have overrun their own budgets. Sorry to put this on you gentlemen but that is the truth of the matter."

Degel, sits back a bit into his chair. "I see. Well, we will continue to progress in all haste, but we will need to come up with glowing reports for Göring. Hopefully he doesn't see through them though."

Lilly responds with a strong business overtone, "We shall skew the production reports to match our committed schedules. Understood? On top of that, Göring doesn't take conclusions from top management alone. He will surely pull aside anyone of you individually and ask you to be frank and tell him how it really is. It's one of his management ploys."

As an engineer and designer, I am not used to this task of skewing my status to meet some fantasy commitment. It does seem that Messerschmitt has oversold the company to the RLM as a wunderkind operation, but in reality, we are the same as any other plane design company; we don't always know how to get to point 'A' to point 'B', so we plod along. 'Fake it till you break it' comes to my mind as our real company motto. Especially with new-fangled technology like a jet and a rocket-plane. Moreover, we don't have the engineering staff in numbers to carry out all the tasks. Lily then issues a demand,

"Sometime next week Göring will be here for his production schedule review and you four are to meet him and his girth head on." I chuckle inside as I have never heard the Baroness utter a crude analogy but Göring in my mind deserves whatever we can verbally throw at him.

"Next week," Lily continues, "all the senior managers will be off at the Rechlin testing grounds and with Willy gone, you four are our first line of defense and response. Please prepare yourselves appropriately."

Lily ends the conversation, rises from the table and in good etiquette, we all rise as well. As she steps out we cast glances at each other. Wolfgang breaks the silence, "Ok everyone. The bill of goods has been sold to the Luftwaffe and they want to see their eggs hatching. That or Messerschmitt's contracts will be rescinded and that would wreak havoc on us all."

"I don't think our respective teams have any choice," I say. "We doctor our reports and paint a smiling picture of design progress and high production output. We just need to be on the same page as to what we will say if Göring pulls one of us aside."

"Agreed Armand," says Wolfgang. "Since we don't know who or which plane project Göring will pick on we'd all better be prepared for a visit next week."

A collective 'ja' goes out amongst us and we start talking about our individual plane project issues. When I speak, I address the 262 and 163 planes, "Gentlemen, I believe these are the most exciting planes out there and I personally want total Luftwaffe buy-in into our planes. Sorry, but our planes are more exciting than the giant glider or the next version of the Bf 109."

"Well, we here in the Gigant glider section," say Degel, "believe this bird is just what Germany needs to supply our dwindling defensive front."

"And in the bomber section wants the Amerika bomber to be the next big production priority. Who doesn't want to hit back at the USA with a bombing raid on New York?" asks that team leader in a rhetorical tone.

"Alright then," I say, "with no directors or superintendents around for the next few days we are all on our own to prepare our story to the Luftwaffe. May the best team win out."

With that, everyone gets up and starts walking back to the drafting Hall. Back to where the pencil and pen meet the vellum. Back to where we figure out how much bomb payload can be lifted by our planes; how many machine guns can be inserted into the wings or nose cone and how much fuel we can fill into every corner of a planes' body.

★★★

With Göring coming to the plant likely in the next few days, I am spending my Sunday evening looking over the production logs and design improvement reports. How am I going to make this all sound like it's going wonderfully smooth? I am already imagining sitting across from Göring, or more likely standing in front of him, as he pours through these reports. I know his key questions will be, 'how is the fast bomber production going?' Yet we at the design bureau have been spending more time on the interceptor fighter and the reconnaissance variation. How do I hide this?

As I ponder over the sheaves of reports and plane diagrams, I hear the pitter-patter of small steps coming down the hall. I look up and I see my son, Emil, now eight years old, looking at me waiting for my permission to enter my study. Giving him the nod he runs over to me,

"What are you working on now?"

"Oh, some new jets and rocket planes."

"Sounds nice, father. I wish I could tell my school friends, but I know we are not supposed to."

"That's right. This is all very hush, hush and it's important to Germany winning the war."

Emil then up looks up at me and then says,

"Could I look at your drawings?"

"Sure, hop up onto my lap." Emil climbs up and then starts flipping through the drawings.

"These are really neat planes. There are so many lines and shapes. Do they fly fast?"

"Oh yes, the fastest of any planes out there. They are so fast that you can barely see them go by when they are close to the ground."

"Wow, that is so cool. You are probably designing the most interesting things of all my friend's fathers."

I hear another shuffling of little people's feet at my door and I see Angelika with her baby doll in tow. She goes everywhere with this doll and usually it is being held by one hand while the rest of it dangles unceremoniously. Angelika approaches Emil and indicates her desire to be lifted onto my lap. Angelika, now seven years of age, looks over the drawings with less curiosity but with enough insight to say, "Papa, do these planes carry lots of people."

"My sweetheart, they only carry one pilot."

"Why so few people? They look like interesting planes to fly in."

"Well, they are for defending Germany."

"Couldn't they be used for families like us instead, dadda?"

"I am sure if I changed around the shape I could fit a whole family like ours."

"Papa, do all your planes have guns and bombs?" asks Emil.

"Why yes, there is a war going on and they are for defending our German skies."

"Why couldn't you draw up planes for families, like Angelika says? I would like to ride fast in the air too."

With this commentary, I am reminded that when I joined Messerschmitt I wanted to design passenger planes, that is where I wanted to go. Getting uncomfortable with my children's thoughts, I call up for Vanessa and she promptly appears. She sees the children pouring over my technical drawings, then she looks at me and notes my exhausted look. Vanessa calls over the children and whooshes them down the corridor into their rooms. Once she puts them into bed, I hear Vanessa bustling in the kitchen with the pots and porcelain cups. I look up from the desk and I see Vanessa entering my office carrying a tray stacked with a teapot, a teacup and some biscuits. Her light brown hair is haloed by the hall light as she enters. As she lays them on my desk, Vanessa comes over to me and runs her fingers through my hair. "Have something to drink and nibble on. It will give you the energy to continue onward with your work."

"Thanks darling. I am getting closer to being ready for the Göring 'surprise' meeting. I am just a little uptight about it."

"That would be understandable. I don't envy your position right now. I know you will be able to handle him well and deliver the right message."

"Thanks for being so understanding about me taking up the whole Sunday with this. I know this is usually our only family day but lately, working on Sunday's is getting more frequent. Now with the Professor out, it's all hands-on-deck for us production managers."

Vanessa looks at me with tenderness in her eyes matched by a supportive, soft tone, "I've always believed in you, Armand and I always will no matter what happens in this war." With that she kisses me on the cheek and leaves the office, and walks into the dark corridor, slowly fading from my view.

★★★

Frau Schnelling appears by the edge of the drafting hall looking anxious, "Herr Kindermann, he is here."

"Who is here, Frau Schnelling?"

"The man we have all been waiting for."

"Göring is here at the plant?"

"Yes, Herr Kindermann. And he seems eager to get on with a tour of the 262's production process."

I put on my suit coat, grab my project folders and walk up to the executive offices. Upon entering the room, I see four Luftwaffe officers seated at the conference table. Göring is seated at the head.

"Herr Field Marshall, I am Armand Kindermann, engineering production manager for both the Me 262 and Me 163. I am at your disposal for information and observations."

Göring makes a comment to the aide next to him and then finally turns his attention back to me. "Herr Kindermann, you look familiar. Ah, yes, you were part of the presentation team we saw at Herr Messerschmitt's estate last month. Very nice delivery and quite a convincing show of the jet's merits."

"Thank you, sir. That is my job as lead production engineer for the jet and the rocket plane."

"Very good. Today we are here to inspect the progress of the jet and the rocket glider. That all your directors are gone today is very propitious to my probe," Göring says this with a smile breaking across his full face as he looks at his surrounding staff. "Please sit down and do tell me what you know about the production and design status of the Me 262 jet."

I take a seat at the far end of the table opposite the foursome. What does he mean by probe? Is Messerschmitt under investigation?

"Most certainly, Field Marshall." I pull out from my folder of bulky files documenting the design and schedules for my planes, "I have all of our latest technical drawings along with assembly plans and production schedules. Where would you like me to begin?"

"I want to start with the 262 jet Kindermann." Göring clasps his fingers together and places his elbows on the table, leaning forward as much as his wide girth will allow him. "Now, last week we met with Directors Hentzen and Kokathi, but I didn't tell them that I would be back this week. I always like to surprise my industrialist contractors with a quick, if not unexpected follow-up visit." Göring looks to his staff who seem to enjoy watching him play this cat and mouse game I have been caught in. "Even more surprising for us though was that your Professor Messerschmitt is out on some unplanned medical leave. What that may be I was not told, but I am sure I will find out soon enough. Anyway, this will help clear the way for us to get right down to the heart of the matter, Herr Kindermann."

"I am at your service; Herr Field Marshall and I am certain to be consistent with what my superiors told you last week."

"Alright Kindermann, let's see how consistent you will be. So first, what is the status of production for the fast-tactical bombers, our Storm birds? You Messerschmitt folks put on a good show last July at the Rechlin Airfield and you all heard the Führer's command to give him a fleet of fast bombers."

"Yes, I heard word of that."

"Ok, then. Then show me the final design drawings and assembly plans."

I lean toward my first large folder and reach in to pull out a thick report. "Here, this report documents our current assembly plans, material tonnage needed per month, component factory locations, number of technicians employed, final assembly factories and acceptance flight testing schedules." Flipping the report's pages in front of the foursome inquest, I then place the documents in front of them as if making an offering at an altar. Göring does not reach for the report and instead looks at me.

"Alright, Kindermann, you have this all down on paper so show me the sections pertaining to the Stormbird and at what monthly rate will the company be producing the birds."

"Yes, Field Marshall. I will do so in a second. I just need to locate the heading for the Stormbird. Ah here yes, in this section, sir, you find all our estimates, quantities and timelines."

Little does Göring know that the ink in these reports is still drying and that the production schedules are extremely optimistic. I keep a calm and straight face, being conscientious of any unusual body movements I may make that could throw off his trust in me. Göring flips through the pages, grunts a little then I hear him say, "Ah ha. I see you are planning to start wing assembly of the Stormbird this January but where are your engines? I don't see any commitment dates on the turbines from BMW."

Göring has picked up one of the flaws of this whole coming together of the jet's assembly. The BMW turbines are not only low in thrust; they are also highly prone to flaming out on tight turns. I then comment,

"Sir, we have tried many prototypes of the BMW jet turbines but none of them have had satisfactory performance. We are now in the process of switching our sourcing of the turbines to Junkers. The prototype Jumo turbines seem to have the power and reliability that we are looking for. But it will be a matter of time before Junkers can provide us with a model that can be mass-produced."

"Oh, so you are placing blame of the delays on Junkers now?" says Göring. "Have you been pressing Junker to move on schedule? Have you gone to their factory and seen the fabrication of their turbines for yourself?"

"Sir, that is not my job to initiate. That would have to come from a Director for us to demand an onsite Junkers turbine inspection."

"Then you should have done such, Herr Kindermann. Where is your German loyalty to the cause? Do you not understand your allegiance is not to Messerschmitt but to the Third Reich? And when you are committed to the Reich, you will cross lines like this to achieve our national goals."

Appalled by his party rhetoric and illogic, I realize I am up against not only a highly manipulative and bullying leader of the Luftwaffe, but I also am up against the National Socialist fervor that sees their way as the only right way. Not wanting to put up a tussle with this almighty, I defer to and acknowledge his wisdom.

"Yes, Herr Field Marshall. I will personally visit Junker's turbine factory and inspect why they have not produced a reliable jet engine yet."

"Now we are talking, Herr Kindermann. I am glad you appreciate our Socialist cause, goals and more importantly, our means to the end. Now tell me about the jet interceptor variant, as you here call it the 'Swallow'. Why do I sense that the Professor would rather have the Luftwaffe invest in the interceptor version?"

"Well sir, the flight testing units are relaying back good results; once they can get the engines to stay consistently burning for fifty minutes. Based on their field trials the pilots are reporting that the Swallow has a great rate of climb, it rides very smoothly, the engines accelerate evenly, the flight controls are integrated and that the armament is deadly."

"Ok, enough of the unadulterated adoration of the jet. Let me hear the problem areas." says Göring in a gruff and flat tone.

"Alright sir. The negatives are that it requires a long runway to take off and it takes some time for it to reach fighting speeds. In the air, while smooth on the controls, the jet cannot turn as tightly as we had hoped. And even if the airframe could structurally hold a tight turn, the jet turbines flame out. On landing approach, the turbines have been taking a long time to burn out and lose their thrust. So, pilots spend a fair amount of time slowing down and carefully lining up their landings. But by far the biggest drawback is the amount of time in the air. The balance of plane weight, engine thrust, weapon payload and fuel storage has limited the jet to fifty minutes of flight. And with that a pilot will likely only get two, maybe three runs at a bomber fleet before he has to start slowing down and descending."

"Ah, so you designed a great interceptor but it's too limited on time. Perhaps you engineers designed too heavy of a machine?"

"Well, it does weigh 16,000 pounds fully loaded and that is almost 8,000 pounds heavier than the Bf 109. We are now currently looking at using aluminum and wood in some parts of the airframe."

"Very well, Kindermann, your report is much appreciated. Now just one last item I want to hear your opinion on. We know the Führer wants more fast bomber versions of the jet than fighter interceptors, but between you and me, what do you think of the fast bomber version of the 262?"

"May I speak freely sir?"

"Why of course. I want nothing more than your complete honest engineering appraisal."

"Well, Herr Field Marshall, and with all due respect to our Führer's wishes for a fast, tactical bomber jet, the 262 airframe was designed from the ground up to be a fighter interceptor. Its design intention was to fly up quickly to altitudes of 30,000 feet in a matter of minutes and then swoop down on bomber fleets and their escort planes. As I said earlier, all our field unit testing to date confirms that the plane performs wonderfully in this role. If the Führer wanted a fast, light bomber, then that should've been on the table back in 1939, when Voldemar Voigt first designed the plane. To tack on the role of tactical bomber at this stage is like putting a wig on a pig. Sorry for the crude analogy sir."

"Ha, I like that, Armand. You engineers can be funny sometimes. I do appreciate your frankness and I am starting to see your point. Maybe we need to reconsider prioritizing the fighter jet to a higher level? I do need this kind of information. You know airplanes have changed so much since I flew them in the Great War. Flying in an open cockpit bi-plane made of wood is one thing but flying these craft of aluminum and high-thrust engines is beyond me to comprehend as an ex-combat pilot. Just don't let anyone know I said that, alright." Göring breaks a small smile, leans back in his chair and then rises. "Armand, I think we are done with our little interview here. Why don't you take me on a tour of your most vaunted design offices and show me some of these plane sketches under development."

"Why yes, Herr Field Marshall. The drafting floor is where I have professionally 'lived' since I was a teen. Taking you there and showing our work will be like me showing you my own home. Please follow me this way and we will start with the 262 project bureau first."

With that Göring and the three staff officers rise, and we head out to my studio, my home, to the world where I merge with technical design and drawing. The wonderful world of lines, geometries, trigonometric calculations and a Cartesian plane that I dwell in.

FEBRUARY 25, 1944

I wake up this Thursday morning early and rise out of bed without disturbing Vanessa and then head over to the kitchen for breakfast. The news that other German cities are being bombed and that our Luftwaffe does not have enough fighters to defend us is worrying me. I pace around the flat and look out the dormer windows into the winter scenery.

It is freezing out, nearly zero degrees Fahrenheit. A frosted pattern etches the window and beyond I can see smoke billowing out against the cold as the sun meekly peers out over the horizon as a thin orange wafer. All of Augsburg seems nestled asleep under their red-tiled roofed apartments. I've lived here now for eleven years, raised my kids and this feels like home to me as any place has. Our new flat on Stetten Strasse is a step up from our first one since we first moved here in 1933 and we now have a separate bedroom for the children.

While I think that I will likely walk to the plant today and not bear bicycling down there for the three miles, my thoughts turn to how the mood in the plant has turned from hectic to desperate, on everyone's part. Not just Messerschmitt and the top managers but we engineers, designers, and the production crews. We just can't keep us this madness of designing and producing planes and working fourteen-hour shifts six days a week, sometimes all seven days a week. On top of that, men from the plant are being conscripted into the Army and exacerbating our labor shortage.

When is this going to end, how will we win the war, can we turn it around? How did I get myself trapped into this? I should have left for Italy before the war started; at least I could've worked for some low-key, ineffective plane manufacturer down there.

But now I feel like we are a big red target for the American and British air forces. Their Lancaster and Halifax bombers have enough range to reach well within Bavaria and continue even then onward to safely land in Tunisia. And while we try to keep our Augsburg plant production a secret we know that our slave labor or foreign guest workers may have snuck the word out.

I look around the house, my wife soundly asleep and my two children nestled away in their dreams. I decide to get ready for work and leave the house early so perhaps I can get back and catch a bit of time with the kids for a later dinner.

I walk down to Haunstetten toward the various buildings of the factory complex. Upon arriving at the studio, it is quiet and there are only a few people populating the space. The humdrum of pencils and triangles slapping the tables along with rolls of paper being torn are all but absent at this early hour. Now I can settle into drawing up the latest version of the cannon mount inside the engine cowling. How should I figure out the curve and radii of these attachments as I handle my compass?

My morning reverie is only disturbed when Wolfgang walks in and shouts out, "Well fancy seeing you here, Armand at this hour. I thought you only worked best on the late shift?"

"Oh, Wolfgang, you know this hurts me more than it does you to see me here. I woke up with these design problems in my head, and I couldn't shake them off. So, what else to do but come to work early."

"Well, we welcome you to our early crew, Armand. Can I get you a cup of coffee from the commissary? The word is that they have cooked up some apple *pfannkuchen* this morning, and I am certain to be the first in line."

"I'll pass on the *pfannkuchen*, but I will take a cup of coffee. Say, Wolfgang, what do you think of the Allied bombing campaign and where they are going to hit next? I am just starting to believe that we are sitting ducks here in Augsburg. I mean, do you think our meager lines of anti-aircraft batteries are going to put up a shield for us as our Wehrmacht claims?"

"Oh, don't go worrying about that. I have complete faith in our pilots to fend off any bombing raid we may come under. Heck, don't you believe in our products. Our Bf 109's can do massive damage to those bomber fortresses."

"Let's hope so. I do have complete faith in our plane design and product, but I am much less confident about the Luftwaffe command in deploying them correctly."

"Ok, Armand, hold that thought and I will have that hot coffee in your hands in no time."

When Wolfgang comes back with my coffee, I notice there is a long convoy of transport trucks rolling up to the assembly buildings. I take my coffee and stare out the window from our fifth floor.

"What is this? Did we just hire five hundred workers in one day? Where did all these people coming from?"

Wolfgang also pulls up to window and looks out alongside. "Oh, here they are, it's the first batch I was told about."

"What batch are you talking about?"

People start disembarking from the transports, but the first ones are soldiers, and they are barking out commands and waving guns. Then a downcast male populace disgorges from the trucks, people in forlorn clothing with the heads down and a slow trodden pace. They are prisoners of war! Upon this realization, I say to Wolfgang,

"Prisoners? Coming here to work at our plant? What has this war come to? Don't we have enough Germans and foreign workers to fill our assembly lines?"

"Armand, I think we have just acknowledged that Germany cannot win this war without bringing in massive amounts of forced workers from other nations."

"And what about this group being dropped off down below?"

"This group must be the Italian prisoners of war. You know, the poor bastards who were caught in the middle when the Italian government capitulated to the Allies."

My first thought is of my cousin Rodolfo, Capitan Lorenzini. What happened to his company when Italy switched sides?

Wolfgang continues, "But we will also be receiving impressed civilians from our conquered territories like Greece, Hungary, Poland, the rest of the Slavic countries and southern Italians. As long as the northern Fascist government holds in place though, I don't think we will see many northern Italians impressed here for factory work. Unless they are under some guest worker program, which is a nice way of saying forced workers from our own axis partners."

Italian prisoners of war and impressed civilians working on the factory floor while I draft away in the project bureaus? Yet here I am, half Italian and now my brethren are going to be working hard under the tough yoke of the SS guards stationed to our plant. The ethical dilemma of my situation painfully sinks into me like the hook of a scythe.

"So, we can expect many new and different people on our factory floors," I say.

"Not only on our factory floors, Armand, we are also impressing engineers, scientists and technicians from captured territories. Especially French, Dutch and Czechoslovakian. So, we may be working alongside some of them right in our drafting hall."

Feeling a wave of disgust swell inside me, I say to Wolfgang, "I need to speak with Gerhard Coulis right now."

I turn to walk to the executive offices and head straight to Coulis' secretary. I present myself to her.

"I would like to speak to the engineering superintendent, please." She makes me wait a few minutes and then I am flagged in to see Coulis.

I enter his office.

"Gerhard, I see that a shipment of Italian prisoners of war has arrived."

"Yes, Armand. Why do you seem agitated? You know it's a production necessity."

"I gather that but I have Italian relatives, cousins, in the Italian Army. One of them even came up here on a Fascist brotherhood tour of Germany some years back."

"Yes, I know Armand. It's a bad twist of fortune for the Italian soldiers. But their Government capitulated on them right while they were in mid-campaign. So, we grabbed them before they became pawns of the Allies."

"I understand that necessity, Gerhard, but I need to know if one of my cousins is on the docket of Italians shipped here to Augsburg."

"Well, even if you found out he is here what could you do about it?" says Coulis with a bureaucratic tone. "They are under the control of SS's Stone and Earthworks company and then leased to us."

"I guess we cannot do much, but my heart will feel better if I knew. And perhaps I could get word back to my uncles in Italy."

"So, what are you asking for then?"

"I want to see the manifest list of Italian officers. If he is here, then I request an interview with the prisoner for a short time."

"Alright let's look at the manifest first and then I'll see if I can get the SS guards to grant you some security clearance to meet with a prisoner. Just be aware, Armand that asking to see a prisoner will raise a flag with the SS and they may put that on your record."

Coulis calls in his assistant and asks for the manifest of prisoners being brought in. A sheaf of papers is brought in.

"What would be his name?"

"His name is Rodolfo Lorenzini and he is a captain in the army."

After a few minutes of perusing, Gerhard looks up and says, "I think we have him. He is with the Northern Italian Army, Second Division. We are planning to put them to work on the assembly lines for the next version of the Bf 109s"

My heart is relieved but also mortified that my cousin is locked up somewhere on this plant complex. I then say to Gerhard, "As soon as Degel explained this to me, I had a feeling that he would be here. Now can you please make arrangements for me to meet with him? This would give me, my mother and his parents some comfort."

"Alright, I will call up the Captain of the Guards and arrange for you to meet with him. I doubt they will give you a lot of time though. I am sure they are eager to put them to work."

I head out of the Administration building and walk over to the security offices and await an escort. A sergeant comes out and walks me toward the prisoner's yard and then into a building that straddles the barbed-wire fence line. I am sat down in a bare wooden room and quietly wait. The door facing the prisoner's yard opens and a guard escorts in my cousin Rodolfo. He walks in with a straight gait and keeps his head up while he approaches me for an embrace.

"*Primo fratello.* What has happened to you?" I say to Rodolfo. He looks slenderer than when I saw him last, his hair is tousled and his Captain's tunic is worn and dusty.

"*Cugino* Armando, I knew you would find me eventually. So good to see you after some years."

"They have been some interesting years, Rodolfo. I just never thought things would turn out this way."

"It's alright, Armand. I am doing ok, considering, and please let your mother know I am well. A little worn from long marches but I am still alive and responsible for my unit here under imprisonment."

"That's good to know Rodolfo. You do look basically the same since I last saw you. Just a little exposed to the elements."

"Nothing I can't handle. Fighting in battle was harder than marching for weeks till we got here. Worse was the sense of betrayal that our Government turned on us and left us hanging out to dry, right while we were stationed with German units. Then to have what were once our allies, turn on us and take us prisoner. It was like double of ironies. *La vita pazzo.*"

"I guess it was a good thing I didn't come to work for Fiat in Italy then, yes *Cugino*?" I say to Rodolfo with a warm smile trying to lighten the conversation.

"Looks my company and I will now be doing some heavy lifting for your Messerschmitt enterprise. I never thought I would be working for you *Cugino*."

"Please, Rodolfo, you may be working for Messerschmitt AG, but without pay and no freedom."

"I know Armand. I am an officer in the Army, trained to lead. And now the War has landed me a job on the assembly line. I will let you know if your designs are awful to assemble."

The guard motions to me that our time is up.

"Rodolfo, I am not in the executive ranks of Messerschmitt AG, yet, but I do have a few friends up there and hopefully I can request that they take care of you."

"While you are at it, tell them if they can take special care of my whole company that is here. I am still responsible for them and I intend to bring them home safely."

"I am proud of you, Rodolfo, for keeping face despite this dilemma. Your father and my mother were right to say you would make a good officer. I will pass on a word to my mother as soon as I can get some communication out of here."

Rodolfo and I embrace, and the guard takes him back into the yard. I feel I did the right thing in tracking him down and hopefully I can pull some strings to ease their life here. Still, the disgust I feel inside at how this War has twisted my Italian family's fate into this surreal circumstance gnaws at my innards.

★★★

It is early evening in the drafting hall and many people are still working away. The winter sky has turned a dark blue to match the frigid February temperatures. As a group, we lift our heads from our drafting tables as we perceive a steady buzz growing in the air. A sinuous howl then shatters our silence as air raid sirens blare on.

Alarmed, we make a mad dash to the concrete bunker at the base of the project bureau building. Deep inside the bunker, we can hear the airplane buzz growing deeper in pitch. The sound of anti-aircraft gunnery crackles through the air, letting us know that they are heading our way. Within five minutes of the air raid sirens going off, we hear the whistle of bombs being dropped. The ordinance starts exploding west of the plant, then closer till finally, they are right overhead. The Allies are wasting no time in trying to stop the production of our planes.

We huddle within the bunker but the door opens as more engineers and a few laborers hustle in. We are all in this together now. I know or recognize many of the workers in the plant, and I can see they are just as exposed and scared as we are. While the thuds of bombs and deep vibrations radiate through the ground, concrete dust crumbles from the ceiling, the pendant light swings in perturbations. We stare at each other with big eyes initially and then grimacing faces as the bombs explode.

Eventually, it is quiet overhead, and we pull out of the bunker onto the airfield awaiting a scene of destruction. The plant has been hit in various places; the factory, the hangars, and the design offices, but not the headquarters tower. There are twisted fallen trusses, strewn piles bricks, wood beam splinters and broken windows throughout as firefighting teams scramble about.

I run off to find and aid any injured. I look about the rising dust and start hearing cries and moans of help. When I finally look away from the smoke, dust, and rising fires of the plant, I realize that the city of Augsburg has been bombed as well. How can this be? Attacking our plant is one thing, but why attack the center of Augsburg? I see smoke billowing north of the factory toward the city center. A pale orange lights the underbelly of the dark, devilish clouds now lurking over the city. While I want to run into the city center and find Vanessa I must stay near the plant to help rescue people. Worse, from the looks of it, the city is aflame in a whirling hot, red morass of consumption. What can I do but wait it out and pray for a miracle?

★★★

By morning we have contained the conflagration at the plant, and it is now time for me to seek out Vanessa and the children. I step through the smoldering rubble of what was Haunstetten Strasse leading to the center of Augsburg, knowing with each step that I am closer to the truth, what must be an awful truth. Still, I plod along with blank eyes as firemen and excavators dig through bricks and timbers of what were houses only last night.

I come to our block and I see a smoldering and rambling pile of bricks, wood beams and shattered household items. Smoke wisps out of random sections of the rubble. Disconsolate and losing my grip, I run toward the heap that was our apartment and I start to pull bricks and wood shards out,

"No. No. My God. It can't be. This can't be happening to me."

I start to sob, my chest heaving up and down, my voice wailing. I feel a hand grab my arm. It is a fireman and he is trying to pull me away. The look on his eyes express a quiet sympathy. I look at him ready to explode into a rage and pull my arm from him and dive back into pulling bricks out. As I toss rubble aside I see broken windows, pieces of table legs, curtain fabrics all pressed under the heavy weight of building detritus.

I see a hand and I reach out for it. It is plastic though, a plastic doll. I pull it out and realize I have found Angelika's doll. A clear and painful image of my daughter holding her doll while trotting down the corridor sears my mind and heart.

"No God. Not my children. Not my Vanessa. What has this war brought to me? What good is that I have risen up the ranks of Messerschmitt when all I get in return is the loss of my family?"

I cry out and drop to my knees. I place the doll in my arms and cradle her as if it was Angelika herself. I look up to the sky, my eyes filling with tears and then I drop my head onto my chest in resignation. I feel the fireman's hand on my shoulder again. This is all I will find of them. Why didn't I give them one last kiss yesterday? An emotional void filled only with sorrow pervades the pit of my soul.

★★★

The following Sunday there is a memorial held for all the Augsburg and Messerschmitt people killed in the bombing raid. Various city leaders speak, first burger meisters, then Party officials like Scheide. But, my attention is most centered when Willy Messerschmitt walks up to the podium and addresses the gathered,

Messerschmitt's Apprentice

"My dear Germans and fellow plant employees. I am deeply saddened by the death of so many of our community of workers. I feel deep pain for each surviving members and for the sorrow that all of you must be feeling. Lilly and I extend our sincerest condolences and sympathies to you and your families.

"This morning I received a telegram from our Fuerher. He extends his condolences to all of you on the loss of our factory and family members. But he also congratulates us for our resolve in restoring order, production and most importantly, faith. Faith that the Reich will proceed ahead no matter what the Allies throw at us.

"This is a war. A war that tests Germany's will and sense of purpose against the rest of the world. But we are the superior peoples with the superior intelligence, organization, technology and military prowess. We will come ahead and vanquish our enemies shortly. All of our sacrifices of time, loved ones and property will be worth the struggle we are enduring. While you work long hours, wonder about your relatives on the frontlines, you are all directly contributing to a greater Germany through your assembly of warplanes. One where we will be able to live our Aryan ideals in a 1000 year Reich. I keep this in mind every morning, every late night, and with every plane rolled out off the factory floor, I know surely, that our German sacrifice has moral bearing."

Messerschmitt looks up from his podium, a cold wind sweeps over and blows a few strands of his hair into the air. His speech papers rattle in the wind. Messerschmitt continues with fervor in his voice,

"Yes, we are in an epoch-defining war where every factory worker, every engineer, and every production manager is fighting together toward one singular cause, goal and direction. The victory of the Third Reich over our enemies. Our contribution of fighter planes toward this war effort is essential and by extension making all of you an integral part of the war.

"And while the bombing and killing has been tragic, we are not to be dissuaded. No, we are actually stronger today than the day before the bombing. Because we are Germans and we are a resourceful and dedicated people. No bomb or fire can stop the fervor of our advanced culture. It will surely last another thousand years as will our worker's solidarity. My blessings to all the people of Augsburg, Haunstetten and Messerschmitt AG. Heil Hitler."

There is an emphatic applause followed by a spontaneous standing of 'Heil Hitler's' from the more aroused members of the memorial. Nonetheless, I notice that some in the audience fail to feel consolation from this Party rhetoric. Messerschmitt seems to have totally bought into the National Socialist's vision more than ever now. But now my Party activities reveal themselves as token and involuntary efforts to show my company allegiance. This is not what I had signed up for when I committed my career to Messerschmitt. Now, I have lost my wife, my children and my home. Reich visions of imperial glory will never replace my families' love and companionship. What can replace Vanessa's voice, her touch, her constant support, her hugs at bedtime and to arise every morning knowing that she believes in me?

As other officials continue with their memorial speeches, I think of how my hometown of Mainz has been repeatedly bombed by British and American planes for the past two years. I have not heard from my parents since January and nor am I allowed to travel there. How will I get word to them about cousin Rodolfo being imprisoned here? Worse yet, I don't even know yet he and other prisoners fared during this wave of bombing. But I am fearing the worse for my parents and the potential of losing them along with my own family would be a deep chasm for me to crawl out of.

PART 3
SCHEMATIC REDESIGN

APRIL 1944

"Herr Messerschmitt," I say, I am asking for a transfer to another plant location." I look at him across from his desk while we sit in his sparsely decorated executive office. Messerschmitt leans back in his chair and puts down his pen.

"What is wrong, Armand?" responds the Professor. "We have plenty of work to do here in Augsburg and we need your skills on the two-seater jet variant."

"Yes, I know, Professor, but the memories of my wife and children are wrapped in this town. We had been together here for ten years."

"I know it must be hard but just think of how proud your Vanessa would be if you stuck to your mission of defending Germany's skies with our jet."

"I do feel proud of that and I am very committed to work on the Swallow, and the Komet for that matter. It's just that I am feeling so depressed lately, I can barely get up in the morning. And at night, I wake up sporadically, usually from nightmares of the bombing."

"I know your wife believed in you and she must've been the rock in your life. Come to think of it, if I lost my Baroness, I would be very shaken up as well."

"Exactly sir. I am sure you can imagine how distraught I have been these days. I dare say that I don't think I am even being as productive as I could be. I find myself drifting in thought throughout the workday."

"So, you think a transfer to one of our other plants will help your spirits?" asks Messerschmitt.

"I do sir. I can only think that a change in scenery would help me start anew and keep a positive outlook on my work."

"Very well. You are one of my trusted engineers here and I know that I can trust you out in the field as well. Recently, the Armaments Ministry ordered that we move out significant portions of our design and production into dispersed, rural locations."

"I have heard rumors of that directive, sir, and these had me thinking that a move to a forest location would be good for me. A place where I won't see my wife and children's faces appear to me at every street corner."

"Alright, Armand, there is a group of engineers being assigned to a new forest factory in Horgau, some thirty miles west of here. It will be under the direction of Gerhard Coulis and the unit will continue production design on the jet and the rocket. Moreover, they will be performing final assembly of the single-seat fighter jets. Nearby in Offingen, the Metallblau plant will be producing components for the two-seater jet variant. And in Burgau, they will be performing the final assembly. As for the Me 163 rockets, they will be continuing testing in nearby Leipheim as well. So Horgau would be a good base for you to work out of."

"This sounds like a good fit for me and I would welcome that assignment."

"I will draw up reassignment papers for you and hand them off to Gerhard Coulis for implementation. I will miss seeing you around every day but I am sure I will be visiting Horgau regularly."

"Do you have plans to move out of Haunstetten as well, Professor?

"Yes, and it may not be of my own doing."

"How so, Professor?

"Minister Speer has proposed taking aviation industry production away from the RLM and putting it under his Armaments Ministry. It's all about production and rationalizing of our resources right now. The pressure is on us to produce more fighters with a less-skilled workforce and a geographically stretched out assembly process"

"But haven't we already been working feverishly on increasing and streamlining craft production?" I ask.

"Even so, we are not meeting our production goals for 1944," says Messerschmitt. And I am getting taken to task at every production meeting I attend in Berlin. By Milch, by Göring and even by Himmler. Our competitors are standing at the door ready to take over our contracts if we slip. It doesn't help that our own employees are ratting on me for usage of automobile gas on personal trips."

Messerschmitt leans back, let's out a sigh and looks out his window and says, "Soon Messerschmitt AG will only have my name on it but not my leadership. I just learned last week that a special SS Commissioner, Gerhard Degenkolb, will have full authority over the Me 262's production and allocation of resources. And with that, the Ministry wants me out of Augsburg and out of executive management. Even my old 'buddy' Milch has been demoted as they have formed a Supreme Fighter Production Staff to wrest control from the RLM."

"So, where are you being reassigned?"

"I am being relocated to Oberammergau to focus on advance jet plane developments. I guess this will be better for me. And besides the Raulino estate was heavily damaged during the Augsburg bombing raid, so the Baroness and I need to find a new home anyway.

"Good luck Professor on the move. God knows when the Allies will be back with another bombing gift for us," I say. "When they do, they won't find much of us here."

★★★

As the lorry drives through a thick pine forest late at night, we approach a large hill that is vaguely outlined by the moonlight. My new design team disembarks from the trucks and we assemble around Doctor Voigt for directions. The hill offers no clue as to where to go next but the Doctor walks up to an outcropping and then lights come on. A sergeant emerges and directs us inward toward a tunnel system that winds down into and enormous man-made cave. The cave is still under construction as hundreds of slave workers shift around as one slow mass digging out rock. We are led to a staging area where Doctor Voigt is met by a colonel who then signs off on his security papers. With that we are cleared to move out and we disgorge from the tunnel where we are transported to Horgau some ten miles away.

This forest factory is nestled under tall spruce pine trees with camouflage netting spread between the trees. Some twenty-one, wood buildings have been constructed and I learn that 800 people will be based here; 300 engineering and technical staff along with some 500 assembly workers. Many of the factory workers will be impressed workers brought in from other Axis countries like Italy, Spain and Romania and some are concentration camp workers. Likewise, there will be foreign engineers and technicians brought in as guest workers or as collaborators.

After we cross through a barbed-wire perimeter fences, I see a complex of assembly halls, warehouses, sleeping barracks, design studios and a kitchen commissary. Our design bureau staff will be stationed in a large wooden vaulted structure making this my new production home. Happily, Walter will also be relocated here to continue work on the radio and radar systems for the night fighters, and we will be sharing the same barracks.

The Horgau *waldwerk* complex is on a flat area next to a creek called the Aspenbach. To the north, the land rises quickly, and the surrounding hills backdrop the plant. The landscape is a dense planting of pines, so thick that you cannot see further than one hundred yards into them before all the pine trunks close in on your view. Further screening us from air raids, is a canopy of camouflage netting interlaced with branches casting a dense interplay of shadows onto the ground.

Now that we are all in the Horgau plant, a waldwerk isolated off in this tall pine forest, I can see that we are detached from the rest of the world. A barbed wire fence surrounds the plant and our engineering staff are only permitted to leave through guarded checkpoints, and only for specific assignments to other plants or airfields. As we all live together around the clock, much like a military base, the plant camp becomes a world of its own.

There is one platoon of SS soldiers consisting of one Sergeant and twenty-five men assigned to watch the slave laborers. But for such an extensive network of buildings and with eight-hundred people working here, I wonder how can they cover everything twenty-four hours a day?

★★★

I look at the Komet drawings in front of me and I know mechanically what must be done to complete the fabrication drawings. Existential questions abound though. Why am I still alive while they are dead? I lift my pencil and take the triangle to draw a line between the two circular parts. Where am I going to gather the energy to stay focused and motivated to complete all this work? How should I space the bolts connecting this rib to the wing fairing? Why did they leave me now when I needed them most? The anguish of their loss seems to be eating away at me, draining my life source. Draw. Erase. Measure. Letter. Next sheet. Repeat. I have created a world of geometry for myself but now it feels more like a box that is keeping me locked in.

Yet at the same time, drawing and design work seem to be the only reason I exist. These functions are my essence and the rationale for my existence since, currently, I have no love or deep connection with any other. My drawings breathe of me and I breathe of them. But drawings and ideas have no emotion, no compassion and no soul. I need to cross this line, the boundaries I have set myself in and break free somehow.

"Herr Kindermann, excuse me but may I have some of your time to look over this fairing connection detail?" interrupts one of my team members. He is a recent graduate of the university and his eagerness reminds me of when I first started here. Seeing that it is late, I admire his persistence to keep at his drawings and knowing when to seek my input.

"Sure, why don't you place your drawings on my table and let's look through the details," I respond.

The young man plops down a roll of drawings and I start peeling through them, so I can hone in on the problem.

"The Komet's wooden wings are pulling away from the fuselage from the tight turning forces," he says. "So, I've been creating alternate attachment structures that should hold them in place even as it approaches Mach 1. But there is only so much bearing place surface area for us to make an attachment, so I am proposing we increase the number of rib structure members to better hold the wings on. What do you think of that Herr Kindermann?"

"Well, you know that adding more weight to the Komet will slow down its velocity, make it heavier to launch and increase the volume of fuel used. So, every added pound has a cascading effect."

"I see, but would it be worth it to run the calculations to see if this added rib can be born with greater benefit?"

"It is a balancing act of fuel versus plane weight so go ahead and run the calculations and I trust you will find the right balance. Alright?" I say this with a fatherly and encouraging tone to the junior member of our team knowing that soon he will be on his way to better understanding plane design. "By the way, it's well past nine PM, you should stop for the night and rest up in your barracks."

"Yes, Herr Kindermann. I appreciate your review and I will stop for the night. Have a good evening Herr Kindermann."

As the young man pulls away from my desk and walks out of the drafting hall, I realize that I am the last person in the hall. I look at the Komet's drawings in front of me. Such tediousness of detail that I must endure through, but this is my career path.

As I continue drawing into the evening, I realize that I have no desire to go back to the barracks to endure a conversation with my bunkmates. But I am starting to feel drowsy and my energy levels are dropping like a plane running out of fuel. So, I decide that I will put my head down on the drafting table and take a few minutes' break.

As I take in some deep breaths with my face on the table I drift momentarily into a suspended mental state. Feeling a presence watching over me, I lift my head up to see who this visitor may be. To my surprise, I see Vanessa standing in front of my drafting table.

"Dear, what are you doing here?"

Vanessa seems calm and full of loving energy. "Armand, I want you to know that we are all ok. We will always love you. Our lives' paths have diverged now but you have more here to explore and to learn from."

"But Vanessa, I miss you and the kids so much. How am I supposed to continue here, at least happily and with resolve?"

"Armand, you have a mission to fulfill here and your time has not yet come. We will be waiting for you and in no time, we will all be together. But for now, know that we love you and that you are free to move on. You need to continue your path here on Earth."

I stand up from my table and extend my hand toward her to reach out and touch her, but as I do so Vanessa evaporates like a shimmering mirage. I plop down on my drawing stool, place my head over my hands and start sobbing. 'Please come back, Vanessa. I need you and the children. I am so lost right now.'

Am I going crazy? Was that just a wild image generated by my imagination or better stated, my sorrow? I've never heard Vanessa talk like that before, what was she trying to relate to me? Telling me it's alright to move on. Finally coming back to awareness of my surroundings, I realize the drafting hall is dark and empty. I am alone of heart and this is a worse pain to endure than social isolation. The vision of Vanessa initially gave me a mix of hope and comfort but now I just feel emptiness. I decide to retire for the evening and head to the barracks for a night of what will hopefully be a restful sleep.

JUNE 1944

As we move on with the Me 163 Komet's development into a buildable fighter, I continue the fuselage's production drawings. On this morning, I realize that for me to finalize the strut assembly, I need the thrusting power of the rocket engines and the amount of moment arm force they will create on the wings. I am told by Coulis that for those questions I should speak with one of the foreign guest workers who is on another end of the drafting barracks. Wolfgang tells me that he is also working on the Komet's rocket engine with the remaining Lippisch's team. He also mentions that he is one of the engineers brought in from Fiat's Milan aviation division.

Walking past a grouping of French and Belgium engineers, I approach the Italian engineer's drafting table. I see that his location is isolated from the rest of the rocket engineers, and I approach him cautiously. His hair is dark, bushy and disheveled and his smock is tattered, as if second-hand. He is of dark complexion and has equally deep, dark, penetrating eyes. Based on the lines on his face, I would say he is in his fifty's.

"Doctor Da Zara, may I have some of your time?"

"Yes sir, how can I help you this day?" he responds.

His voice is sing-song, belying his Italian heritage but he is deferential, and he does not raise his eyes off his desk. Having been to Italy many times, I note his accent is northern Italian but of what region I cannot tell. Not Genovesan for sure.

"Doctor Da Zara, I understand you know the properties of the Walter's rocket engine characteristics and I need your help in figuring out how to mount the motor within the fuselage. It will exert dead weight, momentum, and forward thrust. So, I need to calculate the frames that will hold it in place."

Da Zara stops, looks up and says, "The equilibrium between the thrust vector and the centroid of mass can be calculated through sectional area analysis at each major profile cross section. Determining that will give you the center of gravity and thus the key points on where to structure the rocket motor."

"Why thank you, Doctor. That does sound like a reasonable approach. I will go back to my table and run through a few calculations and see if that resolves it for me."

I find that Doctor Da Zara is highly knowledgeable on this subject matter, so I ask him where had been trained. Da Zara responds obliquely,

"From the beginning of powered flight, I have been there."

He then puts his head back down to his calculation pad. There is something valuable hidden away in Dr. Da Zara, and he puzzles me with his direct and succinct technical answers and his refusal to be sociable with anyone. Nonetheless, he performs his job wonderfully, plowing away at calculations on how the turbines will perform with the Komet.

As I saunter back to my studio I ask Gerhard about the Doctor Da Zara fellow.

"Oh, you haven't heard, Armand? He was given over to us by the Social Republic of Italy that is still in power in the north. He is technically a guest worker. After Hitler demanded that Italy provide Germany with their aviation talent, he was one of the engineers taken from Fiat in Milan. You know Da Zara; he's the fellow from Venice that started Italy's flying clubs back in the teens."

"Oh, that Da Zara. That's him? Yes, I do remember reading about him in my youth. I never saw a picture of him before nor have I heard much about him since. So, how did Messerschmitt AG end up with him? We already have French and Czech aviation engineers working for us, but I didn't know we've pulled in Italian ones as well?"

"We need every technical expert we can get our hands on, German or not. We are even bringing in Jews back onto our assembly lines straight out of the concentration camps. But when the RLM requisitioned Da Zara, they didn't know he was Jewish, as he was busy working away on Regia Aeronautica planes."

"Ah, so he is Jewish," I say back. "We haven't had any Jewish engineer's here since they all left back in '38, for the sake of their lives. So, he must be under of diplomatic protection of some sorts then. And that must be why he is so aloof with the rest of us."

"Da Zara is an avowed supporter of Mussolini and he is a wealthy landowner in Italy as well. But as he is Jewish, he was brought here forcibly, and he is 'contracted' to us for a year. I've heard he is quartered with the commissary and other housekeeping staff. Good thing or the guards would abuse him like the rest of our slave laborers. At least he's well fed and in comfortable working conditions."

★★★

The next day I must confer with Doctor Da Zara again on the latest Walter HWK 509 A-2 rocket engine characteristics for thrust force on the Komet wing attachments. Following his run-through on the moment forces and vibrations caused at various speeds, I make a friendly gesture to him,

"*Dottore* Da Zara I understand you hail from Venice. My mother is Italian, and I enjoyed many trips to northern Italy as a child."

"*A che buono, un piacere,*" he says warming up with a little more life in his voice and a straightening of his posture, as he moves around some of his drafting instruments.

Continuing in Italian to further break any formalities, I say,

"I've never been to Venice, but my mother has family in the Veneto province. I also recall reading your name in aviation books mentioning your work with the Italian flying clubs.

"Yes, I am from Padua, near Venice, and there I had started the first flying club in Italy. I have Italy's seventh aviator's license, so I was in the game pretty early on. I am the old man of aviation, Armando. It's been quite a life-long passion for me. In those first years, I risked my life several times in those flying contraptions. Such exciting times. And those bi-planes, so maneuverable yet so delicate. Like a lady, very pretty but prone to frail moments in a flash. *Capische?*"

"Well I am now widowed Doctor, but I do recall how a woman can be fickle. But it's always worth the effort for the man."

Da Zara breaks into a melody, "*La Donna e mobile, qual plum al vento.*"

"I recognize that tune, Dottore. Giuseppe Verde's Rigoletto act three, the Duke of Mantua *canzone.*"

"Well guessed, Herr Kindermann. I see you know your opera."

"Oh, yes. My mother loved Italian opera and she would love to hum a tune or two for me. I even loved going to the opera with my mother."

"Your mother has good taste I see. But of course, she is Italian. How old are you, Armando? You seem young for a widower."

"I am thirty-four, and yet it seems I've been here at Messerschmitt all my adult life."

"You are a young man by my standards, and you still have much life to live. Like my daughter, who is twenty-eight. She is so adventurous and young at heart. She is such a dreamer even with all this nonsense of the war going on. You must meet her sometime. Her name is Rosa, and she works in the commissary kitchen. A far cry from her nursing studies four years ago but, we are all making the best of things now. You know we are guest workers, although these days I fear that status may be lost."

"Yes, I heard that you and many other foreigners are now working here in Germany as guest workers." I pause looking to mitigate the direction of this conversation. "Dottore Da Zara, I would like to hear more about your flying club days sometime, but I must get back to my drafting table for now. *A presto.*"

★★★

It is a bright day and the rays of the morning sun filter through the pine trees surrounding our barracks. I enter the commissary and approach the serving table and I notice a woman serving eggs and pancakes. As she fills each plate and passes them on to the men in my design bureau, I see her slender neck, thin waist and black hair set against a light skin tone and most striking of all, her bright olive eyes.

I hear a supervisor call out, "Rosa, more pancakes are ready to be served. Come back quickly."

Her thick, curly hair and bright green eyes are paired with dark eyelashes and a thin dark eyebrow line that jumps up with changes in her expression. Her face is slender, her chin slightly pointy and her eyes sparkle in resonance with her broad smile. She seems happy at her work and chats with the staff, accentuating a charismatic smile. From her movements, I can tell she is slender but with womanly curves around her hips and breasts. Rosa is wearing a light-blue serving frock, standard issue for kitchen workers, along with a kerchief tied around her head. From the edges of the kerchief, her hair billows out, belying a large mane of curly hair. My eyes travel below the skirt line, and I notice she has slender legs with smooth skin. 'What I am doing looking her over?' I ask myself as I continue moving down the serving line.

As she serves me, we exchange glances, and her eyes widen just a little. She exudes energy, pep, and amiability despite all the ruins of this war, perhaps because her father has been able to secure her some level of safety and comfort compared to the rest of her people's fate.

I feel a slight tinge growing inside me, but my mind immediately blocks it off and focuses back on getting breakfast going. I need to make this meal quick and move on to design matters in the drafting Hall.

★★★

I am working on the next version of the Me 262, number five to be exact. It is 10:00 PM and with everyone working fourteen-hour days, I decide to keep working past everyone's 9:00 PM departure. The landing gear connection to the fuselage has been the Achilles heel for many of our recent versions of the jet, and I feel that I am closing in on the solution.

There are no overhead lights on in the vast drafting hall, just a few table lamps that highlight the rolls of drawings, the triangles, and moveable arms mounted on every table. All the other tables are empty of people but not their sheets or personal drafting instruments. I don't mind the solace for now since during the work day it is too noisy and distracting to concentrate. The slaps of my triangles on the vellum, the sharpening of my lead pencil and the moving up and down of the parallel ruler all sound much louder as they echo through the hall.

A shaft of light beams into the room as someone from the commissary enters, pushing a cart of beverages. At first, I just see the backlit figure of a woman with a halo of black hair.

I hear a female voice say with a strong Italian accent reaching out to me through the dark,

"Herr Engineer, would you like a tea and a biscuit for an evening snack?"

As she pulls into the umbra of my drafting table light, I see that it is Rosa Da Zara with her wavy hair gently bouncing on her shoulders out of her headscarf. As I look at her face more closely I can see a lack of expression. She seems leery of me and cautious of my reactions. As she approaches, her eyes narrow and he mouth remains tightly pursed.

"Why yes, I would like a cup and a biscuit. I am feeling a bit tired right now so thank you for coming out."

She approaches my drafting table and pours me a cup of tea. She places this on my layout table and then reaches into her cart for a selection of biscuits. She avoids any eye contact with me.

"*Grazie per il cibo. Un piacere*," I say to thank her for the food. She stops with her service and looks at me cautiously. Rosa then says in Italian, "I am only here to do my job. I don't speak to German men so please don't ask me for anything more beyond my food offerings.

"I was only complimenting you on your service *Signorina*."

"I've heard that many of the engineers here will take advantage of the camp women, so I am not taking my chances with anyone. Especially German men. Even if you can speak Italian."

"Well no, I am half Italian, *Signorina*, so I speak with sincerity toward you."

197

Rosa pulls back up straight, stiffens her back and continues looking at me through narrowed eyes. "Italian or German, you are here as a German working for this industrialist company. I am practically enslaved here by your company so why should I trust you?"

"My you are a feisty one. I hope you don't speak this way to the other German engineers here."

"No, I don't but I heard of you already through my father, so I know your sentiments and that I can be more forthright with you."

"I guess your father's reference to me was not that flattering then."

"Oh, they were fine, *Herr* Engineer. But I don't know if I should trust you nonetheless. Why don't you just leave me alone and I will continue doing my kitchen duties?"

"Very well *Signorina* Da Zara if that is what you want. But between you, your father and me, I am horrified to see Italians working here. I risk my own neck saying that to you, but I want you to know that it is safe to chat with me."

Rosa continues staring at me and then says,

"Look *Herr* Kindermann, I am a Jewish woman and from what I can tell, all you German men want to do is kill us off or take advantage of us women before you do the final deed. I don't know why my father trusts you or anyone at this camp."

"Perhaps because he can sense my Italian heritage makes me sympathetic to your situation? I say.

"You know sir; I am not sure what I dislike more about you," hisses Rosa. "That you are a German industrialist enslaving my father and me. Or that you are an Italian who has voluntarily come over to the German cause to do their bidding. Either one is not a pleasant or flattering one to you. Good night, *Herr* Kindermann."

Signorina Da Zara walks out of the hall toward the kitchen her heels making sharp taps on the floor.

I guess that did not go over as I thought it would. Nonetheless, inside I feel a push to move on as Vanessa had urged me. But right now, I feel like running back into Vanessa's arms and staying there forever.

JULY 1944

Doctor Da Zara and I decide to continue our working conversation over lunch, so we head over to the commissary. From a distance I see Rosa wearing her light blue serving frock and serving tables. Da Zara and I sit in a far corner of the dining hall away from anyone and continue our discussion about the rocket engine's forces on the fuselage structure. Rosa comes over to our table to serve us and greets her father.

"*Ciao babba, cosa disiderano per mangiare?*"

Leonino responds to her and says,

"*Mia figlia*, this is the gentlemen I mentioned to you that has family in Genoa. He speaks pretty good Italian, albeit with a slight Teutonic twist."

Rosa pours us glasses of water, "Yes, I had met him on the drafting floor the other evening. She avoids my glance and continues her service.

I pick up the conversation in Italian,

"Yes, in fact, a few nights ago, I had the pleasure of her serving me some tea and biscuits while no one else was left in the drafting hall. It was quite the night reprieve and it kept me focused for hours after that. Thank you for thinking to come out to serve me, Rosa."

Rosa does not respond to me.

"Then you know that my lovely daughter has an incredible skill for cooking," jumps in Leonino. "Although, she studied medicine to become a nurse before this whole war started. But I can see she is using her chemistry talents very well in this kitchen."

"I have tasted first hand her wonderful cooking skills," I say.

Rosa remains quiet, but her father continues and pulls her into our conversation further, "*Figlia*, I have been enjoying working with Armando over these last few weeks. He is quite the adroit designer, and I am enjoying hearing his tales of Italy. Remember that time you and I went to Milan one summer and we saw the Da Vinci sketches? Well, it turns out that Armando here was equally impressed with them. We are now sharing our commentaries on those intricate drawings." Rosa jumps in on that comment,

"*Si padre, mi ricordo tutto.* It was quite the trip, and his human anatomy drawings are why I went into medicine."

I chime in, "Well, his mechanical drawings are why I got into industrial design."

Leonino says, "Well, we all have one master in common. And it is not Jesus Christ, ha."

"Ah, you are funny Leonino," I say smiling at him. "I can see you are quite the daredevil not only with planes but also with social conventions."

"Ah, social conventions. *Putta di madre.* I've never conformed to them very well. I would say I am a bad Jew, not much for all those kosher laws. I mean really, I am a scientist, and everything has a rational basis behind it. Newtonian physics is what governs our world; it's what makes our planes fly per our design. *Si, e vero?*"

"Oh, I totally agree Dottore Da Zara. I would say I am a bad Catholic likewise in that I don't give much heed to those Papal decrees. My only God is physics, and he seems to rule us humans rather consistently with those laws."

Rosa drops off her food plates for us, turns to start walking away and then says over her shoulder, "Pity we have no opportunity to appreciate our shared visionaries while we are all segregated in our own camps."

She walks away with a soft sway of her hips, my eyes lingering a bit too long as Da Zara looks at me apologetically.

"*Che forte.* She is quite strong-headed and always says her mind. Just like her mother. Now I have a little remembrance of my wife always."

"So Dottore where is your wife? Did you leave her behind in Venice?

I see Da Zara's face turn from wistful to melancholic. "Ah, that my son, is not such a happy story."

He pauses, looks at his coffee cup and takes in a long breath, "My wife and the rest of our family were killed when their train was strafed by American fighter planes. They were on route to join Rosa and me in Milan, but they never made it. I was working at Fiat on Regia Aeronautica planes at the time when I heard of the tragic news."

"I can only imagine the pain Dottore. I am so sorry to hear that."

"No worry, Armando. Rosa and I make for a close family now. She is my living heritage, all that I have left now."

"Well, unfortunately, Dottore, that is one more thing we share in common. After losing my own wife, I struggle with how to express the loss of them in my day to day life. How do you honor them and hold on to a bit of them as you try to move on?"

"Armando, we must live on and enjoy what we have now. Don't you think so my young man? You are only, what, thirty-four? So much to live still. You know Jewish people have one thing going for us. We know how to thrive even after we've been brutally put down. This war too shall pass, and we will find our land of salvation. *Che fa.* Maybe someday you will come visit Rosa and me in Venice and enjoy some Pinot Grigio da Veneto."

"That is a nice idea, Dottore, and I will keep it in my mind as we work through these long evenings. So, tell me about how you got up here to work in Germany? You are Jewish, right?"

"Yes, but you must know that I have been a big supporter of Mussolini and the Fascist movement. Back in 1936 I wrote a book in support of Mussolini and his Fascist goals. So, I do have friends in high places, at least when Italy was totally under Fascist control. Right now, it is in a disarray, the southern side has switched over, and in the north, there are pockets of Fascist control. But this is typical Italian politics, a little messy to say the least and always in flux like a good salsa."

"Yes, I know. I keep track of Italian politics since I have family in Genoa. I even have a cousin who is a captain in the Army. Right now, though he is a prisoner of war working away at one of our Messerschmitt plants."

"Likely circumstances my young man. Strange things always happen to us Italians. Bizarre twists of fate, surreal passages of life, the world turned upside down. You know, little things like that."

"So Dottore, how did you end up supporting Mussolini?"

"Well, maybe you don't know this, but my father was a very wealthy landowner in the Veneto province. He was a Baron by land title and I used his money wisely. I invested much of my young fortune on airplanes. What could be wiser? Back when they were new and odd contraptions; no risk at all.

"Yes, I had heard that you had started up a flying club near Venice."

"Padua specifically, but close enough. Yes, I was quite the daredevil in my twenties. But back to Mussolini. During the Great War I had offered my land to the Italian government for use as an airbase. It was Italy's first airbase. Then during the War, I served in the Communication Corp at my airbase as a second Lieutenant. And from there the government was indebted to me. So, when I came out in support of Fascism and Mussolini, I was golden. And that is all it takes my son."

"Yes, maybe for you Dottore but I do not have a title, extensive landholdings nor a large family endowment."

"True, Armando and you are also not Jewish. Which in my case is a detriment at this point in my life. You know, I never determined if those wealthy, old money Venetians really liked me or whether they just liked my title, my money and my plane flying. Because at the heart of it, if I didn't have those, I would've been just a Jew who would was shunned by those old patriarchs. So I enjoyed flaunting my trappings and status in society at them."

"I gather that didn't fly with the National Socialists of Germany though?"

"No, now we are talking a different breed of fascists. They have one thing in mind and that is racial purity. No, when the RLM took effective control over Fiat in Milan, it was over for me. Fiat handed over all their engineers and technicians to work here in Germany. They were particularly interested in the jet aircraft that we had been working on. When the Germans figured out I was Jewish, however, Fiat managers and Regia Aeronautica generals had to step up to keep me alive. Thus, a diplomatic deal was struck, and I am now on a foreign guest worker pass. Fiat wants to make sure I come back alive.

"Fascinating and trying story Leonino. You are an interesting man and I hope your life's adventures keep continuing. Can I ask you something about your daughter?"

"And what would that be, Armando?" says Da Zara with his eyes narrowing.

"She seems very distrusting of us German engineering staff."

"Yes, she is a very cautious person given that Germans have rounded us up and forced us to work here," says Leonino.

"I can understand that, but would you let her know that I only have full sympathy for my brethren Italians stuck in this situation. Jewish and Catholic ones, regardless."

"Sure, Armando, I will pass that on to her. That's all you wanted me to tell her?"

"Well," I say as I reach into my shirt pocket, "I do have this token of my family heritage I want to give to both you and Rosa."

"And what would be that piece of heritage, Armando?"

"This is something that my mother gave me in 1938 right after Krystal Nacht. It's a mezuzah for you to place on your door post in normal times but for now keep it hidden. I thought you two could use the protection and remembrance of your Torah scriptures while you are held here."

"Armando," says Leonino, "that is very heartfelt of you. Are you sure you want to part with something your mother gifted you as a symbol of what I gather is your long, lost Jewish heritage?

"Yes, Leonino, from my mother's side. I can find no better place for this mezuzah than the temporary quarters that you and Rosa now find yourselves in. You need the protection and remembrance of who you are while you are so far from your land."

"Why that is very biblical of you, Armando. And I thought you were a bad Catholic, but I am impressed by your theological consideration of our plight. I am sure Rosa and I will find much comfort in having this hiding in our barracks somewhere. Thank you dearly my son." Leonino leans over the table and puts his hand around my neck and bows his head toward me. I bow my head as well in equal deference to him and our foreheads touch.

★★★

It is after 10 PM and I am in the drafting hall alone. The door opens from the commissary and this time I know who is approaching. Not knowing how she will react to me today, I decide to keep my tone and conversation down.

As Rosa approaches she says,

"Buona sera Signore Kindermann."

"Buona sera Signorina Da Zara. I appreciate you coming out this late."

"It's fine. Would you like a tea or coffee Signore?"

"I will take tea, please."

She then says in a half whisper, "Thank you for the mezuzah. That meant a lot to me and my father. I think I misjudged you earlier." She then looks down at her cart and says, "You know we have a few fruit tarts left over from Herr Messerschmitt's recent reception with the Luftwaffe. Would you like one of those instead of a biscuit?"

I am a state of reverie, half endless detailed thoughts the other half lulling off to sleep, but I respond to her,

"This is a real treat and *grazie per tutto*. It is just what I needed so I can keep going on this fuel tank design."

Rosa looks at me. "You do know your Italian well. When have you been there?"

"*Lei e justo.* You are right, I spent many summers there as a child. *La mia madre e Italiana.*"

Rosa's bright olive eyes widen slightly as if to look me over more carefully and then says,

"But I can see your father must be German then, eh?"

"Yes, he is. They live in Mainz, or what is left of it now. I've known of your father, Rosa, from before, and I am very impressed by what he did with the airplane club in Venice, Italy's first. I've been watching glider and plane shows since I was little. You never know when those childhood events can catapult you into one direction for the rest of your life."

Rosa responds, "He was very brave to do what he did and thank you for noticing. Why are you working so late Herr Kindermann?"

"Oh, I am just trying to resolve these fuel tank pumps. The engineering superintendent is all uptight about having me fix these as soon as I can."

"Well, then I better leave and let you get back to your work. *Un piacere conocerti.*"

And with that salutation Rosa pulls away, out of the light's penumbra, back into the darkness and through the light shaft upon which she entered. The great hall is quite and dark, but I feel an afterglow of warmth lingering in me. Feeling a mixture of excitement with tiredness, I wrap up my drawing materials and head back to the barracks for a night of sleep.

★★★

Like in a play that repeats itself night after night, I keep seeing Rosa each night in the drafting hall usually well after 9 PM. This is starting to become a regular event for me and I am enjoying chatting with her a little bit more each time. This night, Rosa approaches from the commissary and says,

"Signore Kindermann,"

"*Ciao signorina.* It's great that you work the late shift like me. Was that by accident or by design that you were put on this schedule?" I inquire.

"No, it is more my nature to be up late. My mind tends to be more active and creative late at night. So, this works out well for me. And I see it is the same for you, Signore Kindermann."

"Rosa, please you can call me Armand or even Armando if you like. My mother and Italian relatives call me by that."

Rosa reaches into her cart and puts out a teacup and a biscuit on my side table. I continue, "To be honest, I usually dislike being called 'Armando' by anyone except family members. You don't know what it's like growing up half Italian, half German, especially in Germany. As soon as school kids or university friends figured out that my mother spoke Italian to me they would make fun of it somehow. If they wanted to get at me all they had to do was to say, 'Armando' with an affected Italian accent. And then they would snicker. I knew they were just making fun of my mother's accent and how boyish it sounded to hear my name called out like that."

Rosa stands by my drafting table with a smile, her eyes beaming at me as if she is absorbing it all in.

"Oh please, Rosa, make yourself comfortable. Grab that stool over there and let's chat. I am almost done with this drawing."

"Well Armando, I don't want to get you in trouble," she says in a sing-song lilt that is both teasing with a hint of playfulness. "But at your invitation and approval, I won't say no. Besides, there is no one else back in the kitchen. The supervisor lady has gone to bed already, and I am left alone on clean-up."

Rosa takes a seat in front of my table and pours herself a cup of tea. "Well, you can imagine growing up Jewish in Italy had its awkward and confusing moments. Especially since my father, a Doctor of Science, was a modern, thinking man and he taught us children to have similar attitudes. So, living in the ghetto of Venice with all its kosher and rabbinical traditions could be quite suffocating and full of contradictions for my family."

"Ah, so you felt a little like an outsider within your own community?"

"Oh *si, certamente*. My father's liberal position on Judaism put him and our whole family at odds with the rabbinical society. I mean, what could they say about him flying bi-planes and creating flying clubs for all sort of *goyim* to join in."

"I am sorry Rosa but what does *goyim* mean?"

"You know, non-Jewish people, Christians, like yourself. I am sorry, it is a Hebrew word."

"I suppose, but I never thought of myself as predominately or singularly as a Christian. That's kind of a simplistic way to categorize our faith. Here in Germany, there are Catholics, and then there are Protestants. And the two don't really like each other much less appreciate each other's masses."

"I suppose but to me, it all seems to be the same religion. With your mother being Italian I suppose you are Catholic then?"

"You guessed right, but as I told your father, I am not a very strict one. In fact, I can't stand going to mass at all, and I only attend masses on major holidays like Christmas, Easter, and Lent."

"Ah, much like me. I only attend the High Holidays, Yom Kippur and Rosh Hashanah along with fasting for Passover. There is so much more to understanding God than just reading scriptures that he and our prophets left behind. We all have an adventure here on Earth to figure out what God and faith means. Sometimes those experiences do not adhere to any social conventions and they can involve great personal risks."

Rosa says this holding her teacup up to her mouth as her mouth breaks into a playful smile while her eyebrows dance upward for an added effect. I think to myself, we both have the same irreverence for religion.

We hear footsteps of someone in military boots coming toward the drafting Hall. We can see the shadow of a soldier with a rifle strapped over his shoulder walking into the room. Rosa stands up and acts busy with her cart and moves around plates from one level to the next, avoiding looking at me. The guard continues, his steps fading away until he turns out of the building.

I say in a whisper, "Alright, we are good now. Please sit down again. Where were we? Yes, you seem like a very playful and happy woman Rosa. How do you maintain that under these conditions?"

"I have not given over my mind or soul to anyone, no matter where they physically detain me. While I work away in the commissary, cooking, serving and cleaning, I just count my blessings that my father and I are still alive. And what better way to make people happy than to serve them good food along with a dash of happiness. Even though I don't care for the people I am serving."

"Nicely stated. I had no idea a cook could be so philosophical. I never think about my work as being happy per se, more that there is the satisfaction of creating something from your own vision."

"Well, it must be pretty engrossing as you seem to spend many hours here, Armando, more than most of the other engineers in Horgau."

"Thanks for noticing Rosa and I do appreciate your stopping by at such a late hour. You know on Sunday, my friend Walter Ignaz, and I take walks along the creek at the north edge of the camp. Maybe I will see you out there some Sunday?"

"*E possibile*. But shouldn't we be careful about talking in public, Herr Kindermann? I am a foreign guest worker who is Jewish, and I wouldn't want to get you in trouble."

"You are right. We will have to be discrete. Just slip me a note whenever you want to chat during our break time."

"*Molto buona, Armando*. It's been nice talking to you, and I will see you around for sure."

"*Buona notte Signorina, un piacere mio.*"

With that Rosa places the cups back in the cart, heads to the commissary and I start gathering my coat to head over to Barrack 19. As I walk back, my heart is all a flutter. I am starting to feel the impending flow of a river pushing its force of destiny washing me downstream.

★★★

Bonnie Colintroppo, from the university, is standing in front of me, chatting away about her Italian Nona. We are in a large hall with many people but they all seem faceless. The music being played is nondescript, more of a blur of sound. I reach out to Bonnie and ask her to dance with me and we walk to a dance floor that has magically appeared. What hall is this, some university building? As Bonnie and I stroll out together I see Vanessa walking toward me. I am startled and almost ashamed to be with Bonnie at this moment, but Vanessa continues walking up to us. Expecting Vanessa to be angry and to let me have it, I am surprised when she stops in front of us and looks at me calmly and says,

"Armand, you look so well dressed tonight and I am glad to see you enjoying yourself."

I say back with a tinge of guilt in my voice, "Vanessa, I didn't think you would come to this dance, but I am glad to see you too." Inside I feel the conflict in my heart knowing that I should have stayed focused on one woman over another. Vanessa continues with understanding and patience in her voice,

"And Bonnie, how are you doing?"

Bonnie also responds with some hesitation, "Ah, Vanessa. So happy to see you as well. We must chat afterward."

"No problem, we will work it out." says Vanessa in a soft yet flat tone. "I just wanted to let Armand know that it will all work out in the end." With that Vanessa approaches me, puts her arms around my shoulders and places a light kiss on my cheeks."

I reach out to pull her in as all my heart wants to hold her, caress her and make her mine. Why is she so detached yet understanding of me? A surge of anxiety rushes into me, I feel I can't breathe and this wakes me up from my dream state. I quickly sit up in my bunk bed gasping for air, my skin is soaking from sweat and my heart is aching to touch Vanessa. But I can't, she is gone. Awake but with all my bunkmates asleep, I am sitting up in the bed and I am overcome with grief. I start to sob softly, putting one hand wiping my brow and mumbling out,

"No God, no, I want to be with you and our children. I just can't keep going on. I feel so empty without you. Maybe I'd be better just dead myself? What's the point of living except for my nameless work?" I throw myself back onto the mattress and softly cry myself back to sleep.

AUGUST 1944

Walter and I take a walk into the pine forests on a trail that leads to the Aspenbach creek, the small stream that pours out of the surrounding hills. It is a pleasant, sunny August day and we are happy to know that the Me 262 is finally combat operational. We discuss how we've had this jet ready for two years and only now have we gotten the RLM's approval to put it into full production and assign them to fighter units such as Commando Nowotny's. More so, we are happy that this first fighting unit has made so many kills with the jet already, and we feel vindicated over all the doubts expressed about our designs.

As we continue our walk under the tall, thick array of pine trees, our lungs deeply breathe in the resin-scented air. The sky is blue, the clouds are puffy, and we feel the light crunch of the needles under our shoes. The Aspenbach is off to our left with the hills rising beyond the creek. It is nice to be here with Walter at this forest plant, our waldwerk, and we enjoy our few moments of free time.

After a few quiet paces with our heads down Walter asks me, "You know, Armand, I was wondering how you are dealing with the loss of your family? It must be hard and being your friend, I just thought I should let you know that you can talk about it to me anytime you need to."

"That's great of you to offer, Walter, and I appreciate it. Their deaths have cut me up like a sharp knife. At some point though, I must move on. So many other German civilians have lost families, and I know I am not the only one. But yes, it drags at me, and it gets me down often.

"There is no way I can replace them, and I just need time to heal. I am very grateful you are here, Walter, since you knew Vanessa and my children. It gives me a sense that you share in some of my sorrow, or at least comprehend its depth. Although, in the last few weeks I do feel a glimmer of relief and resolution inside, ever since the weather has turned nicer and perhaps from being here in the woods away from Augsburg. "

We walk a few more paces just hearing the crunch of pine needles beneath our feet.

"Luckily, we have our work," I say, "and every day my mental capacities are pushed to the limit. It is a good distraction now. Once I get on the drafting table and hold my pencils and triangles I can focus on, even dream about, how to make these planes better."

"Oh, Armand," says Walter, "you don't have to force yourself to move on and try to feel all good about things again. I know you generally are an optimistic and happy guy but give yourself some time. I will be there to help you out whenever you need it."

"Thanks, Walter but can I tell you something I almost feel ashamed about?

"Yes, what could that be, Armand?"

"Well," I hesitate, "there is a woman in the commissary. That has my attention in a strange way because for the first time in six months I felt something move inside me. It was a stirring that I wasn't expecting, but there it was deep in my chest. An attraction for another woman. Do you think it is disrespectful toward Vanessa for me to feel this way?"

"Armand, this war and the level of death has created a world of bizarre situations for all of us. The last five years have felt like ten, and I feel that much older. Who knows what is right or conventional anymore. It's all turned upside down. So maybe your attraction to another woman is perfectly normal in this abnormal world we are in."

"Thanks for your philosophical views Walter but I think you have just given me the confidence to go with what I am feeling inside."

We end our walk and head back to our barracks for an evening of reading our books.

★★★

The next Sunday, as Walter and I are on our pine forest stroll, we come across a group of women camp workers with blue scarves on their heads. It is composed of domestic women workers from the commissary, and as we quickly come upon them, we sound off a friendly group 'hello'. I notice that Rosa is in the group, and I catch her glance. She holds her gaze at me and beams a big smile. Inside I feel a buzz of warmth and before I know it, I am smiling just as broadly back to her. Not being able to contain myself I speak out in Italian to her,

"*Ciao signorina, bella giornata, no?*"

She responds back affirmatively and turns to a woman next to her with a cupped hand to her face and then seems to whisper hiding a big smile. We walk side by side along with the other women for just a few steps and then Rosa comments to me in a friendly tone, "*Si he un giorno bello per due.*"

As Walter and I pass the group, he turns to me and whispers, "What did you two just say to each other?"

"Nothing too unusual, just daily niceties. I told her it was a beautiful day, and she responded back that it was a beautiful day for two."

"I don't know, Armand, but that sounded a little flirty to me, on both your parts. You sure are putting your Italian to good use. But you better be careful, she is a camp worker, and she is Jewish. If party officials find out, they will have the SS out here to snatch you away, forever."

"Ok Walter, you are right. I need to be cautious, and I need your confidentiality. I feel I am falling for her, and I can't stop the momentum. If anything, it is gaining on us both. I can feel it, but it is also exciting to have someone be attracted to you. Besides, I am so lonely and distraught these days, this Rosa gal is the one bright spot in my daily life."

"Of course, Armand you have my complete confidence and I can see why you are falling for her. Let me guess; one, she is beautiful, two, she has a dark Mediterranean look that reminds you of your Italian roots and three, you two can speak away in your own language without most of us understanding. Great, you lovebirds are going to carry on this affair right in front of our noses at the commissary. Just keep the tone flat so people don't pick up on the emotional heat you two are kicking off."

"Well, it's not unheard of here for the engineering staff to be having dalliances with the camp workers. I know some of it is just playful fun or quick moments of sex."

Walter chuckles. "Oh yes. I am starting to pick up on where some of the fellows disappear to on Saturday nights. We are all caged up here like Roman legions in a foreign camp, and there are few German women here. We are far from home, locked up yet still feeling some desire in our bodies. In fact, the other day I was checking out a Greek worker myself, and I started having visions of her undressed. I know, I am feeling it, too."

"I know this stuff is going on but with Rosa this is different, Walter. Yes, I do feel a physical attraction for her, but it's deeper than that. We really do connect on so many levels. We can talk for hours, laugh and just smile into each other's eyes. I don't want to make this a one-night stand with a camp worker."

"Sounds like you are looking for a deeper connection, Armand or should I say Armando." He looks at me teasingly, his eyes laughing even more, making light of my desire to have a significant relationship with a woman. "Look, Armand, I am keeping things non-committal here. I haven't married yet, and I think it is an ideal situation to be in until this war is over. But if you want to entangle yourself with a woman whose situation is so untenable and so in flux, go ahead. Just be warned my friend, we don't know how this war is going to end much less where we are all going to end up."

"Ok, I've been warned by a sage greater than myself, Walter the Oracle. Should I take a number for your services? Ok, enough sharing with you. Let's finish up this walk and head back to the barracks for our books."

★★★

This Sunday afternoon, I decide to walk on my own around the pine forest path and head toward the Aspenbach creek. There I see the group of women from the commissary resting on the banks of the water. The area around the stream is open enough so that sunlight pours down on it in contrast to the surrounding dark forests. To the south of the Aspenbach the land is flat but to the north and away from our waldwerk, the hill slopes up gently. Like sentinels guarding the edge of the forest, the pines stand tall casting coolness and security onto all who walk under. The stream runs along at a slow pace, burbling as it splashes over a few rocks while eddies quietly spiral along the banks.

I hear the chatter of the ladies; Italians, Greeks or Romanians, and they have all seemed to have figured out how to communicate with one another. As I approach them, there are some quick glances between them and like a gust blowing flower petals away, they drop off their conversations and slowly scatter away. As the ladies part, Rosa is revealed still sitting on the banks of the Aspenbach. She is looking at me with a delightful and welcoming smile, her eyebrows lifting.

"*Signore Kindermann, viene qui,*" she shouts out to me in a playful manner while patting one hand down on the grass.

"*Certo Signorina Da Zara.* What a beautiful day and the creek is so tranquil looking. I'm sorry, I didn't mean to scare off your friends."

"Oh, don't worry about them. I am sure they will find another spot on the creek to catch up on the week's events. You know life in the commissary can be very interesting. We overhear all the talk by the chief engineers and Luftwaffe officers and from there we can piece together what is going on with the war."

"I am sure you are also homing in on other camp social matters as well," I say inquisitively as I have guessed the kitchen staff know everything about everybody in our waldwerk.

"Of course, Armando. We love to hear gossip, it's entertaining for us while we cook and clean. But news of the war is even more important for us. We all dream of going home someday and the sooner the better."

"Well, someday this will be over and sooner than we all think, I gather. I've been enjoying your coming by the drafting hall at night. Now I am staying late just to catch you for a tea and biscuit. You have permanently altered my work schedule."

"Sorry, I can have that effect on men."

"Oh, you do? Have you had some significant relationships in the past?"

"Well, sure, a few light-hearted ones and one very long-term one. I was engaged with another Venetian fellow, Jewish of course, when I was twenty-two. That was back in 1938 before all the anti-Semitic laws spread to Italy. We were in love in a youthful way, you know your first big romance, and you think this is it. Time to be a wife and mother now."

"What happened to that engagement?"

"Well, we didn't break it off on our own. His family left Italy to get away from the ongoing persecutions. One day I found out he was gone, no letter, no warning. He and his family had to keep everything quiet. They couldn't even tell me. I later learned they headed to South America, Bolivia I think."

"How sad, Rosa. You must've been heartbroken."

"I was very distraught, I was only twenty-two and the world seemed to have collapsed on me. But that was six years ago, and I've moved on. I had to accept what was dealt to me. And you know, I've become stronger because of it."

"I am impressed. You do come across as very focused yet you are also very content."

"I think I get that from my father. He is like the happy Geppetto, building more planes and whistling away while he works. But on my own I realized that the only way to get over the loss of my fiancé was to move on, be happy and connect to the people around me," as she says this she moves one arm toward to her domestic worker friends, now off in the distance.

"Sounds like you and your dad are a package deal then. Sorry if I am getting nosy Rosa but since your fiancé, have you been in other relationships?" I know this is pushing my boundaries, but something Italian in me needs to know.

Rosa looks at me, tilts her head to read the intent of this question. I am starting to regret that I asked it but she takes the question head on,

"Oh, there have been a few men since my engagement but nothing significant. Now I am here in this Horgau camp detained and with nowhere to go so what can I do?"

A pinching feeling of jealousy creeps up my belly, and I strain to put it down. I was married eleven years, eleven years of conjugation with an incredible woman, so whom I am to be jealous?

"Well, my former wife was my only experience with another woman. I was quite the studious mechanical engineer. Funny that I even ever got married since beforehand I was a no-date-wonder."

"You were just a boy then Armand, but now I can see a man before me. A man who knows what he wants, who knows where he is going and knows how to get there." Her eyes focus in on me, penetrating my inner thoughts. I blush a little as she has just given me a huge compliment.

I stutter a little, take a swallow and respond, "You know, in the last few years I do feel like a new person. I feel like an entirely different man from when I was twenty-three. In fact, I can hardly relate to the person who I was at that age. As a man, there is a meaningful threshold you pass somewhere around thirty years of age."

"And I see and sense it perfectly in you, Armando. You are perhaps more of a man than you realize right now."

She glances into my eyes, her head getting closer to me. This woman is six years younger than me, yet she can read me perfectly. She is tuned in with my inner soul's development. How did this happen? I am the 'older' man here, but Rosa seems so much wiser and more perceptive than me.

"Tell me how you got here, Armando, at this Messerschmitt company? Why didn't you seek to come to Italy and work for Fiat like my father?"

"I entered the commercial aviation field because I wanted to design passenger planes. Ones that were fast and large, beyond what was currently being offered. It all seemed so possible and likely to happen. But over the years Messerschmitt AG had morphed into a military plane company, and here I am, head of the production engineering section for fighter jets. I was a boy really when I started here, and now as a man I am intrinsically wrapped up in the fate of the Luftwaffe's effort to stop the Allied air bombing campaign. And nothing against your father and Fiat but the Messerschmitt company is open for dreams, and they accomplish them."

"No, I take no offense to that, Armando. Papa complained all the time about how ineffective Fiat's plane division was. It was almost like they really didn't want to help with the war or the German cause. A bit of a subconscious resistance on all their parts. I think even initially many Italians had second thoughts about us allying with Germany. We are just such different people at the heart of the matter." As Rosa finishes this sentence, we hear a group of engineers coming down the path and Rosa, and I exchange one last long look with smiles on our faces.

"Well, we better stop here. How about you go catch up with your friends, and we chat later?"

"*Si Armando. Dovremmo incontrare piu tardi,*" she says with her olive-colored eyes looking playful and inviting, her smile turning sharply upward. "Hopefully we can make some more private time together," she says as she picks herself up off the bank and walks along the path to catch up with her group.

I am left there having to say usual niceties to the passing engineers while my heart simmers over what we have just discussed.

As Rosa said, Germans and Italians are such different people yet here I am, a blend of the two. At times, I look at my fellow Germans and question why they don't just take it easier and enjoy life as it happens. On the other hand, I look at my Italian relatives and wonder why they can't be more organized and productive with their time. It's like I see the faults of each people and in me, I see a bit of both their traits.

★★★

It is Saturday night and outside of the commissary, a make-shift Biergarten has been set up by the workers. What else are 300 men to do on a weekend night after long weeks of drawing over a table? Tivoli lights have been strung around the edges of the garden casting a yellowish glow out to the surrounding barracks and bordering pine trees. Picnic tables are lined up in rows for seating within a roped fence; Germans like to define the area of where conviviality can happen. A small platform acts as a band stage, and an older gentleman plays the accordion. A crude bar has been set up to serve beer and steins are lined in rows ready to be filled. Camp kitchen staff are assigned to work as beer tenderers for us.

A good number of the staff are out here enjoying the warm August evening. We hear the welcome news that the Me 262 is being deployed to new fighter groups and that they are quickly seizing the air war. There are toasts made to Major Nowotny and his Commando unit for knocking down so many B-24s and Mustangs in just one week. More toasts go out to our fearless General Galland, the real leader of the Luftwaffe in our minds. Talk goes around how stunning the jet is performing and how maybe we can stem the attacks of the heavy bombers in short order. But as the evening pours on with the beer, talk of the war stops and everyone turns to light-hearted jokes, jabs, and incidences of the week.

I sit with Walter and Wolfgang drinking a beer and think that there is so little time to be lazy at this waldwerk. We work fourteen hours a day, six days a week so this is precious lazy time, and I am going to enjoy it. Walter tells me of his last weekend when he had leave to go to Munich and stay by the University. He says that half the University has been bombed away and that they are still teaching classes, but many are being held in makeshift shacks. Nonetheless, in good German form, the Hoffgarten still had its Biergarten up and running with many Fräuleins added to the mix.

As the commissary staff man the beer and food service for us and I notice Rosa amongst them. She is carrying steins and pretzels out to the men seated at tables. She is dodging her way around the tables carrying heavy loads while deftly swaying her hips around benches and the edges of tables. We call over for another round and Rosa walks over giving me a restrained look of warmth in her countenance. We order some steins and after she takes off, Walter turns to me and says,

"She's looking rather lovely tonight, Armand, and I caught that second-too long gaze she gave you. Maybe this will be the night you too hit off for real. I am getting tired of all this romantic talk of sweet walks and chats. Come on, Armand, that doesn't make for great chit-chat at the pub the next day."

"How many beers have you already had, Walter? The world of women is not all about just having a quick roll in the hay. There are so many more dimensions to appreciating a woman. You are just stuck in the first dimension, ha."

Walter slumps back staring into his stein. "Well actually last week in Munich produced nothing, nor did the previous weekend. I think I am on a dry spell. So, tell me, Armand, what am I missing out on by taking it slowly with a woman?"

"A lot, Walter. And it takes years of being with one to appreciate them. But anyway, I don't need to lecture you my friend. I think you could help me tonight and provide me some cover. Yesterday at breakfast Rosa left me a note stating she is waiting for our next moment together. When that is, I don't know but tonight may be the night."

"Alright, Armand, now you are talking. I would be glad to help out."

"Ok, Walter, if I 'disappear' this evening or don't come back to the barracks till late at night just tell everyone that I was feeling lonely and went for a long walk."

"Yes, a long walk and you were feeling lonely. Sure, friend, whatever you would like me to say. I will cover for you. Don't worry, Armand. You won't be the only man staying out late for a 'lonely' walk tonight."

As we 'prost' out steins together Rosa comes over to our picnic table and drops off our pretzels. She gives me a quick glance and then looks down at the pretzel with her brows popping up quickly. Once she leaves, I look to my sides to see if anyone is looking and I lift the pretzel slowly. Sure enough, underneath there is a note folded up. I unfold it and read what it says, in Italian. 'Meet me behind the Commissary at 10 PM'. I fold the note up quickly and stuff it in my pocket and then pick up on the conversation going on at the table. I have half an hour, and then it will be time to make my break.

At 10 PM I tell Walter that I feel like being 'alone' now and will go for a contemplative walk. Walter winks his eyes at me and salutes me off. I walk a good 100 yards from the Biergarten and then as the Tivoli lights become faint, I dodge behind a barrack out of site from everyone. I walk with assured steps toward the rear of the commissary, and as I approach it I see Rosa standing beside a tree, her large eyes glistening in the moonlight. I walk up to her, look her in the eyes and then without any preamble, I kiss her lips, first gently but as she opens them more, my kissing turns into a hungry search.

Rosa pulls back and whispers, "That was just what I wanted from you, Armando. But don't you think we should move further away from the camp?"

At this point my heart is full steam ahead and her words of caution break me from my reverie.

"Oh, yes. Come with me. We will head toward the Aspenbach."

I grab Rosa's hand and off we run at a quick pace, her skirt flowing with the wind. In a few minutes, we are close enough to the Aspenbach, close enough to hear the water streaming by. Rosa puts her back to a pine tree placing one foot on the trunk while kicking out a knee toward me. Her hands are behind her back as she teases me to come get her. I oblige and step toward her. As I do, I place her chin in my hands and lift her head up and we look deeply into each other's eyes. Her eyes are longing, expansive and glassy with emotion. I feel her breath starting to become deeper and her body quivers. I place my lips on hers and we start to kiss deeply. I clasp her right hand, our palms facing each other, and I can feel the softness of her fingers. I place my other hand around the small of her back and pull her body in closer to mine. Her breasts touch my chest and I can feel her breathing rising to meet my body. Rosa takes deep gasps between our long kisses; a slight moan rises from her chest as her upper body starts to sway her head turning, changing our kissing position.

Rosa pushes her breasts against my chest, her back arching forward as she drops her foot from the trunk letting me press my hips close into hers. My legs sense her curves and she allows me to press into her inner soft thighs. I drape my free hand down the sides of her hips and then I move them over to the top of her buttocks. They are smooth, firm and full of feminine grace. I move my hand slowly up her back and forward to her front just below her breasts. They are heaving, desiring to be touched but I resist for now. Rosa continues kissing me, her breath getting stronger and faster. She stops, pulls away from my lips and looks at me her eyes focused on only me as if I meant everything to in her at this moment. With her lips pouty and her mouth slightly open, Rosa exclaims in a whisper,

"Take me now. I want you here. I want to know you as a man."

A surge of excitement rushes into me with her assured request. We drop to our knees and I take off my shirt and place it over the pine needles covering the forest floor. Upon placing my shirt down, we continue kissing with even more eagerness and animal lust than before. Rosa paws my chest and strokes my back digging all her fingers into ever muscle fiber.

I decide to let the joy and sensuality of kissing play out for a little longer and I pull away, stroke her face, lightly kiss her cheeks, then her earlobes, gently stroke her eyebrows with the edges of my lips and then nibble on her lips. Finally, I plunge forward with a deep, hard kiss giving me the feeling that our souls have touched and are merging into one. It is as if we have come to an oasis and the water of life has just been given to us thirsty, wayward souls.

I wrap both my arms around her waist and Rosa exhales, her breast heaving deeply with anticipation. I know I cannot let us wait any longer and I start to unbutton her smock, undraping her. I see her slender yet curvaceous body glistening in the moonlight. While still on our knees still we continue kissing but we mutually finish undressing each other by sliding off our undergarments.

Rosa leans back on my shirt and the bed of pines while I gently place my body over hers. I feel the full length of her beautiful soft body under mine and I have the urge to cover her with my kisses and bless her with my passion. I have never felt such wild, animalistic passion for a woman before. She is having a magical effect on me, releasing all my inhibitions, sadness and remorse and converting them into pure energetic, sensuality.

We embrace, she opens, I penetrate, we merge, we mesh, we move, she arches in pleasure and then, I seismically release. We lay on the ground embracing, sweating, deeply breathing, my cheeks are flushed, hers are hot. We are peaceful, just sensing each other's heartbeat, feeling our breath brush by each other sensitive cheeks. This exquisite moment of pleasure and the languid after-moment feels like the brink of infinity, a pool stretching out to the horizon. It is full of life's dimensions, energy, replenishment and with a vibrant connection to each other's soul. I have found her, she has found me. And we are in the middle of a forest.

SEPTEMBER 1944

It is Sunday morning. I awake in the barrack and I feel peaceful and revived. Rosa and I have met again on a Saturday night after an another Biergarten event and it seems we have found the perfect downtime from watchful eyes. Feeling awake and satisfied, I get up and prepare for my day's walk with Walter.

As Walter and I walk through the pines we come across the commissary women and there is Rosa. I look at her and she looks back with some shyness today, but I can tell it is an 'I am fine' look. The group of women get up and join in for a walk with us and then Rosa and I pull off to the side to be alone.

"*Buon giorno bella*. You look so beautiful today and your smile is sparkling." I say to Rosa.

"*Grazie Armando*. I think you are making me feel more beautiful than usual."

"I believe the pleasure is mine Signorina. Or should I call you *Principessa?*" I say with a broad smile and stare into her eyes.

"Of course, I am a *Principessa*. I was wondering how long it would take for you to realize that," says Rosa with playful indignation.

As Rosa and I stroll amongst the pines, I ask her more questions about life in Italy and how had it been for the last five years.

"To be honest there had been minimal war activity in Venice. We cannot understand it but we are happy nonetheless. There have been no attacks, shellings, air raids, nothing. Unlike in Rome and Florence."

"What about the treatment of the Jews in Venice? Were people being rounded up and in imprisoned?"

"I heard that was the case in Florence and Rome but only after 1943 when we capitulated back to the Allies. However, in Venice there has been little persecution of the Jews. Perhaps because there are so many Jews in the city or perhaps because the Italians there are not cooperating with the German Army."

"After the Roman government changed sides, the fascists in the north set up a government that is cooperating with the Germans. They are freely consenting to hand over their engineering talent whenever Germany requests such. This includes the Milan Fiat plant and design staff where my father had been working at up until earlier this year."

"Hadn't Mussolini purged Jewish engineers like we Germans have done already?" I inquire.

"No, Mussolini did not do so, initially, only when the Germans demanded it did he. And while we are technically on guest worker passes, with the war deteriorating we are concerned that our status will not hold up. It all depends on how ardent and thorough the SS becomes."

December 1944

I slip out of my bunk and look at my watch. It is almost midnight, our agreed upon meeting time and I put on my jacket. With the colder weather, Rosa and I have found a storage room in the commissary that is solely used by the kitchen staff. From Rosa's barracks there is a connecting corridor allowing the domestic staff to directly enter the commissary. In there we have set up our trysting place, our magical getaway spot where we are bothered by no one, can forget our work burdens and indulge in each other's minds and bodies.

As I walk into the service door of the commissary, I look around to see if any guards are watching. All quiet and I see no one walking around. I approach the storage room and give a four-knock signal, but nobody responds so I enter in and wait for Rosa. Within five minutes I hear Rosa's knock and she enters in with her eyes looking straight at me. Under her winter coat she is wearing something non-staff issued. It's a simple dress and she is wearing some shoes with heels as well.

We embrace and give each other a long kiss. How I love to feel her body in my arms, she grows more beautiful with each passing day. As we kiss, I feel connected to her and emotionally fulfilled. Rosa seems both happy and relieved to be with me as she strokes the back of my neck and firming her kisses on me.

A cot is set up in the back and we lie down together without taking our clothes off. We are so excited to be with each other we are just content to be united physically. Throughout our long work days, we must act nonchalant toward each other, it's a game we play in public knowing that later at night we will be able to express our full emotions to each other.

We undress and slip under the covers and start to indulge in caressing and kissing each other's bodies. After these long, regimented workdays, it is a delight to relieve this stress with our intimate touches. Our sensuality bonds the emotional depth of our relationship. We have moved into a deeper relationship, one where we freely share our thoughts, bodies, wishes and dreams.

Following our intimate time together our bodies beautifully collapse into each other and we doze off for a few minutes. While I am partially awake, I decide to let us linger in this peaceful state. Upon stirring some, Rosa turns to me and whispers with her eyes still closed, "Armando, that was beautiful. I love how your body feels against mine."

"Rosa dear, yours is even more beautiful than my words can express. Your beauty transcends my whole body."

"You have such a way of making me feel complete and at peace, Armando. When this war is over I must bring you to Venice. Have you ever been to the Venetian Carnival?

"No dear, I have not. Am I missing much?"

Rosa slides off my chest and we face each other on our shoulders, our legs intertwined, our feet lazily stroke the others'. Rosa opens her eyes and she says with some awakening energy, "*Oh si, certamente.* The procession of the boats and gondolas is a spectacle of lights, decorations with all Venetian society dressed in their gayest of costumes. Although, some costumes can be rather dark, devilish and sinfully playful. There are also long parades through the winding streets ending in the Piazza San Marco. Finally, in the evening there are various costume balls, one for each society."

"Did you go to these masquerade balls and get all costumed up?

"I did. As my father was a reformed Jew, a Baron and a local aviation celebrity, he freely engaged in many of these Venetian societies. So, he encouraged me to act as full citizen of Venice and to readily partake in the festivities. Besides, our Purim is closely related to the Carnival. Some historians think that that the whole Venetian Carnival came from Syrian Jews who migrated to Venice over a thousand years ago. I mean, don't you find it odd that Purim and Carnival occur so closely?"

"Well maybe much the same way that Passover and Easter are so close on the calendar. There is always that uncomfortable evidence that our two religions have vestiges of the other's past. Maybe Venice is why you are so playful."

"Perhaps it is. Your city's character can have a big impact on your own. I remember going to a Carnival ball in my early twenties dressed as a unicorn. You know that magical character? I had feathers down my back as the horse's mane and above my mask, I had a paper Mache horn that was painted with gold and silver swirls. It was quite the attention-getting accessory." Rosa mimics a unicorn by placing her hand with a finger extended from her forehead. She then prods her 'unicorn' toward me and swishes her hair around my face.

"You make for a mischievous unicorn. I bet you garnered the attention of many men that night."

"That is how I met my fiancé, the night of the Carnival Masquerade Ball. I was being very flirtatious and being a masked ball, I played out my character without any social concern. You know, I really enjoyed being a unicorn. If I liked a man, I just dipped my head slightly and then tossed my horn to and fro. I think they got the idea quickly."

"It does seem that Italians do love a good masquerade. Maybe because it allows them to take on another character beyond the one they are confined to in life."

"I'd say it's more that Italians" she says, "appreciate the bizarre, the surreal but all in good fashion."

"So, the masquerade led to meeting your fiancé?"

226

"Yes, I was dancing and chatting with various men that night, but he caught my attention with his Ottoman soldier outfit. He wore a flowing robe, scabbard, sandals and a turban for a headdress. It was all very dashing looking. "

Looking off in the distant Rosa then focuses back at me and she changes her line of thought, maybe to move away from where this is story leading to.

"So, is there something like a Carnival in Mainz where you grew up?"

"Oh, yes. Our *Fastnacht* is a five-month celebration. We can't get enough of it.

"Armando, you know where I've always wanted to visit with a lover?"

"No darling, tell me."

"I've always been fascinated by the city of Verona and the operas performed in the old Roman stadium. I've heard that they've been performing opera and theater performances in that ancient stadium for over three-hundred years. People have told me that the sound quality of the opera is fantastic and that they have some of the best opera singers in all of Italy."

"I have been to Verona, Rosa and I would love to take you to the opera. There is a beautiful town center, the Piazza Ebro, where there is a quaint trattoria serving the best in Veronan foods and wines. You know in that Piazza there is a Venetian winged-bull statue on a tall column. Long ago the Venetians took control over the Verona kingdom and they didn't want the locals to forget about it."

"Ah, so you know the city very well. You would make my perfect tour guide. I like it when a man knows what he is doing and can show me around. If you haven't figured out Armando, I like it when the man plays the role of a gentleman and treats a woman like a *Principessa*. When I was little I dreamed of being a *Principessa* and you know, even though I am twenty-eight I still want to be treated like one."

"Then I will take you to Verona in my coach and I provide my *Principessa*, a grand tour of the city. Another beautiful point in Verona is the panoramic view from the old Castel San Pietro. From there you can see the River Adige and look over all the spires of the city. And down below, you can overlook Ponte Pietra, an ancient Roman bridge which spans the river. Last time I was there, I took my sketchbook and created various scenes of the piazzas, bridges and castellos"

"I would like that very much. You would be my perfect gentleman to escort me. The two of us sightseeing, watching the opera, dining with Soave wine and you sketching scenes of the city. Would you draw me into your sketches?"

"I am not that good at drawing people. So, if you don't mind looking like a mannequin, then I would happily model you into the sketches. You would be the fashionable lady shopping to her heart's content."

"You missed one other cultural treasure in Verona."

"Oh, and what is that my *Principessa*?"

"It is the legendary home of Shakespeare's Romeo and Juliet."

"Ah, yes, you are right dear. But they are just legendary, they are fictional characters made up by a writer. I did see the Juliet house and they have 'identified' a balcony where Romeo comes to woo her. But I didn't give it much cultural importance."

"Legendary or not, it is a beautiful story and so romantic. I want to see Juliet's balcony with you. I will stand under the balcony and call out for my Armando. And then you will leap out in your prince outfit and whisk me away."

"Yes, and I will take you away from your Capulet family and I will abdicate my place with the Montague family. From there we will establish our Barony, the Kindermann-Da Zara fiefdom. A place where we will tend vineyards, cook wonderful meals for our guests and set up a school for the arts. Sounds like a great place, I want to move there now."

"Yes, let's go now," whispers Rosa as she puts both hands on my chest as if to push her demand onto me.

We hear a truck rumble by and then the sound of delivery crews speaking to each other. They are dropping off foodstuffs for the commissary. Like a stone plopping into a placid pond, we are awoken

228

from our reverie, our night-time daydreaming evaporates into thin air. Our ephemeral adventure wanes and we start to focus on this reality. The harsh situation of where we are and our confined quarters.

Rosa shifts to a more realistic and sad tone, "I am tired of this war. I want to get back to Venice and continue my life."

"Well, I don't think this war will last beyond next summer, another six months and the Americans or the Russians will sweep over our land. Then we can make plans to be together in a full, public relationship."

"The sooner they come the better. Then they will liberate us from your Messerschmitt AG 'employment'."

Rosa's words sting as she ties culpability of her forced labor upon my company, the one that has brought me so far in life. I so want to liberate Rosa, her father and all the Italians being kept here under my Government's will. But at the same time, I am desperately working to produce the next fighter interceptor that will halt or slow down the bombing campaign.

"It wasn't my idea to enslave people from all over Europe. I detest it, love. How could I? I am half-Italian and it pains me to see what my government has done. But I am caught up in it much the same way your father has been roped into producing rocket fighter jets. We are all following along like cogs in this war machine. So yes, while I am working away in this waldwerk, living in a barrack under some sort of military rule, I do cheer when we knock down those Liberator bombers. And yes, I do lament the death of our pilots knowing that they are facing tremendous odds against the Allied fleets."

"But Armando, it is one thing to have to do your work, like I do here. It is another to have your heart and soul in the cause behind this all. Where do you stand on this dear?"

I pause and think this out carefully. This is the crux of the matter behind all of us Germans fighting in this long, drawn-out war. Are we working so hard to continue the Reich's political goals or are we doing this for our fellow countrymen before we are blasted off the map of Europe? I finally say to Rosa,

"My love, I am fulfilling my job and I am doing this to protect my fellow countrymen. Damn the National Socialists and their goal of German living space. I only dream of a day where you and I can freely move between borders and live both in Italy and Germany."

"I understand, dear. Sorry to have pressed you. I am just impatient with the situation. I love our moments together and I think I let my feelings run away with the thought of us being together after the war is over."

"I know my dear, I have been thinking about what happens to us after the war is over. I have fallen for you and I want very much to continue our relationship beyond all this. I see a beautiful future for us and I want to do everything to make it happen."

"It is all so unknown," says Rosa softly. "How the war will end and what will become of us camp workers. I think it will be a mess; people trying to get back to their home countries while foreign soldiers occupy our countries. But I am willing to make it work, Armando. We have something special."

Changing tone, Rosa then looks at me more seriously and asks, "So, are you fully over your past wife, Vanessa? It's only been nine months since she has passed away. Are you going a little too fast by jumping into this relationship with me? I am just being realistic, dear. Maybe I am filling an empty hole in your heart and it's not so much about me?"

Rosa does have a point. Maybe my love is lust that placates the pain of losing Vanessa. But it just doesn't feel that way. I know in my core this real, intrinsic and that there are strong roots growing between us. I say with honesty,

"I did love my Vanessa and I will always hold her in a sacred part of my heart. She was my first and only love to that point. But the war has dragged on, my work demands have increased and I am faced with the reality of having to move forward. No Rosa, I will never un-love Vanessa and I am sorry to say that. But if you could understand that and live with this intrusion in our relationship, I would deeply appreciate it. I am ready to move on and I am ready to love you fully."

Rosa strokes the back of my neck as I say this. "I am ready for this, Armando, ready for us. You understand and accept my past fiancé and I understand and accept your Vanessa. I believe our hearts will be in balance like on the scales of classical Greek times."

Relieved and impressed at her wisdom, I pull her in closer, pressing my chest against hers and give her a long, searching kiss.

January 1945

As I walk toward Gerhard Coulis Superintendent's office, I grasp his hand-written memo in my hand and look at it again, 'Please report to my office first thing in the workday. I have an urgent matter to speak about with you.' My heart is beating a bit faster now and I start fretting over what could be so critical for Gerhard to talk with me right away? As I pull into his office, he has me sit down in front of his large desk. Gerhard starts off,

"Armand, you are in serious trouble." He looks me straight in the eyes, his face looking dark and agitated.

"How so sir?"

"There are reports and rumors surfacing that you are carrying on an affair with a camp worker. And some indicate that the woman is Jewish."

A swell of icy anxiety swells down to the pit of my chest. "I don't know what you are referring to."

"Oh, come on. I know many of the engineers are running off with the camp workers for a tryst or two. But our Reich laws being clear, no relations with Jewish women are allowed."

"How can our laws govern who you love?"

"Look, I want to help you on this one. I can't lose you to an execution wall or being thrown off to the front lines for this indiscretion. But, with your past request to see an Italian prisoner of war, the SS have you pegged already as unfaithful to the purity laws. Or worse yet, that your Italian side of you demerits you being a trustworthy and loyal citizen of Germany. "

"Ok, Gerhard, I admit I am in a relationship with a camp worker. I don't think it has affected my job performance in Horgau. If anything, she has uplifted my soul and given me much needed solace from the loss of my wife and children."

"I was figuring that. Look, you are a decent man and in all your years at Messerschmitt you have always put the company first. But this is why I am concerned. I need you here. If you get ratted out and reported to the SS, they will drag you from Horgau and you will not be the same man when they are done with you, dead or alive."

"I am sorry, but I love this woman. What do you expect me to do? Deny myself this one thing I have left in my life, the one thing that has given me my humanity back?"

"Alright, let's be reasonable. I have a plan in mind. You may not like it, but it could save your lover's life."

"That is gracious of you Gerhard. What do you have in mind?"

"Well, we all know the state of the War is precarious. The Allies just broke through in northern France, they are also halfway up the Italian peninsula and the Russians have crossed the Danube River. Even our foreign guest workers are not renewing their work contracts and each week slave workers are escaping by the dozens. It's going to get crazy here with the SS guards trying to control their concentration camp and forced laborers. I suspect some of them will start carrying out their ultimate solution on the Jewish people, guest worker passes or not."

"So, you are suggesting they get out of here now before we implode? How would they do that?"

"Yes, I think they should get out of here and soon. If they want to live to see Italy again, now would be a good time to escape Horgau."

The thought of helping Rosa and Leonino escape is like cutting off my hand to spite myself. But maybe Coulis has a good point. This may be the only long-term way to save our relationship.

Gerhard continues, "Now I didn't say this to you, Armand, but there is quite an active smuggler's network around Bavaria and I've noted that they have been good at getting people to the Swiss border. I would start with our food transporters as I suspect they work with sympathetic farmers and warehousing groups."

I stand up. "Alright, I appreciate your understanding and your recommended action. Thanks, and I will take an appropriate course."

★★★

It is late Saturday, almost midnight, and Rosa and I are lying in the cot nestled away in the commissary storage. It is well past one in the morning and we decide it best to start dressing. As we get our clothes on, I approach Rosa with my plan,

"Rosa, I am concerned for you and your father's safety. I've heard talk about that in places, where the Allies have broken through, that the SS are killing off the Jewish workers and concentration camp prisoners."

"Yes Armando, the talk in the commissary is that the German Army is collapsing into their borders. It is not safe for my father and me. Diplomatic agreement or not with Socialist Italy, I don't think the guards will care. Besides, the northern fascist government of Italy, which set up our guest worker passes, is now politically defunct."

"As much as I love you and love having you here, it is better for your safety if you flee from this waldwerk."

"I know. Father thinks the same. But how would we do this? We would need some outside help; that is, local Germans who are willing to smuggle us across the border."

"I could find some for you. I have a friend in transportation and he told me that there are local truckers and farmers who are assisting in this. We just need to get word and we could arrange a surreptitious rendezvous."

"Are these people we can depend on? And what if we get caught at some checkpoint?"

"It is dangerous my dear, but I believe it is worth the risk. Getting you as far away from the SS guards as possible is most important thing. At this point they have not marked you with Stars of David armbands and you do still have your guest worker visas."

233

"No, I agree, Armando. It is far riskier to stay here with a squadron of SS guards as the army collapses. It could be hell here for us Jews."

"Good, so you think that I should set this up for you?"

"Yes, please go ahead," says Rosa.

"I think we could get one of the commissary food suppliers to load you into one of their food trucks. They typically deliver well past midnight when there are few guards or any staff around. From there they would relay you through various other sympathetic suppliers. I will check around with my close friends in plant administration. The administrative staff know you are guest workers and I could persuade one of them to help me uphold our obligation to Italy for you."

"Oh, Armando, but then we will be separated. And who knows when we will see each other again."

"I know my, *Principessa* but I am concerned about you and your father surviving this collapse alive. We can always search and find each other after there is order again. I will look for you, I promise."

"But, you don't even know what will happen to yourself. If the Americans sweep into Bavaria, their number one target will be the Messerschmitt plants. They've already targeted them for air raids. And anyone associated with Messerschmitt planes will surely be of interest to them."

"Oh, I wouldn't worry about that my dear. I am too low of management level to be of interest to them. I am confident I will be working in this plant to the very end. They may want to chat with me for a little, but I am sure they will just leave me alone."

"It is all very uncertain. How my father and I will make it out of Germany, how we get back to Italy and what happens to you in the next few months. I pray we will be reunited again. For now, I agree we should get smuggled out of here. After that we can deal with the next steps in our lives."

"I love you Rosa. You mean the world to me. I will miss you terribly. To think I am actively sending you off far away from me into an uncertain future."

"Let's think positively, Armando. Visualize that you and I will be together after the war settles down."

Rosa pulls me in close to her and she presses her face against my chest. I stroke her curly flowing hair, close my eyes and for once I feel a prayer emanating out from my soul to our almighty. Who else can I pray to at this point? Germany is about to collapse, and it is evident to every employee, every common folk and even the camp workers. But our agreed plan must go ahead, and I will be sending off Rosa to safety and to our separation.

★★★

I check my wristwatch and it seems that midnight cannot come any faster. I turn to Leonino and Rosa who are with me in the commissary pantry. It is dark in the room and the Da Zara's have small packs next to them, ready for their travels. I then run through a checklist,

"Alright, the first truck will take you west along the road toward Leipheim," I say. "There you will stay in a beer barrel maker's shed in the upper loft. From there the barrel maker will take you toward Stuggart for further instructions on your travels."

Leonino and Rosa look serious and quietly listen to me. They are relying on my plan and the consequences of messing up this escape could cost them their lives and my heart.

Leonino speaks, "Armando, thank you for what you are doing. But don't worry so much about us. You know Jews have survived many calamities. It is in our nature to be resilient. We thrive through adversity."

"Thank you for trying to take the pressure off me. Once you leave though, the pressure will be on yourselves to survive."

"Armando, you must look at this more philosophically. Who shall live and who shall die is all written in the Book of Life. We are just playing out our parts till the book hits us on the head."

I approach Leonino and give him an embrace, "Thank you Leonino for all your companionship and encouragement to date." I then turn to Rosa and put my arms around her waist. We look each other in the eyes and then embrace our cheeks pressed together and our hands clasped. Rosa looks at me,

"I believe in us, Armando. I believe in the love you and I started here. It will take us beyond this war, beyond the imprisonment we are both in."

"Yes, your love has made me whole again, Rosa. I can't express how much you have meant to me. In a strange way, you have come into my life at the right time."

"I believe we were meant to be," says Rosa. "Whether in this forest or in another time. We are timeless together."

"Yes, my love, you have my soul in your heart and I will be with you throughout your travels." With that we kiss, our hands still clasped together, and we take in a deep breath, our souls intermingling with this breath of air.

We finish this deep breath together, our eyes closed in thought. We then hear the crunching sound of a truck pulling up to the loading door. As we had practiced earlier, Leonino and Rosa hide in large crates of straw. I take one last look at Rosa, give her a quick kiss and then I embrace Leonino much like a son embraces his father.

They work their way under the straw with my help. The truck driver enters and asks if the moon is full and I respond, "It's only a waxing gibbous moon tonight."

He nods, understanding my pass and gets to work, loading up the crates onto the truck bed. The truck then pulls away into the darkness of the pine forest. Now for the first time, these pine trees feel like gate posts to a prison. A prison I didn't know I drew myself into.

★★★

Gerhard comes to my drafting and hurriedly says in a low tone, "Meet me in the bathroom one minute after I walk away." Coulis says this without looking at me the whole time and then promptly walks away. I look side to side to see if someone is watching or following him. Seeing none I get up and walk to the bathroom where I find an apprehensive Gerhard.

"The local Party leaders are here to investigate the escape of the Da Zara's. You are not to say anything about our discussion, understood?"

"Most certainly, Gerhard. You entrusted in me a plan and I will in no way break your confidence."

"Fine. If they interrogate you, keep a poker-face. Remember, I was away in Augsburg at the time and you were in Lager Lechfeld checking out jet deliveries."

"I got it. So, who all is here and what are they up to?"

"Kreisleiter Schiede and his assistant, Dieter Fleischen. They are in the entry shack waiting for me." says Gerhard. "They are here to conduct a preliminary investigation as to how the Da Zara's escaped and who may have helped them. Word is that Schiede has now been made a Major in the Volkssturm militia of Augsburg and that he is enjoying his new-found position. "

"If they call me in," I say, "I will keep to the alibi we agreed upon."

"Good. They are going to start with me and I don't know who else may be called in. Just keep working away at your table until and if you are called upon."

Gerhard then leaves the bathroom while I wait another minute before I head back to my station.

An hour passes by with no word from the Party officials or Gerhard. As I continue working out wing details my mind is racing on what Schiede or Fleischen could be up to. Finally, I see the two of them walking by on the outer edge of the drafting hall. From a distance, Dieter sees me and indicates to Schiede to wait for him in the corridor. Dieter approaches my desk and says,

"Armand, my my, you do seem to be swaying ever so consistently away from our Party ideals. I should've turned you into the Party back in the days of the SA brown shirts, for some trivial disloyalty. I suspect something bad has happened here and you may be involved in it."

"I don't know what you are talking about, Dieter. If anything, I have stayed the course of industrial design and continued onward with plane design. You seem to be the one who has swayed."

"Don't get funny with me, Armand. Do you know what position I now have with the Party? I am a Captain in the Volkssturm, reporting directly to Major Schiede. Do you know that Hitler will soon be authorizing the Party to directly recruit and command the Volkssturm units?"

"No, I haven't heard that, Dieter. I've been too busy putting out new fighter jets to protect our homeland."

"Fighter jets are all fine and good Kindermann, but the destiny of the Reich and our National Socialist Party are the primary goals that must now be preserved. You think you are so important designing your jets but don't let it get to your big head. Our final fight to defend the Fatherland is the most important task now."

"Thank you for reminding me of your position's priority, Dieter. Is this the only reason you came over?"

"No, it is not. We are investigating how two Jews have escaped from Horgau and who helped them out. God help you if you are incriminated in this traitorous act."

"Thanks for your update, Dieter. I have men to direct now and plans to review so we can stay on production schedule. Would you mind excusing me from our little chat?"

"Sure, Armand. Work away on your strategic craft. But don't think your essential armaments status will protect you from any traitorous actions or even conscription, my old friend." Dieter's face then releases its tautness and softens one bit, "One other thing, Armand. I am sorry to hear about the loss of your wife and children. You are not the only one who misses Vanessa."

With that Dieter, spins around and walks stiffly toward the exit door where Schiede has been waiting. As I look out the windows, I can see the two of them enter the back seat of a kubelwagen, while a driver then peels off exiting out of the Horgau camp.

What the hell did he mean he misses Vanessa? That was way back in the University years when they met. The night that I first met Vanessa as well. I feeling of disgust comes over my chest as I try to fathom of Dieter's having any interest in my past Frau. How did I miss this all these years. Or perhaps I didn't want to or couldn't see it. And what did Vanessa do to inspire this life-long yearning in Dieter? This is all an unsettling thought as my heart still holds a sacred place for Vanessa. Even though I just risked my neck for Rosa, I would do anything to have my wife and children back. Did Dieter really think I would welcome his condolences with that extra comment?

Looking down the drafting hall, I see Gerhard waving his hand motioning for me to come over. I figure he has more tell me now, so I quickly walk over and follow him into his office.

"Armand," says Coulis scanning his window view, "I think they are on to you. They don't have any hard evidence, but I can tell from their line of questioning that they have sources pointing toward you."

"Goddammit," I snarl. "So much for trusting any of my engineering barrack mates. They would turn in their mothers if they had to."

"Yes, we have a slew of Party supporters amongst us Messerschmitt people. Their likes have even ratted out Messerschmitt for use of gasoline for personal trips. Anyway, I have an idea on how I can delay or hamper any further investigation of you."

"And that would be what, Gerhard?"

"I think the best course for your neck, and talents, would be to have you transferred out of here and sent off to the top-secret research facility where Professor Messerschmitt is now stationed. This will get you out of sight from those two fellows as few people have access to that facility"

"What about my work on the jet and the rocket fighters? I still have yet to finish up the design work on the two-seater version of the jet."

"I think you have taken both to a good point where others could pick up. From what I know about the research facility is that they

239

are busily, if not desperately, working on the next generation jet fighter. I already have a request from them to provide an industrial engineer position and you may be the right man."

"Given that the Party fellows are on my tail, this would be a good time for me to abscond to this secretive base, Gerhard. I agree with your idea and I will gladly accept the transfer."

"Alright, the base is in Oberammergau, south of Munich. I will execute the transfer papers effective for next week. On your way down, I would like for you to stop at the Lager Lechfeld airfield and check out the flight performance of our two-seater jets. Fritz Wendel oversees flight acceptance for the Me 262's we are producing, and I am sure he will treat you well."

"I am sure Fritz will be a great guide. Then I will make my transition arrangements for my work out of here and prepare myself for the new location. Thanks for helping, Gerhard. I hope no harm comes to you from this investigation."

"Don't worry about me, Armand. I've been around long enough to know how to deal with the Party apparatus. I am more concerned about the Party catching up with you and exacting a measure of their punishment."

PART 4
FINAL SOLUTIONS

FEBRUARY 1945

It is my day to transfer and I pack my bags and say my goodbyes to Walter and the other engineers. I walk into the commissary and notice that there is no cheery Rosa to greet me with a serving of food and a secretive smile. As I board the lorry, I take one last look at the wooden shacks of the Horgau complex and think of the first night I arrived here not knowing what to expect and feeling displaced from Augsburg. But then I contrast this with how I feel now, a man whose heart was captivated here and in some strange way, healed from my loss of Vanessa. I look over to the commissary building and a series of images of Rosa chatting with me and meeting her out at the Aspenbach roll by in quick succession.

My mind then wanders onto how Leonino and Rosa have done with their escape out of Germany. Did they make it into Switzerland? Are they safely in Italy? Will I ever see her green eyes and feel her lush hair again? With these final thoughts, the truck transport pulls out of the camp and I rumble down the road toward Lager Lechfeld, my first stop before heading onward to Oberammergau.

★★★

As I walk onto to the Lager Lechfeld tarmac, I see from a distance Fritz Wendel climbing into the cockpit of a jet. This plane is fresh from Horgau and I observe that he is going through a checklist before flight testing. It's satisfying seeing what we've been working on getting readied for action.

As I approach closer to the jet I yell out, "Hello old friend, are you staying out of trouble or making trouble here?"

Fritz pulls his head out of the cockpit while he continues to stand on the ladder, "Oh, I am sorry. Plant personnel are not allowed to see us test their products. It's a conflict of interest and you are not welcome here. If I don't accept this plane, Messerschmitt AG won't get paid," jokes Fritz.

"Well, we engineers don't trust those test pilots to really understand nor appreciate all our design nuances. So, we need to check up on you to keep you in line."

Fritz comes down from his ladder and he gives me a big embrace. For his twenty-nine years of age he is a well-built specimen of a man and I receive a crushing hug from him. He releases me and gives me a broad smile and hello.

"Good to see you, Armand. What brings you down from Horgau?" Fritz asks.

"I am here to gather operational field data on the two-seater night-fighter. But also, I am being transferred over to the research complex at Oberammergau. I've done what I can with the Me 262 and its time for me to move onto the next generation of jets being planned there. Plus, I needed a change."

"Nice to hear, my friend. And I hear that it's in a beautiful and quiet setting. That's where the medieval passion plays of old are held every summer. Maybe you will catch a good show and be forgiven for all your design mistakes on this jet, ha," says Fritz.

"Oh, now they are my mistakes? This jet wouldn't have made it to this airfield in time if it wasn't for my engineering crew's late-night hours in the drafting hall."

"You engineers think you deserve all the credit, but us test pilots are the real heroes. Every time I take one of these newly manufactured planes out I never know if your production crews were awake enough to know what they were doing that day on the assembly line."

"Ah, well, I think you have hit on the crux of the matter, Fritz. We can't always control the foreign and prison workers' quality. If anything, we are constantly watching out for sabotage on the production lines. So, tell me how life is here at Lager Lechfeld?"

"I love it here, Armand. I'm treated very well here by upper management and the Luftwaffe officers. I have a full say on what jets get rejected and which ones are ready for combat. I am the first and last word on it. If the jet has to be reassembled that's my call."

"Not too bad and it seems like a step up from being at the Leipheim airfield. I see that there is now a jet fighter unit stationed here."

"Yes, they are forming a night-fighter unit here to intercept the bombing runs over Munich. The English are incessant with their nightly bombing. I don't think there is much left standing there, yet they keep coming back night after night. And then the Americans come during the day and do it all over."

"It's just crazy, Fritz, how many planes the English and Americans have. I feel now that our jet's main role is to defend our homeland from this bombing terrorism."

"It's what keeps me testing these new planes twelve hours a day," responds Fritz. "We need to stop or slow down these bombers. They are killing women, children and ordinary townspeople. Most days I test out six planes but lately, since you and your waldwerk have been so productive, I have to do eight to nine a day."

"So long days are standard here too? You have time for lunch, Fritz? Let's catch up and I need your help in writing up a report on the night-fighter's performance."

"Sure, Armand. Let me finish this cockpit inspection and I will soon meet you in the dining hall."

As I walk over, I see a few batteries of anti-aircraft guns posted around the airfield. To my surprise, I realize that there are women manning the stations. There are also women on the airstrip flagging planes for takeoff. Further along the tarmacs rows of jets wait for testing. In the lineup are the variants of the Me 262; the bomber, the night-fighter, the interceptor and the reconnaissance plane. I think to myself that it would've been so much easier if the Luftwaffe had just given us one type to work on and then let us run with that into mass production. We have so few resources left to build our planes and the Air Ministry's indecision has increased our load like a pack of overburdened donkeys in a mountain pass.

I then pass the pilot's dispersal huts where groups of twelve or so pilots are seated waiting for flight orders. Off on the runway Kettenrad track vehicles pull Me 262 jets back to their line-up to await their next flight. From there, I head over to the commissary. I've heard much about how well the Luftwaffe staff are treated and I want to see it firsthand. As soon as I open the door I can barely see in. There is a thick haze of cigar smoke, music plays from a Victrola and loud chatter is punctuated by the bellows of deep laughter. The food is served in large quantities: hasenpfeffer, kartofen salad, schnitzel, goulash and large circles of hard cheeses all spread generously throughout the tables. Each table has bottles of beer, wine and what looks like French bourbon. Men are gathered around with their pilot and officer uniforms smiling, embracing each other as they chomp their cigars and hold out shot glasses of some deep-burgundy liquor. I hear an occasional '*prost*' followed by some cheering, or was that some singing I heard? It's only twelve in the afternoon and yet I feel it could be ten in the evening.

With women auxiliary crews here to help flag the planes and set up field signals, I see that each table has at least one young lass sitting amongst the men. Each man seems to best his comrade with jokes and outlandish stories. The women appear to be none too shy and enjoy the off-color jokes along with the direct flattery that is freely being doled out to them. Ah, so this is the life of the pilots: daring, gallant and I would, say, sex-filled.

After being in the more austere Horgau plant for the last ten months, I got used to the spartan life we had with the Saturday Biergarten being our only indulgence. A thought of Rosa pierces my chest as I think of the event that finally brought us together. I then look at all the jovial women around me, red-cheeked with straight flaxen hair, and I feel no attraction to any of them.

I sit at a table with only two other pilots at it and patiently wait for Fritz. I make some small talk with the pilots and they tell me they feel honored to be part of the jet fighter units as only the elite of the Luftwaffe pilots have been asked to join.

I feel a tap on my shoulder and it is Fritz as he pulls up a chair to the table. Fritz takes a quick look around the dining hall as if to see if we can pull in some Fräuleins into our table.

"Fritz, such joviality here. It's like there is no war going on here just party planning."

"Ah yes, I forgot to warn you. Life on an airbase is like no other in the military. The officers and the enlisted men here have done away with rank formalities, there is much camaraderie and there are beautiful women supplied right on base. But, on the other hand, there is much death and these guys live like today could be their last. And for many lately, it has been. I am just trying to make the reason for it being their last not my fault. Or yours," he says with a penetrating look at me.

I realize Fritz has a direct relationship with the combat pilots while fellows like me in engineering are removed from this day-to-day existence of fighter pilots.

We order our food and drinks while Fritz continues, "On a more serious note, Armand, we are losing jet pilots at a tremendous rate. In fact, I think soon your plants will be producing more planes than we have pilots to fly them. When these guys go up to take on a bombing raid, there are up against 300 to 500 bombers and typically 150 to 200 fighter planes. What can twelve fighter jets do against air fleets of this size? Granted, their fighters are piston engine aircraft and fly 120 miles slower than our Swallow, but being outnumbered thirty to one takes away our speed advantage at some point."

"I've heard that statistic Fritz and it is chilling. The faster we make them, the faster they shoot us down."

"I don't blame these pilots for living it up on the way they do," says Fritz. "For many it's only a matter of time before their plane gets blasted down by a Mustang or a Thunderbolt. The Americans have been studying our jet's performance and they figured out that the jet can't make a tight turn and that it's very slow on take-offs and landings. So, they've been taking tighter turns, circling around the jet and the lining up their sights with deadly aim. And when we are landing, they swoop down on them and go for a kill shot. Unfortunately, I've noticed that every week the Americans are getting better at this."

"So what can I as a designer take with me as I go off to Oberammergau and work on the next jet?"

"Well, for one, I can't believe the Air Ministry, has plans for another jet. There just isn't enough war left for us to put it to use. Look, where are the Americans now, at least as of two days ago? It appears they are ready to cross the Rhine River and when they do, it's all over for our Fatherland."

"I know, logistically it's almost over but our design efforts must continue. We are always looking at producing a plane for some two years down the road. It's our way of being. We don't think about planes for tomorrow but for ones that are way out there in time."

"Ok, enough talk of the war. Let's enjoy our sauerbraten and wash it down with this Dortmunder beer. Can you believe we have this here? I don't know how they shipped it down from Essen. The bottles must've had a treacherous trip to get here, so let's *prost* to our tasty, well-traveled beer."

I am impressed how Fritz flips from a serious war realist to living it up like a university student. I remind myself that he is not yet thirty and entitled to retain a bit of youth.

I then question inside, where did my youth go? I think it was swallowed up somewhere along the lines of me getting involved with this armaments industrialist. I cast a glance at the all too rowdy men in the hall and think maybe I need to loosen up a bit and forget about Rosa, Vanessa and what will happen to me at the end of this war.

I then turn to Fritz. "A *prost* to you my friend. The world's best goddamn test pilot ever."

After we clink glasses I take a large drink from my stein and hammer it down on the table. I turn to Fritz. "You know, I've never flown in my baby, the Swallow. I drew it up and you get to fly it. Something is not right here. How about you take me up in the two-seater night-fighter you are checking out? What do you say Fritz?"

"Well, I am under strict orders to only fly with authorized personnel or with those under military orders."

I take another deep gulp of beer and feel its warmth giving me comfort, "Well, I oversaw the integration of the Siemens Neptune radar console into the operator's cockpit. And my friend Walter, explained to me how it works, at least on paper. So, I understand the basic operation of the short and medium range radars it has."

Fritz looks around the room and then pulls in closer to me, "I guess we could say you needed to observe the performance of the two-seater cockpit for navigation characteristics, first hand."

I reply with my stein swinging toward him, "That sounds good enough for me. Let's do this. Where do I get my hands on one of those flight suits?"

My, Armand, you have gotten a bit bold lately haven't you."

"I've lost too much already, Fritz. Time for me to forget about what I've been through. I've played good boy long enough. Look at where it has gotten me. So, yes, I am now willing to bend the rules."

Fritz and I finish up lunch and we head over to the base commander's office for my flight authorization. Having achieved this approval, we head over to the quartermaster's area to snatch up a flight jacket and a helmet. I change in Wendel's locker area and off I walk onto the tarmac toward the night-fighter jet. Its stag antennae are ready to poke me or anyone else that gets too close to it. Wendell tells the mechanics to load up the jet with fuel, arm it and prepare it for flight. I am excited as I see the mechanics run through the preflight checklist knowing that I will be in this jet in no time.

The plane's turbines are pre-started and a low-level whir emanates from them. The mechanics first help Wendel in and then move the ladder over, so I can climb up and into the rear of the cockpit. As I slip into the seat I am impressed at how tight it is. Once you are fitted in, there is no room to wiggle your feet, legs or shoulders. The mechanics buckle me in, check my parachute, adjust my air mask and then close the canopy. A hush comes over the cockpit and we can now only hear a low muffle of the jet turbines. Wendel's communication with the control center breaks in through my headset as I hear him communicate his flight plan.

Being in the rear of the night fighter, I have no flight controls, only gauges and two radar screens in front of me; a medium and a short-range radar. I can see Fritz is running through a flight checklist, flipping switches and dials while he watches them respond. The turbines are still in a low whir but as he finishes preparations, he pushes the left control forward and starts to rev up the engines. I hear the whir rise to a higher pitched whistle while the plane's body starts to rumble with the anticipation of flight.

Fritz speaks over the headset and instructs the ground crews to prepare for his take-off. He then releases the brake and the plane jerks forward at first but then moves smoothly down the runway.

"Ok, Armand, the controls and gauges look good, so I am going to taxi to the take-off strip. After that I am going to accelerate the engines and we should lift off shortly afterward. I hope you people put extra care into this machine."

"How ironic it would be for a plane designer to crash in his own design," I respond. "I will cross my fingers that production quality was good that day."

We taxi the jet to the take-off strip and with a few final flight control checks. Fritz pushes the turbines into a higher thrust as the craft barrels down the mile-long runway with increasing speed. We must be going at least 100 miles an hour, but I know the plane needs to reach 130 miles an hour before it can take off. As we approach this speed every bump in the runway feels exaggerated and we are tossed up and down on set intervals. As we approach the latter half of the runway, I feel a slight deceleration as Fritz taps the brakes to get the tail up in the air. He does so successfully and then I feel an uplift along with the silencing of the wheels.

As we take-off, I can see a light brown and blurry exhaust streaming out of the turbines. The J2 coal mix burns this color and I know just how many gallons are being burnt per minute to achieve the 1500 pounds of thrust needed for take-off. As we rise a few hundred yards up the turbines kick into a higher thrusting power and I can now feel the acceleration pushing me deep into my seat as we not only speed up but also increase our rate of climb. Fritz then activates the landing gears for retraction and he pulls the Swallow into a steep ascent.

As Fritz levels off the plane at 10,000 feet he radios into the control center, "This is Shark Tooth. Can you read me, Beagle? We have leveled off at 10,000 feet." Over the headset I hear a cackle burst through, "Affirmative, Shark Tooth. We have you on radar and all is clear. Proceed ahead."

As I look below me at the checkered German landscape I see snow-covered fields broken only by little hamlets, winding roads and an occasional reflection of the sun off the Lech River. Further to our south I can see the snow-peaked Alps, their white peaks piercing the horizon. Up here in this streaming state I feel liberated and full of potential; everything seems so manageable now. No war, no factories, just the blue sky, cloud formations and a landscape that continuously rolls under our position.

The turbine sound is constant as the plane cuts through the air. For looking like a shark, I can feel how the Swallow is a deft and agile aircraft that only requires a smooth touch on the controls. On the left levers, Fritz pushes the turbines now to maximum thrust, pulls the control stick down and then I see the indicators read that our velocity is just over 500 miles an hour. Yet still even at this speed the ride is gentle. General Galland's comment comes to mind, 'It is like having an angel push you along with its hand.'

Fritz puts the plane through a series of dives, climbs, then starboard turns, port turns and finally a ceiling climb of 30,000 feet. The turbines hold out well and the plane feels sturdy with no unsettling vibrations.

"I am now going to test the cannons and air-to-air rockets. Hold on for a few bumps." Wendel then pulls into a starboard dive, flips the safety catch and presses the firing mechanisms. He fires of two sets of rockets from each wing and I feel a push back as the missiles jump off into the sky. He then fires the four cannons out from the nose and they shudder the whole plane with more determination. All the glass on the plane rattles including the gauge windows and the canopy itself. It is a good thing the cannons only need to fire for three seconds to make a kill. Otherwise, I think the airframe would start unbolting. I then hear

Norman Emilio Barrientos

him over the headset, "Armand, flip on the radar screens and let me know how the panel lights up."

I reach in front of me and locate the on switch and turn on the display panel. Having a basic understanding of the Siemens Neptune radar instrument, I tell Fritz, "Everything has lit up. Do you want me to adjust the distance or sensitivity?

"Yes, lower them both, wait for ten seconds then increase them to maximum gain."

I do so and see a bar of light rotate around the short and the medium-range screens. "Ok, Fritz, both screens are working."

"Give them a few seconds to do a few sweeps and then let me know what you see." I then hear Fritz radio into the air controller, "This is Shark tooth. Do you read me Beagle? We have completed the climbs, dives and weaponry. We will now be testing the radar system. We are at 20,000 feet up, twenty-five miles south and heading due north back to the base."

A crackling voice comes over my headset in response, "Affirmative, Shark Tooth. All clear in the skies. Continue operations."

After staring at the screen for a minute I see a light beep on the far edge of the medium-range screen. Then another light beeps up. I say, "Fritz, there are two objects detected on the medium-range radar screen."

"*Scheisse,* where could they be? I am scanning the horizon and I don't see any enemy planes. They must've detected our firings. What are the coordinates, Armand?"

"They are approaching quickly from ten o'clock. They are out some ten miles and coming from the east-north-east bearing. They are heading our way. I estimate their speed to be 350 miles per hour and their altitude at 20,000 feet."

"Must be P-47's, Thunderbolts," mutters Fritz. "Either they have tracked us, or they are just keeping a close eye on the flights from Lager Lechfeld. I am not going to make this their lucky day."

"This is the real thing, Fritz, isn't it?" I ask not wanting to know the truth.

251

Fritz then calls in on his radio, "Any sign of enemy planes on your radar? Our radar is indicating two planes."

The controller responds after a short delay, "Affirmative. We just picked up two enemy aircraft. We will activate the anti-aircraft batteries around the base."

"Yes, this is real, hang on tight and brace yourself. We are going to take some evasive measures. The best evasive tactic we can take is an offensive one." exclaims Fritz

He then radios back, "We only have twenty minutes of fuel, so it is enough to take one pass at them. Then we will have to hightail it back to the airstrip." Fritz cuts the call and then to me says, "Armand, keep reporting their positions to me."

"Whatever you need me to do, Captain," I take an anxious look at the screen and note that they have a dead bearing on us. "Fritz, they are now some five miles out from us but now they are turning parallel to our flight path."

"Looks like they are planning to turn around us and sneak up on us from behind. I know this tactic all too well. I am going pull up into a rapid climb to 30,000 feet and then make as tight of a port turn as I possibly can. I want to end up on their tail just as they complete their own turn."

I feel the jet increase its rate of climb as I am pushed back against the seat, the blood being squeezed out of my chest and my ribcage feels like it is being pressed by a barrel. As he levels the Swallow, he then makes a tight left turn and then accelerates downward. This time, my stomach lurches up my throat and I feel like it might pop out my mouth. My head starts spinning and I feel like the blood has been drained from my head. Downward we flow past layers of cloud formations with intermittent streaks of blue sky flashing by. Finally, I catch a slight of the Thunderbolts making their turns some three miles out from us. As Fritz had projected we have ended up on the duo's tail and I report out to him,

"The P-47's are out two miles...one mile...3,000 feet...1,000 feet. We are coming up fast on them, Fritz."

Fritz pulls down the Revi 16 gun sight, flips up the safety cover on the stick and then yells out, "I got them in my sights." He levels the planes descent and comes in at a slight angle and from behind on the Americans at over 100 miles per hour faster than their planes. I can now distinctly make out the American Airforce star on the wings and then I feel the hammering of the four nose cannons firing out for three long and riveting seconds.

"I hit one!" yells Fritz and as he says this he immediately pulls off to starboard and starts a descent. I look out the canopy and see bits of metals spinning through air and a thick, black tail of smoke spewing out of the wings of one of the P-47's.

The other one though, immediately pulls off to port and ascends out of our way. Fritz speaks, "Damn it, I couldn't get them both. The other pilot is trying to pull around to my rear now. We only have enough fuel to head straight to Lager Lechfeld. He calls over to the control center "We are on our approach to the airfield with an enemy on our back."

"Affirmative. We have the batteries activated," says the controller.

"Check your parachute release, Armand, and keep a hand on the canopy opening lever. If we must bail, roll out of the plane in a tucked position and fall for a good five seconds before you open.

"I've never had parachuting lessons, Fritz. Why five seconds? I may hit the ground at this low elevation."

"The Allies are shooting parachuting pilots in mid-air."

"Great. I am tracking the other plane and he is about three miles behind us and it looks like he his diving down on us as his altitude is dropping quickly."

"Sure, the only way for a Thunderbolt to catch us is in dive mode. But right now, we must start heading to our landing. Which means I have to bring back the throttle and start deaccelerating for our approach."

"He is out two miles and we have ten minutes of fuel.

"Alright, now is our time to drop low, treetop low," exclaims Fritz. "Keep an eye out on the altimeter. We may scrape a few trees. I need to get that Thunderbolt within range of our batteries." Fritz then places the plane into a dive and levels out at about 1000 feet above ground. I can see Lager Lechfeld on the horizon coming up on us.

"The American is behind us, one mile out...3,000 feet...1,000 feet." As I say this a series of pulsing lights race by the side of our canopy. A second later I hear the rattle of the machine fire that is the cause of these tracer bullets. Fritz then takes a sharp port turn and says, "I am going to pull up and then around again."

As the Swallow accelerates and pulls up I ask Fritz, "Will we have enough fuel to land?

"As long as we approach the runway, we can glide from there on a dead stick." At this point the P-47 is pulling around to pursue us but he has come in range of the batteries as Fritz had hoped. It is then that the ground opens up from five different points with sheets of flames darting up into the sky. As I look back at the Thunderbolt I see that it is enveloped by fire and shrapnel.

"Serves him right," says Fritz.

"Looks like he has flown thrown through all the flak, Captain. But he has aborted his chase on us and is flying away from the base."

"Ok, we are clear to bring the Swallow in," says Fritz. He continues pulling a hard port turn and starts heading downward as well. It is then that we hear a 'pop' sound and a sudden deacceleration.

"*Scheisse*," says Fritz, "We just flamed out the portside Jumo turbine. it was too tight of a turn."

"These can fly with one turbine, right, Fritz?

"Sure, I just need to trim the tail rudder and oversteer to the right. No sweat."

"Just get us home and I will owe you a big one." As he pulls the plane level for the approach to the airfield, I continue scanning the radar control.

"Where is that P-47 now?" asks Fritz.

"He is out some ten miles making a big turn. Oh, wait, there are two new blips of light showing up on the radar. Looks like he has reinforcements coming in."

"Alright, our batteries can hold them off while until we land. Then we will need to make a mad dash to the first slit bunker we can find.

"Fritz, we are almost hitting empty."

"Come on Swallow," prays Fritz, "just give me three more minutes. I am switching over the port fuel tank to the starboard one now."

As the airfield quickly approaches us, I can see Wendel is constantly shifting his steering stick. As the concrete runway appears beneath our wings, the jet is still moving at over 150 miles an hour and the lines are a blur. Fritz approaches with the nose pointing up, the back two wheels land first and then he lands down the front wheel. The plane deaccelerates on the runway and we approach the control center. It is at this point that the starboard engine run out of fuel with a pop sound. With only momentum left, we come to halt some 2000 feet out from the base's center.

I take one last look at the radar panels and report to him, "The three planes are out five miles, they will be here in minutes." Fritz cranks open the canopy and we start unbuckling our gear, tearing off our masks and the parachute strappings. We climb out of the cockpit and jump off the wings.

"Run toward that track, fast!" yells Fritz. As a hauling track comes toward us, we hear propeller planes whining with increasing intensity. A burst of machine fire hits the tarmac starting at the command center and then rips it way down the airstrip. In a growing line of explosions, the runway cement is pulverized into flying dust and pounds toward our Swallow, now a sitting duck. The bullets miss us and the jet allowing us to continue our sprint.

As the American plane pulls up and away, Fritz and I jump into the track and the driver spins around back to the base. Close on the heels of the first Thunderbolt, the other two planes then dive down onto our Lager Lechfeld base with equal and determined vengeance. Fritz points over to the nearest slit trench and indicates for the driver to head over there. Two lines of strafing strike downfield hitting a plane which explodes into a yellow, fiery ball. Our anti-aircraft guns are blazing away at the Americans even as they pass just hundreds of feet over us but this doesn't halt their attack. Fritz, the driver and I jump into the slit trench as this double line of strafing pounds its way up to our stationery jet. The ground shakes as fragments of concrete fly into our trench and debris spits upward as the runway unzips before us.

We then hear another explosion and the sky turns white-orange, temporarily blinding us. Bits of steel come flying down onto the tarmac causing a shattering of metal rain that thuds down with pings and rattles. As the propeller planes' sounds fades off into the distance, we lift our heads out of the trench. Before us we see that the night-fighter Swallow is now a hollow frame of fire and billowing black smoke.

FEBRUARY 1945

"Armand. Good to see you. I am glad you have finally made it here safe and sound," exclaims Professor Messerschmitt from a distance waving his hands at me with broad gestures.

I impressed that he has come out to personally greet me right after the guard shack. Before me are eighteen or so two-story Alpine buildings covered in white stucco and framed with heavy timber along with carved wooden ornaments. If it weren't for the two guarded checkpoints you could mistake this for a mountain resort. The mountains behind the Oberammergau Complex also look taller and steeper than the pictures I had seen beforehand.

"I heard about your near disaster with Fritz. I am happy that you made it, but what got you to thinking it would be okay to fly in these conditions?" asks Messerschmitt as he shakes his head.

"After all these years, Professor, I wanted to feel the jet and experience it firsthand. Sorry if I took such a risk."

"That you did, and the consequences could've been grave for our development efforts."

"Think of it this way. If I hadn't been operating the radar controls, we would've had a harder time tracking the P-47's. They were bound to show up and I think I actually helped Wendel survive the attack."

"Well, I agree with that, reluctantly," says Messerschmitt. "Maybe we should consider Wendel lucky to have had you on board rather than you to have been unlucky."

"Just think about how much more I know now about how the Swallow handles under combat conditions."

"I can't believe this happened to you, Armand. We came so close to losing you at Lager Lechfeld. You had us all worried when we heard the reports."

"I am sorry sir. I took a bit of a risk and I regret having to worry you."

"Well, at least you are alright, and we have plenty to do here. Welcome to our Upper Bavaria Research Institute. Coulis said that you would have a report on the night-fighters."

"Yes, Professor. I have a report already for you on how the extended fuselage of the trainer version affects flight controls. I personally know how well it actually does."

"You know, I don't even get to fly around these days. As it is, the Luftwaffe has commandeered my beloved Mtt Bf 108, so I don't even have access to a liaison plane."

"Really, I am sorry to hear that. I guess it's an indication of how this war is going."

As we pick up our stride and head through a courtyard, the mountains peering beyond the rooflines, Messerschmitt responds, "War or no war, we and the RLM have ambitious plans to produce successors to the Me 262. If we could only get a reliable fighter in the air to intercept those *viermots*, we could take command of the air war again. And I would like nothing more than the 'Me' designation to be affixed on the next generation of fighters."

I am impressed that the Professor still is holding on to a chance of winning the war. Is he so confident in our machines' abilities or has he become delusional about the war? Or is it his pride in having his name attached to all these planes?

"Well, I am here reporting for duty, Professor. Whatever plane needs a realistic set of production drawings, will be my pleasure to work on."

Messerschmitt flashes a smile and pats me on the shoulder indicating for me to follow him. He walks me toward one of the buildings and we enter what looks like a school building with a long corridor and classroom-like studios on each side. Before this was taken over by Messerschmitt AG, it was a training facility and set up like a school. We walk past a few 'classrooms', each being a distinct project bureau with people frenetically working away on some advanced aircraft. Finally, he turns into a project bureau and I see in the room twenty or so men focused on their drawing tables.

Messerschmitt approaches Hans Hornung and Moritz Asam where they are in a corner looking over a sheaf of blueprints,

"Hans and Moritz, look who has finally made it over from Horgau in one piece."

Hans gets up and shakes my hand. "Good to see you, Armand. You are only two weeks later than we wanted and equally late on your assignment," he says with a laugh.

"Sounds like the pace of life hasn't changed with research and design groups," I respond. I have my portfolio of drafting tools ready to go. Just tell me where to sit."

Messerschmitt starts up, "Armand, here is the gist of the matter. Hornung and his project bureau worked on a series of designs for a variable-wing jet where there is only one turbine right in the fuselage. And while we have not fully completed this concept design, we are pressing ahead with construction of one prototype while we finalize design on other aspects of the craft."

"That seems rather risky," I respond.

"The urgency of the war and our lack of supplies is forcing us to plunge ahead," says Messerschmitt.

"I assume you have some working concepts of the moveable wing assembly," I ask.

"Armand, that's why you are here," say Messerschmitt. "We have not been able to develop a workable gear mechanism that can move the wings back after takeoff. Even harder is getting the wings to swing back at speeds over 300 miles per hour. Ideally, we would like to have the wings sweep back to three positions to achieve different flight characteristics for take-off, cruising and attack."

"So, the next challenge is to develop this variable position gear into a working concept?"

"Yes, and we believe you are just the man that can crack this nut. The last designer threw his hands up and stated that he couldn't think of what else to try. But I've seen you tackle mechanical problems like this and I know you are will figure this out."

"What is your timeline to get this plane to into prototype construction?" I ask, trying to size this problem up from all angles.

"We have committed to the RLM to have a flying prototype by the end of this April and then conduct test trials later in summer. We already have a mock-up of the fuselage, but the wing construction is much further behind."

"So, I am already behind then," I say. "What is the project number and name of this plane?"

Messerschmitt moves over to a wall where there are layers of drawings tacked up. Some are hand sketches, others are calculations pages and while others are blueprint copies made by the technical drafters. Stopping at a three-face drawing, Messerschmitt says, "The plane is numbered P 1101 and we don't have a name for her yet. Last July the Air Ministry put out a proposal for a successor fighter jet to the Me 262 that can approach Mach One and perhaps even in later versions, break the sound barrier."

Hans continues the overview, "My initial concepts back in July were for a plane with the jet turbine encased into the fuselage with circular intake aspirators forward of the wings. The cockpit is mounted toward the front of the nose and atop the turbine housing for better viewing. For the wings, we have been studying a 40' sweep that halfway out, turns into a 24' sweep. But lately, we have changed our direction and we are now exploring a variable-wing fuselage where the wing could be mechanically adjusted by the pilot in mid-flight."

I think to myself, 'These fellows in Oberammergau have been very busy and dreaming big'. Having been kept out of the development loop myself, I am now starting the realize how far out there these Messerschmitt researchers have gone. At this point, Moritz Asam takes over the talk, "And this is where you come in, Armand. In November, our Construction Bureau took over the concepts from Hornung and we've been working on making detailed designs of this jet so we can produce prototypes here in our experimental workshop. The wing design is the most critical part of the design process right now. One expedient approach would be to use the Me 262's wing assembly and pluck it onto the P 1101's fuselage. But there could be much gained from developing a working variable wing design. It's just so mechanically complex and we don't have any designers with the expertise or time to address this."

Looking at all three of them I say, "Oh, so my knowledge of the Me 262 wing assemblies and my past record on the landing gears has gotten me nominated for this one?"

So, I am to help in creating the world's fastest, swiftest, and most powerful jet fighter that will even surpass the performance of the ME 262. Difficult to believe that another craft could exceed my baby, the Swallow. Before me lie the drawings, which portray a jet plane that so revolutionary, so advanced that I thumb through the drawings carefully looking at the all the unique features of the P 1101 in awe. Quickly thinking this over, an idea comes to mind on how to align a series of gears to shift the wing structure. I lift my head up.

"Gentlemen, I believe there is a way to accomplish this. Give me a week or so of getting to know the plane better and I will start exploring solutions."

Messerschmitt seems satisfied, "Just let me know what resources or technical staff you will need, and I can set them up for you."

"Thanks for your offer, Professor. I will shortly let you know what draftsmen and fabricators are needed to create my working prototype. One more thing, could I see the experimental workshop where they are currently assembling the fuselage?"

"Most certainly and I think you will find it enlightening. Hans and Moritz, would you take Armand to the assembly halls down below? I must be going to attend another project bureau's meeting. Great to see you here and if I haven't stated it yet, welcome to the Upper Bavaria Research Institute."

Hornung and Asam direct me toward an elevator at the end of the hall. From there we descend to what seems a good fifty feet. When the doors open, I see a labyrinth of rooms cut into hewn rock. A flurry of people and occasionally small carts travel around a network of vaulted streets blazoned into this bedrock city. It is a large tunnel complex right underneath the 'Alpine Resort' above. Amazed and peering left to right, I follow Hans and Moritz as they pass by many other prototype planes under construction. This Piranesean underground development center is labyrinth-like, full of platforms, stairs, bridges, traveling cranes, storage cages, steam pipes and jets prototypes. They stop in one of the underground hangars and there I see the fuselage of the P1101. It is a full-blown mock-up complete with the pilot's canopy, a test turbine mounted in the nose section, fuselage plates, a tail and even landing wheels. But it has no wings on it: that is where I will come in on this prototype.

Being the managing production engineer, Moritz says with pride, "This here, Armand, is how far we have taken the variable-wing jet. We've modeled it, wind-tunnel tested it, structured its inner workings, completed the flight control systems, have the beginning of its avionic systems in place and machine-gun mounts installed. We are just waiting to complete the design of the wings."

"And this is where I pick up the story." I interject. "I know I can figure this." I run my hands along what is completed of the fuselage and look at all the ribs and spars that create its structure. A moveable wing mechanism is within my grasp. "First, I must say gentlemen, you have taken this pretty far already. What needs to be completed now is nothing more than a few details. Right?"

They laugh, enjoying my attitude toward this challenge and Hans says, "I like your confidence. This is the 'can do' section of Oberammergau and that is how we all think. Dreams are possible here. Alright, Kindermann, we will set you up with your design table, equipment and skilled workers. Let us know if you need anything else. We usually have Monday morning progress meetings and on Friday, we have open critique sessions, so all the engineers can help each other out with problem-solving. Have a good first day."

With that, Hans and Moritz point me toward where my station will be and I walk off thinking, I am in a design wonderland far removed from air raids, heavy production, and seemingly no budgets to limit my thoughts.

MARCH 1945

I look up from my drawing table and I see the professor chatting with Moritz but then he turns toward me and comes over to my station.

"How is it going today? Are we getting closer to finalizing the moveable wing mechanisms?"

"Morning, Professor. Yes, I have it in concept but instead of a continuous movement I have figured to just have two positions. A more forward one for take-off and landings and a second one that sweeps back allowing faster flight speeds."

"What happened to our mid-flight and dogfight speeds positions?"

"They are doable, but they will require so many more machine parts and controls. And with that comes more production complexity, more weight and more chance of failures for the pilot."

"So, you think we need to compromise the design criteria to get this bird on the production floor?"

"Yes Professor, that is how I see it. Plus, the fuselage prototype is basically complete, and I am holding up the train with this wing assembly."

"Ok, when do you think the experimental workshops can complete it Armand?"

"I should have these drawings wrapped up this week and then we can start a prototype of the wing assembly. From there we will have a flyable model out by mid-April."

"Mid-April? But that is almost a month later than what we told the Ministry. I just had a meeting with them last week and I told them we would meet our contractual deadline of March 30th for a flying prototype. And from there they want to produce a series of pre-production models by January 1946."

"Professor, I have needed every day to work on this since I've arrived here. And I only have one other drafter working with me when ideally I would have had three."

"I know. Every project bureau has the same problem. The Volkssturm units are activating up and calling up our technicians and fabricators left and right. Each Monday morning that I come to the Institute I never know who else will be missing from the workshops." Messerschmitt seems to have hit a nerve and his jaw clenches as he exclaims to the ceiling,

"How does the Ministry expect us to get our work done while Party militia units keep pulling away our people? Just last week Kreisleiter Schiede was here demanding that I provide him eighty-one engineers to form a new Volkssturm company. How the hell am I going to spare that number of designers? Then I receive this scalding letter from fat head Schiede questioning my loyalty to Party goals. What, me not loyal to our Fuhrer and the Party? *Mein Gott!* His hands form fists and he looks up to the ceiling as if seeking an answer.

Messerschmitt sweeps his arm across the drafting table. Papers crinkle up and flutter to the ground, pens and erasers go flying across the room, hitting the tiled floor with unceremonious taps until their echoes fade out.

"Oh *scheisse*! What the hell are we doing, Armand? It's almost over, the war. It's just a matter of time before we lose. Why are we continuing to design? In what war will these planes fly in?" Messerschmitt bends over the drafting table his face dropped to the table's surface covered by his arms.

"I don't know Professor; the War is getting desperate now that the Allies have crossed the Rhine River. Why do we continue doing what we are doing?" I ask. "Is it because we have RLM contracts lined up?"

While still facing the table Messerschmitt states in a muffled tone, "Even the RLM contracts ring hollow at this point. They are just a bunch of bureaucratic cogs who continue their neurotic planning even while the heart of National Socialism is being squashed out by Sherman tanks. I mean literally, Nuremberg is under siege as we speak, and my lovely hometown of Bamberg was run over last week."

"And what does that make us?, I ask. "Cogs of the cog? The dog that is wagged by its tail?"

"Something like that. We just don't have the guts to stand up to the rats at the RLM and tell them that their game is over. We just keep running around them and taking their contracts and payments. We act like this war will continue for years but who are we fooling now?" Messerschmitt lifts his chest off the table and waves his hand above his head as if he is commanding actions to happen magically.

"Professor, if I may ask you something that is concerning me as the end is surely imminent?"

"Sure. I've been thinking of this reality too for some months now. What are your thoughts?"

"Well, all these drawings and designs that we have been developing. They are worth something to someone even after the War. Maybe more so to the victors."

"Yes, they are invaluable, and I can't stand the thought of all of my, yours and the everyone else's ideas being taken over by nations that had nothing to do with their creation. Especially since some of these countries are next to barbarian status."

"Exactly. We've come up with these wonderful plane ideas but soon there will be no RLM or German court to govern them."

"Just a bunch of marauding American cowboys who are still trying to figure how to develop a flyable jet. *Dummkopffen*," sputters Messerschmitt. No, they don't deserve our jets and that's why Speer has instituted a secret plan already. At first sight of the Allies in the Oberammergau Valley, we are to remove all the drawings from our tables and files, roll them into metal tubes, label them by project number and then abscond them into a nearby mineshaft. I've already picked out an abandoned shaft to bury away our ideas, our German ideas."

"I am glad there is a plan. Let me know if you want me to help out."

"I have another concern though," continues Messerschmitt. "How will I and the company maintain our copyrights and patents with no effective German government in place. I am concerned the Russians or Americans could run off with our blueprints and never pay me any royalty for what I am properly due. I would hate to have this all done only to benefit the Allied countries."

As the Professor continues looking dour, I then console, "Perhaps the Allies won't be able to make much sense of our German technical terms and concepts?"

"I am sure they will make every effort to reverse engineer them. These blueprints embody our technological ideas and create potential for them to be re-created by many. Wherever the blueprints go and whoever has them, carries with them the real prize of our German aviation intelligence."

Changing thought, I ask, "With the Allied front pressing in, have you given thought about your own safety or the Baroness'?"

"I thought of fleeing but where to? Austria? No, I am just going to stand my ground here at this beloved Institute. I can't part from my ideas, our design team. What else do I have, Armand? This is my creation, my child, my life."

★★★

It is morning and Hans and Moritz walk into our Project Bureau studio. "Everyone is to report to the dining hall for an Institute-wide assembly, immediately. Drop everything you are doing, this is a highly urgent matter," says Hans.

I am in midstream of drawing a compound curved line but based on the urgency of their voices, I drop my pencil and French curve. What could this assembly be about? Has Germany surrendered? Are we under imminent attack? Anything is possible these days ever since the Fuhrer has issued orders for the German people to all revolt against the invading Allies.

As I and other engineers pour into the dining hall, I surmise that this is a Party matter. At the head of the hall, a red swastika flag has been unfurled and I see both Party officials and Volkssturm officers standing at attention waiting for us to assemble. As I focus on who is leading this Party meeting, I see Kreisleiter Schiede at the center with his arms behind his back and with eyes scanning the men coming in. As I look further down the line, I see Dieter Fleischen in a Volkssturm Group Captain uniform and next to him are a few other militia officers. What is he doing down here in Oberammergau and not in Augsburg where I thought he was overseeing Volkssturm recruitment and training?

Schiede steps forward and bellows out in his squeaky, raspy voice, "It is a good day for Germany, *mienen Herren*. Today Herr Messerschmitt has agreed to cooperate with the Party and provide eighty-one riflemen for the Augsburg Volkssturm militia unit under my command as Major. There, you will be joined by other Messerschmitt men from the various plants to form a battalion of three companies. Now, while Messerschmitt AG has provided such exceptional service to the Party with their planes, we are even happier that the Professor has agreed to provide his talent to our ultimate cause, the continuation of our Third Reich. Of the three Captains under my command, Captain Dieter Fleischen, will form up the Oberammergau company."

With that Schiede has Fleischen come forward and he reads off the list of men to be conscripted,

Fleischen steps sharply forward, clicks his heels, spins ninety-degrees and walks to the center rostrum. He snaps out, "The following men are to gloriously commit their lives to the fighting cause of Germany. Step forward and fall in line behind Lieutenant Heinrichs who is standing here in front. From here you will be marched out to an assembly outside and then given four hours to gather your belongings."

Standing ramrod stiff, Dieter unrolls a sheet of paper and starts calling off names of those to fall into service and I am horrified as my name is called off. My head bows down in resignation, but I lift it back up, keeping decorum, and start walking toward the Lieutenant. How could Messerschmitt have chosen me, I thought I was essential to the P 1101's development? Is it because I am younger than most of the engineers here? Or perhaps is because the Professor knows there is no use in continuing plane development with the war crumbling apart?

Worse yet is my dismay that my old university competitor and company turncoat is now leading Messerschmitt personnel and me into what could be our final fight. I fear that Dieter's ardent National Socialist beliefs will make for a demanding and dogmatic leader of our company as we stand up against the closing Allied front. Maybe Schiede selected Fleischen personally so that Messerschmitt would feel the full brunt of the Party's power and a bit of revenge. And maybe they are onto me for my actions with the Da Zara's? *Da Zara's Jewish family from Italy*

Armand to the front ★★★

We are marshaled under the barks of a sergeant and transported to the center of Augsburg near the train depot. As can be expected, the City is in turmoil, as the Allied front is only eighty miles away in Stuttgart. Horse-carts and trails of betrodden people stream out of the City in anticipation of an impending invasion. I pass by streams of foreign workers who are seeking to exit Germany and I also see SS guards marshalling concentration camp workers being hastily relocated. They form a long line of workers in striped outfits looking more worn and skinny than the average slave worker. They are being pressed on by their SS guards as they trample their way on the edge of the roads through Augsburg. *the Passion Play*

Once all the Oberammergau men have disembarked from the train, I am drawn into a line with many others from the Augsburg plants. In all, there are about 300 men pulled from various Messerschmitt AG locations, enough for the three companies. Each company is then divided into platoons of twenty-eight men each, assigned our Sergeant and then our weapons. some men are just given Panzerfausts, the anti-tank launcher, instead of rifles. We are then placed in temporary bunkers for the night with orders to report in the morning for the start our basic training.

Surviving Jews were spared because out of Europe, as well

★★★

In the morning, we are lined up by a sergeant and our two commanding officers, Major Schiede and then Captain Dieter Fleischen come forward to address the three platoons. To date, Dieter has not addressed me individually, looked at me with any recognition, nor acknowledged in any way our past associations.

Schiede comes to the front of our company ranks and addresses us, "You are now soldiers of Germany and you are under the direct command of the National Socialist Party. You will leave behind your past social class, your work status and even your families for this great cause. Now, I have heard some grumbling from town officials that drafting you at this stage of the war is a bit of a lost cause. That is not how we at the Party see it nor me as a Major in the Volkssturm. Every American, every Russian we kill and every hamlet we defend is worth the effort. Our great Führer has plans for a great comeback of Germany and we are to hold on to every inch of homeland until he releases his surprise secret weapon.

Upon hearing these words, the company does not waver in its stance, but I sense from the group a feeling of dread emanating from our chests. He continues,

"Your officers will be your all and end all in combat. You will follow every order faithfully, quickly, without question and with all your country loyalty. After this address, we will commence with a week of basic training and then you will be sent to the western front, somewhere toward Stuttgart. There our Augsburg Militia battalion will be combined with a regular Wehrmacht regiment."

Schiede then ends his introduction with a threat, "This war is nowhere near over and we are to fight to the last man. Your Führer demands it and I demand it. In my Volkssturm battalion I will expect complete adherence to this. You may have heard that Russian officers shoot their men if they retreat. Well, I will practice the same on anyone showing cowardice, insubordination and worst of all, retreat. There will be no surrender option in my battalion."

Schiede's eyes are slanted, his lips pursed as if he is already imagining pointing his Luger at some hapless fellow. My gut tightens as a lump moves down my throat.

Following this rousing assembly, we break and begin with marching in formation followed by weapons training. I am assigned to a mortar squad along with learning how to fire my Karabiner.

At the end of the day, I hear that more men have been pulled from the plants including the one in Horgau. I inquire around and find out that Walter too has been conscripted into this Volkssturm battalion. I ask for leave of our barracks and head over to his company. I see Walter cleaning a rifle while standing up against a barrack wall.

"Walter. Great to see you."

We embrace and pat each other on the backs.

"Can you believe it?" I ask. "They finally got us. Those Party people got what they wanted out of Messerschmitt and here we are. Plane designers, advanced plane designers at that, and we are now shining rifles and marching in formation. How are guys like us going to defend our hamlets before the Americans run us over?"

"I know," says Walter. "This is a crazy turn of events for us. But it's great to have you here, at least in the same battalion."

"What is your officers like?" I ask.

"I think they are just following orders to pull together this band of poorly trained soldiers and get it over with. We are all from the Augsburg region and many people know each other. So, they seem to be more concerned that we just make it back alive."

"Can you believe Dieter is now commanding a company? Who would trust that guy?"

"I thought we did him in after his being caught as an informer and spy but hey, maybe this is how things work at the Party level.

"Well now I must bow to his command," I say to Walter. "The guy is a zealot. He always has been. Today, he and Schiede stated they will shoot anyone retreating or surrendering for that matter. Where did we get people like this into our army?"

"This is not a regular army unit," says Walter. "We are under the command of local Party leaders. It probably would've been better to have been drafted into the Wehrmacht instead."

"Agreed, but since Messerschmitt sheltered us from being conscripted into the regular army, we get this as a reward instead."

"Armand, I think we have been sheltered in the plant world. It's one thing to get bombed but it is another to be holding a gun where we will be shooting at Americans. Meeting some of these veteran officers has been quite chilling. They have been through so much and it shows on their pallid faces. But word is that we will be merged with a regular Wehrmacht regiment before we march out of here."

"Hopefully that will bolster our resolve. Just so you know, I've got your back out there. You do the same for me?"

"Certainly, I will do so however I can. We will be marching out in a week, so I will keep a close eye on you. Hey, how was your time at Oberammergau?"

"It was going well until I got pulled off my project thanks to Schiede and Fleischen messing up my little getaway there."

"I gather they pegged you as being an accomplice in the whole Da Zara escape. I am sure Dieter's sense of retribution is more subtle than we imagined."

"Yes, and combine that with Party methods of justice and here I am, a foot soldier."

"We all are now," says Walter. "No more being sacred cows from military service. Speaking of the Da Zara's. Have you heard anything about their whereabouts?

"No, I have no idea if they made it out of Germany. All I know is that I miss seeing Rosa. She was a special and significant woman for me."

"Sorry that you had to let her go. Hopefully you two will be able to reunite after this War. But things are getting more chaotic here by the week."

"That bit of uncertainty keeps me restless at night," I say. "But I have to keep up hope that they made it out and that I will be able come out this Volkssturm service alive and well enough to track her down."

With that I head back to my company barracks and prepare my equipment for tomorrow's training. I am already starting to feel sore in my arms.

APRIL 17, 1945

From the trench emplacement at the top of the Kornberg hill, I can see the valley below is laced with a string of hamlets stretching out to Stuttgart. Our three Volkssturm companies have been merged with four Wehrmacht companies to form a regiment. Yesterday, we marched twenty-six miles west from Ulm to the top of this defensive installation. Just to our backs and down the hill is the village of Gruibingen, a small farming hamlet nestled in this bucolic valley.

Westward, through the haze of smoke, I can see the spires of Kirchheim some ten miles away, peering through in ghostly form. It is apparent that there is bombing going on as we hear the rattle and rumble of booms echoing through the valley.

"Sounds like American Sherman tanks," says my squad Sergeant as he stands next to me in the trench. Jens Bauer is a burly man of forty with a squat, broad frame and a scar on his neck. He is a Wehrmacht veteran who has been called up for Volkssturm duty after his two war injuries. "They must be sieging Kirchheim. In no time, they will be rolling up this valley. Probably take them a day."

I look out through the field binoculars I have been assigned with my mortar role and scan the road winding through the valley. "Sergeant, I see a stream of men out about three miles. Take a look."

"Those are our retreating men," grunts Sergeant Bauer. "I am sure they will fall back into our lines."

I respond, "I am sure we could use more veterans amongst our ranks."

"You plant fellows will do fine," says Bauer. "Just listen to my commands, don't expose yourself unnecessarily and when I say fire, fire all out. Now, Kindermann, go double check the sights on your mortar."

"Yes, Sergeant Bauer," I say as I turn and walk through the trenches back to my mortar team below. My mates consist of a forty-five-year-old sheet-metal worker from the Leipheim plant, named Horst, and a fifteen-year-old boy who is still in secondary school, named Ewald. Horst is a lean man, with sunken cheeks that makes his face look more like a skull. From his factory work, though, he is sinewy, and his calloused hands have the texture of work gloves. He told me earlier that when he was drafted in March, he was working on making jigs for the fuselage plates of the Me 262.

Ewald tells me that his whole class in the Augsburg secondary school was called up in early April1. Some of his classmates are spread throughout the three companies of our battalion. For being fifteen, Ewald seems to be swallowed up by his uniform. His greatcoat slouches over his shoulders, the Volkssturm cap comes down to his ears, his hands barely make it out of his sleeves and his pants are crunched up at his boots like accordions. His blonde hair, light blue eyes and reddish cheeks seem almost feminine amongst all the older, plant workers in this unit.

"Lieutenant Heinrichs thinks the Americans will be here by day's end," I state to Horst and Ewald as they clean off the unassembled mortar equipment.

"Oh, we will be ready for them," says Horst. I think these regular Wehrmacht fellows know how to put up a good defense. We just have to have stick to our parts."

Ewald looks less assured as he continues looking down at the assembly of pieces we are cleaning off. With hesitancy, Ewald says, "I don't feel we have enough training. I've had more training on how to hitch a horse than I've had on how to fire off this mortar."

"It's easy, Ewald," chides Horst. "We just make sure it's clean, secure the legs down, sight it properly, drop in the shell, and off she goes. All you have to do is keep hauling the shells over from that pile."

"Just stay close to us, Ewald, and as a team we will get this mortar to work," I say to him feeling a bit like a teacher to him.

"I like our lieutenant," says Horst, changing the subject. "Seems like a spirited fellow and a good leader for our platoon."

"I agree," I say, "He is very encouraging yet realistic as to what we can do as a new unit."

"But I do not feel any warmth for our company commander," says Horst. "Every time he struts by he just looks down his nose at us and tells Heinrichs that he has to push us harder."

"Unfortunately, Horst, I know our captain all too well and you are right on the mark."

Ewald picks up on this and asks, "You know him from before? Maybe you can get him to give us a favored position in this defensive line."

"Sorry, fellows," I respond. "From what I know of Captain Fleischen, he will enjoy making our lives harder than it needs to be. Plus, he is a Party member to the core and I don't see him giving up without a major fight."

Sergeant Bauer comes by and shouts out, "Ok, enough time cleaning out your mortar. Time to get back to digging in the entrenchments."

"Yes, sergeant," we say in unison as we leave behind the mortar equipment and grab our shovels and pick axes.

"Your squad is to continue digging in at this mid-level line of the hill over to that line of trees. We then need to dig one communication trench between our company and the next one, so the major can move between them."

"Shall we spend the rest of the day doing this, sergeant?" asks Horst. "What about our completing the upper-level trenches we started yesterday?"

"I know men, it may not make sense to leave the upper trenches incomplete," says the sergeant, "But those are orders from Major Schiede. I think the Americans will hit us here in the middle of Kornberg hill and that the upper ones are only for when, and if, we retreat uphill."

As we walk over to the mid-level trench works, I turn to Horst and comment, "Nice view of Kirchhiem from here. I've heard this hill is 800 feet above the valley floor."

"Let's hope this isn't too high. Maybe the Americans will deduce that we are likely on the highest promontory in the valley and aim right for us."

"At least we have the higher elevation for firing down on them," says Ewald as he carries a pick-ax over his shoulder and a shovel drags from his other hand. "I couldn't imagine trying to charge up this hill myself. Even if I knew the defenders didn't know what they were doing."

Looking back uphill at the upper trenches some 200 feet higher, I see that there are anti-aircraft guns and anti-tank howitzers positioned in nests with camouflage nets strung overhead. The top of Kornberg hill is a grassy, flat knoll with no trees, so those trenches are open to the air. Fortunately, down at this mid-level there is a thick patchwork of broadleaf trees.

As Horst, Ewald and I work on the communication trench, we can hear the whir of engines coming from Kirchhiem. Sergeant Bauer's ears pick up on this and he asks for the binoculars from me. As he scans the valley floor he says, "Those are not retreating Germans. These are American troops heading our way. Let's see, I would say they are some three miles off. They are making their way faster than we thought."

There is a shuffle of activity running through the whole company as the command post eagerly tracks the American's early arrival. As he continues looking out the binoculars, Sergeant Bauer comments,

"There is a long convoy of trucks, jeeps, tanks and howitzers. Must be a full regiment of men. Some men are walking alongside but it appears many are being transported in the trucks. Now they are moving off the road and fanning off into the woods. Not a good sign. They probably have figured out this hill is fortified. Now we won't be able to use our pre-sighted cannon fire along the road passes. These Americans are getting too wise for that trap."

Standing next to Ewald and me, Horst says, "They just don't know that our regiment is composed of so many inexperienced men, young and old.

I say in response, "At least we have some Wehrmacht regular companies here and thank God they are manning the artillery placements."

Horst grunts out, "We have Party members leading our battalion. These characters have vowed to keep the Fatherland fight going to the end."

"They and the likes of Fleischen," I say, "are pledged to fight to the last bullet. This is madness, Horst. How did this war reduce itself to these babbling idiots with no semblance of reality?

"I know," says Horst looking at Ewald with pity. "We are now going to throw our elderly and youth at a professional, well-armed and well-fed army while we barely know how to shoot our weapons. How am I going to get a good shot at tank downhill with this Panzerfaust"

Ewald's growing worry on his face turns to surprise as he looks up and points toward the western skies, "Look, fighter planes, coming in low. They are over Kirchheim and heading this way."

We then hear the growing buzz of Mustang fighter planes flying low and over the valley's road. As we count out six echelons of fighter planes, we hear orders for the upper positioned men to descend to our lower trenches. As these men start pulling out of their trenches and run to the lower ones, I hear a high-pitched sound coming from the other direction; it is our Me 262's from the Leipheim field beginning to take on the Mustang planes. First three, then three more Me 262's zip by on a steady climb upward for higher altitude as they are just gaining speed.

As I watch the jets soar overhead, I exclaim, "It looks like they will attack the Mustangs from a higher altitude and then swoop down on them. Everything we have been working on for the last five years is now in action above our heads."

"Yes, and I probably built the fuselage for some of those jets with my own hands," says Horst. "God help us find some justice in that."

Then Ewald cries out, "Heavies! There are waves of bombers behind the fighters. Must be hundreds of them."

As I watch this floating armada blanket the western skies, I realize they are likely heading to Augsburg and the Messerschmitt plants.

With the Me 262's high up above the Allied planes, we see that they are starting to descend upon the bomber box formations and not the fighters. Ewald looks toward the lower level fighters and says, "What, the jets are not going to take on the fighters?"

"Sorry, son," says Horst. "Shooting down bombers are the jets' priorities. We are on our own for this attack."

Lieutenant Heinrichs shouts out, "Everyone take deep cover in your trenches!" Within ten seconds, we hear a high-pitched drone screaming down on us with increasing intensity and then hot cannon fire rips through the trees and flips up the ground in a fast-moving wave. A truck explodes and rolls over while our anti-aircraft guns let out a fusillade at the low and fast flying planes.

Heavy machine gun fire erupts from the batteries in a frenzied attempt to defend our position, but waves of fighter planes keeps pouring rounds into the upper trenches. Most of us, though, are now hundreds of feet below in the relative protection of tree coverage and darkened areas. After a few more strafing passes, the P-51s disappear to join up with the bombers at higher altitudes.

From there we can see a long trail of American bombers stretching across the sky. There must be 300 bombers all tightly grouped into formations. I can see our Me 262s looking just like swallows attacking a hawk, diving down on the *Viermots*. Reports of cannon fire echo through the air and we start to see the first bombers spewing smoke. First one bomber starts spinning down, then a second blows up in mid-air and finally a third starts losing altitude and trailing smoke from one wing.

Other Me 262s are making broad turns after the P-51s and blasting away in short bursts. The P-51's are flying tighter turns and getting in position behind some of the jets and even starting to fire onto them as well. The jets continue their turns and come in for a second run at the bombers. More bombers explode into balls of fire or dismember in mid-flight. With their two passes completed, the Me 262s zip off to the east, likely to Leipheim, while the American fighters vainly try to pursue them. The dogfights continue over the horizon and out of our sight. And with them the long wave of bombers heads off east toward destinations we are likely familiar with.

Captain Fleischen stands up and orders all the platoons back up the hill into the uppers trenches to assume a higher defensive position. A whistle of shells pierce the air, tree branches crack followed by reverberating thuds. This time the earth shakes as their shells are heavier than the one let loose from the P-51s. As more shells drop and explode around our trenches, we all simultaneously turn around and head back to our lower trench placement.

Captain Fleischen then orders us to stay put and starts telling his lieutenants to form a defensive line at this lower level. Lieutenant Heinrichs comes over to the platoon of twenty-five men now as two have already been killed by the air attacks,

"I've been on both fronts and I can tell you that all that training, marching and even that air attack was just a cake-walk compared to what we will see now. The American's are well armed, and determined but at this point they have very young officers leading their companies and I've seen them make many blunders. For one, the junior officers will lead, coming out first and then you will see their men marching behind them. So for the best effect aim at the first man out as he likely their commander. This should cause some chaos in their ranks."

Heinrichs then yells out where each squad should dig in and mount their weapons. We have two machine guns and one mortar to fortify our platoon, but we only have two-hundred rounds and about thirty mortar shells for each. On top of that each of us has forty bullets, although I see that bullets are being redistributed from our earlier casualties. Some men are armed with Panzerfausts but until the tanks get closer, I don't see what use they will be now.

"Major Schiede has ordered that we are to hold this position at all costs. We cannot let the Americans take Ulm because from there they will go straight to Augsburg. At best we can fall back only to the trenches up the hill. There we still have the heavy weaponry and some surplus of cartridges and stick grenades."

Everyone in the platoon has a sunken face of dreadful determination as if we are preparing for a sacrificial tribute. We know that this is the hour we will be put to the test. A test that we have not had time to study enough for. I think to myself, 'Will everyone else hold together mentally? Damn the rest, I just need to keep my cool and stay focused.'

As Sergeant Bauer adjusts his machine gun post with a magazine of bullets, I squat down next to him. "Sergeant, with all due respect, that comment about holding this position at all cost seems suicidal."

"I know, Armand, but that cursed Schiede is a committed Party member. I sometimes think they don't believe we deserve Germany ourselves."

"Ok, I understand your position and you have my word I will fight for every man here."

"People of their kind will never surrender, and they will drag us all down with them in the process. But as a non-commissioned officer I have no choice to but follow his orders. Now man your mortar post, Kindermann," responds Bauer.

Heading back to my trench emplacement, there is a break in the cannonade. From out of the quiet we hear the crunch and rattle of armored vehicles pressing through the woods. My ear strains to figure out how far they are: it seems like a good 1000 yards. Still, we cannot see the American soldiers but we know they are closing in on our hill position.

The whir of machinery and the clanking of tank tracks increases in sound blindly through the thick forests in front of us. The Americans are not hiding their distance from us and they must be preparing to take the hill head-on. I jump into a low-lying pit next to my mortar mates, Horst and Ewald. Ahead of us, Sergeant Bauer signals for us to prepare to load the mortars and to set the sights for 500 yards out. I hear the cranking of machine guns loading magazines in place and the hammering back of gun bolts. We crouch low, peering into the forests but still we see no sign of American armor or troops.

Then a series of whistling sounds rip through the silent and suspended air breaking trees and branches while terminating with thunderous bursts of fanning explosions. The earth around us appears to heave up in a phantasmagoric gasp belching out its decomposing soil. I lower my head into the ground to avoid the flying dirt while hot shrapnel flings through the air. There is a brief five-second pause and then another round of high-pitched screams ending in explosions protruding around us like fountains of fiery columns. This time the line of fire hits beyond us toward our upper entrenchments and the heavy weapons.

The next round comes in and the explosions are now starting to fall on our lower entrenchment. I see a Kubelwagen flip into the air and men's bodies get thrown out like rag dolls. The bombardment goes quiet and we lift our heads to look out. I hear commands being barked from the sergeants and the officers telling us to load our weapons and search the woods for incoming troops. Even though my ears are ringing and the dust in the air makes it hard to see more than 100 yards around me, my mind starts to make out the cries of injured men. I can't see them, nor do I want to at this point. I've never seen a man blown to bits by a shell and I feel it will be too disgusting and disheartening for me. I am scared enough as it is and all I can do is grip my Karabiner tightly. I look to Horst and Ewald and they both have shocked and frozen looks of fear across their faces.

There are shouts running through the ranks, 'Amerikaner!' Sergeant Bauer motions for us to man the mortar and start loading it. Horst moves ahead to act as the forward spotter and yells back that the troops are downhill 400 yards out. Ewald and I then set the distance to 350 yards, hold a mortar shell ready in our hands and await the go-ahead.

While the troops are being spotted off in the woods, we hear the crunching of trees and branches as Sherman tanks start rolling out of the haze. Knocking down trees, they halt, shift their turrets, and then I hear the retort of tank fire with a corresponding explosion in our ranks.

At this point the officers yell out for us to shoot and our platoon and all the others let out a flame of small-arms fire out into the woods. The American troops are still hard to see as they disappear behind the many trees while some hide behind the tanks.

Sergeant Bauer brings his hand down, giving us the go-ahead to fire the mortars and I drop a shell in. Horst, while looking through his binoculars, points his thumb up indicating that we need to raise our sites. I load another shell while Ewald braces the mortar and then Horst gives us the 'ok' sign that we are on target. I then keep dropping in shells as soon as they fire off.

With the rattle of our machine guns blazing away, a Sherman tank seems to notice us and starts rotating its turret toward our direction. Sergeant Bauer flags us to aim toward the American tank and we adjust our sights for 300 yards. After Ewald adjusts the angle, I drop another mortar shell and I can see that we landed it right in front of the tank. Close, but not enough to stop it. The tank then lets out a flash from its muzzle and our machine gun nest explodes into the air. Lieutenant Heinrichs is thrown to the ground, rolls a few feet and looks dazed but he isn't injured.

Now the American troops are getting bolder and they start scrambling forward. I can hear their small arms fire. The whistle of bullets snaps through the air around me as branches and trunks start splintering with the onslaught. A haze of yellow sawdust envelopes me, limiting my view and an acrid smell of sulfur stings my lungs.

Horst yells at us to set the sights at 250 yards and to start dropping shells on the incoming soldiers. Damn the tanks, the soldiers are going to swarm us now. I drop a few more shells and I realize we only have ten more left.

Upon the last mortar shell drop, I grab my Karabiner rifle, pull back the safety and throw myself into the trench just ahead of me. When I look down upon the forest I see there are troops some 200 yards below us, a little far for my sights. The tank is still firing away at our position, but it has been stopped in its tracks.

Now for the first time I start firing my rifle into the oncoming enemy, but I find myself wildly shooting at anything and before I have even lined up a good sight. I am both petrified and excited in a strange way as I keep pulling the trigger without aiming.

As the Americans pull within 100 yards of us, they start pouring out their rifle fire and some with deadly aim. Sergeant Bauer pops up on the edge of the trench and positions himself in with one foot forward while he drops the other knee down on the ground. While exposing himself to the Americans, he starts firing away at them but then I hear a slap like an oar hitting the water. Bauer falls back into the trench, his body limp, his arms sprawled out as he slides over the crumbling earth. Horst is right next to him and yells out, his eyes wide with shock,

"Bauer has been hit! My God, I think he is dead. As Horst says this, I hear another body slap and Horst lurches over holding onto his stomach. Blood seeps through his fingers and a dark red blotch grows around his hand.

I step over toward Horst and try to bring him down gently to the bottom of the trench. He grits his teeth and takes in short breaths through pursed lips. Ewald comes over as well but we both are ignorant as to what to do.

"Medic! We need a medic," I shout out, but no one comes forward. There are no medics stationed with our platoon I realize.

As bullets whine over our heads and pilfer the earth around us, I sit next to Horst and hold his shoulders, "Horst, hang in there. I will get a medic to come over from the next platoon."

"Armand," gasps Horst, "It hurts, badly. Oh lord, I don't think I am going to make it," his eyes rolling upward.

"You will, Horst. It will be fine. We just need to bandage you up," I console him with nothing to back up my offer.

"He's turning pale and starting to shiver," states Ewald as he comes to his other side. "Here, take my overcoat to stay warm."

Horst hangs his head lower over his chest still breathing in gasps while writhing with the pain, his boots digging into the earth. We hear commands to move up to the higher trenches and Ewald says, "Horst, we have to leave you. Stay low and keep my coat on. We will come back." With that Ewald and I follow commands, grab our rifles and magazines, and then start climbing.

I scan the troops moving uphill, it seems that our platoon is half the size at this point and I am assuming we have just left behind many of our dead or wounded men. As we start scrambling up winding our way through the trees we hear the whistle of bullets interspersed by tank shells bursting and hissing through air around us. The upper trenches are in my sight but as if in a bad dream no matter how fast I run they do not appear to be getting any closer. Still, Ewald and I step hurriedly into the uneven ground to move upward while clinging to our rifles and magazine boxes.

As our company and the other ones make their way up the hills, our artillery and anti-aircraft guns let loose on the Americans downhill. They start firing before many of us get into the lines, but they are aiming just over our heads. As I jump into a trench, I look back and see that our artillery is having a withering effect on the attackers. Tree trunks are mowed in half, large branches snap off and rows of American soldiers collapse like scarecrows onto the ground. A Sherman tank comes under our anti-aircraft gun's fire and explodes with an upward flame throwing the turret into the air. Our large caliber machine guns burst open up with frenetic life with a shredding sound and it now seems the Americans have stopped moving forward. I believe we have them pinned or at least halted. Our upper position over the enemy has given us the advantage over the land troops, for now.

Men are running behind the trenches passing out more magazines of bullets along with more stick grenades. Our company of three platoons is in disarray and reduced in size as Captain Fleischen strides close behind the trench line barking out commands for us to assume our rifle positions and prepare for another attack.

I point my rifle down the hill and scour between the trees for any moving Americans. Between the loud reports of our guns, their guns, their tanks and our artillery, I cannot make out the sounds of my rifle reloading and firing. In fact, I think I just 'fired' off five rounds before realizing that my cartridges have been empty for some time. I look over to Ewald, he seems frozen and is not even shooting as he keeps his head pressed against the dirt wall of the trench.

It goes quiet and the sound of wind rustling the leaves becomes apparent for the first time since this battle began. I say to Ewald, "The American shouts are getting fainter. I think they are retreating."

"God, let's hope so," says my younger mortar mate. "I don't know how much longer I could've held out."

"It's alright, Ewald. We are much safer here at this higher elevation." As I say this, I only wish I could believe what I just said.

"Do you think Horst will make it?" ask Ewald. "He didn't look too good and what if the Americans entered his trench?"

"Let's pray he has made it this far. I felt awful leaving him there but we had no choice." As we keep a low profile in our trench, we can start to hear the moans and wailings of men crying out for someone to help them. The haunting and disturbing sound wafts through the air like a poisonous gas and demoralizes me more than seeing the men being shot at.

"Is someone going to help them?" says Ewald while his cap sinks over his left ear.

"We don't have orders to leave our position right now," I respond. Listening to these pleas for help causes my heart to ache. Those are our fellow plant workers lying on the slope below us and we are impotent to help them

Lieutenant Heinrichs, covered in mud, comes by. "It looks like they have called off their attack for now. But we must sit tight as they may just be regrouping and figuring out a different strategy. It could be that they call in for reinforcements. In the meantime, we have to be vigilant and keep a watch out for their next attack. I will call out names for those who will act as sentries. Armand, take a headcount of who is present, wounded or disabled. Also count out the weaponry we have left.

"Yes sir," I respond, and scurry off along the trench counting our men, magazines, machine guns and mortars. Following my quick survey, I come back and report to him, "There are twelve of us here but two are pretty shot up. I don't think they can hold on, much less fire a weapon."

Heinrichs looks concerned, his calmness being only a thin veneer hiding his worries. "We could be overrun by another surge of theirs. Right now, these artillery pieces are keeping us entrenched and fighting. We've sent a request in for reinforcements, a company of men. They should be coming up the Gruibingen pass from Ulm, and they will also be carrying more ammunition for us. Our scouts are keeping an eye out for them. Estimates are that they will be here by midnight."

I think to myself, 'If we can only hold out until midnight.' It's only five in the evening, the Americans could surge again upon our hill at any time. At this point, Captain Fleischen walks up from behind and starts to confer with Heinrichs right in earshot of me,

"Lieutenant, your platoon is the nearest to the downslope of the pass and Major Schiede is anticipating that the enemy will be targeting this point for a counter-attack. I am going to cluster the other two platoons within a hundred yards of your platoon to fortify this position. It's critical to hold them off at all costs. They can't break through here or we lose Augsburg."

"Yes, Captain. Understood. I will position my men to take deadly aim at any uphill attacks. Where will the heavy artillery be placed?"

"We will bring one cannon and one anti-aircraft gun over here. But we can't afford any more manpower to be moving the pieces around. We also suspect that they may try to outflank us and come up the backside of the hill."

"Captain, the Americans will barrage us again and then follow that with an attack. With only about half our company in place, the next attack could decimate our defenses."

"Enough Heinrichs," growls Fleischen. "Don't even think of that possibility. This is it. We are to stand or die here. And remember, I will shoot the first man that turns and runs, refuses to fight or stands up to surrender. Is that clear?"

"Yes sir. We will fight to the last."

Fleischen swings around and heads off. Heinrich slumps down into my trench pit, looks at his feet and takes a deep breath.

"You know, we don't stand a chance in holding off another attack, sir," I say.

Heinrichs says while still looking at the ground, "I've fought on the Russian front. I've fought on the French front lines but there was always a point where we could say, 'fall back to the Fatherland.' Now we are in the Fatherland and there is nowhere to fall back to."

"How about back to our hamlets and families?" I ask.

"What hamlet and families? They've been bombed off the face of the earth." says Heinrichs as he sinks on his hunches deeper into the trench.

Dusk grows upon the hill as we can see the sun setting over the valley highlighting the church towers of Aichelberg some five miles west.

As hoped, at midnight a company of soldiers comes up from Ulm bringing with them the much-needed supplies along with morale-boosting. Under cover of dark, we also make our way down the hill to collect our dead and wounded, ever cautious of snipers. As Ewald and I crawl into our lower trench position, we find Horst still under the greatcoat. Ewald lifts up the coat and puts a hand on Horst, then looks at me and says, "There is no life in him. He's dead." Ewald's eyes look up to me for an explanation. "He was alive just six hours ago. I thought he would make it longer than this."

"Ewald, take your coat and the other weaponry here and let's head back up," I say to him. "Maybe we can give him a proper burial tomorrow. For now, let's try to get some sleep in our rifle pit."

APRIL 18, 1945

The sky is a dusky orange when I am awoken by Ewald mumbling in his sleep. The boy is muttering something in a rapid and agitated tone. "Ewald," I say as I shake his arm. "Wake up and grab your gun."

"What?" says Ewald as he comes to. "Oh no, I am still here in this hell hole."

"It's ok, we've condensed our position with the other platoons. We will get out of here soon enough."

"Herr Kindermann, I don't think I can take another day of this fighting. I just want to go home and be back at my school today."

"I am sorry, Ewald. I can't make that happen. I would rather be back in my design barracks as well. But here we are, fodder to this desperate defense bid the Party has created."

As I say this, a screaming sound pitches through air as shells break their way onto our lines. A bombardment of thirty minutes follows while we duck our heads into the shallow holes we have dug for ourselves. Some of the shells hit their targets and we lose more men and some artillery pieces. I press my hands against the pit's walls, dig my fingers into the soil, and worry that Ewald and I could be buried if a trench wall collapses on us. Then the barrage ends and officers bark for us to pop up and man our weapons.

I grab my rifle and look down the hill, sure enough, the Americans have closed in on us while we were being bombarded. This time I see a line of four Shermans some 300 yards out tracking their way up the hill with trails of men behind them. Our artillery and anti-aircraft blast the incoming line, but the Americans press on through the hail of fire.

Unlike yesterday's attack, the Americans call in an airstrike just as they attack the hill. Without my noticing it, airplanes dive on us and a gun rattle breaks through the air. A strafing line pops up alongside the crest of hill, ripping up one of the anti-aircraft stations. Another set of planes launch off rocket-propelled missiles from their wings and these land high of our position. This is followed by another barrage of artillery fire to the rear of our trenches making the soil vibrate and crumble. I feel like the earth is going to swallow me whole and that I will not be able to stand up or run away.

As our defensive line fires away, the American troops and tanks fan out all around us. They are going to try to flank us but this time on both sides. Which way to turn and to defend ourselves? Soon they will be surrounding us. Now within 100 yards of us, their rifles are starting to pick away at us. Within a half hour of this, men drop dead up along the trench and I realize that my platoon is nearly gone. Ewald and I along with two other remaining members of our Volkssturm platoon, decide to run over to join the one next to ours. As we scurry through a connecting trench it appears there is a lull in the American attack.

Approaching the next platoon's placements, I realize that all three companies are huddled here for a final defense. Ewald hesitates before we arrive to this company grouping and looks downhill. I notice his eyes are wide with fear and his chest is heaving deeply. He then says to me,

"I am leaving this now! I can't take it." And with that he runs with his hands up toward the Americans. I call out to him and say, "Ewald! Don't. It's dangerous."

Coming from our company placement, I hear two cracks of a pistol. Ewald's back and head arch back as his body tumbles down the hill and he slouches into a lifeless heap. The shots have come from our side and I see Major Schiede still holding out his smoking Luger pointing in the direction of Ewald.

"Any more cowards coming forward?" exclaims Schiede.

I look at Schiede with disbelief. He just killed a German, a boy at that. A boy who had no capacity to handle this horror. How could have he done this?

As I look around the remaining battalion, I see that half of them are prostrate, dead or injured. It is a mad scene of carnage; men writhing in pain, blood stained faces and torn uniforms, body parts lying in the bottom of bomb craters, trees denuded of branches and leaves and an endless cacophony of explosions. The able men continue to fire but many are starting to reload in their rifle pits and are taking stock of the matter. I see uncertainty in their faces and as I connect my glances with theirs and I sense we are on the same page. This must end, now.

With Captain Fleischen pulling up to his side, Major Schiede continues pointing at our soldiers and approaches one that is holding his arm while crouched in the trench. Is that Walter? I can't tell with all the dirt in everyone's faces.

"Up you *schwein*. Is this the way to serve your Führer? I will shoot every insubordinate before I let the enemy take this hill."

The soldier, who is bleeding from the arm looks askance at Schiede as if saying, 'what more do you want me to do?' Schiede bellows out, his eyes bulging, "Get up and fight or I will shoot you." He lifts his Luger, lines it up on the soldier in the pit, his eyes ablaze.

I think it is Walter. Suddenly my mind erupts with fiery, burning images of my flat leveled, my lovely wife dead, the Party rallies I had to go to, fathead Göring at our plant and I feel my temples swell with pressure. My heart races, my chest pounds, adrenaline flows icily down my arms into my fingers. I can hear American voices off in the distance. Bullets hiss by me, men scream, my ears are ringing. I rise out of the entrenchment, raise my Karabiner, line up the sight on Schiede's chest and without further thought, pull the trigger. A retort goes out and he staggers, his mouth opens in shock, not knowing where the shot came from. As Schiede looks around, he notices me standing there, he looks me in the eyes with disbelief. I then fire a second shot into his forehead. His head flips back with his mouth wide open, his glasses fly off and he lands flat on his back.

"Kindermann, you traitor!" yells out Dieter as he raises his pistol and lines it on me. I only see his face partially as his Luger is lined up straight on me. I lower my Karabiner and continue staring at Dieter. We look at each other, for seconds but it feels like minutes, reflecting on our all year's past. Where did my old roommate go? Is this really him in front and about to kill me? This will be an absurd way to die. I am breathing heavily expecting this to be my last. I throw my gun down finally as Dieter continues pointing his pistol at me.

Shots are still incoming from the American's downhill and we can also hear their calls and shouts. I don't take my stare off Dieter, he seems to be breathing heavily as well. A shot rings out, I see a flame from his Luger and then a whizzing sound passes over my head. Dieter has shot past me. His face then contorts into pain, confusion and finally sadness. He seems to be losing his bearing, his stature as Captain. He slowly lowers his pistol, finally throwing it down as well, and then he raises his arms up in surrender.

With this action, the remaining company stands up along the entrenchments as their arms rise in a wave pattern. The Americans halt their firing and then start running around our lines, encircling us. We all have our heads bowed, our rifles at our feet. I hear the shouts of the Americans while they wave their guns at us from a distance. They look cautious as if concerned that this is a ploy but we all tilt our heads down upon our chests in resignation and avoid their glances. Within seconds the American troops rush in pointing their rifles at us and ordering us to line up. Their medics rush in too and they start dressing our wounded men. One takes Walter out of his pit and lays him down to start cleaning the bullet wound in his arm.

As I am standing near Walter I say in a quiet tone, "I did it for you Walter. But you ended up saving the rest of our lives,"

Through gritted teeth and heavy breathing Walter responds quietly, "Thanks, my friend, you took care of me. You watched my back just like you said you would." Walter places his head back on the ground and closes his eyes from pain and exhaustion as the medic starts dressing his wound.

I look over toward Schiede's body lying on its back, deflated and lacking any soul. Did he ever have a soul?

The Americans then continue their round up of our company, our battalion and then our entire regiment. As I scan the lines of downcast German Volkssturm soldiers I notice that the Group officers look dejected while the common citizen soldiers like myself, seem highly relieved it is over. While many men witnessed my assassination of Schiede, no one says anything to me. If anything, they keep quiet about it and to me, that lets me know that I did the right thing for our folk. The Reich's Volkssturm is over for me.

MAY 1945

I stand looking through the barbed wire strung through wooden posts that corrals us German prisoners. There are probably over ten-thousand German men grouped into their regiments throughout this wide-open farm field. American soldiers with an MP insignia band, are searching through our clothing and detaining any personal effects that could be used as weapons. They ask us basic questions as to our knowledge of battle plans and defense works behind the lines. Most soldiers reveal the least they can and I follow suit.

Officers of a different insignia from the ones that captured then run through the camp and pull aside soldiers and officers. From what I can tell they are from an Airforce intelligence agency and that they are not foot soldier types. Apparently, someone had mentioned to the Americans that I was a designer at the Messerschmitt Plant and now they are keenly interested in me. My main concern is to figure how I can get out of here, contact my parents and then track down the whereabouts of Leonino and Rosa. I barely got out alive out from my one battle engagement and I hope to stay alive until I find Rosa.

A sergeant approaches me and commands me to follow him into his Jeep. I am taken to a makeshift field office and eventually an officer sits me down for an extended interview. A translator sits next to him and the he speaks,

"Herr Kindermann, I am Colonel Watson from the Army Air Forces Information Office. I am here to investigate what you know about the Messerschmitt company and its planes. Capturing your regiment and the Volkssturm company was quite the treasure trove. A whole company of Messerschmitt plant and engineering workers. You couldn't have made my job any easier. Colonel Watson learns back in his chair and takes a puff from his cigar.

"Tell me what you know about the Messerschmitt planes? What was your level of involvement?"

"Sir, I was a draftsman of various planes produced at Messerschmitt AG, but I know little of the engineering principals underlying them. I only drew at the direction of the engineers and did what they told me."

"Well, we've been told from various plant laborers, that you were one of the key designers of the Me 262 jet and that there may have been some prototype under development of the next generation Me 262? Can you tell me anything about this next jet?

I break a sweat as I know where this conversation is going and where the Americans' interests lie. They want to replicate our jets and get a jump on them before the Russians do. If I divulge the full amount I know I will be taken in for further interrogation, perhaps even an internment camp. The war may be close to over but it's still on and I am still a German. Or I could act ignorant. I am not an officer or Plant director with higher levels of authority.

Colonel Watson continues after my silence, "I will tell you that we have captured the airfield at Lager Lechfeld and there we confiscated nine Me 262s in perfect shape. As we speak, they are at a French port being readied for shipment to America. Mr. Kindermann, it appears you need to think about this some more. Could I offer you some brandy, from my home State of Connecticut? You see, America needs your intelligence more than ever. And now that we have bombed your cities into rubble, we now will have to scramble to beat the Russians out of here. It is essential for your people's long-term defense against Communist Russia to work with us Americans and provide us the technical data on your advanced weaponry. Give up your allegiance to the Nazi government and work with us to save Germany and Europe from a Red takeover. Your other option is waste away in a prison camp for God knows how long."

He leans back and lifts a snifter of brandy up and offers me a '*prost*'. I 'prost' back and smile with a slight chuckle.

"Surely you don't think a mere drafter such as me would have much to offer American scientists?" I then down my snifter with a bit of relish knowing that I may have deflected his keen interest. Or do I?

"Mr. Kindermann, you will stay in the intelligence detainment camp for a few days and we shall sort things out. But you may receive a few more visits from very interested members of my agency, the Army Air Forces Intelligence Office. We have formed a task force called LUSTY and it stands for Luftwaffe Secret Technology. Our goal is catch up and recreate your jet for ourselves. Or as we say exploit, Nazi technology

As I tip back the snifter, Colonel Watson continues,

"You know Herr Kindermann, I've flown the Swallow and it is a beauty of a craft. That bird is smooth, fast and easy to control. I am amazed at how you Messerschmitt engineers put that one together. And we were bombing the hell out of your factories at the same time while you were developing it."

"The production of the jet from design to fabrication was quite a story," I concede finally. `

"Well, my whole unit has garnered a new nickname since we have been buzzing around Europe with your jets. They've started calling us 'Watson's Whizzers' and I like the label." The Colonel then takes another sip of his home State liquor. "I think that moniker is going to stick. Thanks for the jet planes, Herr Kindermann."

With that comment, I know that Watson already has keen intelligence on my involvement with the Me 262 and that further denial of it is just going to make my life more miserable. With resignation I say,

"We worked hard on the jet and I must see where this war ends up before I divulge everything I know. I am a Volkssturm unit member, so I am something of a prisoner of war by Convention."

"The way things are looking, it is a matter of weeks before the war is all resolved. And as a prisoner of war we will detain you at our pleasure. Thanks for chatting with me."

I am led to a set of barracks with other Messerschmitt engineers and managers along with a growing group of Luftwaffe officers. A sergeant then instructs us that this will be our 'home' for the next week. We are assigned bunks, provided sheets and some American rations to keep us fed and settled.

As I enter the wooden holding barracks I see slumped bodies sitting on the benches awaiting their fate. As I work my way past the many ashen, downcast faces, the blue, gray haze of the room starts enveloping me like a set of chains. I approach an open seating area I realize that the man there on the bench is Professor Messerschmitt. He has a brown US Army blanket draped over him and he is looking down into the floorboards. He doesn't notice me until I sit right next to him and I state in a hushed tone,

"Professor, it is me, Armand. Good to see you again but not under these circumstances.

"Armand, yes. His sentences and thoughts seem to fall short; he doesn't look me in the face but only lost in a distant thought.

"I don't know what to tell you now. It's over, isn't it? All that we worked on, dreamed about, that kept us up at night and day bent over our design tables. So many plane ideas, so much more that were just getting going on. It is like having your teacher call the time and pulling your drawings out from under you. Only that you knew you weren't done. You had more to go, more to explore. Just one more change, one more iteration. Who knows where it would all end?

"How could we have ever finished our work? I now realize that I set myself up for failure by continually changing and designing new features on the planes. Because this war was like a big clock in which our assignments had to be done in a certain time or everything was marked as a failure."

I start to say something supportive and even to contradict the Professor, but I realize that this is not the time to rally him.

"You did a great job, Armand, no matter what happened with this war. You know that our plant design bureaus were all in their own little worlds. It didn't matter that the Americans took Sicily, the Russians took Kursk or that English finally crossed the Channel. That was their war. Ours was with time, technology and possibilities that only we could imagine. A designer's quest for the truth and to make the future a reality now."

I listen in admiration and sorrow for the professor. Even with the defeat he still has fire in him to pursue the jet plane designs, war or no war. It wasn't about the war to him, the Nazi Party, and fat Göring's Luftwaffe edicts. It was his planes, his company and his team of designers."

Messerschmitt heaves his shoulders in a long sigh then lifts his head up toward the dusty, dark rafters overhead. I can see he is envisioning other worlds, other possibilities and realizing that for now they have come to an end.

"You know, I was only fifteen years old when I built my first glider with that architect, Harth. It was a grand and formative time for me. I was so focused on getting those gliders to hang in the air for just another five minutes longer. What I wouldn't do to tinker and tweak with those planes. I banked the whole family wine store on my first factory, but I always knew that I would come out ahead. I just knew that my designs were superior to anyone else's. Well looking back, they weren't as superior as I thought, I was just one step ahead of everyone. And I stayed that way for years."

Messerschmitt pauses again, and I stay quiet, looking ahead as well. He then starts up.

"So many beautiful planes. The Swallow, my God. We designed the airframe in 1938, even before the war started. Imagine if Germany had a fleet composed of those jets instead. Imagine the outcome of the air war?"

"Yes," I say, "but we never could get the RLM to fully buy into the jet. And when they finally did, it was too late."

"True, but beyond the Ministry and Luftwaffe politics, I think I lost my way. I got avaricious. I couldn't control my appetite of designing for design's sake. I can't even remember how many planes we had under development. Many times, I personally bankrolled the prototyping of the advanced planes. I am sorry, Armand. Some of these I can't tell you about even now because if our interrogators find out, you may be dragged down this hole even further.

What, there were even more planes that I was not aware?

"All I can say, is that we were beyond the jet turbines. Anti-gravitics, flying discs. Let's just say you never heard of the Hannebu Bell projects in Breslau. We even kept a few discs in our Augsburg hangars."

"Ok, I have no idea what you are referring to, so yes, I never heard of those technologies."

Messerschmitt then continues with his soliloquy,

"Good. I will say that the Americans are very interested in the Me 262 and our Project 1101. And while Hornung masterminded the 1101, I still feel deeply attached to this design. But now there are foreign troops swarming all over the Oberammergau complex and the P 1101, like flies feasting on a dying elk.

"You know, when I was captured, it was because I couldn't leave the Oberammergau complex. Everyone else heeded the warning to leave in advance of the Allies. But feeling like a captain on a sinking ship or perhaps more like a mother bird hovering over her chick's nest under attack, I couldn't leave. I just wandered the halls aimlessly until a captain approached and told me to halt. I wasn't going to stop until the other side saw me."

"Were you able to wrap up the blueprints into tubes and place them in a mineshaft?

"Yes, we were ready as word reached us an hour ahead of their arrival."

Messerschmitt takes a long pause, visualizing the planes he left behind, his mouth slightly agape.

"At some point though, I lost it. I lost my touch with the planes' design needs, how to draw them, how they were built in the factory and how the pilots experienced the controls. I threw myself at Party politics, ingratiating the Luftwaffe staff, besting my competition, chasing contracts and keeping my board happy."

"I think if I had stayed directly involved at your level, right at the point where the pen meets the vellum, down to the anchor attachment of each truss, that's where I could've made the difference in getting our planes to the frontlines faster."

"Professor, I think you are a being too hard on yourself. I can only imagine what an effort it must've been to manage the company, to win those contracts, to keep the money flowing in and then keep up on all the plane projects. No, you did a job worthy of Ulysses and just as epic. I think our company will always be remembered for the great planes we put out."

I decide to pause just in case I have overstepped my position for the professor. But at the same time, I want to console him and give him some reassurance at this dark hour, that he made the most incredible effort beyond any of us in the design bureaus.

Changing his mood, the professor whimsically asks me, "So, you had a good time at the Munich Technical Hochschule? I had such good times myself at the university and Munich was a great place to be as a student."

Funny, after all these years, the Professor and I have never reminisced about our shared college experience. I reply, "Oh yes. It was both the most challenging time professionally and the most exciting time socially for me. Not to mention that I met my dear Vanessa. Did you ever celebrate the end of a project at the Hoffbrau Haus where the polka bands play? God, did I have some raucous nights there. That's where I first met Vanessa. Although not successfully at first."

"I was quite the run around myself in college," says Messerschmitt, "and I stayed that way well into my late twenties. Yes, lots of festivities and young women. They all seem so fascinated with my plane building. But once I met Lilly, my life changed, and all the other women meant nothing to me. Armand, if I never told you, I am so sorry that you lost Vanessa. I could only imagine that if I lost Lilly, I would be like a plane without a rudder."

"Thanks for mentioning it, Professor; it was hard to lose her and the kids. I have felt very empty without her and the children. I hope it didn't affect my performance at work."

"No, not at all. With everyone having lost loved ones after that winter bombing I assumed everyone was grieving. In fact, I didn't know where to start offering condolences to people. It was overwhelming, and

I didn't have the energy to let out my sorrow for everyone. So please forgive me, Armand."

"I understand, but it is thoughtful of you to ask now. Yes, it's been hard to adapt to not having her or my kids in my life. Such a deep sense of loss, it's a hole that can never be filled. I've been struggling with the reality of it for over a year now. But I did have some comfort in meeting another woman at the Horgau plant this summer. I just don't know where it is going now."

"I heard rumors about you finding love right in our forest camps," he says, turning his head to look at me and a slight break in his mouth reveals the first light of a smile.

"Ah well, that is still an unresolved issue for me. I didn't know how many people knew about it. I mean, you know it was against the governmental laws for me to be fraternizing with non-Aryan women."

"Oh, Armand, I knew, but I didn't feel it was mine or anyone else's business at the plant. I mean, look at Lilly and me. When I fell for her, she was married to Raulino and I created quite a stir in conservative, Catholic Bamberg. But we wanted each other, and we knew that this was it for life so we continued our course despite the town's disdain for our not getting married."

"Yes, I did fall in love with Rosa. But at first, I didn't know if it was just loneliness and filling the void of Vanessa. But as time went on last fall, I realized that we were meant to meet in life and be something significant to each other. So I became bolder and I am sorry if others noticed."

"Armand, those damn anti-Semitic laws have dogged my company all along. Right away in 1936 I lost some of my best engineers because of them. But you and this woman Rosa, hmm... was that the daughter of the Italian aviation engineer, Da Zara?"

"Yes, it was her. The woman with the lush, wavy hair and green eyes."

"Not bad taste, Armand. I can understand your desire for her. Well, now that this war is over maybe you two can still make it happen. I think you should track her down and try to make a go of it. If you feel that strongly about her, damn the social conventions and do what is best for your heart."

Right woman is worth fighting for her

I am surprised by what Messerschmitt has just told me: that the right woman is worth fighting for no matter what the rules are. Inside, I get a surge of inspiration, an inspiration to find Rosa. I should've kept the relationship going and not to have let them escape. Now I realize that my deep-seated hollowness is not from losing my way, not from losing my family but from losing Rosa. How can I bring her back now?

"Since they escaped from our Horgau camp I've thought that I would never see them again," I say reflecting my growing pessimism. "I've been thinking either they fled west toward Stuttgart or they headed toward the Alps to eventually get back to Italy. It all depends on which direction they headed out. But if they had any sense they would've headed to the American front and surrendered themselves. If the Americans pick up on his rocket plane experience they will likely snatch him up just like they are doing to us."

Shifting my thoughts towards what I am going to do once I get out of the camp, I ask the Professor,

"Do you have any idea where we are heading to next and how many more agencies are going to interrogate us?"

"This is just the beginning, Armand, but I think some American defense group will try to pick you up for their projects. Your knowledge of how to assemble, produce and modify the jet is extremely valuable to them. I can tell from the interrogations that they are not as far along as we were with a jet fighter. And now they want to take our knowledge, advance their designs and hopscotch the Russians. We had them, Armand. I knew it. We had them." Messerschmitt lifts his head up and closes his eyes while his hand forms a clinched fist.

Messerschmitt continues with stronger emotion now, "Do you realize that what the Americans are doing right now is probably the greatest technology transfer to happen in this whole century? And they are going to do it without paying us a *Pfennig* for our intellectual property. They view our design work as their war booty."

And even though many of us were loyal National Socialist Party members they seem eager to incorporate us into their aviation industry. For you though, Armand, your path is much clearer. Mine is tainted with my cooperation with the Party and the use of slave labor. The colonel I last met with yesterday threatened if I didn't cooperate I would be up for war crimes against humanity. The fellow I met with today had a lawyer with him and he said that regardless of how much I cooperated, I would be charged with war crimes. So, I am screwed either way. I stand to lose everything we built together. The plants are closed, the employees are afield, I have no rights to my design licenses and our estate has been seized. Poor Lilly is living in some shack in a hillside right now.

"From what I heard, Armand, I am likely to be shipped off to London for an inquest there. They also mentioned that they don't want the Russians to get a hold of me first. I could become a target of kidnapping by the Reds. Considering this, it could be years before I get back here."

Outside, we can hear a truck pulling up to the barracks, followed by an American soldier barking out orders. I respond to Messerschmitt knowing his departure is imminent, "Professor, you have been the greatest teacher in my life and I don't regret our time together. I became a man here at Messerschmitt AG and I will always be a Messerschmitt man at heart, no matter where I end up. Thank you dearly."

We give each other a tight embrace. As we let go, an officer walks into the barracks.

"The following are to stand up, grab your personal belongings and follow me to the truck waiting outside. Wilhelm Emil Messerschmitt…"

Messerschmitt arranges his bags and then gives me a smile along with a wave. He steps out into the bright outdoors with the barrack's haze of dust enveloping his silhouette. I surmise that this will likely be the last time I see Professor Messerschmitt. My Icarus has flown too close to the sun, and now his wings have melted.

NOVEMBER 1945

"We are now approaching your destination. Wright Field in the State of Ohio," yells out the American sergeant in broken German. "In a few minutes Captain Wenzel will be addressing you on what will happen at this de-boarding."

I look out the train window and I see a flat terrain dotted with farmhouses. 'So, this is the great United States that beat our country?' I say to myself with my forehead pressed to the window.

Ever since I arrived in New York City, I have been under the watchful eye of the US Army Air Forces. First, they gathered up more German plane designers, added a few rocket scientists into the mix and once they had a train car full of us, they packed us up on this train. From what I can tell, Wright Field will be our new settlement camp for the time being. I don't know any of the other engineers or scientists on this train, but I have been chatting with a few and getting to know their backgrounds. We are all a bit confused as to what the end game will be: where we will be working; for whom, and for how long. Currently, we are wards of the Air Force's intelligence officers and they have our fate in their hands.

My attention is drawn to the front of the train car and I see a captain of the Air Forces stand at the head of the row of seats. Having a boyish face and looking like he is in his late 20's, he begins in German, "Good afternoon, gentlemen. I am Captain Lloyd Wenzel and I will be your caretaking officer for your stay here in Wright Field. All your living arrangements, work assignments, immigration procedures, communications back home and how you all live together will be my responsibility."

My seatmates all look at each other as we mutter, 'He actually speaks German pretty well'. One of the senior scientists raises his hand, "How do you know German so well young man?"

Captain Wenzel responds, "I am from the great State of Texas, south of here, and I grew up in a community full of German immigrants. So I grew up speaking English half the time and German the other half. Also, I flew seventy fighter missions in Europe and went toe-to-toe against some of your planes.

The men on the train look at each other with an 'Ah, that explains it' expression and corresponding head nods. Captain Wenzel then continues,

"Now as I explained, I will be taking care of your living arrangements here at Wright Air Base up until the point you are assigned to a job. Your work assignments will be decided by a higher up level of command beyond my authority. The new jobs could be at another airbase, a government research center, a university or some private defense industrialist.

"So, while you wait here under our military custody, my job will be to acclimate and prepare you for a new life in America. We will be having classes on the English language, imperial unit conversions, our government structure, our free-market system and how private enterprises operate. On top of that, we will try to make your life on base comfortable with recreation, music performances and occasional field trips.

"I know that for many of you this is a big transition; a new country, new language and you have no family around here. Some of you have wives and children back in Germany and we will be working on reuniting them with you.

"I will do everything in my power to keep us an active, supportive community. If you have any ideas that could make living here easier for you all, please let me know. If any of you are feeling depressed, anxious or just plain homesick, please come talk to me in my offices. My government's orders are to keep you intact, of sound mind and in good spirits.

I think to myself, 'This will be no different than being at the Horgau camp: barracks, guards and military custody over our lives. This

304

Captain Wenzel fellow, seems like he really cares out us though, or at least our intelligence value.' Captain Wenzel then continues,

"Probably the stickiest point we must address before you are assigned to your jobs is your status as enemy aliens. I will be upfront that many in our country are not too happy that we have German nationals now working in higher levels of the industry. So, my Air Force intelligence agency is dealing with the President, the State Department and the Justice Department to obtain clearances for you all.

"As of right now, it appears the job of winding this through those agencies belongs to me, the man right in front of you. So please be patient with me and I will work hard to get you your immigration visas. All clear, everyone?"

The group lets out a collective '*ja*' and we start chatting with our seatmates about what life will be like at this Wright Air Base. More so from the older Germans, I hear mumblings that they just want to see their wives and kids again. Captain Wenzel then wraps up his speech,

"One last thing. On the weekends you will be allowed to leave the base to enjoy Dayton. We ask that you please not talk about your wartime activities, particularly political ones. We are getting word that some of the Dayton residents are not too keen about having Germans in their midst and some are actively lobbying to get you men sent away.

"Ok, I will be walking down the aisle to chat with each one of you briefly. I will be gathering dossier information, such as your education, past employer and functions, and design expertise. Eventually, we will be developing a resume of your skills, minus any of your involvement with the Nazi party."

The captain strolls down the aisle until he reaches my row.

"Hello there. What is your name and background?"

I respond feeling a bit of pride and indignation of having to continuously submit to this line of questioning. Yet another interrogation type 'conversation'.

"I am Armand Kindermann and I worked as production chief of the Me 262 for Messerschmitt AG."

Captain Wenzel lets out a whistle and says in English with a drawl, "Woo-hee. Those Watson Whizzers were thorough in rounding you folks up. Man, we have some incredible talent on this train"

Switching back to German he says, "The Me 262, yes, that was quite the fighter. When we first sighted that jet we thought it was a wonder-weapon. Like out of a super-hero comic book. Amazing work you people did. I am glad you are on our side now."

I think to myself, 'Am I on your side?' I don't really have any choice in the matter, but this is better than being swept up by those crazy Cossacks. I say to the captain,

"Yes, my expertise is in taking aerodynamist concepts into prototype production, or as we would call it, experimental mock-ups and construction."

"Well, I am sure there will be a few American aircraft companies that will want to get their hands on hot-shots like you. Ok, tell me a little more so I can determine where to assign you for orientation."

"Well, I worked alongside chief designers like Voldemar Voigt, Robert Lusser, and Professor Messerschmitt to create production drawings for all the inner workings of the wing and fuselage assemblies. As we were always changing the engines, weaponry and avionics in this craft, I had to create an endless series of improvements to this plane."

"Interesting," says Captain Wenzel nodding his head. "Any other planes you worked on?"

"Well, sure. I worked on the BF 108, the BF 109 and the Me 163, the rocket-plane glider."

Wenzel's eyebrows pop up in interest and exclaims, "Are you referring to the fighter that Alexander Lippisch developed?"

"Yes, he was the lead designer. It was quite an advanced fighter, maybe too far ahead of its time. We really didn't achieve many kills from it after all that design work."

The Captain leans closer to me. "At Wright Air Base, we have a Me 163 intact at a hangar. Our scientists are still trying to figure it out. So far, they've judged that it's not worth further back-engineering. But with you here, maybe you can give them insight into its concepts and

306

design. You know what, I am going to put you on the tour for Building 89. You are going to be impressed with the planes you see there."

"Yes, Captain. I would be happy to see what's there. I knew many of the men who put their talent and lives into that screamer of a craft. From what I was told, it was like having a rocket strapped between your legs It wasn't called the Komet for nothing."

"Couldn't be any more exciting than riding a bronco buck at a Sunday fair."

"I am not sure by what you mean, 'bronco buck'."

"Oh sorry. It's a fun little activity we like to have in Texas with the wildest of horses. The ones that refuse to be tamed. Kind of like you Germans who fought to the end."

"Thanks for the analogy, Captain. I will take it as a compliment."

"So, do you have a wife or kids in Germany? Part of my other duties will be to round up and reunite the families."

"No, sir. I lost them both during the war." I've gotten so used to saying that that is has lost much of its impact on me, but now that I am in an alien country it hurts deeply. The loneliness of being without a family is now sinking into me.

"I am sorry to hear that, Herr Kindermann. I am sure they were special people and that you loved them dearly."

"Thank you, Captain Wenzel for your thoughts. Many of us are in the same boat. It will be interesting dynamics with all of us getting over losing the war, losing our families and then losing our Fatherland."

Captain Wenzel understands my German well enough to know that Fatherland and home country mean the same thing to us Germans.

"You Germans are a respectable lot and I will treat you all with the same sentiment. Ok, Kindermann. Good talking with you. Time for me to talk with the rest of the men here. We will see you around the base. You will be assigned to a set of barracks built by our National Youth Administration works program. We will have you all together and out of the public's view."

He gets up, shakes my hand and gives me a smile. I look back out the window and see that we are approaching a larger city. A sign zips by that says 'Dayton, Ohio'.

The fellow next to me then says, "I heard you worked at Messerschmitt AG. Interesting place I bet. I was at Arado working on our version of the jet but you devils beat us to it"

"It was a close race, wasn't it?" I say to the gentleman.

"Too close for us. But hey, it's all over now. You know, I heard at my last interrogation about some Messerschmitt people being brought over here."

"Oh, really? I would love to hear what you know."

"Well, this is all hearsay as it's under tight wraps, but I heard that three test pilots and an engineering superintendent of Messerschmitt have all voluntarily come over."

"Do you remember their names?"

"Yes, I do. The test pilots are Karl Baur, Ludwig Hoffman and Herman Kersting. And the superintendent is Gerhard Coulis."

"Yes, I know them all, especially Coulis. He was my boss' boss. I wonder where they will end up?

"Wouldn't we all like to know that one," replies the gentleman. The war is over but our next phase in life is unknown. We are in the hands of the US military.

Once we disembark from the train, we are split into different groups for orientation and tours. Captain Wenzel boards my bus to lead the tour and we are taken to Building 89. It is off to one side of the airfield and it is more an assembly of large hangars. Feeling like ants approaching a cave entry, we walk through the gaping hangar door out of the sunlight and into the din of the voluminous shed.

As my eyes adjust to the darkness, before me appear the forms of various planes. Eventually, as if in a dream, I see our Messerschmitt planes along with others lined up like prisoners awaiting their own interrogation. These once proud, advanced, German fighter crafts look saddened and de-fanged as if they are raptors in a cage with their wings clipped.

I walk by a Me 262 reconnaissance jet, a Me 163 Komet, an Arado 234 and a Heinkel 162A, all stoically facing up to the ceiling as if not willing to share their secrets. The irony of seeing our Messerschmitt planes captured here along with our arch-competitors saddens me. While I was not supportive of the Nazi Party or the War effort, I put all of my heart into the design of these fighter planes. Plus, for over ten years we battled against Heinkel and Arado and now with the war over, the hulks of these planes are tombed up in this American mausoleum waiting for autopsies. Only that, we German engineers are going to be the ones helping the American conduct this forensic examination. Professor Messerschmitt's last words with me that 'we had them' rings hollow as I now see that 'they have us'.

MAY 1946

The hotel room's phone goes off with a loud clang that I am not used to. I stumble over my luggage heading over to the phone and I wonder who could be calling me, I just arrived in Niagara, New York, and I've only met a few people at the Bell Aircraft plant so far. I pick up the phone and a German voice rings through the earpiece, "Armand, is this you?"

"Hello, yes, who is this?"

"It is your old superintendent, Gerhard Coulis. I am here at Bell Aircraft just like you. Welcome, my friend. We will be working together again."

"Gerhard?" I say, "I didn't know you were here as well. The list of Germans being brought over is quite hush-hush. I've only heard bits and pieces so far."

"Well, welcome to the club, and it's a growing one. You will have plenty of old companions around. And we will have plenty of work to do as well."

"It's great to hear a familiar voice, Gerhard. I've been detained and shipped around for months now."

"Well let's not speak so long over the phone. How about we meet for dinner and I can fill you in."

" I would love that. Where do you want to meet?"

"There is a diner down the road from the plant on Niagara Falls Boulevard called Augie's Sunrise. We can meet there tonight at six."

"I like the name of that place. Anything to do with Augsburg sounds good. I will finish unpacking and see you there later today."

I hang up the phone and I hear extra clicks continuing after Gerhard has hung up. Looks like my new bosses are going to keep a close eye on me here. I did sign the papers to commit myself to the American defense industry for the next five years. It was that or a prison camp. So a little monitoring here and there will be worth the price for freedom and coming from Nazi Germany, we were all used to it.

Gerhard and I meet at Augie's Sunrise and we are each excited to see a comrade from the Messerschmitt company. But in such a different setting. The restaurant décor has aluminum finishes everywhere, almost factory like and there are stools where there should be chairs. Plus, the Americans seem to like having records play throughout their meals. Gerhard and I struggle to order dinner as our English is just nominal. We end up pointing at photos of the food printed on plastic sheets.

After the waitress leaves, Gerhard opens, "Armand, it is great to be alive, well fed and working on our dedicated professions, isn't it?

"I guess we will be continuing on where we left off in Oberammergau," I reply dryly.

"I think that is the agenda. We were way ahead of the Americans and now they are eager to incorporate our designs into their planes. Too bad being ahead of them didn't win us the war."

"Maybe we will end up helping them win their next war?"

Gerhard nods. "Exactly. We've jumped from one military juggernaut into one that is even larger. I really don't know where you and I fit into this yet but we are definitely top strategic assets for the Americans for now. So, dinner is on them today and tomorrow and the next day. As long as you and me and all the other Messerschmitt fellows keep cranking out advanced jets, we will have our meal ticket."

"That part sounds good. We might as well ride this one out then. And by the looks of it, life is good here in America after the war. I've never seen so many cars on the road, and they are so large. I heard back in Germany people are starving to death, living in bombed out buildings, and no one has any work except to clear out the debris. It sounds dreadful, perhaps worse than the war itself. I wonder how everyone is dealing with having all these American soldiers on bases throughout the country?"

"I am sure it is very humiliating, but for the folks who never bought into the Nazi vision, I am sure it is a relief as well. Losing the war was the only way to get the Nazi party off our backs."

As Gerhard says this, I have a flashback of the Kornberg Hill battle and the outrage I felt toward Major Schiede quickly rises inside. I still feel I did the right thing. I decide to change the direction of the conversation,

"So, Gerhard, how did you end up here, at Bell Aircraft?"

"Well, like you, I know production of Me 262 jet intimately and after you left Oberammergau, I too worked on the moveable wing jet, the P 1101. And that is just where Bell Aircraft is trying to go. It's just that Bell was three years behind us and now with us on board they can hopscotch ahead to a moveable wing jet. I've also heard that Bell Aircraft is aiming to break the sound barrier, Mach One."

"No, they are? That's what we were shooting to do. Oh, now they are going to take all the credit."

"Yes, that is their goal. I think we have landed in a unique company, one that wants to accomplish singular goals with their planes. I don't think this company is keen on producing the next mass-production fighter jet. They seem more interested in developing something that is radical, on the leading edge. Kind of what Professor Messerschmitt was aiming for."

"So maybe this is a good fit for us? But still it seems like yesterday you and I were fighting these Americans and their P-51 Mustangs off our backs and now here we are helping them out. It's just so ludicrous."

"You will get over it, Armand. You and I are nothing but pawns for whoever controls us. They want fast jets; we give them fast jets. They want to break the sound barrier; we will break it. They want a war with Russia; we will give them warplanes."

"So, that's what my next few years will be all about then, breaking Mach One? No more arming jets with cannons, machine guns and seeing how fast and easily we can produce them. Like in a wheat field if necessary."

"No, America seems to be a big country with bountiful resources. We no longer have to think about using coal-derived jet fuel or avoid using titanium for our turbine blades. We can just design and not worry if there are too many exotic metals in the planes or how long it would take to produce them."

"So, Gerhard, how did it all end for you?"

"I was in Oberammergau with Willy at my side when the word went out that the Americans were riding up the valley. Willy ordered that everyone leave the complex and that the jet blueprints be hidden away in a nearby mineshaft. I left and made my way to the Austrian border where I was picked up by an American regiment heading into Germany. As I drove away, Willy told me has going to take one last look at the P 1101 prototype we were working on. It was not quite done. The fuselage was complete but we were still awaiting the wing assemblies. The Professor looked despondent and demoralized."

"Well, if I hadn't been conscripted into the Volkssturm, I could've whipped up that wing assembly in just two more weeks. You know where I ended up the last month of the war. Thanks to Herr Schiede and those damn Nazi auxiliary militias. They really knew how to make the war's defeat worse for all of us."

"Yes, I heard, and I knew of the selection ahead of time. Sorry that you had to go through that. I can't imagine a worse time to have been in the Volkssturm. I think Schiede singled you out because of his suspicions of you helping the Da Zara's get out."

"Well thanks for sticking your neck out to protect me, Gerhard."

The investigation heat picked up after you left," says Gerhard, "So I too transferred myself out of Horgau and went off to Oberammergau too."

I start to wonder if Gerhard heard anything else about my doings at the Kornberg Hill battle. But he doesn't say anything further, so I assume that word stayed within the regiment.

"What about your friend, Walter Ignaz?" asks Gerhard. "Have you been in touch with him?

"We've exchanged two sets of letters since the war," I say to Coulis. "He is struggling like the rest of the people in finding a regular job and good housing. But he also tells me that he has met a nice lady from the Red Cross and he has been dating her steadily for some time."

Coulis smiles. "Well good for him. I didn't think he had it in himself to settle down. In that way, maybe the war was good for him."

"Well, I do miss him as a friend and I am hoping someday to have him come visit. I even told him that I would pay for his plane ticket once I start making some money here. It does seem that more Germans are coming to the United States for employment in the defense industry. Gerhard, do you have information on who is being brought in? I had met many at the Dayton Field but information on other Germans being brought to other American bases is being kept highly secretive."

Gerhard looks over his shoulders first and then in a soft voice responds, "Well, there are two groups of Germans here now. There is a large contingency from the rocket research complex at Peenemunde and they were brought in under Operation Paperclip. Then there is a smaller group revolving around the jet and rocket plane production brought in under LUSTY. I don't know many of the engineers from Peenemunde except for the director, Werner Von Braun. But on the LUSTY program I heard that many of the test pilots came over and that they picked up on Lippisch and his delta wing rocket crew."

I think about Leonino and Rosa Da Zara. Could they have been picked up as well by Operation LUSTY? Up until now I've not heard any information as to what happened to Doctor Da Zara and Rosa.

"So, do you know which plant or company Lippisch has gone to?

"I don't have a clue yet but it's possible I will find out once I get in touch with more of our ex-Messerschmitt comrades. Given Lippisch's focus on delta wing, rocket planes we just need to figure out which aircraft company is developing one of their own. I am sure that is where Lippisch will show up."

Coulis gives me a deep look as if wondering if he should say something, "Are you hoping to track down Doctor Da Zara and his daughter?"

I look up at Gerhard and respond with a sigh. "I have a slight hope lingering in me that eventually we will connect again. But it's been over a year and I don't know where they are and if they even made it out." I look down at my plate losing my interest in eating. "Back in Germany, how did the Watson Whizzers group pick up on you?"

"Much like you. They detained me, interrogated me, threatened me with war crimes, long-term prison sentences that or employment in United States. So there wasn't much choice, was there? Plus, the aviation industry in Germany is dead."

"Yes," I concur. "One month we are their enemy and the next we are their treasured assets. Strategic ones at that."

"Well you know," says Gerhard, "President Truman went on record that no Nazi Party members were to be allowed to enter the United States even if it were for military purposes. But my well-placed sources told me that the Air Force Intelligence Office lied to Truman by doctoring our dossier clear of any Party involvement. And I don't know about you but in my pre-release, interview I was told to avoid talking about my Party affiliations if not outright deny them. In fact, I caught a glimpse of my new resume and there is nothing on there that says I belonged to the Nazi Party."

"Oh, so we are all absolved of our involvement in the Nazi party, not that I cared for the whole lot of them. How kind of the Army Air Forces to do that for our sake. And we can't even confess even if we are pressed to."

"So, Armand, you, I and other Messerschmitt folks here will just play along and act dumb on our wartime activities. Agreed?"

"Yes, Gerhard. For the sake of all of us I will keep my mouth shut. So, can you tell me who is here in the United States now?"

"Well, you will be meeting many of them soon but some are off at other companies and plants. I know for sure that Hans Honnerung and Heinz Bauer are here. We even have a Wehrmacht General coming to join Bell Aircraft, Walter Dornberger."

"What about Professor Messerschmitt? I haven't heard anything more about his outcome?"

Coulis looks around and leans over the table. "I understand that he is under house arrest in London. I am sure they are trying to soak every bit of information out of him. Probably had the same group of Watson's Whizzers that you and I experienced all over him like bears to a bee's nest. But worse for him though. It looks like they are deliberating pressing charges against our Professor for war crimes. Specifically, the use of slave labor brought in from our conquered nations."

I think of the day when the impressed foreign workers were first brought into the Augsburg plant. The consequences of that abuse will fall upon someone's shoulders and the Allies will be looking for someone's neck to hang for that. But did Messerschmitt willingly do so? Did he have any choice given that the workers were brought in by the SS straight to the factory gates? Could he have made conditions better for them? I then respond to Coulis,

"I only wish the best outcome for the Professor and hope that his neck is saved at the ongoing Tribunals in Nuremberg."

Gerhard looks up with eyes wide. "Good thing I was not in a corporate role or I would be locked up with the Professor right now too. Still, it didn't stop those Whizzes fellows from using it as a threat to pursue charges against me."   *Whizzes*

Gerhard and I go silent, each thinking about the intense interrogations we went under. Breaking our thoughts, the waitress serves us our ground beef sandwiches, which the Americans call 'Philly Steak' and we take a break in the conversation to savor our food. A five-year meal ticket: this is good. I think over how the Americans have actually treated us very well ever since we left the detainment camp. They have given us stipends for new clothing, rent, food allowances and lodging expenses. Our salaries are minimal but everything else is well-covered. And the management of the company seems to be excited to have us onboard.

Later, I head home back to my hotel and ponder my discussion with Coulis. It's May of 1946 and my life has changed so dramatically; no wife or kids, no more Messerschmitt company and now I will be working in another large drafting hall with but with American engineers. I am excited much the way a school kid feels on the first day of class. Maybe next weekend on my free time, I will check out what everyone is telling me to go see, the large falls in the center of Niagara.

APRIL 1947

"Everybody, that is Niagara Falls, Canada across the bridge," yells out Captain Wenzel over the sound of rushing water. "You are to disembark from this bus, walk across the bridge and then present these visas to the Canadian border officials." It is nice to see the captain again and this will be his last official act with the LUSTY engineers in obtaining our work visas. "Once you leave United States and re-enter here, you will no longer be considered enemy combatants. Thanks to our smart fellows at the Army Air Forces, you will be fully free to work in our country now. My work with you will also be completed."

In the year and a half that I have been working at Bell Aircraft I have made friends with many engineers but with the ex-Messerschmitt folks I still feel a deep bond. Frequently, we meet after work, have a few Schlitz beers and spend many of our weekend hours together as well. Usually talk goes around to what is happening back in Germany or who from the old aircraft industry has emigrated here. While Operation Paperclip and LUSTY have brought in hundreds of German engineers, many more have come on their own accord in the last year.

How, I a Nazi plane designer could come and work right in the middle of the United says with a military contractor is still a bit of mystery to me. I was an enemy combatant two years ago, and now am under contract to design jets for Bell Aircraft company here in the State of New York.

★★★

In the Bell Aircraft research center, Gerhard and I listen to a former fighter pilot address our design team. "I caught wind of the jet as I approached the Essen airbase," says the test pilot, Chuck Yeager. "He had just finished a run on our bomber fleets and was coasting back to his base with ever decreasing speed. So, I pushed the stick of my P-51 down hard and came to his level in a matter of seconds. I think he noticed me as he started rolling his plane as if to decrease his profile me. But that poor Jerry had no chance by that point. As I let my Browning guns rip into his fuselage. I was going a good eighty miles an hour faster than him and I just blasted him like I was at a turkey shoot."

"Are you done now, Captain Yeager?" I ask as I sit across the table from him. I look at Gerhard next to me and he too is pushing back into this chair with has a grimace of discomfort.

"Well, I thought you German designers ought to hear what we experienced on the tail end of your Me 262's."

"Yes, thank you," I respond. "That was a very graphic and riveting account. How did the pilot fare?"

"Oh, he made it alright," says Yeager. "I heard after the war while I was verifying all my kill shots, that the pilot successfully bailed out, even at that low altitude. I heard he even went on to fly more missions. I would shake his hand I ever met him."

"Captain Yeager," I ask, "I have been in America for a year and year and half and your accent is very distinctive. Even for a German like me."

"I am from the deep back-woods of West Virginia. So deep, you need a pipe to get down there," says Yeager with a big toothy smile.

Gerhard smiles and then turns to me and says, "Armand, we need to head to the briefing now.

"Thanks for the field input Captain Yeager. It is much appreciated." I turn to Gerhard for a quick look and then slap my hand on the project portfolio, "I think we are done with field data collection and I look forward to hearing what you think of our X-5 prototype, Captain."

Gerhard and I then walk down toward the executive suites and enter a large conference room with a table for twenty people. At the far end of the table are seated ten executive-level managers with Bell Aircraft all already working their way through the agenda. Gerhard and I sit opposite of each other at one end of the long table. A senior manager from Bell is speaking,

"The Pentagon has given us approval and funding to pursue the variable wing jet and at the same time they have funded our X-1 jet for

Chuck Yeager

supersonic speed testing. The variable wing jet, numbered as the X-5 jet, will be headed up by Gerhard Coulis and the chief production engineer will be, Armand Kindermann. Gerhard, would you please give the management an overview and update on the X-5?"

Gerhard rises and walks to the head of the table where we have placed large blueprints and illustrations on the wall.

"The basis of design for the X-5 is the Messerschmitt P 1101 as we last left it in April of 1945. The jet turbine is to be placed directly in the fuselage with aspirator intakes as circlets on each side. While in development at Oberammergau, we initially explored a split V-tail, but we abandoned this as we believe it created a negative spin factor on the flight. The cockpit is streamlined into the front of the fuselage as much as possible to minimize aerodynamic drag. The farthest swept back wing position is forty-degrees but we are finding this steep angle can initiate a spin. Finally, we solved the wing movements with a jack-screw, a horizontal travel bar, and disc brakes.

"Schedule-wise, our team envisions having a mock-up built at the end of this year and then a prototype built in 1948. "From there we will start with the first series production of the X-5. From a staffing point, Armand and I will be the lead design engineers on the project, but we have just heard news that one other Messerschmitt P 1101 engineer is emigrating to the United says to work here on this project. That is Voldemar Voigt and he relays his excitement and gratitude to be working with Bell shortly."

Gerhard did not even tell me this. Then I think to myself that Bell has really rounded up the core crew behind the P 1101. Coulis continues his presentation with a series of technical drawings illustrating the orthographic projection of the jet in plan, port elevation and nose elevation. The management asks a few pointed questions as to what the end merits of this jet will be and Coulis responds, "This jet is the next generation aircraft after the Me 262 and is its direct successor but with a single turbine and a refined tail design. What we learned at Oberammergau about the 262's flight performance for combat was all integrated into this design. We will end up with a point interceptor jet that will fly over 600 miles an hour, perform acrobatic attack maneuvers and carry heavy weaponry to blow up bombers and chase off other fighters."

Coulis completes the presentation while upper management at the head of the table continues discussing the jet amongst themselves.

We are excused and Gerhard walks along next to me. "Armand, I've located information about Alexander Lippisch this morning. Come over to my office and let's chat there."

My heart skips a beat as I know where this trail can lead to. We walk into his office and I pull a chair to his desk.

"You know how our test pilot Heinz Bauer who went over to Convair in San Diego?"

"Yes, I knew Heinz left last month to test fly their latest jet planes."

"Well, he sent me a letter indicating that Alexander Lippisch is located there. So, there is your lead, Armand. Just contact Heinz and he probably will be able to connect you to Lippisch."

"Thanks, Gerhard, this means so much to me. Perhaps now I can piece together what happened to Doctor Da Zara and his daughter."

"Well I know it's been bothering you for a long time so I hope this helps out."

Thanking Gerhard, I exit out of the office and walk to my drafting table and pull out some stationery and start writing Heinz inquiring as to the whereabouts of Doctor Da Zara.

★★★

It is three weeks later when I hear back from Heinz that, yes, Doctor Da Zara is working at Convair and that he arrived there two months prior. He and Lippisch are working on a Delta rocket plane that has some resemblance to the Messerschmitt sanctioned ones. I search around the office to see who has the phone number for Convair in San Diego and finally one of the ladies provides me the number.

I have Coulis sanction my use of a company telephone to make a long-distance call and I start dialing the number. After a few receptionists' transfers, I finally hear the voice of Leonino Da Zara and say, "*Dottore, ce Armando qui.*"

Leonino's voice quickly rises in tone,

"Armando? *Non lo credo, e possibile?*"

"Yes Dottore, I am here safe and sound at the Bell Aircraft company in Niagara Falls. I am so happy to have located you through Heinz. How are you and is Rosa with you?"

"We are doing fine and surviving as usual. Of course, I know your interest in Rosa is probably greater than the one you have in me, ha. But yes, Rosa is here in San Diego with me. She will be so happy to hear from you, Armando, as I am too. We have so much to catch up on."

"I know, Dottore, the last two years have been one big displacement of our lives but we finally have reconnected. I didn't even know if you two made it out of Germany or if you were in Italy."

"We made it alright but not without some adventure. Trying to avoid all the major roads and hiding in barrel carts had its moments but we finally made it to the American front lines and turned ourselves in."

"Well that is wonderful to hear, Dottore. Remember you once stated that at the end of the war we would have a Pinot Grigio da Veneto in Venice someday?"

"Ah, yes we did talk about that. Sometimes I can be very optimistic."

"Well I am still dreaming about it and the thought of it keeps me going while I work here in this strange new land."

"Strange it is for all of us, Armando. This is probably too much change for a man of my age, but Rosa seems to be challenged by the change in setting. I think she never really fit into the traditional Venetian society anyway. Too independent-minded, *capische?*"

"For sure, Dottore. Oh, it is so great to hear your voice, but you are right, I confess, I really want to know about Rosa. How is she doing?"

"Well, aside from taking all this change in culture in stride, I'd say she is actually a little down of heart these days. You know love has eluded her now a second time in life and as a parent, I feel her sorrow so much. Right inside my chest."

"I do miss your daughter terribly, please send her a big *abracio i bacio* for me. I want to get in touch with her soon. I will send her a letter separately."

Leonino gives me their current address and then, being at work, we wrap up on our conversation. I put the phone down and shout in joy, 'yes.' I have located her after two years of separation. I wonder if our feelings for each other will be the same or if time has eroded them somewhat. Either way, I am going to write her a letter tonight after work.

★★★

A few weeks later, I return home from work and I find a letter from Rosa. It is a *par Avion* envelope with blue and red edging and there is a woman's handwriting covering it. I open the letter, being careful to not tear the paper. My hands shake in anticipation of what she has written. As I unfold the letter I see her handwriting, the one that captured my heart the night she left a note at our makeshift Biergarten. The letter reads:

May 10, 1947
Los Angeles, USA

Dear Armando,

I received your letter yesterday and I have taken a day to think about it. I am happy to hear from you but so much has happened in the meantime and I needed to think about what you may mean to me now.

Papa had told me that you contacted him to let us know where you are now. I am glad you have transitioned well, and I wish you happiness in Niagara. I too am adjusting to my new surroundings and find it both adventurous and challenging at the same time. While everything is so different from Italy, I can see that California is a pleasant place to be. I just need time to make new friends and perhaps start a family.

I was not sure I would hear from you again, Armando, and while our moments together in the waldwerk were memorable, I knew that to be happy in life again I would need to move on. You know that I am a realist and maybe even too practical but haven't we all lost a few our dreams from the war?

A little bit on how papa and I ended up here in San Diego. After we had escaped the Horgau camp, that food transporter took us to his livestock shed and had us sleep up in the rafters where they kept hay. From there we were smuggled at night in the truck of a barrel maker and then stayed in their warehouse. Even though we wanted to head toward the Switzerland border, our guides took us toward Stuttgart not knowing that American forces were lined up in the forest about to assault the city.

As we approached Stuttgart we stumbled onto an American picket where we promptly surrendered ourselves to that unit. Being that papa was a man, they pulled him aside for questioning to see what he knew about the German forces. I too was questioned some but not as much as papa was.

When papa revealed to them that he was Italian and had worked for Fiat Aviation, they became keenly interested in him and detained us for five days with them. A few days into this, a major from an intelligence agency pulled us into a tent of interrogation. Papa and I were then separated for a day while they learned he had also worked at the Messerschmitt plant, worked on the Komet rocket, and was an active fascist supporter of Mussolini.

At that point he decided that further hiding this information from the Americans was futile. So, at the risk of being held for further interrogation, Papa decided to tell all of what he knew about the Messerschmitt planes and production process.

After that, we were promptly moved to an American airbase where they put papa to work analyzing captured German planes. At the end of the war, the Americans told papa he could either face prison time for working with Messerschmitt and supporting Mussolini or commit to working with them. How ironic, being that we are Jewish, and our peoples where being liberated elsewhere.

Eventually Papa's work was connected to that of Doctor Lippisch and with Lippisch working in the USA, he was offered to work with him again. And *since we have no family left in Venice for me to go to, papa felt it best for me to join him. Papa got the Americans to agree to this and here I am now living in San Diego while papa works for Convair alongside Lippisch.*

Anyway, Armando, what about us? It's been over two years since we have seen each other. So much as happened along the way. Does what happened in the pine forests at the waldwerk still hold in our world today? Can what happened in a German pine forest hold true in a San Diego dessert? It was very meaningful to me but to be honest I am not sure I want to look back at the horror of the war. Is it time for us to just move on? You know I've been hurt before, with the loss of my fiancé and then you. I have just started healing over that pain and I am not sure I want to open it again.

And while I say these words of doubt, I sincerely welcome hearing your feelings further.

Yours sincerely,
Rosa

I am a bit stunned at the letter; it was not what I was expecting to hear. Maybe I've romanticized the affair over time, maybe I've been holding on too long. Perhaps Rosa is right: I should move on. We are in a different world now and we each could each just happily progress along our own paths. Or could we?

Over the last twenty years my life with design, planes and women have been intertwined. I am now on the brink of a new chapter of my life, a new employer, a new plane type, a new country. Now could be an opportune time for me to redraw the geometry of my life and cross new thresholds of opportunity. So should I pursue Rosa or just move on as she suggests?

I look out the room of my newly rented apartment, my briefcase open with sketches and technical memorandums on the X5 jet. Further out of my window I see broadleaf elm trees arching over the streets while children play stickball. Groups of boys play ball on side of the street while girls cluster around a hopscotch game. The boys seem to ignore the girls, but I know all too well that they are near them for a reason. I look back into my living room and see that I have no artwork or photos on the wall. I have no memorabilia left. All my pictures of Vanessa and our kids are gone in a pile of rubble somewhere in Augsburg. And even now some bulldozer has probably scrapped that site clean.

But I did have one lasting moment in the waldwerk that still resonates deep within my soul. A moment of infinity on the brink of a pool, something so powerful, so sweet yet so connected.

I grab my pen and stationery and begin this letter,

May 17. 1947
Niagara Falls, USA

Dear Rosa,

Come to me, forever....

"Liberta"
Bocelli

EPILOGUE

Armand Kindermann has completed his epic journey, one of transitioning from being a kid to being a man. He survived the war, kept his profession intact and reconnected with his love. Who knows what other journeys he may have, but for now Armand and I have finished our communications.

I know that our journey and bond, have been completed when Armand sends me one last sequence of images. It comes to me much the same way as when one watches a movie. Cinematically, there are two scenes being played out, each in slight slow motion that eventually intertwine. Not letting go of his Italian heritage, Armand also relays music to accompany these final scenes. I hear the song titled "Liberta" written and recorded by Andrea Bocelli and realize that the music and words are an integral part of what he is experiencing.

Armand is in the Niagara Falls offices of Bell Aircraft as he puts together technical papers into a briefcase and rests it on his drafting table. He takes a content look at his drawing, it is the beginning of the X-5 jet and he knows it is a good start. Having worked on the Messerschmitt P 1101, how couldn't he be happy. It is almost a direct copy of what he worked on before but this time it will be fully built and start test flights soon. He grabs his overcoat and slings it over it his shoulder and turns to walk out of the drafting hall.

At the same time but in the San Diego engineering offices of Convair Aircraft, Rosa is dressed for travel with her baggage at her side. She wears a short wool overcoat and has a burgundy-colored scarf draped over her shoulders. She thinks about how she wants to look good for him when they finally meet again. Her father, Leonino Da Zara approaches her with a broad smile and both hands out. They clasp hands and look happily into each other's eyes. Leonino knows that Rosa is separating from him for the first time in three years, but he is joyous to have her move on for love. They kiss on the cheeks three times, embrace and then Rosa turns to walk out the office lobby and down to a waiting taxi. Next to Leonino is Alexander Lippisch, who is beaming with happiness for the two of them as he puts an arm around Leonino congratulating him on this moment of transition.

Armand walks down the halls of the engineering offices of Bell Aircraft while many of his co-workers stand up and come to the aisle to send him off. They wave their hands, yell out wishes of good luck. He doesn't stop for anyone, just nods his head acknowledging their salutations, gives them a bright smile and continues at even pace down the corridor. In the entry lobby is Gerhard Coulis, his eyes sympathetic, sensitive and content. Armand stops to shake Gerhard's hands. They embrace and then Gerhard sends him off with his hand waving high in the air. As he exits the glass doors he places his brown fedora hat over his head and throws on his coat, walking quickly to his car making his coat flow in the wind.

Rosa approaches a DC-3 propeller plane parked on the tarmac at the San Diego airport. The small terminal and various airplane sheds behind her slowly recede from her perspective as she marches confidently toward the plane ramp. The only sound she hears is her heels clicking on the pavement. She climbs up the stairs, takes a seat in the plane and a stewardess with white gloves and a cap assists her with the seatbelt. The plane's propellers start off with a puff of smoke and then they quickly whir into a blur. The nose of the parked plane is kicked high in the air but as it taxis down the runway with increasing speed the nose levels off. As the plane accelerates the landing wheels gently lift off the runway and the plane gains altitude. Rosa takes one last look at the San Diego hills and desert landscape below. A slight tinge of sadness from being separated from her father surges into her but that it is quickly overtaken by the anticipation of reunion.

Armand approaches the Buffalo airport in his Packard car and sees a sign for the airport. Various small aviation buildings pop in to view with the control tower being the most prominent one. Nestled between arched metal hangars, he can see commercial planes parked on the tarmac along military transport ones. He walks into the terminal's one large room, a pavilion with boarding gates leading right off it. He approaches the windows facing the airside and looks up into the sky as if to read a message. He scans the clouds with happy expectation.

The DC-3 carrying Rosa sails through puffy, cumulus clouds bouncing the plane here and there. It is sunny, and the clouds below look like a rolling, snowy landscape. Rosa peers out the window down toward the earth wondering what cities and states she is passing by. A polite and cheerful stewardess offers her tea and a magazine to read. Then she asks her if there is anything else she can do to make her journey more comfortable. Rosa smiles and shakes her head. She looks back out at the wing, then the propellers and then toward the endless horizon of cumulus clouds.

Armand catches a glimpse of plane in the far horizon, this must be her. His heart jumps, his breathing become short, a flutter of expectation rises in him. The moment he has dreamt about for two years is about to be finally realized. He continues watching the speck of a plane as it descends toward the runway.

The plane glides down toward the runway, the landing gears are out, the nose of the planes tips back up. The landing wheels hit the ground, smoke wisps up along with a sharp screeching sound and the DC-3 bounces once. The propellers start to slow down and the plane taxis through the runways.

Upon seeing the plane taxing up to the terminal Armand bursts out of the terminal up to a line of attendants behind a rope and he is halted, for now. The plane parks nearby, the propellers are turned off then the ramp stairs are brought up.

Rosa looks out the window scanning the terminal gate for any familiar faces. Then she sees him, a man furiously waving his fedora hat. It is Armand. She quickly unbuckles her belt and grabs her coat and purse. She heads toward the cockpit exit door, ducks her head to get past the door and steps onto the ramp stairs.

Seeing her, Armand runs past the gate attendants and bolts toward the plane in a full gallop, his arms slicing through air. Rosa gently but quickly descends the stair and once on the ground she opens her arms to receive him while she also starts running toward him.

Armand comes up to her so quickly that he practically spins her around as he barely stops in time. He grabs her by the waist, lifts her up and spins her around for a full turn until Rosa is laughing like a child. Her lush hair lifts in the air while she kicks one leg up, the other dangling down against Armand's side.

As he lets her down, they kiss passionately while smiling broadly, they are almost crying with joy. They can hardly speak they are so overwhelmed, they just stare and in Italian, babel short words of affection to each other. No more war, no more work camps, no more separations. He has found her. She has found him. And they are free in America

The Author, July, 2016

Historical Characters' Aftermath

Willy Emil Messerschmitt

Following being detained outside of the Oberammergau complex, Willy Messerschmitt was shipped off to England, where he was held under house arrest for three years. It is likely the Americans kept him this long so the Soviets would not try to capture him. During that time in London he was extensively interrogated about his knowledge on the jet and he cooperated amicably. Lilly lived in a wooden shack in the hillsides surrounding Bamberg until Willy made it back.

He was tried for war crimes, specifically for the company's use of slave labor and concentration camp prisoners. In the end, the multi-national tribunal did find him guilty of war crimes and labeled him a "traveler along in the War journey".

Messerschmitt retained company ownership but after he was released in 1948 his company was banned from designing or producing anything military related. Instead, he focused his business on building homes and then on compact, small-engine automobiles.

Eventually, his past fame caught the attention of other countries and he was hired out as a consultant to design planes for their industries. This included a stint in Egypt and then a multi-year contract in Spain, where he created his last working jet, a successor to the P 1101 series.

Finally, Messerschmitt's company was permitted to design airplanes again but by this point the company was merged in with other consortiums, blocking his ability to ever be the top design executive.

In his later years, starting around the 1950s he started being recognized formally for his work and was presented with many awards and citations by various agencies including ones in the United States. This includes an award given to him at the United States Air Force Academy, where Messerschmitt gave a frank speech on how his jet could've changed the course of the war if they had been put out earlier and in greater numbers.

Willy and Lilly eventually married in 1954 while he was working for Air Hispano in Spain. Willy spent much of his later professional years working on vertical-take-off-and-landing (VTOL) planes and stayed as a consultant to Airbus until his retirement. Lilly Strohmeyer died at age 81 in 1973. Willy Emil Messerschmitt died in Germany in 1978 at age 80.

Leonino Da Zara

This an alternative history of the real Leonino Da Zara, who was born in 1888. The alternative history for him starts after World War I where Da Zara becomes a doctorate engineer specializing in aeronautics and then works for Fiat's airplane division. Also, while the real Da Zara was briefly married, in this book he is a widower and has a surviving daughter, Rosa.

The real Leonino Da Zara was the illegitimate son of a wealthy Jewish landowner from the Veneto province just west of Venice. At some point the father officially adopted Leonino, giving him full rights to his land and wealth. He and his father were referred to as barons and this prestige and wealth allowed Leonino to pursue his airplane flying interests in the first decade of the twentieth century. Leonino became a minor celebrity for setting up Italy's first flying club, building a hangar to store his planes and an airfield to fly them.

During World War I, Leonino offered his family's airfield for the development of Italy's first air force base. He then served in the Communication Corp of that fledgling air force during the first Great War as a Lieutenant. Following World War I, Da Zara became a sympathetic fascist and by the mid-1930s even went so far as to write a book in support of Mussolini. Not much more is known about Da Zara except that he died in 1958 and by that point he had spent all his family fortune.

It is interesting to note that the real Leonino Da Zara, as a Jew, survived Nazi Germany's occupation of northern Italy. This indicates that either the Italians were not so ardent in rooting out Semites from their land or that the Germans gave him some respect due to his title and extensive land holdings, or it is also possible that the Germans did not have Jewish extermination in Italy as a high or immediate priority. Moreover, as a fascist supporter of Mussoluni, he may have been granted special privileges.

Alexander Lippisch

Lippisch is the unsung hero of supersonic delta wing flight. While Messerschmitt's name has more recognition value with the public, Lippisch was far ahead of him in terms of high-speed flight concept development. In fact, there are quotes that Messerschmitt thought that the breaking of Mach 1 speeds would likely not happen in his lifetime. Moreover, Lippisch never benefited financially from plane royalties anywhere near the extent that Messerschmitt did. There are indications that Lippisch felt his advanced ideas were never properly converted to profit and that he may have envied Messerschmitt for having been able to readily do so.

After the War, Lippisch was brought to the United States under Operation Lusty and was put to work with Convair in San Diego. In 1946, he was highlighted in a cover photo by Life Magazine issue highlighting German war scientist's contribution to the American defense industry. He continued creating novel planes, including the ground-effect flyer. Eventually, he ended up working for an Iowa radio electronics company. He died in Cedar Rapids, Iowa in 1976 at age eighty-one, leaving behind a wife and children that married Americans.

It is the author's speculation that Lippisch's work at the Iowa radio company may have been a cover to hide continued work on advanced projects involving delta jets and rocket craft. From researching Paperclip and LUSTY scientists, much of what they did in the USA was kept under guard and not freely disseminated.

Slave & Forced Workers

Over 54,000 slave workers were involved in the production of the Me 262 jet alone. The numbers involved in the other Messerschmitt planes is unknown but likely it is quadruple this figure. Overall, 40,000 forced and slave workers died at Messerschmitt plants throughout Germany and Czechoslovakia to produce their various planes. In fact, at one point during the war, twenty-five percent of all of Germany's factory workers were forced laborers. The numbers of total forced laborers in Germany during World War II reached 6.5 million people and of that amount, 180,000 were Italians.

Typically, the slave laborers were kidnapped or rounded up off their native streets and forced to work in Germany. As a group, these peoples suffered many privations; they lived in simple barracks, typically had one meal a day, could not leave or communicate with the outside world, were uncompensated for their work, under the repressive yoke of the SS guards and worst of all, exposed to incessant Allied air bombing attacks. It was not unusual for many laborers to die within any given day and consequently, a large number never made it back home. Ironically, Jewish concentration camp workers became valuable plane assembly workers and the in some ways, the plane programs saved these Jews from extermination efforts.

So, while a group of maybe 100 engineers were involved in the design of the jet, there were thousands of faceless, imprisoned workers who made each jet a reality. At the end of the war, there was collective legal action taken against Germany for the injustices born upon the forced laborers. Germany eventually did compensate the workers in a class action suit but whether the individuals and surviving family members felt justly compensated is not known.

Other Historical Figures

While Armand and his close friends and intimates are fictional, there are many real people that play a role in this book. The dialogue and actual actions depicted in this book were construed by the author's imagination. Below is a brief listing of these figures:

Herman Göring, Field Marshall and head of the Luftwaffe. Committed suicide after conviction at the Nuremburg Trials.

Adolf Galland, General of the Fighters for the Luftwaffe, decorated fighter from the Spanish Civil War and the Battle of Britain. Commanded one squadron of Me 262's in the final months of the War. After the War, followed other German aviation designers and Luftwaffe pilots to Argentina to work for Juan Peron, a fascist leader.

Kreisleiter Schiede, National Socialist Party district leader for Augsburg. Records indicate that he did demand from Willy Messerschmitt, eighty-one research engineers to assemble a Volkssturm company in the final months of the War. It is not known whether he actually saw combat, but he did recruit Volkssturm units. His assasination by Kindermann is fictional.

Gerhard Coulis, Engineering Superintendent at Messerschmitt AG, later worked at Bell Aircraft in the USA.

Walter Ignaz, production engineer at Messerschmitt AG. Little is known of him except that he was filmed for a broadcast history segment on Messerschmitt plane developments.

Fritz Wendel, Chief Test Pilot for the Messerschmitt AG, first to fly the Me 262 jet. Stayed in Germany after the war. Died from a hunting accident in 1975 but there are some who believe it may have been a suicide.

Robert Lusser, Design bureau head of the Me 262 jet at Messerschmitt. Ended up in the USA after the War and worked for the US Navy on cruise missiles.

Voldemar Voigt, lead designer of the Me 262 jet at Messerchmitt AG, working as a deputy to Robert Lusser. After the War ended in the USA working for Glen Martin Aircraft.

Wolfgang Degel, one the key designers of the Me 262 jet at Messerschmitt. From when he joined Messerschmitt in 1933 he quickly rose in prominence to eventually leading the development of the Me 262. Once Messerschmitt resumed the company again in the early 1950's Degel went back to work with him till 1975.

Hans Hornung and Moritz Asam, lead designers of the P1101 jet and other advance prototypes developed at Oberammergau. Hans Hornung ended up in the USA at Bell Aircraft. Moritz emigrated to the USA in 1955 and worked for Boeing on the Super Guppy transport plane.

Colonel Watson and Captain Wenzel. Watson was the leader of LUSTY, Luftwaffe Secret Technology exploitation unit and his groups was referred to as Watson's Whizzers. Wenzel oversaw Paperclip engineers at Wright Airfield and was of German descent.

Heinz Bauer, Karl Baur, Ludwig Hoffman and Herman Kersting where all Messerschmitt Factory Test Pilots and all came to the USA under Operation Paperclip or LUSTY. Some worked for Bell Aircraft while others went to Convair in San Diego where Lippisch worked.

The Messerschmitt Jet Legacy. The Me 262, the P 1101 jet and others in the 1100 series set the pace for the next generation of jets for America, Britain, France and Russia. Much of this was possible from the blueprints that were obtained from the Messerschmitt Oberammergau complex as well as the direct employment of Messerschmitt engineers involved with the jet and the rocket planes under operations LUSTY and Paperclip. Jet planes that were offspring of Messerschmitt's company include the Sabre jet, the Russian MIG and the BellX-5. Based on this Nazi Germany aviation technology, the superpowers had their jets ready for the next military engagement, the Cold War.

1. obergammergau Passion Plot
   barracks taken over by
   Messerschmint Co.

2. Good Germans put a "warm
   face" on the evil which
   Nazism brought p. 300

3. survivors @spearheaded out
   of Europe, as well
   p. 268

4. falling in love with
   someone Jewish
   Right woman is worth
   fighting for her 301

_____

Next Book
_____

German Jews were proud
WW I - about 2 Jewish
(officers) brother fought in WWI
Kaiser's Army ① Turkey
② France

silker/first
Agreement
1921

Made in the USA
Columbia, SC
19 September 2018